Praise for Mary Daheim
and her Emma Lord mysteries

THE ALPINE ADVOCATE
"The lively ferment of life in a small Pacific Northwest town, with its convoluted genealogies and loyalties [and] its authentically quirky characters, combines with a baffling murder for an intriguing mystery novel."
—M. K. WREN

THE ALPINE BETRAYAL
"Editor-publisher Emma Lord finds out that running a small-town newspaper is worse than nutty—it's downright dangerous. Readers will take great pleasure in Mary Daheim's new mystery."
—CAROLYN G. HART

THE ALPINE CHRISTMAS
'If you like cozy mysteries, you need to try Daheim's Alpine series. . . . Recommended."
—*The Snooper*

THE ALPINE DECOY
"[A] fabulous series . . . Fine examples of the traditional, domestic mystery."
—*Mystery Lovers Bookshop News*

By Mary Daheim
Published by Ballantine Books:

THE
ALPINE ICON

Mary Daheim

BALLANTINE BOOKS • NEW YORK

Chapter One

AFTER ED BRONSKY, my former ad manager at *The Alpine Advocate*, took over the local food bank last March, there was some concern about whether or not he was eating more than he handed out. When presented with day-old donations from the Upper Crust Bakery, the millionaire by inheritance had frequently been spotted stuffing doughnuts into his mouth and sweet rolls into his pockets. I didn't doubt the reports. As Ed stood in front of my desk at the newspaper office, two chocolate-chip cookies fell out of his jacket.

Ed and I both pretended we hadn't noticed. Easing his bulk into one of my two visitors' chairs, Ed's eyes briefly veered in the direction of the floor. "How do you feel about tithing, Emma?" he inquired in his most serious voice.

"You mean at church?" I frowned at Ed, who had picked up a stray pencil from my desk and was idly toying with it. "Don't we already do something like that through the annual archbishop's appeal?"

"Some people do." Ed was now looking gloomy, an expression I recalled all too well from his days on the job. "But plenty of our fellow parishioners at St. Mildred's don't bother to fill out the pledge cards, or if they do, they don't send in the money."

I wasn't surprised. There isn't a lot of money floating around Alpine these days. As an isolated community of four thousand people historically nurtured by the timber industry, Alpine is in an economic slump. In recent years logging cutbacks have put many residents out of work. Two unemployed loggers had stepped in front of Burlington Northern freight trains; a family of six had burned their crumbling house down around them; and spousal abuse had risen dramatically, along with alcohol and drug addiction. From a distance Alpine looked like a picturesque mountain community; up close it wasn't so pretty.

"What's your point?" I asked, hoping not to sound impatient. It was Tuesday, the twenty-second of August, and deadline was upon us for the weekly edition, which shipped each Wednesday.

"Well . . ." Ed dropped the pencil. He all but disappeared on the other side of the desk. I suspected he was scrambling around on the floor, retrieving his cookies. When he surfaced, he held up the pencil and beamed as if he'd found a gold nugget. "Sorry about that," said Ed, placing the pencil on the desk. "You were saying . . . ? Oh, my point." The grin faded. Ed was again the somber man of affairs. It was a pose he enjoyed since reaping his windfall from an aunt in Cedar Falls, Iowa. "St. Mildred's coffers are pretty low. I was talking to Father Den about it last night—Shirley and I had him over to dinner. We were going to take him to that French restaurant down the highway, but the weather's so warm, we decided to just throw some wienies on the grill and kick back."

I felt myself growing tense as Ed rattled on. The door to the editorial office was ajar, and I could hear my current ad manager, Leo Walsh, taking down last-minute instructions on Safeway's insert. Vida Runkel, my House & Home editor, was pounding away on her battered upright. My sole reporter, Carla Steinmetz, had just disappeared with notebook and camera in hand. Our office manager, Ginny Burmeister Erlandson, was delivering the morning mail.

"Anyway," Ed went on, attempting to wedge himself more comfortably into the chair, "Father Den is really pleased with the way I've pitched in these last few months to help out at church. But he needs more than manpower. The parish needs money. You've no idea what a drain the school is. I suggested a tuition hike, but Father Den wanted to think it over, maybe talk to the parish council first."

"I should hope so," I replied somewhat stiffly. "That would be a big step, and a real hardship for many parents."

Ed nodded rather absently. "Right, yeah. You know," he continued, folding his hands on his paunch, "there's a special parish-council meeting tonight. It's going to be held in conjunction with the school board because classes start two weeks from today. Maybe you should come."

In the course of professional life, there are far too many meetings that I'm compelled to attend. I try to delegate some of them, but I still get stuck with at least one a week. The last thing I wanted to do on a warm August evening was sit on uncomfortable chairs in the stuffy confines of the parish rectory.

"Look, Ed," I said, still somehow mustering patience, "I'm always beat on Tuesday nights after we get the paper ready for publication. If something major comes out of the meeting, let me know. It'll be too late for this week's edition anyway."

Ed scowled. "Now, Emma, this is no ordinary jaw session. This is your parish. You ought to have more than just a news interest. Or have you got something hot going with the Man Behind the Star?" Ed wiggled his heavy eyebrows in a lascivious manner.

The reference to Sheriff Milo Dodge annoyed me, but I wouldn't let it show. "I was planning to go over the statements for the new back-shop operation," I said stiffly.

Ed waved a pudgy hand. "That'll keep. The meeting

won't. Tonight could determine the whole future of St. Mildred's. This is big."

So was Ed, I thought, watching his three chins quiver with self-importance. The significance of any activity in which he was involved always became inflated. Still, Ed's admonition gave me pause. Despite the fact that I regularly attend church, that I contribute my fair share of money, and that my brother is a priest in Arizona, I have never been involved in parish activities. Over the years I've used up a lot of excuses: as a single mother, I never had the time; as a newspaper reporter on *The Oregonian*, I never had the time; as *The Advocate*'s editor and publisher, I never had the time. But there were other busy people who made the time. Maybe Emma Lord should become one of them.

The phones were ringing like mad, both on my desk and in the news office. I tried to ignore the flashing lights and hoped that Ginny would pick up my lines. "Have you got an agenda?" I asked, feeling myself weaken.

The beginnings of a smug little smile played around Ed's mouth. "You bet. It's the Good Guys versus the Bad Guys. That's all you need to know." With a grunt, Ed stood up. "I'm one of the good guys. Natch. See you at seven-thirty."

My phones had trunked over to Ginny's line. The cluttered cubbyhole I call my office suddenly seemed quiet. Scribbling in the time of the parish-council meeting on my crowded calendar, I looked up to see Vida Runkel looming in the doorway.

"Well?" huffed my House & Home editor. "What did that ninny want now?"

While *ninny* could have applied to most of Alpine as far as Vida was concerned, I knew she meant Ed Bronsky. "It's some minor crisis at St. Mildred's," I said, motioning for her to sit down. "I should never have talked Father Den into asking Ed to get involved with parish activities. Ever since he's been a regular gadfly."

"Ed had too much time on his hands," Vida said, adjusting the straw boater that sat on her disordered gray curls. "He still does. You'd think that between volunteering at your church and overseeing that monstrosity of a house he and Shirley are building, Ed could keep out of mischief."

Just picturing the Bronsky housing site made me wince. Leo Walsh had remarked that the architectural rendering we had been conned into running reminded him of Hearst's Castle at San Simeon, only more ostentatious. Leo had been exaggerating. Still, the Spanish-style residence that Ed called his "villa" didn't fit in a mountain community like Alpine.

But I knew Vida hadn't come into my office on a hectic Tuesday morning to discuss Ed or his house. She proved the point by handing me a sheaf of copy paper. "See what you think. It's the feature on Ursula O'Toole Randall. The woman is such a pretentious sort that I had problems keeping my perspective."

I couldn't help but give Vida a quizzical look. Despite her critical attitude in private, she always managed to maintain objectivity when writing a story. Apparently Ursula was an exception. I had met her only once, at coffee and doughnuts after Mass. She had struck me as egotistical, but nothing more. On the other hand, our conversation had been brief, devoted mostly to whether raised doughnuts were preferable to the cake variety.

"Okay, let's see," I said, scanning the half sheets filled with Vida's erratic, two-fingered typing. " 'Someone once said you can't go home again,' " Vida wrote, " 'but Ursula O'Toole Randall is trying to prove otherwise. After twenty-four years in Seattle, twenty of which were spent married to the late Dr. Wheaton Randall, Ursula has returned to her hometown.' "

I glanced up at Vida. "So far, so good. Am I missing something?"

Vida's mouth was pursed. "Keep going. You can skip

the part about her being Jake and Buzzy O'Toole's sister, her high-school career, the Miss Skykomish County pageant, the tragic early marriage, the world travel, and how she's engaged to Francine Wells's ex-husband, Warren. Move on to where she talks about being Lady Bountiful."

Lady Bountiful showed up on page seven. " 'Ursula is a firm believer that the more a person has received from life, the more one ought to give back. "I've been so blessed," she said, waving a graceful hand at the art-works and fine furnishings that fill her newly acquired home in The Pines subdivision. "Some days it seems as if God looks down and smiles and gives me a little nudge. So I get in my new Lexus and rush off to church, where I beg Father Dennis Kelly to let me do something for the less fortunate. He—and God—need all the help they can get. My old hometown is full of needy people who need me to pull them out of the hole they've dug for them-selves." ' "

Wide-eyed, I slapped at the copy paper. "Vida—is that an actual quote?"

My House & Home editor nodded solemnly. "There was more, but I didn't use it. Really, Emma, the woman is insufferable. She has a dreadful do-gooder complex. Is there anything worse?"

I've known the type. Filled with energy, zeal, and enormous ego, the good-works moguls plunge into chari-ties and causes. They want to feed the hungry, house the homeless, stop abuse, save the whales, spare the spotted owl. While their goals may be worthy, many actually seek nothing more than self-aggrandizement.

Vida gestured at the copy paper. "Read the last graf. And please don't be ill. I almost gagged when I wrote it."

" 'In the parishes I attended in Seattle,' " Vida quoted Ursula, " 'I discovered that while priests and nuns see themselves a part of the solution to social ills, they are often part of the problem. Sometimes there is a chasm between them and the laity, which creates a vacuum that encourages irresponsible behavior on both sides. In other instances, members of religious orders feel a need to behave as if they are no different from the people they serve. These extremes are ridiculous. That's why it's so important for well-grounded individuals—such as myself—to become deeply involved.' "

There was, in fact, one last, brief paragraph. " 'Ursula and Warren Wells, also formerly of Alpine, plan a December wedding at St. Mildred's Church. The archbishop is expected to concelebrate the ceremony.' "

I gritted my teeth. "It's not your fault," I finally said. "You simply reported what Ursula said."

"I could have censored it," Vida reported with sparks in her gray eyes. "But I truly believe Ursula wanted to be quoted."

I glanced down at the final paragraphs. "Maybe. Unless she's one of those people who speaks without thinking."

"So?" Vida whipped off her glasses with their tortoiseshell frames. "Perhaps this will teach her to think the next time she's interviewed."

"How are the pictures?" I asked, handing the story back to Vida.

"Fair. I took one at the house—it's that quasi-French Provincial that's been sitting vacant ever since Nyquist Construction built it on speculation three years ago. I understand Ursula got it for a song."

I knew the house. It was one of the last to be finished in the subdivision at the edge of town. Once known as Stump Hill, the builders had rechristened the neighborhood as The Pines. By Alpine standards, the homes were very classy. The only problem was that there weren't many local residents who could afford to live in them.

"Go with it," I said, though I suffered a pang of misgiving. "Ursula sounds like a silly, conceited ass."

Getting to her feet, Vida sniffed. "Don't we strive for

accuracy?" With her impressive bust leading the way, she marched out of my office.

The rest of the day was busy and chaotic, but no more than usual for a Tuesday. Leo complained of too many last-minute changes from advertisers, Carla required heavy editing on three front-page stories, and Vida didn't have enough tantalizing tidbits for her gossip column, "Scene Around Town." Fortunately—or unfortunately, depending upon one's point of view—a tourist from Utah rear-ended a carpet salesman from Seattle right in front of *The Advocate*. No one was hurt, and damage was minimal, which meant that the item was more suitable for Vida than for hard news.

By five-ten, we were ready to go to press. Until the first of May, we had sent the paper to a printer in Monroe, about forty miles down Highway 2. But during the late winter and early spring, I had finally reopened the back shop. Kip MacDuff, who had been our driver, was now an Alpine High School graduate. When he expressed an interest in working with the job printing, I hired him on the spot. Most of the added equipment was secondhand, and not quite state-of-the-art, but still light-years ahead of anybody else in Skykomish County. The transition hadn't been smooth, though by mid-June we seemed to have ironed out the glitches. We also had acquired some local desktop jobs, and though we weren't yet showing a profit, I was optimistic about the future.

Thus I felt reasonably sanguine as I left the office and headed out into the muggy late afternoon. Rush hour on Front Street is a relative term. From my vantage point I could see a steady stream of traffic in both directions. It would last for a good twenty minutes. As usual, there were more trucks, RVs, and logging rigs than passenger cars. I was about to get into my aging green Jaguar when the sheriff called to me.

"Emma!" Milo Dodge shouted, applying the brakes of

his Cherokee Chief so hard that we almost had another rear-end collision. "Dinner? Drinks?"

Milo's long, ordinary, tanned face was looking out from the open window of his sport utility vehicle. That face was special, and I had to smile. "Ah ... okay. Now?"

Milo frowned. "How about six? Want me to come over?" He looked hopeful.

I grimaced. "I've got a meeting. It's now or never."

"What about later?" The hope hadn't quite disappeared.

"Okay. Nine-ish? I'll call when I get home."

Milo gave me a thumbs-up sign. The Cherokee Chief took off down Front Street. I didn't recognize the man who sat in the pickup behind Milo's vehicle, but judging from the fact that he hadn't honked, yelled, or cursed up a storm, he knew the sheriff.

A smile clung to my lips as I got into the Jag. Milo and I had been friends for a long time before we became lovers. That was good. In our forties, I thought it was important to have some basis for a relationship besides sex. Intimacy meant many things to me, and didn't always require the removal of clothing. Whether or not I was in love with Milo or he was in love with me wasn't as important as the fact that we genuinely cared for each other. I hadn't done well with passion. Except for fathering my son, the man I once referred to as the love of my life had brought me nothing but grief and frustration. Tom Cavanaugh was married when I met him twenty-four years ago; he was still married, to the same woman who held him hostage to her family's wealth and her fragile mental state. I hadn't spoken to Tom since New Year's, and I didn't intend to. After almost a quarter of a century it had finally occurred to me that he was never going to leave Sandra, and that I was a sap to think otherwise. I could hardly blame anyone who called me a slow learner.

My musings lasted as long as the five-minute uphill drive to my little log house at the edge of the forest. Alpine sits on the banks of the Skykomish River, nestled against the rugged crags of Tonga Ridge. Mount Baldy hovers to the north, its rounded twin crests bare of snow in late August. The town is a mile from the main highway, and fifty miles from a city of any size. Alpine's isolation, particularly in the long winters, causes its residents to look inward, to mistrust the wider world. After six years I'm still considered something of a stranger. Not having been born and raised in Alpine, I will never be accepted into the inner circle.

That's just as well. Journalists have to keep their distance. Though Vida is a third-generation Alpine native and proud of it, she does her best to maintain objectivity, at least in print. It was no wonder that she was disturbed by the results of her interview with Ursula Randall. But the patronizing words had come out of the woman's mouth. It would be interesting to see if Ursula tried to refute them after they were published. People often do. If they can't eat their words, they want them retracted.

I was still thinking about Vida's predicament when I chucked my mail—except for a couple of fall catalogs—into the wastebasket. There was nothing but junk in the current delivery, and I was disappointed. I'd hoped for a letter from my son, Adam. Usually, he spent part of the summers with me, but this year he had chosen to stay with my brother, Ben, at the Navajo mission in Tuba City. Both my son and my brother were amateur anthropologists, spending their spare time on an Anasazi dig. Ben had promised to visit over the Labor Day weekend; Adam had been stalling me since he finished spring quarter at Arizona State in June. I was annoyed and hurt. I hadn't seen my only child since Easter.

There was no phone message from him, either. The answering machine revealed a big fat red zero. I changed clothes, made a meager dinner, and ate while reading *The*

Seattle Times. Normally I don't mind being alone. But the lack of word from Adam somehow drained my log house of its usual cozy comfort. The air felt stuffy after the eighty-five-degree afternoon, and no breeze stirred the evergreens that flanked my small backyard.

A little after seven I assessed my appearance before heading off to St. Mildred's. A change of clothes was in order, since I'd perspired heavily in my cotton shell. Applying lipstick, I considered brushing my hair, but decided against it. I was in the midst of letting the heavy chestnut mane grow out, perhaps to my shoulders. Trying to coax what was left of my perm into some sort of style was hopeless. The rest of my five-foot-four, hundred-and-twenty-pound frame was presentable, at least for a boring session at church.

At seven-twenty I drove the five blocks to St. Mildred's. The church is old, a white frame structure that would look more at home in New England than the Pacific Northwest. The rectory is of the same vintage, but the school is much newer. Built of brick, its two stories overlook the playground on one side, and the church on the other. The convent was torn down a long time ago, and the two nuns on the faculty share an apartment in a building across the street.

To my surprise, there were at least three dozen vehicles in the parking lot. Since the parish council numbered five members, and the school board only three, I was puzzled. Maybe Ed hadn't exaggerated. Something was up at St. Mildred's.

Francine Wells pulled in just as I was getting out of the Jag. As the owner of Francine's Fine Apparel, she feels a responsibility to be well groomed at all times. In a town where designer clothes means handstitching your name on the back of your bowling shirt, Francine tends to stand out in a crowd. This evening she was wearing a simple pale yellow linen sheath that probably cost her a hundred dollars wholesale.

"Emma!" Francine exclaimed as she locked up her dark blue Acura Legend. "What are you doing here? Don't tell me Father Den talked you into serving on the school board?"

My puzzlement deepened. "No. Is there a vacancy?"

Francine fell in step beside me. "There's a move to expand the membership to five, just like the parish council. Didn't you see the notice in Sunday's bulletin?"

I hadn't. It had been very warm in church on Sunday morning, and I'd been inclined to drift. Father Den's conversational skills tend to outshine his speaking talents in the pulpit. Still, he's an enormous improvement over our previous pastor, Kiernan Fitzgerald, who was elderly and not always aware of the city, state, or century in which he was operating.

"Some of the parents are up in arms," Francine was saying. "They don't feel fully represented. Do you realize that almost thirty percent of the pupils in the school aren't Catholics?"

I hadn't known that, either. But I did realize that Francine was leading me not to the rectory, but the school. "Where is the meeting?" I asked.

"The school auditorium," Francine replied. "They expect way too many people to fit into the rectory parlor."

That made sense. Three more cars pulled into the parking lot; I recognized Buzzy O'Toole, Roseanna and Buddy Bayard, and last, but certainly not least, Ed and Shirley Bronsky in their ice-blue Mercedes.

I also recognized most—but not all—of the fifty people who were milling about in the school auditorium. Those I couldn't place were all under forty. I figured them to be parents of St. Mildred's non-Catholic students.

Father Dennis Kelly was wearing his short-sleeve summer clerical garb, which was probably a concession to the gravity of the meeting. Usually, our pastor is seen around town in old sweats or blue jeans and a flannel shirt. He is in his mid-forties, average height, average looks, and superior intelligence. What makes him stand out in Alpine isn't his religious vocation, but the fact that he is African American. Minorities are rare in Skykomish County. Indeed, the previous generation considered a minority as anyone who wasn't Scandinavian. When Father Den arrived at St. Mildred's two years ago, he was met by hostility, suspicion, and fear. Ironically it was his fellow clergymen, especially Regis Bartleby of Trinity Episcopal and Donald Nielsen of Faith Lutheran who had made overt gestures of welcome. Slowly, hopefully, most Alpiners had come to accept Father Den's presence, at least on some level.

As a member of the parish council, Francine had to take her place at one of the two lunchroom tables that had been set up on the stage. Thus I sought a discreetly placed folding chair near the back. If I must attend meetings, it's my policy to sit where an early exit is not only easy, but unnoticed.

However, Buzzy O'Toole sought me out immediately. "What have you heard?" he asked in an urgent whisper.

I stared at Buzzy. He is about my age, but looks older. His auburn hair is graying and thinning, there are deep lines in his angular face, and his blue eyes are always sad. Unlike his brother, Jake, who owns the Grocery Basket, Buzzy has had bad luck in the world of commerce. Three years ago he was forced to close his BP service station. Since then, he's tried his hand at running a secondhand store and a bicycle shop. Both enterprises failed. Lately he's been working as Jake's produce manager. I'd heard a rumor that his wife, Laura, had left him recently, but so far, Vida, my source of all Alpine knowledge, hadn't been able to confirm it.

"I haven't heard anything," I said in my normal voice, which seemed to disturb Buzzy, who signaled for me to speak more quietly. "That is, Ed Bronsky suggested I

attend because there are going to be some important
issues on the agenda."

Buzzy let out a gust of air between clenched teeth.
"For once, Ed's not full of it. This is crucial. I can hardly
afford tuition now." Father Den brought down his gavel.
Buzzy jumped. "Hard times for St. Mildred's," he whispered, and furtively moved off to his seat.

The meeting was opened with a prayer, which seemed
sufficiently harmless in that it wasn't incendiary. Then
Father Den deferred to the parish-council president, Jake
O'Toole. Jake is bigger and better looking than his
younger brother, but when he speaks in a public forum he
has an unfortunate habit of using big words he doesn't
always understand.

"This convocation has been summoned tonight
because of the distension between certain members of the
parish and parents in the school," Jake began. "There are
diverse issues on the agenda. We're going to commence
with one that was raised at the last regular parish-council
meeting August eighth." He turned to Nunzio Lucci, a
grizzled unemployed logger who was seated on his right.
"Luce?"

"It's about money," Luce said in his deep, gritty voice.
"Back when Father Fitz was here, nobody could say
nothin' about how the money was spent. But times has
changed. Father Den here knows that we got rights, too.
This is America, not Italy or one of them places where
the Church runs the whole show."

A small woman with long, straight brown hair waved a
hand at the far end of the tables. "Excuse me, I was in
Italy last month, and I'd like to correct Mr. Lucci. While
the Roman Catholic Church is an influential force in
people's lives, I didn't get the impression that it ran its
members. Of course, I'm a Unitarian, but I do have a
major in sociology. And yes," she added with a sour
expression, "Italian men still pinch. They can't seem to
stop being macho."

Nunzio Lucci sat bolt upright. "Hey! Whaddya mean about Italian men? We *are* macho! So who gives a shit?" He flexed the muscles that showed in his forearms below the sleeves of the frayed cotton work shirt.

"Oh, shut up, Luce!" Francine snapped, glaring at her neighbor to the left. "We're not here to talk about your manly prowess!"

Father Den gave Francine a grateful look. "I think," he said in his mild voice, "it's important to keep to the agenda." His gaze traveled down to the small brown-haired woman at the end of the table. "Let's withhold extraneous comments for now, okay, Greer?"

Greer sniffed, but kept her mouth shut. I leaned forward to tap Roseanna Bayard's shoulder. "Greer who?" I asked, trying not to move my lips.

"Fairfax," Roseanna murmured. "Married to Grant Fairfax, some kind of naturalist who commutes to Monroe. Greer weaves."

I jotted down the names. Nunzio Lucci was still speaking about money. I'd missed part of what he said, but the gist seemed to be that while Father Den was willing to allow the parish council a voice in expenditures, he reserved veto power. Judging from the stir that was caused in the audience, a number of people didn't approve.

The next twenty minutes were devoted to a discussion of whether or not our pastor—or any pastor—had a right to hold the purse strings. Of the parish-council members, Luce was vehemently in favor, as was Francine, who argued forcefully, using all the persuasive powers that kept a handful of well-dressed Alpine women in debt. After some vaguely incoherent remarks, Monica Vancich disagreed. Brendan Shaw of Sigurdson-Shaw Insurance Agency could see both sides of the issue. In his role of council president, Jake O'Toole felt obliged to remain temporarily neutral.

The discussion from the audience grew heated, though

not particularly newsworthy. As I had done Sunday at
Mass, I began to drift. It was now after eight, and I'd told
Milo I'd be home around nine. Trying to focus, I
observed the rest of the people up on the stage. There
was Greer Fairfax, of course, who apparently was on the
school board. So was Buddy Bayard, Roseanna's husband and owner of Bayard's Picture Perfect Photography
Studio, where our film is processed. And of course I
knew the third member, Bill Daley, proprietor of Daley's
Fine Furnishings and one of our advertisers. Trying not
to attract attention, I moved quietly around the auditorium, snapping pictures: Father Den and Jake and
Francine, looking thoughtful; the school principal,
Veronica Wenzler-Greene, raising a point about parish
subsidies; Monica Vancich, gesturing nervously at a
scowling Luce; Brendan Shaw, laboriously taking notes.
I passed on the chance to capture Ed Bronsky sneaking
over to the refreshment table to nab a handful of sugar
cookies.

"Look," Jake was saying in a reasonable voice just
after someone in the front row had called for a vote, "we
aren't in regular session. We have garnered the con-
sensus of opinion on monetarial responsibility and will
duly comprehend your views. Could we move on?"

In the third row, a raven-haired woman who was
almost as smartly attired as Francine Wells put up a mani-
cured hand. "Mr. President," she said in a throaty voice
that was laced with a slight giggle, "may I point out that
you have a mission statement, bylaws, and a contract
with your pastor. A parish council is strictly consultative.
The pastor may listen to advice, but he·has final authority
and is responsible to his bishop. If you have questions, I
suggest you contact the chancery office in Seattle. Otherwise you're simply wasting everyone's time and showing
your ignorance." With a graceful movement, the woman
sat down. I recognized her as Ursula O'Toole Randall.

I couldn't help but look at Francine. Her eyes had narrowed as she stared down on the woman who was about to become her ex-husband's third wife. Ursula tilted her head and smiled archly at Francine. I could tell there was no love lost between the two women. Unless, of course, you counted Warren Wells.

As far as I could tell, Warren wasn't in the audience. I hadn't met him since he returned to Alpine with Ursula in late July. He and Francine had been divorced for many years by the time I arrived in Alpine. Vida had told me that in between Francine and Ursula, Warren had married someone else but it didn't last more than a few years.

The meeting had finally reached its goal: should the school board be expanded from three to five members? Debate was heated. Old-line parishioners such as Annie Jeanne Dupré and Pete Patricelli and Buzzy O'Toole were against the proposal. Vocally for it were most of the younger set I hadn't recognized. At last Jake agreed to take the matter under advisement and to schedule an official vote at the next regular parish-council meeting. He raised his gavel to adjourn, but Ursula Randall was on her feet again.

"Unless I'm ill informed," she said in that husky, purring voice, "school will open before the next council meeting. Wouldn't it be wiser to settle the matter now so that if the expanded membership is approved, the school will have the benefit of knowing who the new board members are and where they stand?"

Three rows behind Ursula, Verb Vancich, Monica's husband and owner of Alpine Ski, got to his feet. "I agree with"—Verb grimaced, then shrugged his narrow shoulders—"the last speaker. Why can't we call for a voice vote right now?"

Verb's presence puzzled me. While Monica Vancich was very active in the parish and school, her husband wasn't. He rarely came to Mass, except at Christmas and Easter. But I knew that the Vanciches had two children, one of whom attended St. Mildred's. The other was a preschooler. Perhaps Verb had decided it was time to get involved. With ski season coming up, it certainly wouldn't hurt his position as an Alpine merchant.

Everybody onstage was looking bewildered. An anxious muffled discussion ensued. Murmurs and a couple of guffaws ran through the onlookers. At last Jake pounded for order.

"We've determined to present a ballot this weekend inquiring if parishioners favor incrementing the school-board members," he said, looking uneasy. "If the affirmatives pass, we'll request candidates to come forth and hold the election the subsequent weekend, September second and third." He glanced at Francine, who nodded confirmation of the dates. "That way," Jake went on, "we'll have the board members in place by the time school inaugurates September fifth." Despite the buzz from the auditorium, Jake slammed his gavel down. "We're adjourned."

It was nine-fifty. I was the first one out the door. It was exactly ten o'clock when I called Milo.

"What happened?" he asked in a sleepy voice. "I thought you said you'd be home by nine."

I explained about the tedious, inconclusive session. "I'd like to choke Ed. He said it was going to be hot stuff. But it was just another Alpine meeting, with the usual insults and long-winded bilge. I get enough of that from the county commissioners and the regular school board." I paused to catch my breath. "Do you still want to come over?" Despite the closeness between us, the veiled innuendo embarrassed me.

"Well . . ." Milo paused, and I could hear him lighting a cigarette. "It's kind of late, Emma. You want to drive over to Leavenworth Saturday?"

It was unusual for Milo to think of a more adventuresome date than a couple of drinks, a steak at the Venison Inn, and a roll in the hay afterward. I was surprised.

"It sounds like fun," I said. "What time?"

"Noon? I'll want to check in at the office Saturday morning. Jack Mullins is on vacation this week."

Jack was one of Milo's deputies. He was also a fellow parishioner. It occurred to me that I hadn't seen him at the meeting. "Okay, see you tomorrow maybe."

" 'Night." Milo yawned. "Hey—I'm sorry about tonight." The gruffness in his voice masked what I assumed was genuine emotion.

"Me, too. I wish I hadn't gone to that stupid meeting. It was a waste of time."

"Most meetings are." He paused again. "It's okay. I'm not going anywhere."

"Neither am I."

"Right. 'Night."

We hung up. I smiled down at the receiver. The exchange between us was about as sentimental as Milo and I ever got. But we knew that under the casual conversation, there was real affection. It was as if we spoke in code. We were too mature to need endless verbal reassurance.

Weren't we?

Chapter Two

CARLA'S FRONT-PAGE PHOTO of the community-college construction site was going to look good when the paper finally came out of the back shop. The administration building, the student union, a lecture hall, and a dorm were all beginning to take shape. After much argument, the state had selected a location almost three miles west of town, beyond Ptarmigan Tract and the fish hatchery. There was a rumor that our state legislator, Bob Gunderson, owned the land chosen for the new college. After a lengthy title search, it was discovered that the property belonged to the state. Nor did Gunderson own the nearby land on which he parked his mobile home. In fact, he didn't own the mobile home either, having been "loaned" it by the car dealership he'd worked for on Railroad Avenue. Naturally rumors had spread that Gunderson was a crook, but he managed to turn them to his own advantage, proclaiming that he was one public official who not only didn't own anything, but couldn't be bought.

I held back on writing about the parish meeting. By our next deadline, the vote would be in on expanding the school board. That was the real news. As far as most of Alpine's non-Catholic majority was concerned, St. Mildred's controversies were unimportant. My article would probably run less than two inches and go on page three.

So, as I often do on a quiet Wednesday morning, I cast about for my next editorial. There was talk of turning parts of the Skykomish River into catch-and-release. The environmentalists were all for it, but the fishermen were against it. I didn't much blame them. The concept of reeling in a five-pound steelhead and then letting it go didn't appeal to many anglers. It was hard enough to catch anything these days in Washington's lakes and streams. Of course the scarcity of game fish was the very reason that catch-and-release was being considered.

I was leafing through news releases from the State Department of Fish and Wildlife when Leo Walsh came into my office. It was only ten o'clock, but the temperature had already topped seventy degrees. Sweat stains showed under the arms of Leo's pale yellow summer-weight shirt.

"I'm guessing we can go thirty-two pages next week," Leo announced, sitting down across the desk from me. "Safeway and the Grocery Basket both have Labor Day inserts, we've got the back-to-school specials, and I've conned some of the smaller advertisers into taking out two-inchers honoring the local teachers. Then there's the full page sponsored by the Chamber of Commerce for the Labor Day picnic and concert in Old Mill Park."

"That's great," I said with enthusiasm. "You come up with some really good ideas, Leo."

If Leo was pleased by my praise, he didn't show it. "That's my job," he said without inflection. "You got enough editorial to fill it?"

"I will," I replied. "Vida's doing a history of Alpine High, Carla is interviewing three new teachers, and we're all working on a where-are-they-now story on former principals, going back to when Alpine had a one-room schoolhouse in its logging camp days."

Leo gave a nod. "Sounds good. I suppose half the principals are dead." The idea seemed to please him in a grim way.

"Some of them are, of course." My expression turned uncharacteristically severe. "What would you expect, when the original school opened before World War One?"

Leo had stood up, running his hands through his graying auburn hair. "I never expect much. That's why I'm rarely disappointed." He started to turn away, then spoke again. "By the way, Verb Vancich took out a quarter of a page instead of his usual two-by-two. He bought up Buzzy O'Toole's bicycles and is selling them off for half price at Alpine Ski."

"I suppose he wants to clear out space before ski season sets in." I waited for Leo to comment, but he merely walked out of the office. A normally gregarious sort, my ad manager seemed to have grown withdrawn of late. He'd had a drinking problem when he first arrived at *The Advocate*, but appeared to have it under control. I wondered if he and I should have a talk.

Putting Leo out of my mind, I mulled over editorial possibilities. With Labor Day coming up, maybe I should write something on the American worker. But despite the college construction, too many Alpiners had no work. I'd already done endless pieces on the lack of jobs. I could compare the contemporary work ethic with that of the past. Glancing through the door, I saw Carla filing her nails. Maybe the work-ethic comparison wasn't a good idea, either. I returned to catch-and-release. At least Milo would applaud my efforts.

By noon, this week's edition was printed and ready for delivery. After seeing off Kip MacDuff and his pickup from the back entrance to *The Advocate*, I headed for the Burger Barn. The air smelled dry and dusty, which was unusual in Alpine. But there hadn't been much rain for the last month. The flowers drooped in the planters along Front Street, a thick coat of grime covered many local vehicles, and there were splashes of red gold on the side hills where the vine maples had begun to turn color. As a Pacific Northwest native, I, too, felt dusty and dry and in need of watering. Though some people, especially those from more sun-drenched climes, think me odd, I swear that after more than three weeks without rain, I can feel my roots begin to wither and my disposition sour.

Thus, while I found my own company less than amiable, I didn't mind eating alone. Milo was busy, Vida had to go to the mall, Carla and Ginny were off somewhere together, and Leo seemed to be functioning in his own little world. As I waited for my burger basket, I thumbed through the August 23 issue of my professional pride and joy.

"How can you put out a rag like that?" The gruff voice belonged to Nunzio Lucci.

Looking up, I assumed he was kidding and grinned. "Hi, Luce. How's the family?"

To my surprise, Luce seemed a bit jarred by the rhetorical question. But then he ignored it, and shook his grizzled, balding head. "You know, Emma, I expect better from you. When some dumb cluck and his fat wife go to Hawaii for a week, you guys write it up like they flew to the moon. But then comes some real news, and it doesn't even get in the paper. How come?"

I turned a puzzled face up to Luce. "Like what? Did somebody jump off the bridge over the Sky and I missed it?"

Without being invited, Luce wedged himself into the opposite side of the booth. "I mean last night, up at St. Mildred's. You were there—I saw you. Now if it had been Vida and her freakin' Presbyterians, it'd probably be on page one." His brown eyes narrowed and he thrust out his heavy jaw with its hint of stubble.

"Look, Luce," I began, ever weary of trying to explain deadlines, "we'd already locked up the paper before the meeting. The story will be in next week's edition."

"Right, sure, gimme a break." Luce folded his arms on the table and leaned forward. "You know what those damned non-Catholic yuppies are up to, don't you? They're tryin' to turn St. Mildred's into a private school.

Get it? Not a *parochial* school—a *private* school. They don't want their precious little brats taught religion, they want 'em to learn Japanese, for God's sake! Look at the old-time parishioners like Polly Patricelli and Annie Jeanne Dupré and Marie Daley—they feel all at sea. Nothing but change, change, change these last thirty years."

I waved an impatient hand at Luce and almost knocked my burger basket out of Jessie Lott's grasp. "Okay, okay," I said, with an apologetic glance for the middle-aged waitress who also happened to attend St. Mildred's. "So which changes in the school bother you most?"

"What changes?" Jessie's plump face was suddenly anxious. "I've got grandchildren in second and fourth grade."

"It's nothing, Jessie," I said in reassurance.

"It's a big mess," Luce declared. "Jessie, bring me turkey on white, with a side of potato salad and some dill pickles and coffee, okay?"

Jessie, apparently feeling put in her place, wheeled heavily on her rubber-soled shoes and headed back to the kitchen. Luce sat up straight in the booth, squaring his broad shoulders. "What about that school board? Greer Something-or-Other, one of those freakin' yuppies. Buddy Bayard shows up in church when he damn well feels like it. The only real Catholic is Bill Daley, and sometimes I think the main reason he goes is to sell carpets and easy chairs from his store. A real glad-hander, that's our Bill."

I was sinking my teeth into my burger and wishing it were Luce's hairy arm. "So you're saying that the school board is already stacked in favor of the less-than-fervent faithful?"

Luce looked at me as if I were the village idiot, which I was not, because at that moment Crazy Eights Neffel wandered into the Burger Barn playing a ukulele. Crazy Eights may not be an idiot, but he is definitely crazy.

Jessie Lott and Doc Dewey, who happened to be sitting next to the door, hustled Crazy Eights out of the restaurant before he got through the first few bars of "The Frozen Logger."

"Look," Luce said as Doc Dewey returned to his table and Jessie Lott picked up the coffee carafes, "that Greer yuppie is one of those antireligion types, and if they add those new board members, you can bet they'll be pagan yuppies, too."

I frowned at Luce. "Are you saying that's the whole point of this proposal? To weigh the board in favor of the non-Catholics?"

"You got it." Luce drummed his thick fingers on the Formica tabletop. "Even if Bayard and Daley keep the faith, the rest of 'em won't. Then where'll we be?"

"We've got Veronica Wenzler-Greene as principal," I pointed out. "She seems like a responsible sort."

Luce uttered a contemptuous snort. "Ronnie Wenzler-Greene's no Sister Mary Rose," he declared, referring to the nun with the iron fist in the iron glove who had run the school for twenty-odd years before her retirement shortly after my arrival in Alpine. "For one thing, Ronnie's divorced. Now, that's not like it used to be with Catholics, but besides that, she strikes me as the kind who likes . . . what do they call them? Innovations."

I had to admit I didn't know Ronnie Wenzler-Greene very well. I didn't really know that much about the school, never having had a child enrolled there. I was beginning to think I didn't know much about my own parish.

"Okay, Luce," I said between french-fry nibbles. "If the vote this weekend favors expanding the school board, we'll run that in the paper, along with the candidates who've declared themselves. What's the deadline for getting on the ballot?"

Luce didn't know. If it had come up at last night's

meeting, I'd been wool-gathering. I'd have to call Father Den or Principal Ronnie.

Luce had now shifted gears, and was grousing about the environmentalists. Naturally Greer Fairfax's name came up again. So did that of her husband, Grant. But Luce refused to call them by their last name. Instead he favored designating them as "Tree-hugging SOBs."

I finished lunch before Luce did, so I left him with promises to watch the developing church story more closely. Since the papers were only now being delivered to individual homes, I had some spare time before the usual irate phone calls started coming in. Now that we had the back shop up and running, I needed to check our insurance. When I called Brendan Shaw earlier in the day, he'd assured me that I could drop in at the Sigurdson-Shaw agency any time between twelve and one. Brendan had brought his lunch.

Over sixty years ago a bucker named Harry Sigurdson had been seriously injured in the woods. Rather than leave Alpine to find work in a larger town, he had hit upon the scheme of selling a form of workers' compensation to his former fellow loggers. Eventually he sold life and home owner's and car insurance. When he finally died three years ago at the age of ninety-six, he had still not officially retired. But his son-in-law, Cornelius Shaw, had been allowed into the business upon his marriage to Helen Jane Sigurdson shortly after World War II. According to Vida, neither the marital nor the business merger had been entered into without conflict. Cornelius Shaw was a Catholic, Harry Sigurdson was a Lutheran, and fifty years ago such a so-called mixed marriage between members of different faiths wasn't looked upon with favor. But Harry had no sons, and eventually he relented. Vida, however, intimated that the main reason Harry continued working into his dotage was because he never quite trusted his son-in-law. The Irish, the old man insisted, were lazy and inclined to dissipation.

But Cornelius had been diligent, and now was in semi-retirement, spending almost half the year with Helen Jane in Palm Desert. Their son, Brendan, who is in his late forties, now runs the business. He is a man of medium size, medium coloring, and startling blue eyes. His handshake is a shade too firm, his laughter a trifle too hearty. Brendan makes much of how hard he works, as if still feeling a need to give the lie to his grandfather's allegations about the Irish.

Sigurdson-Shaw Insurance is located on the first floor of the Alpine Building, directly across the street from *The Advocate*. Ironically I rarely cross paths with Brendan Shaw. Our work schedules must be very different. It was only when I saw Brendan at the parish-council meeting that I remembered to call him about our coverage.

The agency is composed of a small reception area, Brendan's inner office, and a cubicle that's used by the salesmen he sometimes hires part-time. The current receptionist-secretary-assistant is Patsy Shaw, Brendan's wife. She is a ruddy blonde with a comfortable plump air about her that befits the mother of four sons. Idly I wondered if any of them was interested in carrying on the family business.

"Brendan's tied up for a few minutes," Patsy informed me in her friendly, open manner. She leaned forward and lowered her voice. "Mrs. Gotrocks is in there with him. Let's hope she's buying a couple of million-dollar policies. Except for some of the construction workers on the college, business has been sl-o-o-o-w. As usual."

I was puzzled. "Mrs. Gotrocks?"

Patsy nodded, her tightly permed blonde curls dancing. "You know—Ursula O'Toole." Patsy made a face. "I mean Ursula Randall. Soon to be Wells. I was two years ahead of her in school. You know, she was kind of a snip even then. Which is strange, because the O'Tooles were just plain folks. Mr. O'Toole had a corner grocery store in those days, where Itsa Bitsa Pizza is now. But I always thought that Mr. O'Toole was one of those fathers who doted on his daughter. You know—the Little Princess syndrome."

I did know; I'd seen it among my own peers. Sons were taken for granted, expected to be strong and brave and hardworking. The daughter—there was always only one—was protected, pampered, and put on a pedestal.

"So how did Ursula end up marrying a doctor?" I asked. Vida hadn't seen fit to go into Ursula's marital history.

"She got married right out of high school to a kid from Index who'd already joined the army. Six months later, he was killed in Vietnam. Ursula wanted to get away, so she left Alpine. I think it wasn't grief so much as it was her feeling that she was entitled to Bigger Things." Patsy sniffed in disapproval. "Ursula got a job at some big hospital in Seattle and met her first husband while he was an intern."

"I wonder why she came back," I remarked, keeping an eye on the closed door to Brendan's office.

Patsy shrugged. "Maybe she got tired of being a big frog in a big puddle. In Alpine, she can be a huge frog in a tiny puddle. And I gather that Warren wants to—"

The sharp signal I made with one hand silenced Patsy. Ursula Randall was backing out of Brendan's office, bidding him a gracious adieu. When she saw me, her thin face with its high cheekbones grew perplexed. I sensed that she was trying to recall the rock under which she'd last seen me crawling.

"Hi, Ursula," I said in my most cheerful voice. "Emma Lord, *The Alpine Advocate*. We met a couple of weeks ago after the ten o'clock Mass."

Ursula assumed a rueful expression. "Of course! Weak coffee and . . . some sort of stale confectionery." She laughed, that husky, gleeful sound that would have been more appropriate for jumping on bugs. "Tell me, dear, when are they going to run the article Mrs. Rumplemeyer wrote?"

"Runkel," I said with emphasis, not daring to look at Patsy, who was trying to stifle a giggle behind her hand. I was certain that she, too, knew perfectly well that Ursula hadn't forgotten Vida's last name. No one ever forgot Vida. "It's in today's edition," I went on. "You'll probably have it in your box when you get home."

"How nice." Ursula lifted a hand in apparent salute. "I do hope the pictures are flattering. I'm afraid I'm the most unphotogenic person on earth!" With that declaration, Ursula Randall departed the insurance agency just as Verb Vancich came in.

"Hi, Verb," Patsy said in greeting, then noted the harried expression on the newcomer's face. "What's up? Don't tell me the ski shop caught fire! I didn't hear any sirens."

Verb acknowledged me with a tremor that passed for a smile. "Maybe that'd be the best thing that could happen," he said, then rubbed at his high, slightly protruding forehead. "Some creep stole six of those bikes I got from Buzzy O'Toole. I need to put in a claim."

Patsy immediately turned sympathetic. "That's terrible, Verb. Kids, I suppose." She rummaged in a file cabinet behind her desk and pulled out a form. "Have you called the sheriff?"

Verb nodded. "I stopped in there before I came here. I saw Bill Blatt. Dodge was at the courthouse."

Alpine Ski was located next to the cobbler shop, across Front Street from the sheriff's headquarters. Verb took the claim form from Patsy, who indicated that he might be more comfortable filling it out at the desk in the cubicle. Then she ushered me into her husband's inner office.

Brendan was just hanging up the phone when I sat down in the high-backed armchair that looked as if it had once belonged to a dining room set. We made brief, idle conversation for about a minute before getting down to business. The result wasn't as bad as I'd feared. The increase in my annual premium would come to only around three hundred dollars.

"It's going okay for you?" Brendan inquired, now sitting back in his swivel chair and clasping his hands on top of his head.

"I think so," I said. "It's hard to predict. As time goes on, more and more businesses will do their own desktop publishing. But right now not too many Alpiners are equipped for that."

In his usual careful manner, Brendan seemed to consider my words. "You do a lot of nickel-and-dime stuff, I suppose."

"Right. Flyers, posters, that sort of thing. But it adds up. Father Den thinks maybe we can do the school yearbook next spring. I'll have to give him a reminder come January."

Brendan gazed at me with his brilliant blue eyes. "I'd guess the principal makes those decisions, not Den. Maybe you'd better check with the parish secretary first to make sure our pastor hasn't made a promise he can't keep."

It appeared that the division of responsibility was more clearly marked than I realized. "Who is the secretary?" I asked, once again struck by my lack of familiarity with inner parish circles.

"Monica Vancich," Brendan replied. "She took on the job this summer after Marie Daley had that stroke. Have you heard how Marie's doing?"

Marie Daley was a widow who had worked at St. Mildred's for at least twenty years. I knew her by sight, but that was all. I was much better acquainted with Marie's brother-in-law, Bill, who occasionally came into the office to confer with Leo about advertising for his home-furnishings store. I was surprised, however, that Monica Vancich had assumed Marie's responsibilities.

"How does Monica find time to run a home, raise three kids, and handle the religious-education program?" No wonder she had seemed somewhat rattled at last night's meeting.

Brendan merely grinned, revealing very white teeth with tiny spaces in between. "Beats me. Patsy's so worn-out every night that she goes to bed by nine-thirty. I'd fire her so she could get some rest, but I can't afford to right now. I'd actually have to pay a real secretary." Brendan chuckled. "Besides, my wife's darned good. She's spoiled me for anybody else."

It was well after one o'clock, so I made my farewells and returned to *The Advocate*. Judging from Vida's grim expression, we'd already started receiving calls from out-raged readers.

"I am not anti-Catholic," she declared, whipping off her glasses. "You people are very queer in many ways, but that's your business. How dare these papists criticize what I wrote about Ursula O'Toole Randall?"

I managed to find just enough space on Vida's desk to plant half of my backside. "Who? How?"

Vida threw up her hands. "Betsy O'Toole. Kathryn Daley. Buddy Bayard, of all people! To think of the business we give him every month, doing our photo work! And four anonymous. One of them was Annie Jeanne Dupré. Another was Sister Clare. Or is it Sister Mary Joan? Even when they don't wear habits, nuns still look alike."

Given that Sister Clare was short, dark, and dumpy, and Sister Mary Joan was a tall, beanpole blonde, I doubted Vida's confusion. But as usual, there was no point in arguing with my House & Home editor.

"What's the complaint?" I inquired.

Vida tossed her head, which caused the silk pillbox she was wearing to lose its grip and skid down over one ear.

"That I—not that ridiculous Ursula—made Catholics
sound pompous and superior. That Catholics think they
have a direct line to God. That everybody else in Alpine
is a lazy, worthless failure. If you ask me, Ursula's trying
to stir up trouble." Vida righted the pillbox and narrowed
her eyes. "Given the mood of this town, she's going to
get in much deeper than she expects."

Even Vida couldn't guess how close she'd come to the
truth.

Chapter Three

FATHER DEN'S DISTRESS call came through shortly after three o'clock. He was absolutely mortified by Ursula's comments.

"I'm tempted to write a letter to the paper," he said, "but I don't feel it would be appropriate. Are you getting much adverse reaction or am I being paranoid?"

I confessed that we now had heard from at least two dozen people—Catholic, Protestant, Jew, agnostic, and atheist. Ursula had struck a chord, and it definitely wasn't harmonious.

"I could talk about it in my homily this weekend," Father Den said in a dubious voice. "But only our parishioners would hear it."

"What about making a statement at the regular parish-council meeting?" I offered. "Then I could report it in the paper."

"We don't meet for almost two weeks," Father Den pointed out. "That's too late."

I cudgeled my brain for another way. "How about an interview with Ronnie Wenzler-Greene? It's a natural with the possibility of school-board expansion. Carla's already doing an overview of the coming year, but I could write up Ronnie's comments on the board. I'll call her this afternoon."

"Good." I heard Father Den's relief roll over the phone line. "One thing, though."

"What?"

"Don't get Ronnie started on . . . how can I put it? Her educational philosophy. No," he quickly contradicted himself, "that's not right. Forget what I said. Let her talk about whatever she wants."

I was frowning into the phone. "Is there something touchy that I don't know about?"

Father Den sighed. "Everything's touchy these days. Everything has to be politically correct. Whatever happened to right and wrong?" His laugh sounded bitter. "I think I need a vacation."

"Take one. Ben's going to be here for almost a week. He can stand in for you."

"Really?" Father Den brightened. "You know, I might take you up on that. My mother isn't well and I should spend some time with her in Tacoma. When will Ben get here?"

"Friday, the first," I replied. "He plans to leave the sixth."

Father Den said he'd think about it. We rang off and I immediately called Veronica Wenzler-Greene at home. The phone rang seven times before she answered it in a breathless voice.

"I was just coming in the door," she said, "and I guess I forgot to turn on the machine. How are you, Emma?"

I knew Ronnie only slightly. It was dawning on me that I knew most of my fellow Catholics either slightly or not at all. If they didn't advertise in *The Advocate* or provide a news source, they scarcely existed.

Explaining the reason for my call, I set up an appointment with Ronnie for Monday afternoon at one. It would be better for her if we met at the school. She was knee-deep in preparations.

She was also a little wary. "I thought you already had a story about the new fourth-grade teacher. And didn't Carla call last week about an overview?"

"It's this school-board expansion," I said by way of clarification. Or maybe it was really obfuscation. "If that gets approved, then it's going to be a fairly big story. Even if it doesn't, we . . . um . . . will be covering that, too."

"Oh, it'll get approved," Ronnie asserted. "It's absurd to have only three members. We've got a hundred and forty-six pupils enrolled this fall. We're reaching out all over Skykomish County."

I withheld comment. "I'll see you Monday. Bye, Ronnie."

The rest of the afternoon didn't do much to lift my spirits. To break the monotony of listening to scandalized readers, I phoned Verb Vancich and asked for details on his theft. Three ten-speeds and three mountain bikes had been lifted from the rear of the store some time between six P.M. and nine A.M. Yes, they were all locked onto a rack, but the thief or thieves had sawed through the metal. Yes, Verb knew he should have put them inside, but the store was already crowded, and since his ad was coming out in today's *Advocate*, he intended to display them out front on the sidewalk. No, he had no idea who had taken them, but if he ever caught the little bastards, he'd teach them a thing or two.

"Kids?" I asked on the basis of his implication.

"Who else? It's late August, they're all bored." Verb's exasperation was palpable. "By this time of year they're tired of hiking and fishing and skinny-dipping. What do you expect when there aren't any part-time jobs around here for young people? Or enough real jobs for anybody? I bet they'll take those bikes to Everett and sell them off for half of what I paid Buzzy O'Toole."

Verb was probably right. Everett was fifty miles away, but big enough to provide anonymity. "Speaking of Buzzy, did you see his sister coming out of Sigurdson-Shaw?" I inquired, changing the subject to prevent Verb from casting further aspersions on Alpine's errant youth and depressed economy.

There was a pause at the other end. "Ursula? I saw her. Why?" Verb suddenly sounded on guard.

"She's making quite an impression around here with her money and her mouth. Of course, if she spends what she's got in Alpine, that's all to the good," I allowed, aware that I was sounding like a common gossip. "Patsy Shaw thinks great things might be in store for Brendan and the agency."

"Like how?" Verb was now downright suspicious.

"I'm babbling," I said with a lame little laugh. "I guess what I'm saying is that anytime anybody who isn't flat-out broke moves to town, we ought to roll out the red carpet. Alpiners tend to react instead of act. If local entre-preneurs want to capitalize on newcomers, they need to be more aggressive. There are plenty of new businesses opening up farther down Highway 2, especially in Monroe. You have to seize the moment. The window of opportunity can be very narrow." I felt as if I was still babbling, parroting a talk I'd given at the Chamber of Commerce last May. Verb hadn't been in attendance, but the members who were had acted as if they hadn't heard my speech, either. "Do you see what I mean?" Even as I renewed my vow never again to give a formal talk at the Chamber, I sounded as if I were pleading with Verb.

"Maybe." His voice had dropped a notch.

"I'll get off my soapbox now," I said with a phony little laugh. "I shouldn't bend your ear, Verb, but my own business lives and dies with the local economy. This was a fairly good week in terms of advertising. Have you seen the paper yet?"

"No," he replied in a glum voice. "I don't want to— that big ad I paid for is worthless. A third of my inven-tory is gone."

"I'm sorry about that, Verb." The only thing I knew about bikes was that five years ago Adam's Klein had set me back nine hundred bucks. The bike was gone, too, after my son had left it unattended on the University of

Hawaii campus. "Maybe we'll have a hard winter and you can make up the difference during ski season."

"Yeah, I'll get rich." Verb was all but sneering. "Sometimes I wonder why Monica and I stay in Alpine. Seattle may have crime, but it's got jobs."

I refrained from saying that Seattle probably didn't need another ski shop. Maybe Verb wanted to get out of the winter-sports business. He and Monica had moved to Alpine soon after the birth of their second child. They, like many expatriates from the big city, had an unrealistic view of small-town living.

After I hung up, I considered Ursula Randall's reasons for moving back to her hometown. Vida hadn't made Ursula's motives clear in her article. I wandered out into the editorial office, but found only Leo, who had his ear glued to the receiver and was drawing circles on a notepad. He didn't look up.

The phones had started ringing again. It was after four-thirty. Feeling the need to escape, I left the office and walked the two blocks to Francine's Fine Apparel.

"Aha!" Francine cried when I entered the shop. "You've read your own ads! You know the fall line is in. Come on, Emma, when was the last time you did something for yourself?"

"I'm not here to buy," I asserted, though my eyes were straying to a couple of items tastefully displayed along one wall. "I'm suffering from unsatisfied curiosity. Can you explain Ursula Randall?"

I cannot think why it didn't occur to me that this wasn't a tactful question to put to Francine Wells. Maybe it's because she's usually such an open, candid sort of person. Maybe it's because she and I have never really discussed her failed marriage. Maybe it's because I'm an idiot.

In any event, Francine bristled and her eyes grew hard and cold. "How do you explain Satan?" she snapped.

My clumsy brain tried to work its way through

Francine's marital tribulations. Many years ago Warren Wells had left her for another woman, or so I'd heard. But that woman couldn't have been Ursula O'Toole Randall. There had been a second wife, the alleged temptress. Either she had died or divorced. It was only recently that Ursula and Warren had become a twosome.

"Are you referring to Vida's article?" I inquired apprehensively.

Francine gave a flip of her newly acquired champagne-tinted locks. "God, no! That was typical of the bitch. Pardon me, but she's a real piece of work. She always was. Ask anybody around here who knew her when she was growing up." Francine's expression altered as Marisa Foxx, a local attorney and also a member of St. Mildred's, came into the shop. "Later," Francine said under her breath. "Power suits, Marisa? A dress for client dinners? How about something to sway a jury? And where did you get that smart-looking jacket? It wasn't here—I don't carry Max Mara, though I should. You look terrific!"

I wandered around the store while Francine seduced Marisa. Again, I knew my fellow parishioner only by sight. She was in her thirties, tall, slim, and, as certain sniping locals were inclined to point out, somewhat mannish. We nodded pleasantly. Then I tried to disappear in the sale rack at the rear of the shop.

After about five minutes Marisa went into one of the two fitting rooms with a couple of suits, several pairs of slacks, and a blazer. Francine led me toward the front, where Marisa couldn't hear.

"Sour grapes, right?" said Francine, then shook her head. "It's not that—it's that Ursula has lousy timing. We've got big problems up at church, and guess who shows up? The curse of the archdiocese, Ursula Randall, that's who. I talk to people in Seattle, they know all about her. She's done nothing but meddle and stir up trouble. It's all money. Dr. Randall was a hotshot surgeon who raked it in, then conveniently died of a massive heart attack in his mid-fifties. He and Ursula were big contributors to the Church. From what I hear, they could have had kitchen privileges at the Vatican."

My lower-middle-class background hadn't given me much experience with wealthy people. My first encounter with the well heeled had come as a freshman at Blanchet High School in Seattle. Most of those teenage scions had regarded me as if I were a contagious disease. The richest person I had ever known was Tom Cavanaugh's wife, Sandra. If her mental derangement was an example of what money could do, I considered myself lucky to be borderline broke.

"So why did Ursula move here?" I inquired, keeping one eye on the fitting room, lest Marisa emerge and find us gossiping like common scolds.

"Good question," Francine replied with a smirk. "Why did you leave Portland, Emma?"

I bridled a bit. Francine knew the answer, which was fairly simple: My ex-fiancé of twenty years earlier had neglected to remove my name from his Boeing insurance policy. When he had died unexpectedly, I came into two hundred thousand dollars. After recovering from shock—and trying to recall exactly what my onetime future husband had looked like—I quit my job as a reporter on *The Oregonian* and used the money to buy *The Alpine Advocate* from Marius Vandeventer. I'd also purchased my dream car, the then secondhand, now aging green Jaguar XJ6.

"I wanted a fresh start," I responded. "The timing was good. Adam was about to start college."

Francine nodded, a trifle impatiently. "Yes, new beginnings. But not on top of old ones."

"You mean because Ursula originally came from Alpine?"

"That's right," Francine said as Marisa came out of the fitting room. "You weren't retreating. Ursula is." With a big smile for Marisa, she stepped gracefully around me. "Well? How much of it works for you?"

Most of it, I gathered, and sensed it was my cue to depart. But Francine wasn't quite finished with me.

"Emma! Come back tomorrow. There's an Ellen Tracy suit in the back that'd make you look like the cover of *Vogue*. It just came today via UPS. Oh, by the way— Alicia's visiting this weekend. You must come to dinner."

Alicia was Francine and Warren's daughter. She was married to a TV producer and lived in New York. I'd met her once or twice when she'd accompanied her mother to church on previous visits. It had struck me that Alicia had inherited none of her mother's charm and all of her artifice. But maybe I was wrong. I'm not always perceptive when it comes to first impressions.

When I reached the office it was a couple of minutes after five. Everyone but Ginny Burmeister Erlandson had gone home, and she was gathering up her belongings when I picked up the last phone messages of the day.

"Lots of cranks, huh, Ginny?" I commented, riffling through the half-dozen calls that had accumulated in my half-hour absence.

Ginny turned her plain but intelligent face to me. "What is this with Catholics?" she asked, looking and sounding weary. "Why do you—they—cause such a stir?"

I felt myself blink. "Do they? Do we?" I smiled to let Ginny know I hadn't taken her slip of the tongue personally.

Ginny sighed. "I don't know—maybe it's because I'm Lutheran, and most people in Alpine are. Most people who go to church, that is. But who gets excited about what Lutherans do? Or Methodists or Congregationalists or anybody else? But Catholics always seem to get the attention. Is it because of the pope?"

While the query wasn't without merit, I didn't know how to answer Ginny. "We're more international," I said vaguely. "Because we do have a pope in Rome, outsiders regard Catholics with suspicion. It's dumb, of course, but it's traditional. Maybe we seem kind of mysterious. We're not."

Ginny gave a toss of her glorious red hair. "I know that. I mean you're not mysterious and the Bayards aren't, and neither is Mr. or Mrs. Bronsky." She paused, gazing into the editorial office. "Is Mr. Walsh a Catholic?"

I nodded. "He's what we call *fallen away*. It means he doesn't go to church."

"Fallen away." Ginny seemed to savor the phrase. "See—that's what I mean. You have all these weird . . ." She fingered her chin, then suddenly stiffened as the color drained from her face. "Oh! Excuse me!" Ginny raced off, heading for the rest rooms directly behind the front office.

I smiled to myself. Ginny and Rick Erlandson had gotten married in February. While there had not yet been an official announcement, this was the third time in as many days that Ginny had made a precipitate exit from the office. If my guess was right, our office manager would be taking maternity leave sometime in March. I hoped she would decide to return to work, though I wouldn't blame her if she wanted to be a full-time mother. I'd never had that option.

There was hardly any breeze that evening, and the air felt heavy. A few clouds had rolled in over Mount Baldy, but rain wasn't in the forecast. When I arrived home, my little house felt stifling. I opened both doors and three windows before checking the mail and the answering machine. I could have waited longer: the delivery contained nothing but junk, and once again, there were no telephone messages. Annoyed, I sat down to call my son in Tuba City.

Ben's crackling voice was recorded, a familiar and somewhat involved message in English, Spanish, and

Navajo. As my disappointment mounted I started to call Milo. Halfway through his home number, I hung up. My perverse nature dictated that Milo should call me. Emotionally I was behaving as if I were fifteen; physically I felt about ninety. My cotton shirt was sticking to my back. My scalp itched. My feet felt as if they were a size too large for my skimpy sandals. I needed to hear from Adam. I needed to talk to Ben. I needed Milo.

I needed rain.

The rest of the week played out under a relentless sun and the pressure of deadline for the Labor Day special edition. I'd finally reached Ben and Adam late Friday night. My brother was looking forward to visiting me; my son was irritatingly vague. Maybe he'd come standby. Maybe he'd stay in Tuba City. Maybe he was a rotten kid.

Such was my conclusion after putting the phone down. My disposition didn't improve when Milo called ten minutes later to cancel our outing to Leavenworth. With the help of park rangers, he and Dwight Gould had finally tracked down some of the teenagers who had been stealing cars in Skykomish and Snohomish counties. Because of the conflict in jurisdictions, Milo had a pile of paperwork. Jack Mullins was already on vacation and Sam Heppner was due to take off the week before Labor Day. The sheriff was shorthanded, and the three-day weekend always promised its share of highway accidents. Milo was apologetic, but immovable. I was understanding, but irked. I tried not to let it show.

Somehow, I muddled through the empty, overwarm, uneventful Saturday. My good intentions of cleaning house before Ben arrived were hampered by the humidity. Pushing a vacuum cleaner in eighty-eight-degree weather was daunting. So was washing windows, scrubbing the kitchen floor, and scouring the bathroom. My efforts were halfhearted at best; the day ended as it began, on a sour, muggy note.

So mired was I in oppressive heat and self-pity that I had forgotten about the vote to expand the school board. Veronica Wenzler-Greene stood in the vestibule handing out ballots after Sunday Mass. Despite my attendance at the Tuesday meeting, I hadn't really given the proposal much thought. Staring at the sheet with its simple, printed declaration and choice of Yes/No boxes to check, I decided that adding two members was probably a good idea. If there were only three on the board and one of them got hit by a logging truck, a deadlock could ensue. Recklessly I checked the *Yes* portion and handed my ballot to Veronica.

Slipping out of the church, I headed for the parking lot. The morning haze had lifted, and the sun seemed capable of melting the newly laid tarmac that a parish work party had put in a couple of weeks earlier. It occurred to me that the danger of forest fires must be rising. The indicator sign at Old Mill Park had registered HIGH on Friday. I suspected that it had now moved up to EXTREME.

Maybe it was just as well that Milo and I hadn't gone to Leavenworth. On the other side of the pass where the pseudo-Bavarian town was located, the weather was always hotter and drier than in the western part of the state. It would be much better to visit in early October, when the leaves had turned color and temperatures had cooled.

To my surprise, Vida's big white Buick was pulled up next to my mailbox. She got out of the car when she saw me approach the drive.

"Pastor Purebeck is on vacation," she announced, referring to the minister at the Presbyterian church. "The Bible-camp children put on a puppet show. Mercifully the curtain fell down on top of them and it ended early. Really, Emma, can you imagine a Cabbage Patch Kid as the Queen of Sheba?"

After letting us into the house, I offered lemonade.

Vida accepted, and I suggested that we sit in the back-yard under the shade of the evergreen trees.

"But you won't be able to hear the phone," she protested.

I regarded my House & Home editor with puzzlement. "I've got the cordless kind," I reminded her. "But why should I want to listen for it?"

Behind the big glasses, Vida fixed me with her gimlet eye. She was wearing what she would call a "summer frock" of blue, green, yellow, and white floral cotton, and an enormous straw cartwheel hat with a wide silk ribbon. If it was a conscious attempt at a little-girl look, it failed. There is nothing little about Vida, and, at sixty-plus, far less of a girl. She is all woman, perhaps superwoman. Naturally I flinched a bit as she continued to stare at me.

"The vote," she finally said. "Won't they call you?"

I sagged a bit in the lawn chair. "You mean the school-board issue? No, I didn't ask them to call. I can find out tomorrow."

Vida's nostrils flared in disapproval. "Really, Emma! I can't believe what I'm hearing! Everyone in town is abuzz! Where have you been for the last few days?"

I was taken aback. "It's no big deal," I said, waving away a couple of deerflies. "All they're doing is trying to add two more members. Look, this isn't the public schools. We're talking about a hundred and forty kids and their parents. Oh, we'll carry an article, but this isn't earthshaking news."

Over the rim of her lemonade glass, Vida's expression was skeptical. "I'm hearing otherwise," she murmured.

"Like what?"

Vida shrugged her wide shoulders. "It's not for me to say. I'm Presbyterian."

"You're also on my staff," I pointed out dryly. "Cough it up, Vida."

Tipping her head to one side, she put a hand on her

cartwheel hat. "Well . . . there's Greer Fairfax, for one thing. You must know her background."

"No, I don't," I admitted. "She doesn't belong to the parish. I only figured out who she was Tuesday night at the special meeting."

Vida pursed her lips. "Before she married, she lived in a commune. In California." The pause that followed was obviously for my dull-witted benefit. "She's very much involved in social issues and the environment. Her husband, Grant, works at a laboratory near Monroe."

I felt vaguely bewildered. "Did you do an article on the Fairfaxes when they moved here? Did I miss it?"

"Carla did it, four years ago, right after you hired her." Vida tried to appear nonjudgmental. "If I may say so, it didn't capture the real Fairfaxes. Carla concentrated on their dogs."

"Oh." I honestly didn't remember the story. Four years ago I was still learning names and family ties and all the internecine connections of a small town.

"The Fairfaxes had a registered AKC miniature border collie," Vida continued. "I believe it got run over. Or a cougar ate it."

"Oh." I was still feeling rather lost. "That's too bad."

"Greer is an activist," Vida said. "You recall the chain incident at Icicle Creek."

In the early spring an antilogging group had protested clear-cutting by chaining themselves to various trees near the Icicle Creek ranger station. One of the activists hadn't been able to undo his chains, which had resulted in a heated debate over whether or not to cut down the tree to which he was shackled. Greer had been dispatched to drive into town and get a chain saw. None was to be found. Apparently word of the fiasco had already reached the fuming loggers, who had made certain that no implements were available to free the protester. Luckily, by the time Greer returned with the bad news,

somebody had figured out how to undo the chains
without damaging the tree.

"Bill Daley seems sound," Vida went on in her assess-
ment of the three existing school-board members. As
usual, she knew more about my fellow parishioners than
I did. "But that's an illusion. Bill is a businessman, and
inclined to follow the wind. The same might be said for
Buddy Bayard." The gray eyes peered at me. "So what is
the point?"

"Of what?" I was definitely feeling drowsy, lulled by
the heat and the stillness and the bees buzzing in the
fuchsia bush.

A flicker of impatience crossed Vida's broad face. "Of
adding members. If, as I've heard, the goal is to secu-
larize the school, Greer would be for it. Buddy and Bill
would be against. The younger faction needs to offset the
more conservative votes. But can they guarantee the
election of like-minded candidates?"

"Not necessarily," I allowed, watching an Alaskan
robin hop between the branches of the nearest fir.

"Perhaps we're on the wrong track concerning goals.
Maybe it's finances," Vida speculated. "Or a personal
matter, involving your pastor. It might be Polly Patricelli's cracked vase."

Vida had finally penetrated my lethargic state. "Polly's
vase? What are you talking about?"

"Emma! Shame on you!" Vida clucked. "You must
have heard. It's all over town. I thought of mentioning it
in 'Scene,' but it struck me as possibly in poor taste. And
Polly is old as well as unreliable."

Appollonia Patricelli was the mother of Itsa Bitsa
Pizza's Pete and eight other grown children. She was a
gnarled little shrub of a woman, who had come from
Italy as a young girl, but never quite put aside her old-
country ways.

"Sorry," I said, trying to look properly contrite. "I
haven't heard about Polly's vase. What about it?"

Vida emitted a short but deep sigh, then sat back in the lawn chair. "The vase is very old. It's fairly large and ceramic. Polly's parents brought it from their home in Assisi. A few months ago it developed a crack. Polly couldn't use it for flowers anymore because it leaked. But of course she couldn't bear to throw it out or even put it away. So she kept it on the mantel." Vida stopped for a beat, eyeing me in an apparent attempt to make sure I was really in ignorance. When she realized that I definitely was, she continued.

"Early this month—I believe it was a Sunday—Polly came home and discovered that the crack had gotten larger and more detailed. It looked to her—or so she told my sister-in-law, Ella Hinshaw, who admittedly is very deaf—as if it were the face of Christ. A few days later—Friday, as I recall—Polly insisted that despite the fact she hadn't put water in the vase since Easter, the eyes had wept." Vida took a deep breath. "Now what do you make of that?"

I was stumped. But if Polly's vase wasn't a miracle, it was enough to wake me up.

Chapter Four

SATURDAY NIGHTS WERE the worst when it came to couples beating up on each other in Alpine. But the last Sunday in August had set a record for domestic violence. Maybe it was the weather. Maybe it was the economy. Maybe it was the booze. Maybe it was the frustration of seeing another summer pass amid tall stands of untouchable timber.

Whatever the reasons, Milo had spent his weekend doing the part of his job that he hated most. Answering a call involving familial abuse often erupts into open season on law-enforcement officials. Domestic violence is tricky for journalists, too. The best way of handling reports is to list the type of official call, the address where the incident occurred, and the time and date. If readers are sufficiently curious, they can figure out who's thumping on whom. In a town the size of Alpine, most people already know.

"So that's why you didn't call last night," I said after Milo had unloaded a few harrowing family episodes. "I almost phoned you." It was late Monday morning, and I'd stopped by the sheriff's office on the pretext of checking the log.

Across the desk, Milo's hazel eyes showed a glimmer of interest. "You did?"

"I thought I heard a prowler." It was only a small lie. Something—maybe a dog or a deer—had knocked over part of my woodpile in the carport.

"Oh." Milo swung around in his chair and hauled his feet onto his desk. "I thought you might have wanted to see those pictures I got back from the ocean trip."

In late July, Milo and I had taken off for five days. We had driven out to Grays Harbor and spent a couple of days on the ocean at Klaloch. On the way home, we had explored the Kitsap Peninsula, then ferried across Puget Sound to Seattle. One night in the Big City had been enough for Milo. There were too many cars, too many people, too much noise, and not enough trees. He didn't relax until we hit Highway 2 at Monroe.

"Are the pictures any good?" I inquired, knowing that Milo had tried out his Minolta camera's new zoom lens.

"Not bad," Milo allowed. "I got some good sunset shots. Want me to bring them over tonight?"

"Sure. I'll make shish kebabs on the barbecue. It's too hot to cook inside."

"Sounds good." Despite his wounds, Milo looked pleased. "Can I bring something?"

I shook my head. Since the sheriff and I had officially become a couple, he was in the habit of offering liquor, steaks, or, upon one memorable occasion, a pink dogwood tree that had taken me three hours to plant.

"I'm well stocked," I said. "You haven't been over for a week."

"Nine days," Milo said, surprising me with his accuracy. "It's been crazy around here. It'll get worse toward the end of the week, especially now that Sam's on vacation. Jack's back, but he's got a hell of a sunburn. He went to sleep for five hours at Lake Chelan. The shade moved, but he didn't."

I was on my feet, edging out of Milo's office with its mounted steelhead, NRA posters, county maps, and piles of paperwork. "By the way," I said, a hand at the doorknob, "wasn't that Burl Creek Road address in the log where Nunzio Lucci lives?"

Milo cocked his head to one side. "You mean the

ruckus Saturday night? Yeah, that was Luce. No big deal, though. Their twins had a birthday party. Somebody tossed the cake through a window. Luce tried to do the same with the kids. Ron and Maylene Bjornson don't like noise, so they called in a complaint."

As I recalled, the Bjornsons lived next door to the Luccis, though it was a relative term. The houses off the Burl Creek Road were scattered among the fields and woods. Either the Bjornsons had very sensitive hearing or the Luccis had been making more noise than just throwing cake through a window.

"How are the Luccis getting by?" I asked. "He's been out of work for almost two years."

"Della's still cooking at the high school," Milo replied. "Luce picks up odd jobs, mostly driving trucks. Even if there were jobs open, I don't think he could go back to logging. He got hurt pretty bad in the woods about four or five years ago. Still, they seem to be doing okay. The twins got new bikes for their birthday and their TV is newer than mine." The sheriff shrugged. "Of course my set doesn't have half a pizza plastered on the screen, but somebody's probably cleaned that up by now."

Shaking my head at the vagaries of domestic life in Alpine, I returned to the office. Father Den had called in my absence, relaying the final tally on the school-board expansion vote. The measure had passed, ninety-six to seventy-nine.

"So who've announced as the candidates?" I inquired, eyeing the formal notice on my desk that all timber operations had ceased due to the high fire danger.

Father Den cleared his throat. "They have until Friday to submit their names. So far, we've got only two—Rita Haines and Derek Norman."

I'd never heard of Derek Norman, but Rita had been a Patricelli before her marriage to a man named Haines. Since Rita seldom attended Mass, I knew her better from her job as the Chamber of Commerce secretary. Mr. Haines wasn't around, so I assumed they were divorced. There were children, but I knew virtually nothing about them. Rita had always struck me as mercurial in temperament.

"Who's Derek?" I asked.

"He works at the state fish hatchery," Father Den responded. "His wife, Blythe, is a writer who does some tutoring. They have a second grader and a kindergartner. I think they moved to Alpine at the end of June."

More newcomers, I thought. "Do they come to Mass?"

"Well . . ." Father Den's laugh was lame. "They're not Catholic. But they believe in private education. School-board members don't have to be Catholic. In some cases, they don't have to be parents, either."

I jotted down a note for Vida or Carla to set up an interview. Obviously the Normans had slipped through the cracks. "So we'll vote at the weekend Masses? Do you expect anybody else to jump in or will these spots be uncontested?"

"You'd better ask Ronnie Wenzler-Greene about that," Father Den said. "I try to keep out of the school side of the parish as much as I can. I've already got enough headaches." Judging from the weary note in his voice, the pastor was having one now. I didn't want to add to his woes, but felt compelled to mention Polly Patricelli's cracked vase.

Father Den laughed. "Somebody brought it up the other day," he said. "But Polly hasn't said anything. You know how rumors get started in this town."

"You mean . . . Polly isn't taking it seriously?" If ever there was a candidate for a home miracle, Polly Patricelli struck me as at the top of the list. She was what I called an "old-fashioned" Catholic, with a houseful of senti-mental religious paintings, plaster statues of saints, and blessed palms stuck everywhere except behind her ears. Or so Vida claimed.

But Father Den shrugged off the alleged portrait in the

vase. "I've seen the Blessed Mother in a waffle, St. Thérèse in dry wall, and the Holy Spirit flying out of a cigar humidor. Believe me, they weren't miracles, just optical illusions. I'll bet your brother has seen his share, too."

It was true. One of Ben's most memorable "visions" had occurred during his Mississippi assignment when an otherwise sensible young woman had reported seeing the Holy Family in a plateful of chitlins.

On that note of skepticism, I rang off. I had to grab some lunch before my one-thirty appointment with Veronica Wenzler-Greene. Carla and Ginny had already gone out to eat, Leo was nowhere in sight, and Vida was munching radishes and celery sticks.

"Well?" She looked up as I came into the news office.

I knew that she had been dying of curiosity about the school-board vote. "It passed," I said simply. "Who are Derek and Blythe Norman?"

"What?" Vida all but shot out of her chair. "Norman? I've never heard of them! Where did you get such names?"

I recounted my conversation with Dennis Kelly. "They've been here since the end of June," I said with a hint of reproach. "He works at the fish hatchery."

"He can't," Vida muttered, clearly in denial. "The state would have sent a news release." Her eyes darted in the direction of Carla's vacant desk. "She threw it out. I've seen her discard news releases before this. Last week it was the Burl Creek Thimble Club's Fall Remnant Sale! It should have come to me in the first place. Do I have to start going through her wastebasket or will you speak to her?"

"I'll remind Carla," I promised. "But if you have time, can you check out the Normans?"

Vida's entire body quivered. "Of course! It'll be in this week's edition, even if I have to pull the Wickstroms' trip to Salmon Arm. Honestly! Carla gets worse, instead of better." Whipping off her glasses, Vida rubbed furiously at her eyes. "Emma, I really don't see how you put up with that young woman. Have you read her story on the community college?"

I gave my House & Home editor a blank stare. "I didn't know she was doing one. Is there some new development I missed?"

"No." Vida replaced her glasses, removed her magenta beret, and ran agitated hands through her gray curls. "That's the point. The article begins, 'There was no news on the community-college scene this week.' And then she spends five hundred words telling why not."

It probably had been a mistake to assign the college coverage to Carla. But most of the journalistic value was visual at this point, and I did have faith in my reporter's competence with a camera.

"I'll kill it unless we're desperate to fill the paper," I said. "But you have to admit, Carla's done a good job with the back shop. She understands computers."

"Pooh!" Vida wasn't yet ready to admit that computers existed. "Maybe that's what she should be doing instead of pretending she's a reporter. Carla has no sense of news. Such a waste of time, writing about things that haven't happened! I wouldn't put a nonitem like that in 'Scene Around Town.' What have you got for me this week? 'Scene' is very dull—again."

Everyone on the staff was responsible for helping Vida fill her gossip column. Off the top of my head, I couldn't think of anything interesting. "I'm going to interview the principal at St. Mildred's this afternoon," I said. "I'm sure I'll pick up a couple of things there, like how they're decorating for back to school."

Vida didn't appear mollified. "You aren't exactly on top of what's going on there, Emma. I can't believe you waited until just now to find out about the school-board vote."

"They had to count the ballots," I explained. "It was up to the parish secretary, Monica Vancich. She doesn't come in until ten o'clock on Mondays."

"Monica?" Vida frowned. "I thought she taught Sunday school."

I started to pour a cup of coffee but discovered that the pot was empty. It was unlike Ginny to neglect our caffeine lifeline. "Monica is in charge of religious education," I clarified, "which includes Sunday school."

"Indeed!" With an incisive gesture, Vida ripped a half sheet of copy paper out of her manual typewriter. "How can Monica find time to handle all that and run your church?"

"She doesn't," I said calmly. "Father Den does." I inched toward the door. "I've got to eat before I interview Ronnie Wenzler-Greene. I should be back around two-thirty." With a feeble smile, I backed out and ran smack into Leo Walsh.

My ad manager put out a hand to steady me, then pulled away as if he'd been singed. "Sorry," he muttered, and edged on by.

I couldn't help but stare. Vida did, too, though sensing the awkward movement, she spoke up: "Jean Campbell is the secretary at our church, and very efficient she is. I don't know what Pastor Purebeck would do without her. Of course she's been there longer than he has."

Jean Cooper Campbell was a native; James Purebeck wasn't. What little confidence Vida had in anyone else was always assessed in a direct ratio to the length of time they'd spent in Alpine.

But the diversion didn't quite turn the trick for me: I marched over to Leo's desk and forced casual charm into my voice. "I'm getting something to eat, Leo. Come with me. We need to talk. About the Labor Day edition."

Leo's sad brown eyes told me he knew I was lying. Without expression, he flipped a pencil into an open drawer and stood up. "Okay. I can spare twenty minutes."

The Venison Eat Inn and Take Out was in the next block. At twelve-thirty the restaurant was packed with locals and tourists. With some misgivings, I agreed to sit in the bar. While Leo seemed to look longingly at the rows of bottles, he ordered only coffee.

"What's bothering you, Leo?" I demanded after the owner and bartender, Oren Rhodes, had taken my order for fish and chips. "You don't seem like yourself lately."

Leo made as if to pull out his wallet. "That's funny. I could have sworn I had my ID with me. That'd prove who I am."

"It's not funny," I retorted. "It's tough working with someone who goes around like the Grim Reaper."

"Really?" Leo's weathered face showed a trace of amusement. "I thought your previous ad manager always acted like that until he got rich."

"Touché." While working at *The Advocate*, Ed Bronsky had been the eternal pessimist, a pall of gloom in a baggy raincoat. But even when Leo was still drinking, he'd been cheerful. When he began to curb his alcohol intake, he remained chipper if cynical. "You're not Ed. I know that, even if you don't show me your ID. Are you upset about something?"

The question sounded fatuous in my own ears. The fifty-odd years that showed in Leo's face revealed many upsets, along with disappointments, dead ends, and lost causes. Mediocre jobs, a broken marriage, rifts with children, and an uprooting from California to Alpine hadn't seemed to improve Leo's outlook on life. Indeed, it had brought him here, now, drinking black coffee in the darkened bar of a second-class restaurant in a third-rate logging town. I didn't find much consolation in the fact that I was there, too.

"Well," Leo finally said after lighting a cigarette, "it's not the weather. It's been nice. No rain."

That piece of news hardly cheered me. But I was

trying to see things through Leo's eyes, which is always futile. "So what is it?"

A brief roar of guffaws and curses erupted from the bar where a half-dozen loggers commiserated among themselves. I glanced up briefly. It occurred to me that the men who occupied the stools were always the same, or at least interchangeable: burly, belligerent, dejected, discouraged—they sat on heavy haunches with their scuffed work shoes planted on the floor as if they were afraid somebody might pull the shabby carpeting out from under them. Of course in a larger sense, somebody already had.

Leo's brown eyes finally met mine and held. "Look, babe," he began, resurrecting the annoying nickname I realized I hadn't heard in quite a while, "let's say I'm going through kind of a bad patch and let it go at that. I'll snap out of it. I always do. That's one thing about Leo Fulton Walsh—he lands on his feet—even if the rest of him is in the crapper."

I let out a small, exasperated sigh. "I'm probably going to be able to give you a raise before the year is out." When at a loss, editor-publisher Lord can fall back on mundane matters such as money.

Leo shook his head. "I'm doing okay. Wait till you see how this back-shop thing goes. Stop worrying that pretty head of yours. It's not your problem."

I opened my mouth to ask the next obvious question, but Leo stopped me. "It's not Delphine Corson, either. We've kind of cooled it, but that's no big deal."

Leo's romance with the blonde, buxom owner of Posies Unlimited had been an ongoing affair almost since his arrival in Alpine two years earlier. His ex-wife was remarried, and the initial acrimony seemed to have diminished. As for his three grown children, Leo actually had entertained two of them in the late spring. It seemed that in some ways, the big rips in his life had begun to mend.

But of course I couldn't read Leo's mind or peer into his soul. "Okay," I said as Oren delivered my lunch order, "I'll back off. I was afraid I'd said or done something to make you mad. This weather makes me cross."

Leo laughed, a strident and, of late, an unfamiliar sound. "Hell, Emma, isn't it time you got over all that Catholic guilt shit?"

"I don't do guilt," I snapped. "I don't even understand it. That's what confession's for. Guilt stinks."

Leo gave a disbelieving shrug. "If you say so. Hey, I've got to get back to work. All things considered, we're pretty fat for this issue. If not a raise, maybe a Christmas bonus?" He had stood up and made as if to cuff my shoulder, but his hand fell away. "See you, babe."

I ate hurriedly, which is an occupational hazard. I felt just a little furtive, sitting alone in the Venison Inn's bar at midday. Like most of Alpine's buildings, the place wasn't air-conditioned, but it was much cooler than outside. Still, I resisted the urge to linger over a second Pepsi. Without food to accompany the beverage, I might be tempted to buy a pack of cigarettes from the machine next to the rest rooms.

I arrived at St. Mildred's Parochial School just before one-thirty. The main doors were locked, but the office was open. The school secretary's desk was vacant, but before I could wander out into the hall, Veronica Wenzler-Greene called to me from what I presumed was the supply room.

"I'm checking the new textbooks," said Principal Ronnie, brushing dust from her beige blouse. "We're introducing a new math curriculum for fourth through eighth grade this year. It's very exciting."

"Wonderful," I said, trying to exude enthusiasm. In my opinion, math was about as exciting as grout buildup. "Carla's including that in her back-to-school story, I imagine?"

Ronnie nodded with a jerky motion as she led me into

her office. She was a tall, sharp-featured woman in her
early forties whose sandy hair was cut close to her head.
Her mother had been a housekeeper; her father, a mill-
worker. Ronnie's ex-husband, Gerry Greene, was a network technician for US West. The hyphenated name,
according to Vida, was the result of a scholarship to
Loyola Marymount in Los Angeles. Apparently, the
Jesuits had taught Ronnie to think for herself—or like a
Jesuit, which may or may not have been the same thing. I
wondered why she hadn't lopped off the Greene after
lopping off Gerry, but perhaps she thought the hyphen
added importance.

"Carla should have most of our plans for the coming
year," Ronnie said, sitting down behind her orderly desk
and offering me one of two molded plastic chairs which I
assumed had withstood the depressed forms of various
sets of anxious parents. "I honestly don't see what more I
can tell you."

My gaze darted around the room, which was decorated
with cutouts of autumn leaves, photographs of previous
graduating classes, Ronnie's framed doctorate from
Washington State University, a picture of her with the
current archbishop, a crucifix, and a statue of Our Lady
of Mount Carmel.

"I'm interested in the school-board vote," I said. "I
understand the need to add members because three isn't
really representative." Noting Ronnie's quizzical expression, I went on quickly. "That is, with a hundred and
forty-some children enrolled, you'll have a better cross
section with five members, right?"

Ronnie nodded sagely. "That's our hope. It should
have been changed years ago. I've been lobbying the
parish council ever since I became principal. Having
been away from Alpine for so long, I'd forgotten how
hidebound people can be in small towns. Luckily we
have some new blood, and there will be more when the

community-college faculty is in place. I hear they're about to appoint a president."

That was more than I'd heard. Silently I cursed Carla. If the rumor had reached her, she hadn't confided in me. Feigning knowledge, I moved on to the matter at hand. "What do you hope to accomplish with the additional membership?"

Ronnie rolled to one side and then the other in her padded swivel chair. "Excellence, of course. Education for the twenty-first century. Graduates who can compete on the highest level for college scholarships. A love of learning that will sustain our students throughout their lives."

In other words, by eighth grade, they'll stop wetting their pants, I thought to myself. As the mother of a fourth- or fifth- or whatever-year college student Adam might be by now, I had no illusions. "Immediate goals?" I queried, trying desperately to look interested.

"Well." Ronnie placed a long, thin hand against her high forehead. "The curriculum, of course. We're already addressing math. But science is a priority. And computer technology. The equipment we have now is obsolete. The school got it through one of the timber companies before I arrived. It's strictly Dark Ages, not at all what our students need to get a sense of the real world. My dream is to hire someone who can write grant proposals. Greer Fairfax has volunteered, but . . ." The thin hands sketched an arc.

"Math, science . . ." I ticked off on my own ordinary fingers. "What about history, geography, English, and . . . religion?"

"History." Ronnie seemed amused by the concept. "My feeling as an educator is that cultures are far more important. Geography—if you want to use that outmoded term—is factored into ethnicity. English is important, of course, but traditional reading and writing teaching methods are—to be frank—worthless. Again, I feel that

we can give students a richer understanding of the world
around them through books and writing assignments that
are of a more global nature."

In my head, I tried to translate the principal's rationale.
Instead of Dick and Jane and Sally, it sounded as if first
graders were going to get a dose of M'Bawa and Abdul
and Yu Ling. Maybe that wasn't all bad. "But what about
religion?" I persisted.

The patronizing smile that Ronnie bestowed on me
would have rankled a more sensitive soul. "Social issues,
that's the wave of the future. What is religion, but
the cornerstone of organized interpersonal behavior and
relationships?"

I was dumbfounded. "I thought it was more . . . spiritual," I said, unable to keep from glancing at Our Lady of
Mount Carmel. The plaster statue looked ticked off, but
no doubt I was letting my imagination get the best of me.

I felt myself shrinking in the plastic chair, getting
smaller and more insignificant by the moment. No doubt
countless parents sitting in my place had felt the same
way. "What about preparing them for the sacraments?" I
tried not to cringe as I awaited the principal's response.

But Ronnie surprised me. "Absolutely," she asserted.
"First penance and the Eucharist are still important." She
continued speaking, apparently oblivious to my expression of qualified relief. "They symbolize the Church's
involvement in humanity."

They symbolized a lot more to me, but perhaps this
wasn't the time to say so. Somewhere along the line, my
original intention of letting Ronnie offset Ursula Randall's
abrasive remarks had been lost in a sea of educational
hyperbole. Desperately I tried to salvage something from
the interview.

"Are you saying that Catholics should work with the
rest of the community?" The question sounded half-assed
at best.

Again, Ronnie nodded in that sage manner that was

beginning to annoy me. "Definitely. We need to teach our children so that they lose a sense of self without losing self-esteem. It's tricky, of course. But statistically, Catholic-educated students are going to become America's leaders. The public schools are finished. It won't be long before they can't produce pupils who can survive higher education. The graduate programs in particular will be filled with privately taught students. Obviously most of them will be the products of Catholic schools. Everyone else will—alas—fall by the wayside."

"So," I said in a faint voice, "you expect from the expanded school board . . . what?"

"To uphold our mission statement," Ronnie replied without hesitation. "Actually I'm drafting a new one. It should be ready by the time the votes are in on the new members."

"And what is the gist of it?" The small office had grown very warm. If Our Lady of Mount Carmel wasn't breaking a sweat, I certainly was.

"Basically the goals I've already outlined." Ronnie picked up a ballpoint pen and tapped at the blotter on her desk. "However, the long-term objective is to give the school more input in financial matters. Virtually all of St. Mildred's finances are now in the hands of the pastor, with occasional advice from the parish council. That simply won't do as we head for the twenty-first century."

Heading for the door was what I had in mind. I stood up and forced a thin smile. "Is Father Kelly helping you formulate the new mission statement?" I asked.

Ronnie raised her unplucked eyebrows and regarded me as if I'd asked whether a fox was going to baby-sit the henhouse. "The pastor prefers not to get too deeply involved in the school. After all, he hasn't had much experience in elementary education."

It was useless to point out that Dennis Kelly had taught in a seminary before his appointment to St. Mildred's. Indeed, I had the impression that it was useless to argue any point with Veronica Wenzler-Greene. Her agenda was clear. She was empire building. St. Mildred's Parochial School was her territory. Ronnie ruled.

And in all the conversation about Catholic education, one thing had been missing: neither of us had mentioned God.

God help us.

"I flunked," I declared upon entering the news office. "Ronnie is just as bad as Ursula Randall, except in a different way."

Vida and Leo both looked up; Carla wasn't at her desk.

"Oh, dear," Vida said.

"Shit," Leo remarked.

"Watch your language," Vida snapped, then turned back to me. "Perhaps we have a second chance. Ursula wants to see you."

The low, slanting roof of *The Advocate* tends to trap the heat. I felt the perspiration dripping down my back. I also felt my hackles rising. "So? When is she coming in?"

"She's not." Vida wiggled her eyebrows. "She would like you to drop by around three. She promised lemonade."

"Damn!" I whirled around, childishly throwing my purse against Carla's desk. "What is this, a command performance?"

"So it appears." Vida's expression was bland. "Ginny tried to explain that Ursula ought to come down to the office. But Ursula doesn't seem to care for suggestions."

"Okay, okay." I sighed, retrieving my purse. "I'll go see the wretched bitch." Catching Vida's sharp look of disapproval, I waved a dismissive hand. "Sorry. This isn't a good day. How do I find her house in The Pines?"

Vida gave me explicit directions. Fifteen minutes later, after checking my phone messages, I drove off to the development of upscale homes between the mall and the ski lodge. The house that Ursula had purchased was at the end of a cul-de-sac, and bore about as much resemblance to French Provincial architecture as a dandelion does to a daisy. Still, it was handsome by Alpine standards, and there was evidence of recent expensive landscaping in the ornamental evergreens and late-summer flowers.

The interior, however, was more imposing. It appeared that Ursula had moved her furnishings lock, stock, and baroque from her previous home in Seattle. The large living room was filled with antiques, mostly from the seventeenth century, ornate, overdone, and oppressive. The angels that adorned each side of the white brick fireplace could have come from an Austrian church.

"What do you think?" Ursula asked, sinking onto a stark white sofa. "My brothers are aghast." She laughed in her husky, almost hoarse manner.

"Jake and Buzzy?" I said, not merely stalling for time, but somehow unable to comprehend that Ursula was also an O'Toole. For all their flaws, both men seemed firmly rooted in the rocky soil of Alpine.

"Ostentatious, that's what Jake calls it," Ursula said with amusement. "For once, he used the right word. Why on earth does he think that a large vocabulary makes him important? The Grocery Basket is rather successful—or so I understand."

I thought so, too. Despite Safeway's arrival in Alpine a few years back, Jake and Betsy O'Toole seemed to be doing well. Buzzy, of course, was another matter. But that wasn't why I had driven up to The Pines.

"You've certainly settled in," I remarked, thinking that the only thing that was missing in the overdecorated room was a giant pipe organ. "Does it feel good to be back in Alpine?"

Ursula's carefully made-up face turned thoughtful. "Well . . . yes. They say you can't go home again, but that's nonsense. You can if you want to. You can do anything if you want to." Her green eyes were hard.

"And Warren?" I asked innocently. "Is he glad to be back?"

"Thrilled." Ursula suddenly swiveled on the sofa. "Lemonade! Let me fetch you a big glass." She rose, a surprisingly self-conscious figure in a sheer sleeveless tangerine outfit that had probably cost at least three hundred dollars. It was a shame that Ursula and Francine were at odds. The newcomer would otherwise be an excellent customer at the apparel shop.

Ursula went behind a marble-fronted bar at the far end of the room. It looked vaguely like an altar. She mixed and stirred and dispensed ice with all the formality of a priest conducting the liturgy. Producing two tall cut glasses, she served me, then resettled herself on the sofa.

"Now, where were we?" she said with a tight little smile.

"I was asking about Warren. . . ."

"Ah!" Ursula reached into a gilt-edged box and withdrew a cigarette. "But that's not the real reason you're here, is it?" She gestured with the unlighted cigarette. "Would you. . . ?"

I would, but restrained myself. "I'm trying to quit. Again."

"Bravo." My hostess took a deep pull on her lemonade, then flicked at the cigarette with a heavy gold lighter. "You want to hear my announcement, isn't that so?"

"Your announcement?" I echoed in a faint voice.

Ursula exhaled a pale blue cloud of smoke. "Yes." She paused for dramatic effect. "I'm running for the school board. It's the least I can do."

"Oh." If not surprised, I sensed that Ursula felt I should be impressed. I was neither. "That makes three candidates so far. Do you have a platform?"

If Ursula was disappointed by my reaction, she didn't

let it show. "Naturally." Tipping her head back, she gazed up into the rafters of the open ceiling. "It's a very simple one. Traditional Catholic values. I'm sick of these liberal lunatics trying to turn the Church into their private little playground."

Grudgingly, my interest in Ursula's ambitions rose a notch. "Are you referring to trends in Catholic education or everything that goes on at the parish level?"

"Both." The green eyes regarded me with a keen, intense look. "You're not one of the crazies, I trust?"

"I consider myself middle-of-the-road. It's part of my journalistic training. The eternal observer, you know."

"Good. Then I don't have to worry about insulting you. Not," she added with an arch little smile, "that I care very much for the feelings of those who disagree with me. Generally they're wrong."

The self-righteous attitude that I usually found refreshing in Vida Runkel was less appealing in Ursula Randall. Yet under the surface, both women had much in common. I tried very hard not to let my hostess annoy me. Thus I encouraged Ursula to expound on her parochial-school philosophy. She was more than willing to comply.

"It comes down to one thing," Ursula asserted after pouring herself more lemonade. "That's faith. How do you live your life? As a Christian—or not?"

I nodded, still sipping from my original drink. "That's pretty basic. But what about the non-Catholics in the school? Especially if they're non-Christian as well?"

Ursula gave an emphatic shake of her head. "You know the old saying—you can't expose your children to the chicken pox without the danger of having them catch it. Non-Christian parents know what they're getting into when they enroll children in a Catholic school. If they don't want them exposed to religion, send them somewhere else. I've no time for such empty-headed thinking."

In my mind, I was trying to compose an article that would show the less strident side of Ursula Randall. It wasn't going to be easy. "I gather you've been involved in previous school and parish work. Did you begin volunteering when your children entered kindergarten or before that?"

The green eyes were as cool as the ice cubes in the lemonade. "My first marriage was all too brief. Then, when I found happiness with Wheaton, the only flaw was that we weren't blessed with children. Yet the very lack allowed me time and energy to help other families. I've been quite tireless over the years. And I've had my victories. Oh, a few failures, too, but that's to be expected." Her gaze fell, and turned brooding as she studied the pattern of the Portuguese gros point carpet.

It seemed like a propitious moment to take my leave. "Thanks for the lemonade," I said, rising from the damask-covered chair that had offered more ornamentation than comfort. "Do you think there'll be any other candidates before the Wednesday deadline? We have to go to press tomorrow evening, and I'd hate to leave out anybody."

Ursula's sleekly coiffed head jerked up. "You'd hate to. . . ? Oh, yes, I see. You're speaking from the perspective of a newspaper person."

My expression was self-deprecating. "That's what I am."

"Yes." Ursula's narrowed eyes indicated that she didn't entirely approve. "But you're much more. You're a Catholic, and you have a forum. In your place, I'd use it."

"I do use it," I replied with a touch of defiance. "I write an editorial every week."

"That's not what I mean." Ursula was on her feet. I assumed she was going to show me out, but instead, she returned to the ornate bar. "Your power should be exercised to clean up the Church. Tell these people to stop trying to make us into namby-pamby Protestants.

Tell them to listen to the Holy Father. Tell them to go to hell. At the rate they're going, that's where they're headed."

Ursula poured herself another lemonade.

Chapter Five

I'D FORGOTTEN THAT Milo Dodge didn't like rice. Braving the warmth of my kitchen, I'd boiled enough for two, which seemed like a perfect complement to the shish kebabs. But Milo hemmed and hawed and said he'd really prefer a baked potato. Refusing to turn on the oven, I compromised by using the microwave. The potato blew up just as Milo and I were halfway through our predinner drinks.

"Damn it," I grumbled, wiping potato pieces from the inside of the microwave, "I never can do that right! What about noodles?"

"What kind?" The sheriff was leaning against the refrigerator, looking put-upon.

"Any kind. I've got about six varieties of pasta in the cupboard."

"Plain noodles are okay," he allowed after a lengthy reflection. "You know, the sort of wavy ones. But not those curly kind that look like corkscrews."

"Fine." I finished cleaning the microwave, then went in search of egg noodles. "Go check the barbecue. And don't come back in the kitchen. I can't wait to get outside."

Obediently Milo ambled to the back door. "By the way, we found two of Verb's bikes," he called over his shoulder.

I looked up from the sink where I was pouring water into a kettle. "You did? Where?"

"Under the Burl Creek Bridge on the way to the ski

68

lodge." Milo nudged the screen door open with his elbow. At least four bugs flew in. I winced but kept silent. "They were the ten-speeds," he went on. "The mountain bikes and the other ten-speed are still missing."

"Verb ought to be relieved," I said, turning the burner on under the kettle.

"He was pretty riled up about the theft," Milo remarked as I joined him on our progress to the backyard. "I guess he operates close to the bone during the off-season. What's he going to do if Warren Wells opens up that sports shop?"

Since Milo hadn't yet checked the barbecue, I was poking around the foil-wrapped shish kebabs. My hand slipped, almost dislodging the grill. "What sports shop?" I demanded.

Milo had settled himself in the chaise longue. "The one he's talking about starting. It'd go into Buzzy O'Toole's old BP location. But I think Warren'd tear the whole thing down and start over. Buzzy didn't have much space."

I slammed the lid down on the barbecue and waved the long metal meat fork at the sheriff. "Why haven't I heard about this? Why didn't Leo tell me? What's wrong with Vida's grapevine?"

Milo shrugged, though he looked a trifle sheepish. "Damned if I know. Maybe it's because Warren only told me a couple of days ago. I ran into him at Harvey's Hardware. I was scouting new reels for winter steelheading. Do you know that I haven't hit the river in almost a month? It's too damned low."

At the moment I wasn't interested in Milo's latest complaint about the lousy fishing in the Sky or its feeder streams. "Back up," I ordered. "Tell me about Warren."

"I already did." Milo waved off some no-seeums that were flying in formation somewhere in the vicinity of his forehead. His long arms were nicely tanned and muscles rippled below the short sleeves of his thin blue cotton shirt. "He doesn't plan to sit around on his dead ass watching Ursula run your gang up at St. Mildred's. Warren worked as a salesman at several sporting-good stores in Seattle—Big Five, Warshal's, the one that used to be over by the University District."

"Seattle Sporting Goods," I interjected absently.

"Anyway, Warren knows the business," Milo went on. "He couldn't say much in front of Harvey Adcock, because a sports shop would provide competition for the hardware store's outdoor section. I kind of gathered that Warren wants to cover all the bases, maybe even supply the local teams with equipment and uniforms. You know how the high school and the rest have had to go through Everett and Seattle all these years."

Sometimes I am absolutely flabbergasted by the layman's perception of what is news—and what is not. I felt like shaking Milo. On impulse, I jumped out of the lawn chair and did just that. Naturally, I ended up on his lap.

"Hey—what'd I do now?" he asked, half-humorously. One hand tickled my ribs, then strayed to my breast.

"You . . . frustrate me!" I squeaked.

"I can cure that." Milo nuzzled my neck.

"Not now you can't," I said, trying to sound severe. "I've got to put your blasted pasta in the pot." Wriggling free, I went back into the house. When I returned, I decorously resumed my place in the lawn chair. "Warren's plans are news. Big news, in a town that hasn't had a business debut since Starbucks opened two years ago."

Milo brushed at his graying sandy hair. "It hasn't happened yet. What's the rush? I thought you didn't deal in rumors."

"I don't," I replied, "but if I can get Warren Wells to confirm his plans, then it's not a rumor—it's hard news."

"Harvey won't like it," Milo noted, his hazel eyes following a blue jay that was hopping from branch to branch in the nearest Western hemlock. "Neither will Verb."

"I know. But," I pointed out, "once the college is built, they should all be able to withstand the competition."

"That's a year away." Milo's gaze was still out of range. "Harvey should be okay—his sporting-goods inventory is a lot smaller than his hardware section. Verb's situation is different. Basically he depends on whether or not it's a good ski season. Who knows what'll happen this winter? Remember a few years back when there wasn't enough runoff to fill the reservoirs?"

The drought was still fresh in my mind: hardly any snow, very little rain, and endless days of sun had left an indelible dry mark on the Pacific Northwest soul. One of the many casualties had been the ski industry.

"Who do you think took the bikes?" I inquired, my mind veering back to Verb Vancich.

"Damned if I know," Milo replied, now watching me lift the shish kebabs off the grill. "We got some prints, but there're pretty smudged. Maybe the mountain bikes'll turn up eventually. It looks like whoever stole the things didn't bother trying to sell them."

"Joyriders, just like stolen cars?" I asked.

Milo grunted. "I guess. Kids, of course."

"It sounds like it." I returned inside to get the pasta, the rice, and a loaf of French bread. During the course of our meal the conversation veered to other topics. Milo was concerned about the upcoming weekend, which he knew would keep him jumping; I enthused over Ben's visit.

"What about Adam?" Milo asked, buttering his third slice of crusty bread.

My expression soured. "I still don't know if he's coming. Do you ever feel as if you've become disconnected from your kids?"

After the divorce eight years ago Milo's three offspring had moved to Bellevue with their mother. They were now adults, and technically out from under their mother and stepfather's wings. But occasionally they visited Milo during the summer and for holidays.

The sheriff took his time to answer my question.
Maybe he hadn't given the idea much thought. Milo isn't
very introspective. "I guess I don't feel all that close to
them anymore. Isn't that the way it's supposed to be
when they're grown up?"

"Define *grown up*," I retorted, then felt a pang of
remorse. "Never mind—maybe it's different for mothers
than it is for fathers. It's harder for us to let go."

"Could be," Milo said, setting his empty plate on a
metal side table. "You raised Adam by yourself. That
makes a difference, doesn't it?"

"Yes. Yes, it does." I knew I sounded defensive. "It's
that since he's been away—no, since he's been in Arizona," I corrected myself as I realized that the change in
my son hadn't occurred until after his college stints in
Hawaii and Alaska, "he doesn't talk to me the way he
used to. Part of it's because he's got Ben down there, but
that's not the whole reason. It's as if a barrier has grown
up between us. Who built it?"

Milo stretched and yawned. "Nobody, probably. The
kid's gotten older, that's all. It happens."

The sun was beginning to slip down over the foothills.
Clusters of gnats circled above the barbecue. I thought—
I hoped—I could feel a slight breeze stir the evergreens.
Back in March, I'd flown to Arizona to visit my son and
my brother. Adam and I had driven the two hundred
miles from Tempe to Tuba City. I had hoped that the
journey would give us an opportunity to exchange confi-
dences, to resurrect our intimate affinity. And Adam had
talked—but almost exclusively about the Navajos and
the Hopis and the ancient Anasazis. He was all wrapped
up in that world on the reservation, full of pie-in-the-sky
plans to help the Native Americans, to preserve their culture, their dignity, their identity. I'd listened with half an
ear, knowing that my son had a problem finishing anything he started, including college.

During that time in Tuba City—a time my brother and

I had earmarked for a discussion of Adam's career
plans—my son had worked on the dig or hung out at the
local truck stop or visited one of the nearby hogans. On
our return to Tempe, he'd slept until we reached the Arizona State University campus. Ben had told me not to
worry—he insisted that Adam had his head squarely on
his shoulders. I'd laughed at my brother. He didn't know
Adam the way I did. My son had lost his head, his heart,
and his wallet so often over the years that I'd stopped
counting.

Surprisingly it was Milo who broke the long, lazy
silence. The sheriff not only avoids self-examination, he
seldom delves into the minds of others. Silences between
us are comfortable, stretches of time in which I busily
analyze every nuance of phrasing from previous conversations. Milo, however, simply sits, and seems to enjoy
the quiet time. But on this sultry evening, he actually
came up with an unexpected insight.

"You think it's Adam's dad?"

Startled, I almost knocked over my empty highball
glass. "Tom Cavanaugh?" It had only been in the last
year that I'd fully confided in Milo about Tom. "You
mean because he and Adam are finally in contact after all
these years?"

Milo scratched at his cheek. "Well . . . it's a change.
Adam's never had a father figure before. Not even
Ben, since he was off in Mississippi until the last few
years. Now your kid's got two men in his life. One's a
rich publisher, the other's a priest. I mean, they're authority figures. You know—somebody Adam can look
up to. Not dirtbags or con artists or . . . you know what
I'm saying."

I did. For the most part, I felt I'd done the right thing in
allowing Adam and Tom to meet. But I still resented any
influence my ex-lover might exert over my son. Initially
I'd felt it was a case of better late than never; now I wondered if never might have been better.

"I don't know. . . . Maybe." My voice sounded tired, depleted. "Adam doesn't see that much of Tom. They talk on the phone, though. I think."

Untangling his long legs, Milo got out of the chaise longue. "Hey, stop worrying. Adam's not in jail, he's not on drugs, he hasn't knocked up a bunch of girls. You keep pushing him about his college degree. Maybe he still isn't sure what he wants to do."

I looked up at Milo, who was now standing over me. "Did you, at that age?"

Milo's long face screwed up in the effort of recollection. "Twenty-two, twenty-three? Yeah, I did. I was finishing up my college law-enforcement courses then. It wasn't so much that I wanted to be a cop but that I didn't want to be a logger. I'd seen too many guys come out of the woods on stretchers—or not at all." He leaned down and kissed the top of my head. "You want to stay out here and let the bugs eat you?"

I offered Milo a feeble smile. I hadn't talked out my distress over what I perceived as an estrangement between Adam and me. Like most women, giving voice to every angle of a problem was comforting; talking the subject to death was therapeutic. Like most men, Milo dreaded confrontation and dismissed dilemmas with a few pat phrases. "It's still awfully warm inside the house," I hedged.

Milo took my hands and hoisted me to my feet. "Let's pretend we're on a desert island or some damned thing." His arms closed around me. "Let's pretend we don't have kids and that we're not middle-aged and that it's not hotter than a sawdust furnace and that a bunch of drunks won't kill each other on Stevens Pass this weekend. Okay?"

I lifted my face to his. "Okay. Let's."

We went inside.

Coincidences aren't unusual in a small town like Alpine. On my lunch hour Tuesday, I discovered Warren

Wells in front of me in the line at the post office. Never having met the man, I wouldn't have recognized him. But neither did Amanda Hanson, who worked behind the counter and had moved to town a couple of years ago. When Warren identified himself as the recipient of a parcel, I leaned around and introduced myself.

"So you're the one responsible for that interview with Ursula," Warren said with a broad smile. "Isn't she something? No flies on that young lady."

"That's true," I temporized, grateful that he seemed pleased rather than outraged by Vida's article. "Ursula is very . . . frank."

"You bet." Warren Wells's attention was diverted by Amanda, who had retrieved the parcel from the rear of the post office. It gave me a chance to study the man who had gotten away from Francine and now was Ursula's designated consort. He wasn't a heartthrob: Warren was no more than average height; his brown hair was thinning; and his features were undistinguished except for a prominent, hawklike nose. His hazel eyes were nervous, almost shifty, appearing to seek out every nook and cranny of the drab old post office lobby. While Warren appeared fit, there was nothing exceptional about his physique. Perhaps the most attractive thing about him was that broad, engaging smile. Warren had white, even teeth that looked as if they were part of the original equipment.

"Could you wait just a minute until I get some stamps?" I asked as he started away from the counter. "I have a question for you."

Warren gave me a faint look of surprise. "Sure. I'm in no rush."

After purchasing my six dollars and forty cents' worth of commemoratives, I led Warren over to a solid oak table by the door. "I hear you're planning on opening a sports shop. Is it true? And if so, can we print the story?"

Warren chuckled. "I forgot how rumors get loose in

this town. Well, yes, that's the plan. But that's all it is right now. I haven't settled on a site yet."

I stepped aside so that a man I didn't recognize could get a change-of-address form from one of the official postal document slots on the oak table. "I heard you might go into Buzzy O'Toole's former BP station."

"That's a possibility," Warren replied, the hazel eyes still roaming around the foyer. "I really haven't decided. There are a couple of empty storefronts on the main drag, and at least one more at the mall. I've got a commercial realtor from Seattle working on it. There's no rush."

"But it's definitely something you want to do," I said, trying to pin Warren down. "It's not just a pipe dream."

"Oh, no." Warren smoothed his thinning dark hair back from his high forehead. "I'll do it. But it takes planning. It can't be hurried."

"Then I can mention it in the paper?" I inquired.

Warren lifted one shoulder. "Why not? It's no secret. Hey," he said suddenly, the hazel eyes darting in the direction of the street, "I've got to run. Just spell my name right. Ha-ha!" The budding entrepreneur all but ran out of the post office.

I gave the story two inches. Maybe Warren's plan to open a new business in Alpine would smooth some of the feathers ruffled by his bride-to-be's condescending quotes. Vida, however, was annoyed. She couldn't imagine why she hadn't heard the rumor.

"My sources are slipping," she complained. "Or I am. What's going on around this town? Why does everything lately seem to be emanating from you Catholics?" Furiously she rubbed her eyes. Vida's complicated network of relatives, in-laws, friends, and acquaintances usually provided her with any hint of a budding story. I sensed that the recent rash of parish-connected news made her feel as if she were out of the loop.

By deadline, we had yet another St. Mildred's item.

There were two more rivals for the school board. The latest candidates were Debra Barton, wife of Clancy, who owned Barton's Bootery at the mall, and Laura O'Toole, Buzzy's wife.

"Most interesting," Vida commented shortly before sending this week's edition to the back shop. Typically she had calmed down since her earlier outburst. "Laura is Ursula's sister-in-law. What do you make of it?"

I was surprised at Vida. In Alpine, pitting family members against each other isn't unusual. So many people are related that the situation is almost impossible to avoid. "Maybe they want to make sure an O'Toole gets elected. Maybe they have opposing views. Maybe Laura and Ursula don't know each other very well. Was Ursula still in town when Laura married Buzzy?"

Vida's encyclopedic memory didn't fail her. "No. Buzzy married late—for Alpine. And Laura Doyle was a Sultan girl. Unless I've missed something over the years"—Vida's face hardened at the mere idea—"Ursula rarely visited, and if she entertained Jake and Betsy or Buzzy and Laura, I never heard about their trips to Seattle. But that wasn't my point." Now Vida had squared her shoulders and sat at her desk with fists on hips. "Laura O'Toole is a mouse. I can't imagine her speaking up at any kind of meeting. Why on earth is she running for the school board?"

A mental image of Laura crossed my mind. She was fortyish, too thin, more dark than fair, and, as Vida had noted, very quiet. "Who knows?" I shrugged. "Didn't we hear Laura and Buzzy were separating? Maybe they have, and this is some kind of gesture on Laura's part to become independent."

Vida harrumphed, but before she could say anything else, a young woman entered the news office. Her Armani suit, Chanel handbag, and stylish short blonde hair made her look as out of place in Alpine as a Monet at a shopping-mall art sale. It took me a faltering moment

to recognize Alicia Wells, Francine and Warren's
daughter. Vida, of course, was much quicker, and of
course remembered Alicia's married name.

"Alicia Lowell! How nice. When did you arrive in
Alpine?" Vida's gracious greeting sounded almost
genuine.

Alicia's smile was brittle. "This afternoon. I got in a
couple of days early. My meeting in Chicago was can-
celed. How are you, Ms. Runkel?" Without waiting for
Vida to reply, she turned to me. "And Ms. . . . Ward, is it?"

"Lord," I replied. At least she hadn't called me Lard,
as Carla had done in one of her more memorable typos.

"I'm waiting for Mother to close the shop," Alicia
went on, her Delft-blue eyes taking in her surroundings.
Judging from the crease in her forehead, she found the
news office only slightly more edifying than a charnel
house. "She asked if I'd walk over here to invite you both
to dinner Friday night."

"Oh, pity!" Vida cried. "I already have an engagement." She gazed at me over the rims of her glasses. "Mr.
Bardeen. We're going to see a musical in Everett."

It may or may not have been true. Mr. Bardeen was
real enough, however. Vida and Buck, a retired air-force
officer, had been seeing each other for over a year.

Fortunately I, too, had an excuse. "My brother and
maybe my son are arriving from Arizona Friday. How
long will you be in town?" I asked, aware that I was
climbing out on a limb that Alicia probably would be
delighted to saw off behind me.

"I'm not sure," she answered. "My return is open-
ended. I work for myself as a children's-book illustrator,
so my schedule is fairly flexible." The slim figure in the
expensive suit retreated to the door just as Ginny
stumbled into the office.

"I'm going home now," Ginny said in a thin voice.

"Everything's done, and I don't feel so good. It must be this awful weather."

Alicia's eyes followed Ginny out of the office. "The weather? It's gorgeous. What is she talking about?"

Vida's courteous mask slipped a notch. "How long have you been gone, Alicia? Four years? You know we natives don't do well without rain. Don't tell me you've turned into a New Yorker!" Vida made the appellation sound as odious as the Ku Klux Klan.

Alicia had the grace to laugh. "I haven't forgotten. But summer in New York is beastly. If we weren't air-conditioned, I'd die. Blue skies, eighty-five degrees, and almost no humidity seem like heaven to me."

Apparently having succeeded in bringing Alicia back down to earth—or at least with one foot on her native heath, Vida nodded. "I understand. But lack of rain is a serious matter, especially in a logging community. The woods are closed. The forest-fire danger is extreme."

A faintly wistful look touched Alicia's face. "I remember all that. There was one summer that we couldn't even use the barbecue. And some kids I knew from high school got in trouble because they roasted marshmallows upriver from the holding pond."

Vida tipped her head to one side. "Yes, very difficult. But I imagine you have problems in New York, too."

The understatement was taken seriously by Alicia, who still seemed caught up in long-ago summers. "We sure do. You can't begin to guess."

"I believe I could," Vida replied, her smile a trifle smug.

I had done my best to make Veronica Wenzler-Greene sound reasonable, even humble. It was a tricky piece of writing, achieved mainly by describing the more sentimental ornaments in her office and her dedication to the school. By paraphrasing indirect quotes, I toned down Ronnie's more derogatory opinions about public education. Whether or not I had taken some of the sting out of

Ursula's offensive remarks, I couldn't be sure. Maybe this week's controversy would revolve around the catch-and-release editorial.

Milo liked it, though he felt I should have taken a tougher stand. "Go beyond supporting the angler's right to bring the fish home, and tell those morons in Olympia to plant the rivers," he said as we lay in bed after making love Thursday evening. "Get those bureaucrats in D.C. to sit up and take notice, stop mincing around with the Japanese and the Canadians and whoever the hell else steals our fish out in salt water. Jump on those jerks who give the Indians the right to gillnet. Hell, if there's a way to screw the average fisherman, the government'll find it. I think I'll take up golf."

The vision of Milo strolling the greens was incongruous. He was an unlikely golfer, even more so than Ed Bronsky, who had taken up the game as part of his idle-rich persona. But our discussion was brief. Milo had been able to stop in for less than an hour. While the weekend might not have officially begun, criminal activity had already increased: ex-boyfriends stalking ex-girlfriends; campers getting harassed by young troublemakers; stolen checks being passed; DWIs resisting arrest; cars broken into; attempted burglaries; and an APB from King County for three men in their mid-thirties suspected of drug dealing who had been spotted heading east on Highway 2. Milo was up to his ears, at least when he wasn't under my sheets.

"Sorry I have to . . . uh . . . you know . . . and run," he said sheepishly while he got dressed. "Maybe I'll see you over the weekend."

"Ben's going to be here, remember? And maybe Adam." I still hadn't received official notification from my errant son. "Ben's due in tomorrow around three."

"Oh, yeah." Clumsily Milo buttoned his regulation shirt. "I lose track when things get busy."

"Right." The sidelong glance I gave him made no

impression. Milo lost track of just about everything when he was in the sack. Except fishing.

After he left, I got out some of my recipes to plan menus for the weekend. I wanted to try some new things, preferably entrées that didn't require turning on the stove. I was mulling over a Greek chicken salad when the phone rang.

"We're wiped out. It's all gone, even the sanctuary." My brother's usually crackling voice was heavy.

"Ben? What are you talking about?"

"The fire. We had a fire this evening. Lightning, I think. It happened while Adam and I were calling on a Hopi family over at Bacabi. One of those big summer storms came through here and—" Ben's voice broke.

In early March I had visited the small frame church and stayed at the tiny rectory. Both buildings were modest, even by Alpine standards, but Ben had built them up, maintained them, taken pride in efforts that he could share with his fellow parishioners. Pride was essential to the Navajo and the Hopi. Though they might practice the same faith, they suffered from the burden of traditional enmity. I could imagine how devastated Ben's flock must be. I could also agonize with my brother, whose most recent life's work had just gone up in smoke.

"Should I come down?" I offered. "What can I do?"

"Not a damned thing," Ben responded, now sounding more angry than disturbed. "Pray," he added as if in his own anguish he'd forgotten to seek help from a Higher Authority. "Yeah, that's about it. Damn, I probably can't even get a refund on my airline ticket this late."

"They may make an exception under the circumstances," I said in consolation. "I take it there's no chance that you can come a little later? Like in a week?"

"Hell, no!" he exploded in my ear. "I can't leave my people. Adam's out there right now with about forty of them. They're standing around in the ashes looking like lost souls, trying to make sense of what happened, trying to figure it out based on their culture and traditions. Or else muttering that it's God's will. Bullshit, blame it on the weather. Or maybe it was electrical. The wiring's always been patchwork."

"What about insurance?" I inquired, unable to refrain from congratulating myself for checking out *The Advocate*'s coverage with Brendan Shaw.

"I've got to check with Tucson on that. The Extension Society provides us with a subsidy. Remember how they helped us in Mississippi after the flood?"

I vaguely recalled Extension's work with the home missions, including Ben's. "I'll send you a check," I said. "It won't buy much more than a couple of two-by-fours, but maybe I can get Dennis Kelly to take up a second collection. The parishioners here know you."

"Den's got plenty on his plate as it is," Ben said, again sounding glum. "Don't worry about it. We'll manage. These people are wonderful, really. They know hard times, they understand struggle. And I'll have Adam here to help for a few more weeks."

"How is my son?" I could barely keep the sarcasm out of my voice.

"He's fine. Upset, of course. But he's out there trying to keep everybody's spirits up. You'd be proud of him, Sluggly."

Hearing the old childhood nickname forced a small smile. "I doubt that I'd recognize him," I replied. It wasn't merely a slighting comment; the idea of my spoiled son extending himself to others still had a foreign ring. With a few more words of comfort, I let Ben go. My disappointment over his cancellation of the Alpine trip was small compared with what I knew he must be feeling.

The next day, Friday, I thought about calling him back. But I realized I didn't know where to reach him. If both the church and the rectory were gone, so was his phone. Wherever Ben had called from, it hadn't been at the mission. I'd have to wait until I heard from him again.

The long weekend now stretched out before me like a bottomless pit. No change in the weather was predicted. Vida had Buck, Ginny was going home to Rick, and Carla was headed for Seattle. I didn't pry into Leo's plans. Milo would be tied up for most of the three days. I'd left a message with Jack Mullins that my brother wasn't coming to town after all. By mid-afternoon, I still hadn't heard from the sheriff.

When my staff had all left by ten to five, I sat alone in my office staring at the computer screen with its half-finished editorial on coping with graffiti. "If private business owners won't take the initiative of removing the offensive artwork from their walls and windows, they shouldn't expect the city or the county to pony up the funds to clean it for them." How bland could I get? Neither the city nor the county had the funds to get rid of graffiti. "If stiffer fines were imposed on the graffiti artists, the monies collected could be allocated for . . ."

I intended to hit the *save* command, struck something else instead, and wiped out the entire editorial. Frantically, I searched for *undo*. I found it, and restored the text. Then I wondered why I had bothered. The piece was still a bore. Maybe on Monday . . . Except that Monday was a holiday. But with no plans, I could come in for a while and get some work done. The thought held no charm. On a sudden whim, I called Francine at the apparel shop.

"If that dinner invitation is still open tonight, I can come," I said, inserting a false bright note into my voice.

Francine hesitated at the other end. "Actually, Emma, it's not. Alicia and I have other plans. In fact, Alicia's gone into Snohomish to see an old friend who moved there. She's one of the Carlson girls."

"Oh. That's fine, it's just that my brother had to cancel and . . . Have you got someone in the store?"

"Yes, I do. See you in church." Francine rang off.

Gathering up my belongings, I headed for home. The sun fell full and bright on my windshield as I drove along

Front Street with vague thoughts of stopping at the Grocery Basket. Traffic was backed up on Alpine Way, waiting for a Burlington Northern freight to pass through. The train whistled twice as it slowed on its way through town before starting the steep climb through the mountains. By the time I could make a left turn, I decided to skip going to the store. There was hamburger in the freezer. If I wanted to bother heating up the grill, I could cook it outside. If I wanted to bother.

I didn't. Instead, I opened a can of oyster stew. It wouldn't take long to heat. Only then did I check the mail and the answering machine. Nothing. Not even Milo. How many wrecks and drug dealers and stalkers were there in Alpine? I had worked myself up into a full-blown pout by nine o'clock.

That was just a few minutes before Milo called. The report of incidents at the sheriff's office had definitely picked up. Alpine had an accidental death on its hands, and it hadn't occurred on Highway 2 in a mangling collision of steel and smoke.

At the edge of town, the Skykomish River tumbles between big boulders before it begins a meandering course over a bed of smaller rocks and underbrush left by the near-flood conditions of late winter. The river appears benign, almost gentle as it flows into Alpine. Nevertheless, Ursula O'Toole Randall apparently had drowned in six inches of water just below Deception Creek. The sheriff thought foul play might be involved. Did I want to come down to his office?

I was there in less than five minutes.

Chapter Six

RICHIE MAGRUDER, WHO is Alpine's deputy mayor, and a retired logging-camp bull cook, had decided to try his luck at trout fishing after dinner. He had driven up Highway 2 by the Deception Falls turnoff. He'd left his van there and intended to fish as far as the eastern edge of town by the golf course and the Icicle Creek development. Richie was about to quit the river when he found the body.

"I just got back from the scene," Milo said, slipping into his high-backed padded chair. He was wearing his uniform, and looked tired. "We'll have to send this one over to Everett to determine cause of death."

"Where's Richie?" I inquired, not having seen him when I arrived at the sheriff's office.

Milo lighted a cigarette before answering. "We took his statement at the river. He was pretty shook up. It hasn't been that long since his wife had a corpse on her hands at the beauty parlor."

I was the one who had discovered the dead body at Stella's Styling Salon. Stella Magruder had gone through the mill in the aftermath of the investigation. So had the rest of us. Last February had been an ugly time in Alpine.

But my mind was trying to focus on the more recent death. "Ursula Randall," I said in wonder. "That's incredible. Is there any possibility that she did drown?"

Milo was fidgeting with his lighter. "Sure. People can drown in a bathtub. She may have been walking along the river, fallen, hit her head, and landed in the water. It was only her head and shoulders that were actually in the river. But it seems damned odd. For one thing, would you hike along the Sky in satin pajamas?"

I goggled at the sheriff. "Are you kidding? I don't own any satin pajamas. I don't own pajamas, period." I ignored Milo's faintly leering grin. "And if I did, I wouldn't go walking in them. What about shoes?"

"Only one. The other's missing." Milo was back in business. "What do you call those things that are high but not a heel?"

The description baffled me until Milo drew a crude picture on a piece of note paper. "That's a wedge," I said. "Did the rest of it look like this?" I drew an ankle strap and what was supposed to look like a sandal.

"That's it," Milo said. "Sort of, anyway. No strap, except around the heel. The shoes were made of shiny stuff, like the pajamas. Definitely not Alpine hiking gear."

"Did she have a purse with her?" I inquired.

Milo shook his head. "If she did, it wasn't at the river."

"What about her car?" I recalled that Ursula had mentioned owning a Lexus.

"Not so far. Jack's looking for it along that stretch of unpaved road."

I got out of Milo's visitor's chair and went over to the big map of Alpine on the wall next to the filing cabinets. "Show me where Richie found the body."

Extinguishing his cigarette, Milo joined me at the map. A red pushpin had already been inserted in what I assumed was the spot of Richie's gruesome discovery. Ironically it wasn't far from Milo's home in the Icicle Creek development. But it was clear across town from Ursula's handsome residence in The Pines.

"Okay," Milo was saying as he traced the route of the river. "Here's the golf course. Along the train tracks are those dumpy houses that originally belonged to the old

Cascade & Pacific Lumber Company. Railroad Avenue dead-ends just beyond the golf course, but on the north side of the Sky, River Road keeps going for about a mile." Milo pointed to the fairly straight line between the river and the tracks. I knew that shortly after River Road crossed Icicle Creek, the pavement ended, and a single dirt lane continued through the woods. At one time it had been a logging road that had continued up the side of Tonga Ridge.

"There's not much out past the golf course except for what's left of an old water tower, a couple of sheds, and some kind of telephone-company installation," the sheriff continued. "Except, of course, for the new house Ed and Shirley Bronsky are building."

I stared at the map. "That's not on here."

"I know. This thing needs updating." Milo picked up a green pushpin and stuck it in the map. It looked to me as if the Bronsky site was a stone's throw from where Ursula Randall had been found. "See—the body was kind of in between the old dumpy houses and Ed's new palace, just after the asphalt part of River Road ends. Ordinarily a fisherman has to climb up to the road to get to the next hole. But the Sky's so low right now that there's plenty of room to walk the rocks along the river. Richie was going to give it one last try a little further down, where there's a big clump of brush caught on an old snag. He heard somebody had luck there last week."

Ursula hadn't had much luck, I thought, still appalled at the news of her death. "Does Father Den know?" I asked.

Milo arched his sandy eyebrows at me. "Kelly? No. Why?"

"Oh . . ." It was silly, but the thought nagged at me. "What we used to call the last rites, but are now the Sacrament of the Sick can be administered an hour after death. I think. But I suppose it's too late now."

"Hell, yes," Milo replied, returning to his chair. "Doc

Dewey figured she'd been dead at least half an hour, and he made that judgment call around eight-thirty." Milo and I both glanced at the clock, which showed that it was now a quarter to ten. "The body's on its way to Everett by now."

"*Its?*" I echoed. It always struck me as ironic that human beings lose more than their lives when they die. Ursula Randall might have been an arrogant pain, but until now, no one would have dreamed of referring to her as *it*.

Even if he'd been so inclined, Milo didn't get a chance to address the philosophical issue. Dustin Fong poked his head into the office, wearing a perplexed expression on his youthful face.

"We can't find Mr. Wells, Sheriff," the deputy announced. "He's not at Ms. Randall's house. Nobody in The Pines knows where he's gone."

Milo looked pained as he turned to me. "Warren's living there, isn't he?"

"I don't know," I responded, realizing that I hadn't had the sense to check the address on the parcel he'd claimed at the post office. Vida would never have let such an opportunity pass. "There wasn't much sign of a man around the house when I called on Ursula, but I suppose he's living there. Unless they wanted to keep up some kind of appearances until they got married."

"Damn," Milo breathed, then frowned. "Dustin, have you got a local address for Warren Wells?"

Dustin's almond-shaped eyes widened. "No. Jack Mullins told me to go find Mr. Wells at Ms. Randall's house. I didn't check. Sorry." The young man hung his head.

"Check now," Milo ordered, though his tone was relatively mild.

Dustin departed. "I never thought to ask Warren where he was staying when I ran into him the other day," Milo said, more to himself than to me. "I just assumed. . . .

Damn, that's what I always tell my people—don't assume anything."

"You could hardly foresee that Warren's fiancée would end up dead," I pointed out. "It still seems unbelievable."

"It isn't." Milo was looking grim as he poked the buzzer on his intercom. "Dustin—you there? Who's interviewing the neighbors up at The Pines? Dwight? Okay. What?"

I couldn't catch Dustin's words, but I sensed the deputy was being apologetic. Milo switched off the intercom and sighed. "There's no listing for Warren, which leads me to believe that he's living at Ursula's." He got to his feet. "I'm heading back out on patrol. There's not much I can do around here until we get the ME's report from Everett, which probably won't happen until Monday, or even Tuesday, what with the holiday. Jack gave Jake and Buzzy the bad news. Of course," Milo added as he put on his hat, "it was easy enough to find Buzzy."

"How come?" I had joined Milo at the door.

The sheriff nodded in the direction of the big map. "Those old dumps by the railroad tracks? That's where Buzzy lives. He was less than a quarter of a mile from where his sister drowned. Tough, huh?"

Vida wasn't home when I tried to call her at ten-thirty. I guessed that she'd been telling Alicia Wells Lowell the truth about going with Buck to a musical in Everett. I connected with Dennis Kelly, however. He was dismayed, but immediately got down to the business of funeral arrangements. Would Ursula be buried out of St. Mildred's or from her former parish in Seattle? I had no idea, of course. Then the pastor asked if Ben would be able to take over for him since he had planned on visiting his mother in Tacoma Monday and Tuesday. I felt like a fool. I'd been so busy feeling sorry for myself that I'd forgotten to let Father Den know that my brother wasn't coming to Alpine. Thus I hadn't told him of the fire at the

Tuba City mission. Now I didn't have the gall to ask if he'd put out a plea for a second collection to help Ben rebuild his church.

Still berating myself, I sat by the phone and wondered what other duties I'd neglected. I couldn't think of anything, but it occurred to me that someone should tell Francine about her ex-husband's fiancée. It was twenty minutes to eleven when I called, and Francine's voice sounded heavy with sleep.

"Did I wake you?" I said, feeling as if I'd made yet another faux pas. "I guess I figured you'd be waiting up for Alicia to come back from visiting her friend."

"No, it's fine," Francine replied, obviously making an effort to rouse herself. "I just . . . nodded off on the couch. What's going on?"

It occurred to me that I should have rehearsed my announcement. Instead I blurted out the words: "Ursula drowned tonight. Has anyone told you?"

The muffled exclamation at the other end might have been shock—or exultation. When Francine spoke audibly, she asked if she could call me right back. Naturally I said yes.

The phone rang almost immediately, but it wasn't Francine. Doc Dewey's calm, cautious voice was on the other end. "I just checked in with the sheriff's office," he began, "and Dustin Fong told me Milo was out but that you'd been brought up to speed on this Ursula Randall business."

I allowed that that was true.

"I know that you have a Tuesday deadline for your paper," Doc Dewey went on, his careful voice almost lulling me into a somnolent state. "To be frank, I doubt that we'll have an autopsy report by then. With a three-day weekend in a county as big as Snohomish, there are going to be—unfortunately—more than the usual number of deaths. Even if we get the findings in time for your deadline, the pathologist won't be finished. I hope

I'm not speaking out of turn here, but this is a case where the pathology report is just as, if not more, important than the autopsy."

I spurred my tired brain to focus on Doc's words. "Wait—I don't understand."

"Drowning is difficult to determine," Doc responded. "In fact, it's almost impossible for an autopsy to prove that a person died by drowning. What happens is that the medical examiner tries to figure out if the victim's death was caused by something else—a heart attack, a stroke, an aneurysm. Or," he added on a sigh of regret, "foul play."

Though Milo had already prepared me for the possibility, I still winced. "You mean if the person was held underwater?"

"That's always conceivable," Doc allowed. "But it's unusual. What's more likely in such instances is that the victim was already dead before being put in the water. There was no way that I could tell that from my examination at the river. There were some marks on the deceased's face, but they could have been caused by the current and the rocks and the underbrush. Otherwise I saw no sign of injury. But don't quote me."

Don't quote me—journalists hate those three little words. Yet in a small town, sources have to be handled with extra-special care. "Okay," I agreed reluctantly. "What about rigor in terms of establishing time of death?"

"Well . . ." Doc hesitated, obviously thinking through his answer. "There were no signs of rigor setting in, so I'd have to guess that Ms. Randall hadn't been dead very long. It's complicated, though—the weather is awfully warm, which slows rigor, but her shoulders and face were in the water, which is pretty cold. Still, I doubt that death had occurred more than two hours before Richie Magruder found her."

Two hours sounded like a long time for Ursula to lie

undiscovered so close to town. But I was a layman and Doc was an expert. Thanking him for explaining the situation, I'd barely hung up when Francine called back.

"My God, Emma, I'm still shaking like a leaf!" Francine cried. "Now tell me how this happened. Was Ursula in the hot tub? Did she have heart trouble?"

As clearly and concisely as possible, I recounted what the sheriff—and to a lesser extent—Doc Dewey had told me. While I didn't mention the possibility of foul play, Francine was still appalled.

"That's just awful!" she declared. "What on earth was that crazy woman doing in lounging pajamas down by the river?"

"That's what Milo wants to know," I said, taking my cordless phone over to the couch, where I, too, lounged, though in less glamorous attire.

Francine emitted what sounded like a snort. "I suppose I shouldn't be surprised."

"Why not?"

There was a pause at the other end. "Oh . . . I guess it's just that Ursula seems like the kind of person who'd die in some strange sort of spectacular manner. I mean, doesn't she strike you as someone who likes attention?"

The comment struck me as odd. Drowning in the Skykomish River was a peculiar way of achieving the limelight. I said as much to Francine.

"I don't mean it that way," Francine retorted impatiently. "Didn't somebody say once that the way we die is often a reflection of the way we've lived? Well, there's Ursula for you—she spends her life meddling in church affairs, throwing money around like Lady Bountiful, and owning big houses and fancy cars and expensive clothes that even I couldn't afford at wholesale prices. So when she falls into the Sky and drowns, she does it in a pair of Valentino pajamas and it makes page one in *The Advocate*."

"Anybody drowning in the Sky around here would

make page one," I pointed out, feeling defensive and somehow disturbed.

"Ursula will probably get on page one of *The Seattle Times* and the *Post-Intelligencer*," Francine grumbled, then caught herself. "Now I sound like sour grapes again. But it's not that. Not this time."

"Of course not," I said, trying to soothe Francine.

It was only after we said goodbye that I wondered why her remarks weren't sour grapes.

I tried to reach Vida one last time before going to bed around midnight. She answered on the first ring. Before I could deliver my bombshell about Ursula's death, my House & Home editor defused me.

"Really, Emma, it's extraordinary. Ursula Randall was not what I'd call an outdoorsy type. Now it turns out that her car was in the garage at The Pines. How did she get to that part of the river? Why was she dressed like that? Was someone with her?"

"Wait a minute," I insisted, feeling not only tired, but a little cranky. "I thought you and Buck went to Everett. How do you know all this?"

It was, of course, a silly question. "My nephew Billy told me. Buck and I stopped for dessert at the ski-lodge coffee shop. His brother, Henry, sometimes picks up the tab. Very generous of Henry, but of course he is the manager. Buck had chocolate decadence and I ordered the key lime pie. Frankly, mine wasn't quite up to snuff— they've hired a new chef, I don't recall his name, but it's Helmig or Hjellming or something like—"

"Vida!" I interrupted. "Skip the cuisine commentary. How did you run into Bill Blatt at the ski lodge?"

"I didn't," Vida snapped. "Darlene and Harvey Adcock were there. They'd been to a movie at the Whistling Marmot. They heard all about Ursula drowning when they came out of the theatre. They'd run into Jack Mullins. Naturally I had Buck take me down to the sheriff's office, where I talked to Billy. Dwight Gould is interviewing Warren Wells at this very moment. I got home only a minute or two before you called."

"They found Warren? Where was he?"

"At The Pines, of course. Where else would he be?" Now Vida sounded a trifle cross.

"He wasn't there earlier this evening." I paused just long enough to let Vida chew over the information. "What else did Billy have to say?"

"Ursula's car was parked in her double garage. Her purse was lying on the bar with about two hundred dollars in cash. Her car keys were in it, of course." Vida paused. "Let me think. . . . Well, I assume you knew that she was still wearing her very expensive diamond engagement ring when Richie found her?"

I didn't know, because Milo, curse him, had neglected to tell me. Since Vida seemed to have wound up her report, I told her about Doc Dewey's call.

"Doc frets too much," she declared. "His father would have been much more forthcoming." Vida referred to Doc Dewey, Senior, who had passed away some five years earlier. When both father and son had been in practice, they had been known as Young Doc and Old Doc.

"Waiting for those reports out of Everett may screw us up in terms of our deadline," I noted. "What I hate most is that they'll probably be finished Wednesday morning, and then it'll be a whole week before we can print what's very old news."

"We are not without resources," Vida said in a veiled tone.

"Huh?" Midnight was too late for subtleties.

Apparently Vida sensed as much. "We'll discuss it in the morning. Why don't you drop by around ten and I'll fix you a nice brunch?"

"Tea will be fine," I said hastily. Vida's cooking was to be avoided at all costs. "I'll see you then."

Replacing the phone in its cradle, I headed for bed. The house had cooled off some, but I left most of the windows open. As I pulled off the sheet and single blanket, I realized that I was upset. However, my distress was for the wrong reasons: Ursula's passing had shocked me, but I felt no grief. I tried to excuse myself on the grounds that I hardly knew the woman. The rationale was inadequate. The late Ms. Randall was part of the community, both in Alpine and at St. Mildred's. Had I become so callous that the untimely death of a fellow Catholic left me spiritually and emotionally unscathed? Maybe the tragedy would sink in later.

Or so I was consoling myself when I heard a noise outside my open bedroom window. It couldn't be the wind. The air outside had been still and oppressive when I'd taken the garbage out to the can in the carport around eleven-thirty. Maybe it was a deer. Sometimes they came through my yard to reach the next-door neighbor's vegetable garden.

When I heard the sound a second time, I flipped on the bedside lamp and got up. Before I could lift the shade, I heard two or three more furtive noises. Cautiously I peeked outside. A half-moon rose above the trees, but I couldn't see anything unusual in the yard. If it had been a deer or a cougar, perhaps the light had startled the animal. On the other hand, such creatures moved soundlessly. I went into the living room and then the kitchen to look outside. As I stood at the back door I heard a car start on Fir Street. Rushing back to the living room, I peered through the drapes. I saw nothing. The engine faded into the night.

Maybe I was more upset about Ursula than I realized. Her death had made me nervy. Shrugging off the noises, I went back to bed.

But not before I closed all the windows.

Since I'd skipped breakfast, I stopped at the Upper Crust Bakery before going to Vida's house. Carrying my white paper bag with its two Brie-filled brioches, I was heading for my Jag when Nunzio Lucci got out of his pickup.

"What do you think about that Randall woman?" he called across the Jeep Wrangler that was diagonally parked between our vehicles.

"I think it's a shame," I shouted back. *I think it's a shame the news is out before we can write the first sentence of the story.* Naturally I didn't say so out loud. Like most nonmedia types, Luce wouldn't understand.

"Did somebody do her in?" Luce yelled.

I gritted my teeth. At least a half-dozen Alpiners had slowed their step to eavesdrop. Clutching the bakery bag, I made an end run around my car and the Jeep. "Why do you ask?" I finally said in my normal voice.

Luce fingered the stubble on his jutting chin. "Seems to me that nobody drowns in the Sky this time of year without some help," he opined in his gritty voice. "Hasn't she riled up a lot of folks since she came back to town?"

I offered Luce a thin smile. "If everybody who riled up everybody else in Alpine got murdered, we'd have bodies stacked up like cordwood."

"Well?" Luce glowered at me. "We sure as hell ain't got much cordwood, since they put through all those goddamn logging bans."

I sighed. "You know what I mean." Then, to change the subject, I posed a question. "Did you go to high school with Ursula when she was an O'Toole?"

"Naw," Luce replied, rubbing at his hairy forearm. "She was four, five years younger than me. I was in the same class as Buzzy. Jake was two years ahead of us."

It would be up to Vida to ferret out Ursula's peers and get some laudatory quotes for the obituary. "So you never really knew her, I take it?"

Luce lowered his gaze and shook his head. The bright morning sun glinted off the Miraculous Medal he wore around his thick neck. "I'd see her on the street, but she'd never so much as give me the time of day. Maybe she was always snooty—I don't know."

"Maybe she got that way after she married a doctor," I said. "That often happens."

Luce looked at me sharply. "Oh, yeah? And why would she be proud of that?" He slammed a hand against the rusted fender of his pickup. "Why would she be proud of him?"

Startled, I was about to say that I had no idea. But Della Lucci came out of Parker's Pharmacy before I could utter a word.

"Mrs. Lord," Della said with the deference I had noticed she reserved for college graduates, "how are you? Isn't this weather terrible?"

"Yes, it is," I replied. "But I heard on the news this morning that we might have rain by Monday."

Della's plump, round face brightened. "Really? Gosh, I hope so! Somebody told me yesterday that we may have to cut back on using water. And just when I've let the wash pile up."

Judging from Luce's grimy work clothes and Della's stained summer shift, it had been a while since anyone had done the laundry at the Lucci house. But the unspoken criticism gave me a pang of remorse. Who was I to judge what went on with families who didn't have a steady, viable income?

The Luccis climbed into the pickup while I got into my Jag. The contrast in transportation modes made me feel even worse. Sure, my car was aging, but it was still a status symbol, at least in Alpine. So were my Anne Klein II sandals, and never mind that I'd bought them on sale at Nordstrom's discount outlet by the Alderwood Mall. I had a university degree, I ran my own business, I owned my home, and if everything fell apart tomorrow, I could probably go out into the world to start over. That was the problem with so many Alpiners. They had reached a dead end. There was no world outside of Alpine; there was nothing on the other side of the forest.

Vida didn't have a microwave and I didn't want her to turn on the oven, so we ate the brioches cold. She sat at her kitchen table, teacup in hand, looking like a general preparing for war.

"If we can't get any official word before our deadline, we'll have to do some research of our own," Vida stated. "Who saw or talked to Ursula last night? Was it Warren? Put him down first."

Vida never took notes. She had a comprehensive, infallible memory. I, however, needed jottings and scribbles. Obediently I wrote Warren's name on the top line of my spiral notebook.

"Had Ursula made new friends or taken up with old chums since she arrived?" Vida continued. "She didn't mention any names when I interviewed her. Jake and Buzzy might know. Or their wives, Betsy and Laura. Women are much better at keeping track of such things."

"Ursula had only been here a few weeks," I pointed out, writing down the other O'Tooles. "I don't recall seeing her talk to anyone at church except Father Den."

"Ah, yes—add his name to the list. Monica Vancich, too. As the church secretary, she was bound to come into contact with a busybody like Ursula."

"What about her first husband's family? Did they keep in touch?"

Vida shook her head. "His family—goodness, I don't recall the name offhand. Hedstrom? Hegstrom? Hedberg? Anyway, the young man's father was a logger who moved the rest of the family to Idaho after the son was killed. Even if they'd stayed in Index, I suspect Ursula wouldn't have kept in contact. She had not only moved away, but up in the world. Or so she no doubt felt."

Vida's canary, Cupcake, was hopping around and cheeping. She glanced up at his cage, giving him a fond look that was usually reserved for her odious grandson,

Roger. "We have a start on names," Vida declared, pouring more tea. "Let's call on Warren. We really ought to commiserate with him, poor man."

I was familiar with Vida's sympathy ploy. "Why not?" I said, adding sugar to my cup. "I guess he's at The Pines. Shouldn't we phone first?"

Vida shook her head, unruly gray curls bobbing. "The element of surprise is very important. If he's not there, we can chat with the neighbors. Clancy and Debra Barton live next door, and the other closest house belongs to the Carlsons. But I believe Norm and Georgia are out of town."

Norm Carlson was the owner of Blue Sky Dairy. He and his wife were Lutherans, which meant there was no church connection with Ursula. But as what amounted to being a CEO, even if it actually meant no more than that he got to drive the newest milk truck, Norm might have been worthy of his new neighbor's acquaintance. The Bartons' shoe-store proprietorship would put them in the same league, though Debra's announcement as a candidate for the school board might not have endeared her to Ursula.

We arrived at The Pines shortly before eleven. Unlike most of the dry lawns in Alpine, the residents in the upscale development had managed to keep their sweeping swaths of grass a lush emerald green. Along with the second stand of evergreens that had been left at strategic landscaping points, the well-tended neighborhood presented a fresh, relatively cool appearance.

The drive in front of Ursula Randall's house was full of cars, including Delphine Corson's Posies Unlimited van and Dennis Kelly's Honda. Vida parked her big Buick just off the winding street, next to a young Sitka spruce.

"Goodness, such a crowd!" she exclaimed, walking up the drive in her familiar splayfooted manner. "Mayor Baugh's Cadillac, Richie and Stella Magruder's Voyager,

Brendan Shaw's Volvo, and . . . dear me . . . Ed's Mercedes. This doesn't bode well. How shall we get rid of them?"

"I don't like our chances," I said dryly. "Fuzzy Bough will drip with Southern comfort, Brendan is probably here on business, Father Den is no doubt making funeral arrangements, and God knows what Ed is up to. The only ones who might leave peaceably are the Magruders and Delphine, or whichever teenager she's got delivering for her this week."

"The Olson boy," Vida said vaguely as she punched the button that set off Ursula's melodious chimes. Her mouth was very tight and her eyes had narrowed under the brim of her navy sailor hat. "Dear me," she repeated on a little sigh.

It was Brendan Shaw who opened the double doors with their leaded glass panes. "Ah—Ms. Runkel, Emma! Come in, I was just leaving. Everyone is in the living room."

It was quite a crowd, though the Olson boy, whose name I recalled was Matt, had just started for the door. In his wake, he'd left at least five lavish bouquets and a large potted azalea. While I merely nodded to Matt, Vida's greeting was effusive as she retreated with him into the entry hall.

Warren rose when he saw me, and put out a hand. He seemed smaller than I'd remembered from our encounter in the post office, and his anxious eyes looked sunken. I murmured the proper platitudes, then tried to figure out where I could sit without getting stuck near Fuzzy and Irene Baugh or Ed and Shirley Bronsky. I didn't want my ear talked off. But the Baughs, as well as the Magruders, were also on their way out. Richie still seemed shaken by his ordeal of the previous night, though Stella was her usual breezy self.

"This place is air-conditioned," the buxom styling salon owner whispered on her way past the fringed and tufted mahogany bench where I'd decided to light. "I wonder what it costs?" The beauty parlor relied on fans in warm weather.

"Tapestries," Ed blurted, snapping his pudgy fingers. "Look, Shirl—what do you think? Shouldn't we get some of those for the new house?" He jabbed a thumb in the direction of what looked like an authentic Gobelin depicting a falcon hunt. "We could have some made up with pictures of those old castles we saw in Europe this summer."

Shirley, in a black linen sheath that was at least one size too small for her plump figure, gave her husband a mournful look. "Now, Ed, let's not talk about us. We're here to console poor Doubles."

At first, I thought I hadn't heard right. Then Vida was leaning close, speaking softly in my ear: "Warren's nickname—for W.W., his initials."

"Oh," I said, glancing up, though Vida had already tromped over to a Louis XV side chair whose spindly legs looked as if they might not hold up my House & Home editor. They did, however, and Vida immediately took over the conversation.

"Goodness, what a terrible day!" she declared with a shake of her head. "I lost my dear husband in an accident, too." Her gaze rested on Father Den, who was sitting next to Warren on the sofa where I'd last seen Ursula. "Did you know that, Father Kelly? Ernest wasn't much older than Mrs. Randall when he died."

My pastor nodded solemnly. "Emma has told me, Mrs. Runkel. Isn't that when you started working for *The Advocate*?"

"Yes." Vida actually managed to sound wispy. "I had three daughters to support, and my only experience was writing up the minutes for the PTA. But the other parents—and teachers—thought I had a knack. Marius Vandeventer, who owned the paper in those days, kindly gave me a job."

Dennis nodded again, though this time with a slight smile. At forty-six, he was a pleasant-looking man who still had most of his curly black hair and a certain softness of features that concealed inner toughness. Father Den had been an army brat, who had suffered not only the frequent uprooting that his father's job required, but also the prevailing racial prejudices of the era in which he'd come to manhood. Though there were still some in Alpine who might consider him a curious foreign object, Dennis Kelly seemed perfectly at ease in Ursula Randall's baroque living room.

"So," Vida went on as her gaze now drifted to Warren, "I understand how you must feel. Has the shock begun to wear off?"

Warren appeared more depressed than dazed. "I don't know," he answered in a low voice. "Going to the morgue in Everett late last night sure has a way of making things seem real. But this morning . . ." His hands twitched convulsively.

Vida nudged the brim of her sailor hat, which had begun to slip down over her forehead. "So much depends on how the news is broken to you. I trust it was tactfully done."

"I don't think it was," Shirley interjected, sounding indignant on Warren's behalf. "Doubles told us that Dwight Gould was borderline rude. Milo should train his men to be more sensitive."

Of all the sheriff's deputies, Dwight was the most withdrawn. He was a man of few words, and none that I'd ever heard had been impolite. I saw the questioning look that flickered across Vida's face, and knew she was thinking the same thing.

"Where did Dwight give you the sad news?" Vida inquired in her most earnest, sympathetic tone.

"Here," Warren replied, one agitated hand gesturing around the living room. "I'd just pulled in, around eleven. There was Dwight, out in the driveway. I thought

Ursula had reported a burglar." He paused, and took a sip of coffee from an elegant cup. "Then he said he had something to tell me, so we came inside. The next thing I know, he's asking me all these damned questions. It was only after that when he told me Ursula was dead." Warren hung his head.

"You see?" Shirley shrilled. "That's what I mean— rude! Imagine, asking poor Doubles questions! Dwight should have been offering condolences." She wiggled around in her tight dress and turned to Ed. "You should talk to Milo about this. It's ... it's criminal. Dwight needs reprimanding."

Father Den shifted uncomfortably on the sofa. "I'm sure Deputy Gould was only trying to do his job. There's no good way to deliver bad news."

"True enough," Vida agreed. "Tell me, Father Kelly, is the funeral set?"

My pastor's demeanor remained uneasy. "No." He gave Warren a faint smile. "Nothing can be done until we get some word out of Snohomish County. Anyway, the funeral Mass probably will be held in Seattle. Most of Ms. Randall's friends live in the parishes she previously attended."

My antennae shot up. "Parishes?"

Father Den now looked expressionless. "The Randalls moved quite a bit over the years, isn't that right, Warren?"

Warren gave a little shrug. "I guess so. Ursula lived near Lake Washington when I met her. That was after her husband died. I think they were on Mercer Island somewhere along the line, but they moved after the floating bridge fell down."

I recalled the Thanksgiving Day disaster five years ago when the old span that connected Seattle to Mercer Island collapsed during a severe storm. Construction of a new bridge was well under way at the time, but commuters had temporarily faced severe gridlock.

Dennis Kelly was edging off the sofa. "I should be going," he said, putting out his hand to Warren. "Let me know if there's anything I can do."

None too steadily Warren rose along with Father Den. "Sure, thanks, I will, Father. I appreciate it."

Shirley also got up, though it required a good deal of tugging at her black sheath and wobbling on four-inch heels. "We should go, too, Ed. Aren't you supposed to be at the food bank?"

"Food?" Ed echoed, sounding hopeful. "Oh! The food bank! That's right, I'm in charge this afternoon."

While Father Den exited promptly, it took the Bronskys a full five minutes to get out the door. Vida and I remained alone in the living room, waiting for Warren's return. The ormolu clock on the mantel pointed to eleven-thirty.

"Where was Warren last night?" Vida hissed. "We must find out. The flowers are all from people in Seattle. I asked Matt Olson about them."

"Old friends," I murmured, taking in one of the enormous bouquets, which featured pink glads, white orchids, and bells of Ireland. "Delphine must be raking it in."

"But she won't get the big orders for funeral flowers," Vida responded. "Tsk, tsk."

"Why were Ed and Shirley here?" I whispered. "Did they go to school with Warren?"

"Ed did. Shirley was a year behind them. They . . ." Vida's voice rose as Warren returned to the living room. ". . . Never know when an azalea will transplant well in this climate. Well, now! We seem to be the lollygaggers. Don't fret, Warren—we won't stay. Unless you prefer company."

"Ah . . ." The remark evoked an anxious look. "I'm okay, I guess. There are so many people I have to call. I suppose I should go through Ursula's address book. The only one I phoned last night was her husband's sister in

Seattle. I guess she already spread the word, but still . . ." He raised his hands in an uncertain gesture.

"It's a shame you didn't get home sooner," Vida commented with a doleful expression. "You could have gotten some of this out of the way last night. But of course you must have been tied up."

Warren hesitated before responding, then nodded vigorously. "I was." He hadn't reseated himself, apparently momentarily expecting—hoping—to show Vida and me out. "I sure was. I'd decided to take a drive—you know, a sentimental journey around town. It's been twenty-odd years since I've been in Alpine, and I hadn't had much chance to do that until last night. Boy, was that something! A lot's the same, and yet there've been changes, too. Like The Pines—it was still Stump Hill when I left." His enthusiasm seemed forced.

"Indeed," Vida acquiesced. "What struck you as most different?"

"Ahhh . . ." Warren stroked his short chin. "Well . . . the community-college site. The new bowling alley. Those condos across from The Pines. The places that have gone out of business. Oh, plenty of things! The mall wasn't built when I lived here. There was no Safeway or Starbucks or Videos-To-Go. Yes, Alpine's really changed." Warren nodded again, though more to himself than to us.

Vida was now on her feet. "When you put the changes into the context of a long absence, perhaps the town isn't as moribund as some suggest. How did Ursula feel about what had happened while she was away? I didn't ask that question during our interview."

The relief that had crept into Warren's face when he saw that we were on the verge of departure now faded. "Ursula? Oh . . . She thought it was all . . . quaint. Yes, that was the word she used—*quaint*."

"Really." Vida's tone was arch. "My, my." Then, to my surprise, and Warren's shock, she enveloped the bereaved man in a bear hug. "Poor Warren!" she exclaimed, looking out at me from under the sailor hat's brim. "I do hope you parted from Ursula on good terms! Ernest and I quarreled bitterly before his accident. I've never forgiven myself."

I'd never heard my House & Home editor say any such thing. I was still gaping at her when Warren answered in a voice muffled by Vida's shoulder. "We were happy. Very happy." He seemed to have stiffened in the embrace, and when Vida let go, Warren swayed slightly.

"That's wonderful," she asserted. "Most reassuring. Otherwise you're racked with self-reproach for the rest of your days." Lifting her chin in a brave gesture, Vida joined me on the threshold to the entry hall. "If you need to talk to anyone, just call me, Warren. Wasn't I always there for you when I baby-sat?"

Warren had relaxed a bit, but his face was puzzled. "Well . . . Yes, yes you were. Thanks, Vida."

After we got into the Buick, I gave Vida a suspicious look. "You were Warren's baby-sitter?"

"Once," Vida replied. "I filled in for Eleanor Pierce. You know, Nell Blatt, my sister-in-law. She had three-day measles." Steering the car down the winding road, Vida glanced in the rearview mirror. "Warren won't remember whether I sat once or fifty times. Men are so poor at details."

I didn't comment, though I felt that Vida's offer of consolation probably would be ignored. "Do you believe he was out driving around town last night?"

Vida snorted. "Ridiculous! Such a foolish lie. It gets dark before eight-thirty this time of year. Why would he be sightseeing for two and a half hours after the sun goes down?"

"So where was he? Hiding out someplace until the sheriff's deputies came by to tell him Ursula was dead?"

"Perhaps." Vida seemed indifferent to my suggestion.

"More likely he was in a bar. Didn't you notice how he reeked of liquor?"

"I didn't hug him," I replied. "Did he?"

"Certainly. I suspect that even now, he's behind that elaborate bar, guzzling alcoholic beverages. My, my!" Vida shook her head.

Vida's attitude toward liquor was staunchly Presbyterian. "I can't blame the guy for taking a couple of drinks," I said as we left The Pines behind us. "He's just lost the woman he loves."

I could barely see Vida's eyes under the sailor hat's brim. But there was no mistaking her ironic tone of voice as she glanced in my direction. "Has he? I wonder."

Chapter Seven

VIDA DIDN'T ANNOUNCE our destination until we had pulled up in front of Jake and Betsy O'Toole's large but unpretentious old home on Cedar Street near John Engstrom Park. The well-tended front yard dipped down, with stone steps leading to the wide front porch. Vida both rang the bell and shouted through the screen door.

"Yoo-hoo! Betsy! Jake! Yoo-hoo!"

The O'Tooles arrived from different directions. Jake came around the corner of the house, carrying a pair of clippers; Betsy greeted us at the door, holding the telephone to her ear.

"Long-distance," she mouthed, opening the screen with her free hand.

I went inside, but Vida stayed on the porch, offering Jake condolences on the loss of his sister. On this occasion, she sounded sincere. As I sat down on a green-and-white-striped sofa, Betsy rang off.

"This is the pits," she declared in her fast-paced contralto. "We're getting all sorts of calls from Ursula's friends. What can we tell them about how she died? Nobody knows anything until word comes down from Everett. We're on hold, just like everybody else. Why don't they call that moron she was engaged to?"

"Moron?" Vida repeated as she and Jake entered the comfortable living room. "Now, who would that be?"

"Warren," Betsy retorted with a mutinous glare for her husband. "Who else? Don't start defending that guy—

108

your sister had her faults, but he's an opportunist. Don't think I don't know how he treated his first two wives."

Jake, whose chiseled features seemed to have lost some of their sharpness, gave Vida and me a helpless look. "My bride hadn't seen Warren in twenty years, but she knows all about him. It's too bad she cracked her crystal ball."

Off the podium, Jake didn't try to use big words. But his sarcasm wasn't lost on Betsy. "Stick it," snapped his wife. "If nothing else, it's midlife crisis. He's driving around in a hot little red sports car, which is a sure sign of male menopause. Furthermore, I'll bet Ursula bought it for him. Since when has Warren Wells had more than two dimes to rub together?" She lifted her chin in defiance.

"It's a wedding present from Ursula," Jake said in a fairly reasonable tone. "I'll admit it—a BMW Z3 isn't cheap. So what? Maybe he bought her something nice, too. Like jewelry."

Betsy sneered. "I'll bet Ursula bought her own engagement ring. Warren couldn't afford a ring out of a Cracker Jack box."

Vida seemed accustomed to the acrimonious exchanges between the O'Tooles. It was their way when out of the public eye. Like Jake's pretentious vocabulary, the connubial bliss they displayed at the Grocery Basket was something of a front.

"So what do you hear?" Vida inquired, settling into an armchair that matched the sofa.

Betsy's full mouth pouted a bit. At forty-five she retained a youthful manner to complement her flawless complexion and naturally curly auburn hair. "I told you, I've been having my ear chewed off all morning by Ursula's friends. Some of them didn't think much of Warren Wells. For one thing, they felt he talked her into moving back to Alpine."

"Big-city types," Jake grumbled. "They always figure that if you don't live someplace with a trillion people, you might as well go drown yourself." His sunburned face paled and he clasped both hands to his cheeks. "God! What am I saying! My poor sister!"

Somewhat to my surprise, Betsy's piquant features expressed compassion for her husband. "Never mind, Jake. We know what you mean. Or didn't mean." A trifle grimly, she turned to us. "It's lunchtime—how about some chicken-salad sandwiches? I've got enough for an army out in the kitchen. I thought the kids might be here, but instead of mourning their aunt, they're off and running. Of course they didn't know her very well," she added on a note of maternal protectiveness.

I started to decline, but as usual, Vida was ahead of me: "If it's not too much trouble, Betsy. I'll help." She immediately rose, and Betsy could do nothing but follow suit. I was left alone with Jake.

"What do you think happened?" I asked, hoping that my manner conveyed the sympathy as well as the puzzlement I felt.

Jake was rubbing the back of his neck. "I'll be damned if I know," he answered in a quiet voice. "We didn't see much of Ursula after she moved to Seattle. Once every two, three years Betsy and I'd stop in on her and Wheaton when we were on our way somewhere. But she never came up here. Our folks retired to Arizona, you know. I talked to them this morning, and they're really knocked for a loop. My dad had bypass surgery last May, and I'm worried about him. I wish they wouldn't come up for the funeral. It's going to be a big deal, I gather, probably at the cathedral, with the archbishop and everybody but the pope. No, it'll just be too hard on my folks."

The faraway look in Jake's blue eyes indicated that he was now talking more to himself than to me. I waited a moment, but the silence grew awkward. Finally I asked if he'd seen Warren since hearing of Ursula's death.

"No," he replied ruefully. "He called us last night after midnight. We'd just gotten to sleep. We offered to come over then, but he said to wait. When I phoned this morning, a whole bunch of people were coming by, so he asked us to wait some more. I'll try again after lunch."

I decided not to admit that Vida and I were among the "whole bunch" who had showed up on the doorstep of the house in The Pines. "Warren was living there, wasn't he?" I asked.

"No, he wasn't," Jake replied. "He was staying up at the ski lodge. Henry Bardeen gave him a special rate. It's off-season anyway."

I didn't try to conceal my surprise. "Will he stay at the house now?"

Jake shrugged. "Maybe. I don't know. It depends on whether or not it bothers him too much. Ursula really put her personality on that place."

Jake and I were summoned to lunch in the dinette. Betsy had added potato chips, fresh peaches, and orangeade to the menu. "I was just telling Vida how I'd kind of looked forward to getting to know Ursula," our hostess said, passing around the peaches. "My family didn't move to Alpine until I was fourteen. Ursula was almost out of high school by then, and I guess she left town not too long after that. Right, Jake?" Not waiting for her husband's nod of confirmation, Betsy continued in her usual rapid-fire delivery. "So it sounded kind of fun to have a new sister-in-law around. Laura's such a drip."

"Now, don't start in on Laura," Jake cautioned with an air of resignation.

"Look," Betsy said, waving her knife, "I've done my best to help Laura in a lot of ways. Clothes for her and the kids, stuff we'd otherwise throw out at the store or give to the food bank, advice she never takes. And what have they got to show for everything you and I have done? A hovel of a house, a beat-up van, a crummy old Chev, and a bunch of car parts lying around that look like something Cal Vickers forgot!"

"It's not a Chev, it's a Plymouth Fury," Jake murmured.

"Whatever." Betsy made a slashing motion with the knife. "All cars look alike to me. And those pieces and parts look like *junk*."

"Buzzy uses them to keep his own cars running," Jake pointed out.

"Buzzy!" Betsy spat out the name as if it were a household pest that had crawled into her sandwich. "Maybe Buzzy and Laura are the reasons I looked forward to Ursula. At least she didn't strike me as a washout. If I catch your lame, lazy brother in this house with his hand in your pocket one more time, I'll chase him out of here with a two-by-four! Isn't it enough that you've given that loser a job?"

"Come on, Betsy," Jake growled. "Buzzy's had a lot of tough luck, that's all. It's not his fault that the economy around here stinks."

"Hey, big shot—we weathered the Safeway invasion, didn't we?" Betsy countered. "And how did we do it? By working our butts off, that's how. We changed the floor plan, we dropped slow-selling items, we kept up with trends to make the yuppies happy. We even changed our advertising." She glanced at me. "Of course, we had to twist both of Ed Bronsky's arms behind his fat back to do it, but after you hired Leo, we got some really good input from him. Heck, we just hunkered down and did it. Meanwhile Buzzy let Cal Vickers and his Texaco station put him out of business. Even Icicle Creek Gas 'N Go has managed to hold out, and that place is a dump. I was in there last night, and only one pump was working. But Buzzy, even with BP behind him, couldn't make it. His idea of TBA wasn't Tires, Batteries, and Accessories— it was Total Bad Attitude, spelled L-A-Z-Y." Betsy viciously stabbed a peach slice with her fork.

"You're not being fair," Jake said in a relatively mild voice. "He was sick a lot the past few years. His back went out on him, he had pneumonia twice, and then he got shingles. And don't forget, their kids haven't been as easy to raise as ours."

"Ours are easy? Give me a break!" Betsy made as if to fall out of her chair. "Ryan's had two speeding tickets this summer, Tim got caught smoking pot under the bleachers at high-school graduation, and Melissa lost her red-and-white polka-dot underwear during Senior Sneak. I swear, I'm going to put that girl on the Pill before she starts college."

While Vida seemed unfazed by the discord between the O'Tooles, I was suffering from mild embarrassment. Gulping down the last potato chip on my plate, I offered my hosts a feeble smile.

"I think Vida and I should be going. We have to check with Sheriff Dodge to see if he's heard anything."

Betsy acknowledged my announcement with a faint nod, then turned back to her husband. "You check with that dink, Warren. If he needs us, we'll come. Otherwise I'm going over to the store to work on the books for a couple of hours."

Somehow we got out of the O'Toole house without any further verbal sparring. "I catch a little bit of that confrontational stuff at coffee and doughnuts," I said as Vida pointed the car in what I feared was the other O'Toole house, "but that was almost vicious."

"No, it wasn't," Vida replied calmly. "They were just being Jake and Betsy. It's like a show. They're devoted, really. Couples who are secure in their mutual affection can spar and spat without bitterness. The truth is, Betsy and Jake would do anything for each other."

Maybe Vida was right. She usually was. But later I'd wonder about her assertion. If pushed, how far would the O'Tooles really go?

The contrast between the O'Toole families was marked. Instead of neat beds of dahlias, glads, and rose-bushes, Buzzy and Laura's patchy front yard featured rusting car bodies. Two mongrel dogs lay under a scraggly mountain ash. Neither bothered to get up when we pushed our way between discarded mufflers, bicycle wheels, old tires, and a hot-water tank. Only the big TV satellite dish that loomed over the stripped-down chassis of a Dodge Dart looked fairly new.

The small house that stood not far from the railroad tracks wore a weary, untended air. The brown paint was peeling, shingles were missing from the roof, one front window was held together with duct tape, and the porch floorboards creaked ominously. There was a weathered sign above the doorbell that read BROKE—KNOCK HARD.

"Broke in more ways than one," Vida murmured, slamming her fist against the doorjamb. "Tsk, tsk."

Laura O'Toole took her time greeting us. *Stringy* was the word that leaped to mind. Maybe it was the wrinkled shorts and top that revealed her skinny arms and legs, or the limp, mousy hair and the untied sneakers. She ushered us inside in an offhand manner, as if she neither knew nor cared why we had come.

"Buzzy's not here," she said vaguely. "Is something wrong?" Her flat tone indicated that something always was.

The living room was also poles apart from the comfortable ambience of the Jake O'Toole residence. The TV was tuned to a golf tournament, though the volume was turned off and the picture was out of focus. Tabloids littered the floor, along with empty microwave entreé containers. The furniture was old and had never been of quality. Vida positioned herself on a plastic lawn chair, but I chose to remain standing.

"We wanted to tell Buzzy how sorry we were about his sister," Vida said, though her usual glibness seemed to stick in her throat. "How is he holding up?"

Laura's big gray eyes regarded Vida with what might have been skepticism—or perhaps stupidity. "Buzzy? He's okay." She deposited her scrawny figure on a pile of laundry that had been left on the sagging orange couch. The tattered shades were pulled down, and as far as I could tell, the windows were closed. The house felt very warm.

Vida plunged forward. "Was he surprised?"

Laura's angular face definitely looked puzzled. "By what?"

"By his sister's death." I couldn't hear Vida gnash her teeth, but I suspected she was fighting the urge. "It must have been a shock," my House & Home editor added in hushed tones.

"Well . . ." Laura tilted her head to one side, as if she hadn't really considered the matter until now. "Yeah, kind of."

"So close," Vida said after a long pause in apparent expectation that Laura was going to amplify her response. "Richie Magruder found the body so close to your house."

"Oh? I guess." Laura shifted on the pile of laundry. "She was pretty, wasn't she?"

I could tell from the jerk of one foot that Vida was startled by the comment. "Ursula? Yes, in her way."

Laura nodded sagely. "When you're rich, you can afford to look nice. Do you know who gets all her money?"

The guileless question threw me more than it did Vida. "I've no idea," she said.

"There were no children by her first two husbands," I put in, just so that Laura would remember I was also present.

"I'd like to know," Laura said, for the first time showing some animation in her face. "I'd like to know real soon."

"Why is that?" Vida inquired as a door banged somewhere in the house.

Laura's lean features grew cagey. "I just would, that's all."

I nodded toward the sound of the door. "Is that Buzzy?"

Laura shook her head, the almost brown hair hanging limp at her neck. "No. That's one of the kids. Mike, I think. He was over at the playfield."

Having finally seen Laura O'Toole up close, I couldn't resist a question. "Why did you decide to run for the parochial-school board?"

Wiping at the perspiration on her forehead, Laura gazed at me with empty gray eyes. "Luce asked me."

Vida leaned forward on the chair. "Nunzio Lucci?"

Laura nodded. "I didn't want to, but he said it would be good for the parish. Besides, I won't win."

"You never know," Vida remarked vaguely, then gave Laura a coaxing smile. "When do you expect Buzzy home?"

Dangling one of the sneakers from her bare foot, Laura gazed around the crowded, stuffy, shabby room. "I don't," she said. "He's left."

The rumors we'd heard were apparently true. "You're separated?" I tried to sound matter-of-fact.

"That's right." Laura seemed unmoved by the concept.

Vida was now standing up in the middle of the worn carpet. "That's a shame. Where is Buzzy living these days?"

Tugging at her frayed denim shorts, Laura got up, too, but made no move to see us to the door. "In his van."

That was another thought that didn't seem to disturb Mrs. Buzzy O'Toole.

"Honestly," Vida exclaimed as we drove away from the dilapidated house by the railroad tracks, "you Catholics are very peculiar! Nunzio Lucci and Laura O'Toole, running your church and school—how could sensible people elect such a pair of imbeciles?"

"Laura's not elected yet," I pointed out. "Luce is fairly conservative in his views. He doesn't have to be articulate or brilliant. All he has to do is vote the way like-minded parishioners think. Maybe that's why he asked

Laura to run. She must share his attitudes toward the church and the school."

"Laura wouldn't know an attitude if it bit her," Vida snapped. The car slowed as we passed the last of the ramshackle houses on River Road. On our right, we could glimpse the river's tumbling passage as it headed into town. To the left, a new dirt road had been hacked out of the woods. It led to the Bronsky building site.

I had gone with Carla to take pictures when the foundation had been laid in late June. The house was about a quarter of a mile from the Sky, situated on a rise that overlooked the town. I thought perhaps that Vida wanted to see how the construction was progressing. But she kept going past the new road. I realized then that we were headed for the spot where Richie Magruder had found Ursula Randall.

"I brought my camera," she said with a nod toward the backseat. "I'll save Carla a trip Tuesday."

What had started in town as a paved two-lane street was now a narrow dirt track full of potholes. But we didn't have far to go. I recognized one of the old sheds and the remnants of the water tower that Milo had mentioned. Then I saw a small concrete building bearing a US West logo. While Vida drove slowly I kept watch for the underbrush that Richie had figured might conceal a fish or two.

"Right there," I said suddenly, pointing to a cluster of bare branches that rose out of the river.

There was a convenient turnout on the opposite side of the road. Convenient for us, as well as for the vehicle that had brought Ursula to this secluded part of the Sky. Presuming she had been brought and had not come under her own power. Had the elegant wedgie shown signs of covering a lot of ground? I should have asked Milo. Was there any indication of a struggle? The sheriff would have said so if there had been. Could Ursula have been suffering from ill health? Would Doc Dewey or his partner, Peyton Flake, know? A dozen random thoughts tumbled through my brain as I got out of the Buick.

"Milo must have taken impressions," Vida said, bending down to examine the dry brown earth. "Dear me—I doubt that he'd get much. Without any rain lately, I scarcely left any tread marks even with this big car."

There was no bank to descend, just a path from the road that led directly to the rocks and boulders that lined the shallow river. We trod carefully, though Vida's canvas open-toed shoes had gripper soles, and my leather sandals were reasonably sturdy.

But there was nothing to see. Some thirty yards upstream, the Sky rounded a bend, then flowed straight as it headed west. We could hear the river, see the rocks that protruded, take in the riffle where the underbrush was caught on the bottom. But we had no idea exactly where Ursula had been found.

"It was getting dark when Richie came through here," Vida mused, fingering her chin. "Do you know what color Ursula's pajamas were?"

I shook my head. "Richie was probably watching his footing, just like we were. If he saw anything up ahead, he may have thought it was litter. People—especially kids—are so careless about leaving stuff behind."

Vida nodded. "This isn't as isolated as you'd think. Indeed, because of that turnoff in the road, it's the first place that picnickers or fishermen or teenagers would stop at this end of town."

"That's true," I allowed as my gaze wandered from the nearby birch, cottonwood, and vine maples to the fir, cedar and hemlock trees that climbed the mountainside. The rippling water danced among the rocks, swirling around speckled boulders. It was a peaceful late-summer idyll, with the river as deceptive as the scene itself. A month from now, two at most, the rains and then the snows would transform the benevolent stream into a deep, dark churning torrent. The rocky shore would disappear; trees might be swept away; the road itself could be swallowed up. That pretty stretch of amiable water was as mysterious as it was changeable. Ursula Randall wasn't the first secret it had kept and held. "There's no yellow tape to indicate an accident or . . ." I let the sentence trail off, as if borne away on the current.

"No," Vida said. "Milo and his men must have collected whatever they needed last night."

Looking back toward the road, I saw the sun glinting off Vida's Buick. "This part of the river is pretty exposed."

"Yes." Vida glanced over her shoulder. "But no one has gone by since we got here." Taking the camera from her shoulder, she began to adjust the settings. "A pity we couldn't get Richie or Milo to point out the exact spot," she murmured. "But you're not one for using posed pictures."

That was true. Having Richie Magruder reenact his discovery was too contrived. Nor did I see the news value of Milo staring at a bunch of rocks.

"This will do," I conceded. "We'll also run one of the pictures of Ursula we didn't use in your feature. A close-up."

Vida clicked off a dozen shots from different angles. The sun was beginning its midday westerly descent, turning the river to gold. But there were a few clouds gathering overhead, a hopeful sign that the weather might break.

"Okay," I said when we were back in the car, "what did you squeeze out of Betsy while putting lunch together?"

Vida uttered a frustrated groan. "Very little. She's fairly sensible, so I thought she might have some ideas about what happened to Ursula. We're operating on the process of elimination, of course. Was it an accident? Was it foul play? Was it suicide?"

"Suicide?" I shot Vida a skeptical glance. "That seems

really stupid. Who would commit suicide by sticking their face in six inches of water?"

"They wouldn't," Vida answered reasonably. "Not if they had good sense. But we don't know if Ursula did, do we?"

I recalled Francine's waspish comment about Ursula trying to attract attention. A day later it still didn't wash. "We should talk to Milo. That's what I told Betsy and Jake we were going to do."

Vida was now turning onto Highway 187, also known as the Icicle Creek Road. "So we shall," she agreed. "After we've interviewed the next person on our list."

I'd forgotten about the list. "Who's that?"

Vida gave me a disparaging look. "Monica Vancich, your church secretary. She may not be a Jean Campbell, but she must know something."

I didn't argue. Nor, as I had expected, was I asked where the Vanciches lived. Vida already knew, which I did not. To my chagrin, Monica, Verb, and their two young children resided two blocks from me on Fir Street. Like mine, the Vancich house was tucked up against the forest. Unlike mine, it was a split-level with pale green aluminum siding above and Roman brick below. Built in the Fifties, it was one of many homes in Alpine that had been constructed to meet a short-lived housing shortage caused by the boom in the timber industry.

"Let me think," Vida mused as she pulled onto the dirt verge between the street and the lawn with its brown patches of dying grass. "The Dahlgrens, then the Almquists, and finally the Kincaids. They're all gone now, moved away—or dead. Gus Dahlgren was killed in the woods. The Almquists divorced. The Kincaids moved to Alaska." Having summed up the house's history, Vida clasped her hat to her head and got out of the car.

Two small children were playing in a sandbox next to the house. I recognized them from church, but couldn't recall their names. Verb came out of the open garage under the house when he heard us approach.

"Did anybody tell you I got two of those bikes back?" he called, wiping his hands on a dirty rag. "Milo'd better find the rest of them. Or is that why you're here?" His thin face wore an anxious expression.

"I'm afraid not, but I'm sure Milo's trying," I said, thinking that the sheriff had more important matters at hand. "Is Monica home?"

"Monica?" Verb seemed surprised, as if I'd asked after the queen mother. "Yeah, she's inside, sewing or something." He continued to wipe his hands, and his high forehead creased in apprehension. "What's up? No more bad news, I hope. Man, I couldn't take anything else. This has been a lousy week."

Vida fixed Verb with her most owlish expression. "You mean Mrs. Randall?"

Verb gave a start. "No! I mean the bikes. And all the stuff at church. But you go someplace else, don't you, Mrs. Runkel?" The smile he attempted failed badly.

"I'm a Presbyterian," Vida answered primly. "We don't have such squabbles. It's not Christian."

While I couldn't help but bristle, the remark didn't seem to faze Verb. "I try to keep my distance. That's Monica's turf."

The two children, a boy and a girl about five and seven, were calling to their father. Verb excused himself and scurried off to the sandbox. The little girl was crying, a whining sound that indicated her will was injured more than her body.

The front door was open. I waited for Vida to make our presence known, which she accomplished with a push on the bell and one of her ear-rattling yoo-hoos. Monica appeared almost at once from the lower half of the house.

"Mrs. Runkel! Emma!" she exclaimed, pushing the straw-colored hair off her forehead. "Come in. I was doing the mending and thought I heard Verb talking to someone. My sewing room is over there." She gestured vaguely in the direction of the garage. Monica's manner seemed as jittery at home as it had during the special parish meeting earlier in the week.

Monica led us up the carpeted stairs to the living room, which was furnished in what looked like well-worn castoffs. While not as cluttered or oppressive as the Buzzy O'Toole house, there was a general air of untidiness that seemed to emanate more from disorganization than from sloth. Vida and I sat down on half of the tweedy gray sectional; Monica took her place in a lime-rust-and-orange-striped armchair that evoked the worst of the early Seventies. Our hostess wore a curious expression.

"Weekend or not, we're on the job," Vida announced in an ingratiating manner. "Don't be alarmed, Monica, but we're trying to figure out what happened to Ursula Randall. Surely you must have some ideas."

Monica's faded features, which probably had been pretty twenty years ago, became distressed. "About what? Father Den called me this morning to say she'd fallen in the river. I don't have any ideas about that, except that she must have sprained an ankle or something."

"That's possible," Vida admitted, "though Doc Dewey hasn't indicated any such thing. Did you know Mrs. Randall well?"

"Oh, no!" Monica's response seemed both too hasty and too adamant. She must have noticed my surprised reaction because she shifted her gaze from Vida to me. "I mean, I hardly knew her. She's only been in Alpine a month or so."

Vida wore a puzzled expression. "But she was active in your church. Surely you must have dealt with her."

Monica's close-set gray eyes strayed to a framed piece of embroidery that proclaimed, LIVE IN CHRIST, DIE IN CHRIST, DWELL WITH CHRIST FOREVER. Maybe she was seeking inspiration. "Ms. Randall came to see Father Den several times," she finally said in her light, nervous voice. "I hardly talked to her while she waited for him. Not that she waited long—I don't think she liked to be kept waiting."

The observation seemed astute. "Was she experiencing a spiritual crisis?" I inquired, noting a faint nod of approval from Vida for coming up with the question.

Monica's gray eyes widened. "I don't know. I don't think so. Her attitude was . . . assertive."

Vida started to say something, but Monica hadn't finished: "I didn't sense the Spirit moving in Ms. Randall. She seemed more material, more earthbound. Once, I did ask if she'd like to join our Thursday prayer group. She was actually kind of rude about it. She laughed, and said prayer groups were silly." Dismay clouded Monica's face. "I didn't say anything, but she could tell I didn't approve. We've been praying for her ever since."

"We?" Vida sounded ingenuous.

"Our prayer group," Monica replied with a beatific smile. "Sister Mary Joan, Pia Patricelli, Debra Barton, Nina Mullins. There are some others who sort of come and go, depending on whether the Spirit is with them." Still looking sublime, Monica turned to me. "You ought to join us, Emma. There's a real sense of community, of women getting in touch with themselves and each other. Sometimes we feel isolated from the Church proper, as if our role isn't valued. Women sharing their sense of spirituality among themselves is very important to our self-esteem. Marisa Foxx came once and said it was an unforgettable experience. I can't think why she hasn't come back. Maybe her law practice keeps her too busy."

Maybe, I thought, Marisa wasn't a complete idiot. I'd gone to a prayer meeting once, twenty years ago in Portland. We sat around in a circle, with the putative leader urging us all to share our most intimate secrets. By the time they got to me, I'd developed a leg cramp and realized I was stuck in the beanbag chair. Announcing that I felt immobilized, my coreligionists took the statement as a spiritual, rather than a physical, malady and began to pray over me. With kindly pats on the head, they assured me that God would soon lift the veil from my soul. Then they all trooped off into the kitchen to drink coffee and eat cookies while I ended up rolling around on the floor, trying to get on my feet. Needless to say, I never went back to the prayer group. I suspected that Marisa Foxx, who struck me as a no-nonsense kind of person, had had a similar, if less clumsy, reaction. Such incidents definitely could be termed "unforgettable."

I evaded Monica's invitation by pouncing on the mention of Marisa. "Do you have any idea if Ms. Randall had engaged Ms. Foxx as her attorney?"

Monica's response bordered on indignation. "Really, I know almost nothing about Ms. Randall. I don't know Marisa that well, either. She just doesn't seem to be someone who likes to share. The only time I've talked to her lately—except at church to say hello—was when she came to see Father Den a couple of weeks ago."

I could see the alarm flares light up in Vida's eyes, and couldn't resist my next question: "A spiritual crisis?" Spiritual crises seemed to appeal to Vida.

Monica's face hardened. "I don't think so. She brought her briefcase."

"Perhaps," Vida suggested with a straight face, "Marisa had cataloged her doubts."

"Well . . ." Monica considered the idea. "It's possible. She seems very organized." The close-set gray eyes skipped around the living room's disorder, dancing from scattered toys to discarded winter sports catalogs to all manner of books, ranging from children's stories to pop psychology and pap theology. "It's much more important to organize your inner life than to worry about the externals," Monica stated, as if to defend her careless housekeeping.

Looking pained, Vida stood up. "Cleanliness is next to godliness," she murmured, then gave Monica an artless smile. "Of course that's a Presbyterian precept. I'm sure you Catholics would deem it heresy."

"Oh, not necessarily," Monica replied, very serious. "We don't think in those terms anymore. We believe in openness."

"But not in organization." Vida was now smiling broadly, as if she had made a big joke. I knew better, and all but hustled her out the door.

The little girl was on her way into the house. "Mama!" she cried, stepping on my foot as she crossed the threshold. "John Paul broke my shovel!"

Bending down, Monica put a gentle hand on her daughter's arm. "Now, Teresa, don't be angry. Your brother is trying to tell you something, and he doesn't have the right words. Let's bring him inside and we'll share our feelings and say a little prayer. Remember, you must always see the part of him that's Jesus."

"I saw his wee-wee!" Teresa screeched. "He piddled in the sandbox!"

"Teresa!" Monica's voice was firm, though not raised. "First of all, you're not to call body parts by crude nicknames. Second, you must be more open to—"

"Goodbye," Vida called over her shoulder.

The gait that she achieved in getting to her car came the closest to a run that I'd ever seen on the part of my House & Home editor. By the time I got into the passenger seat, I was laughing so hard that I could barely speak. Vida, of course, was fuming.

"I don't believe I can stand interviewing these people," she declared after running out of invective. "My acquaintanceship with the St. Mildred's crowd has been casual, for the most part. At least as far as the younger members are concerned. Really, Emma, how do you endure such silliness? I'm beginning to think Ursula Randall wasn't so dreadful after all."

I started to give Vida a glib reply, then thought better of it. "The truth is, I don't socialize with most of them, and I don't participate much in church activities. In some ways, it's kind of like high school. People are thrown together for one reason. They share a certain thing—getting an education or belonging to the same faith—and they live in a specific geographical area. But that doesn't mean they have much else in common. In a way, it's one of the things I like about being Catholic. The Church—I'm talking with a capital *C*, Vida—is catholic. Little *c*. It has room for all sorts of people, from simpletons to saints. Sometimes it's hard to tell the difference. But I keep my distance because if I hung out with some of those people, I'd go nuts. They're enough to make me lose my religion—or at least to wonder about it. Losing faith is another matter."

"Yes." Vida was thoughtful. "Faith is very personal. I despise talking about it. To be frank, we have a few members in our congregation who are not unlike Monica Vancich. They're younger, like her. But Pastor Purebeck watches them like a hawk. Talking in tongues indeed!"

Vida's remark about Pastor Purebeck reminded me of Father Den—and the visit from Marisa Foxx. "I wonder why Marisa went to see Den," I mused. "I'll bet it had nothing to do with a spiritual crisis."

"You and Marisa should be friends," Vida asserted. "I've often wondered why you haven't become better acquainted."

I'd occasionally wondered that myself. Marisa had moved to Alpine a couple of years earlier and joined the Doukas law firm. Her brisk manner and lack of overt femininity had given rise to rumors that she was a lesbian. But I neither knew nor cared about her sexual orientation. The truth was that we both seemed too caught up in our busy lives to extend a hand in friendship.

"Maybe I'll invite Marisa over for dinner this coming

week," I said. "I can use one of the menus I planned for Ben."

Vida's gray eyes slid in my direction. "Good. Very good."

"Do you want to come?"

"No, no. Not this time. You two Catholics need to be alone. Girl talk. Catholic talk. Talk, talk, talk. It may prove interesting." Vida looked pleased with herself—or with me—as she eased the Buick into a diagonal parking space in front of the sheriff's office. We were lucky to find such a convenient place. Front Street was busy, mostly with out-of-towners enjoying the Labor Day weekend.

Milo had the big fan going, which was good, because his ashtray was overflowing and Vida detested the smell of cigarette smoke. Still, the air was stale and oppressive. The sheriff's offer of hot coffee was refused by both of us.

"I was wondering when you two would come by," Milo said, settling into his swivel chair and putting his feet up on the desk. He looked a bit smug.

"We're here now," Vida responded, adjusting her glasses and smoothing the wrinkles in her striped culottes. "Have you some news?"

The sheriff ruffled his graying sandy hair. "Could be. What do you want to know? Traffic accidents? Attempted break-ins? Bad checks? Crazy Eights Neffel swiping Grace Grundle's underpants off the clothesline and wearing them on his head in the public library?" Milo seemed uncharacteristically playful.

It clearly strained Vida to humor the sheriff. "Actually we had some questions about Ursula Randall. For example, was there any indication that she might have suffered an injury that caused her to fall down? Doc Dewey thought not, according to Emma, but his examination was admittedly cursory."

"Cursory, but on target." Milo reached for his cigarettes, caught Vida's warning glance, and toyed with a ballpoint pen instead. "We heard from Everett about a half hour ago. It seems that some high muck-a-muck in Seattle at the Catholic church headquarters called my SnoCo colleagues and put on the pressure. The preliminary report is in." Milo put down the pen and reached into his shirt pocket for a roll of mints. "Ursula Randall had an accident, all right. She passed out and fell on her face in the Sky because she was drunk. The lady was loaded with alcohol. Hell, the lady was loaded. What more can I say?"

Milo popped a mint into his mouth, held out both hands, and gave us a triumphant grin.

Vida told him he was an idiot.

Chapter Eight

THE SHERIFF EXPLODED in anger. What was so strange about a willful woman who had swigged down a fifth of vodka, wandered away from her fancy house, and collapsed at the edge of the river while she was contemplating her navel or her future or her next drink? People walked in front of railroad trains, meandered across major highways, stepped off curbs in front of buses. Accident or deliberate, the result was the same—they ended up dead.

"Hell, what were you expecting?" Milo demanded, his tone finally becoming less harsh.

Vida leaned forward in her chair, one arm planted firmly on the sheriff's desk. "Foul play. Which, I believe, is what you told Emma in the first place. Do you really intend to dismiss this as an accidental death?"

"I didn't tell Emma any such thing," Milo retorted. "I said it might have been foul play. Look." The sheriff wagged a long finger. "How often do you read—or in your case, write—an obituary where you say something like 'So-and-so died of apparent kidney failure' or 'Memorials in Blah-blah's name should be sent to the American Heart Association'? Sure, it sounds like natural causes. But you know damned well—especially you, Vida—that So-and-so and Blah-blah drank themselves to death. Or worse, they OD'ed on drugs. You never read that a person who died in a house fire caused by a smoldering cigarette had passed out first with an

129

empty jug by his—or her—side. Ask Doc Dewey, ask Peyton Flake. They'll tell you that one hell of a lot of people right here in Skykomish County peg out on booze. You've got almost forty percent of the population living below the poverty level. What little money they've got goes into a bottle." Milo paused, his eyes fixed on the map of Skykomish County. "It wasn't always like this. There used to be jobs, people had pride. A man could hold his head up and support his family—" He stopped altogether. I could have sworn there was a catch in his voice.

"Pitiful," Vida murmured. "But, alas, true. I'm older, I remember even more of the good times." She sighed. "Well, I suppose we ought to be going. Thank you, Milo, for your help."

Milo had turned his attention back to us. "Damn it, you're going to have to trust me on this. It was the booze."

Vida had risen, a majestic figure in the striped culotte costume and sailor hat. With a stretch of the imagination, I could picture her as a figurehead on a New Bedford whaler. "Perhaps," Vida said in a noncommittal tone. "Though I do have a quibble. The people you've been describing are unemployed, uneducated, living in despair. That doesn't really suit Ursula Randall, does it?"

The sheriff's expression was ironic. "You think rich people don't drink? They just buy better brands."

"That's not the point," Vida said with dignity. "I don't think that rich people—such as Ursula—walk three miles from the elegant comfort of their own homes to pass out in the Skykomish River. It doesn't make sense."

"You'd be surprised what weird things people do," Milo replied gruffly.

"No, I wouldn't." Vida's glance veered in my direction. "Ursula's clothes, her shoes, the time of day—none of it fits. But most of all, where was the bottle?"

"The bottle?" For the first time Milo looked jarred.

Vida leaned both hands on the desk. "Of course. Now, I'll confess I've never been inebriated. But my uncle Otto, whose family nickname was Uncle Blotto—well, never mind, let's say that I've had some experience with alcoholism. I do know that if a person walks a great distance in fresh air, they begin to grow sober. 'Walking it off'—isn't that the expression? Now, if Ursula did indeed go on foot from The Pines almost to the end of River Road, she shouldn't have passed out when she got there. Unless, of course, she had brought a bottle or a flask or some such container with her. In which case, where was it? Did Richie find it? Did you? Emma and I certainly saw no sign when we were there this afternoon."

Milo was drumming his fingers on the desk. "She might have dropped it and it broke. If it was a flask, it could have been carried off by the current."

"Rot," I put in. "The current next to the shore is relatively slow. It only picks up toward the middle of the river, where that underbrush is caught. You know that, Milo. You're a fisherman, for God's sake."

Milo had the grace to look sheepish. "It's still a plausible scenario."

"No, it's not," I said, and then saw the disappointment in Milo's hazel eyes. Perhaps he'd taken my long silence for agreement. Trying not to flinch, I plunged ahead. "Look at this from another angle. Most of the local deaths caused by drinking don't benefit anybody. That may not be true with Ursula. She was rich. Who gets her money? She was jumping into what may be a really nasty situation at St. Mildred's. Who is sufficiently fanatical to want her out of the way? She had a history of making trouble. Who might have been seeking revenge? If ever there were motives to murder someone, it seems to me that Ursula Randall is pretty high on the list."

"That's right, Emma," Vida chimed in. "And that's not the half of it."

I gave Vida a puzzled look. "Huh?"

"The classic triangle." Vida nodded sapiently. "Ursula, Warren, and Francine."

Milo and I both stared.

"Bullshit," the sheriff scoffed.

"Rubbish," I declared.

Our disdain had no effect on Vida. "As you will," she said, snatching up her straw purse. "Come, Emma, we must go. Doubtless Milo has criminals to catch." She stalked out of the office.

Milo was leaning across his desk, hissing at me. "Are you home tonight?"

"Sure. Want to come over?"

His answer was a thumbs-up gesture. I was still smiling when I joined Vida outside of the main entrance.

"You two," she muttered in a tone of disapproval. "I just don't know."

"Know what?" My voice had an edge to it.

Vida sighed, then marched to her car. "It's not a good match," she declared after I had settled into the passenger seat. "It was inevitable, of course. But I simply don't understand how you and Milo . . . Oh, never mind. What I think isn't important."

It wasn't. Or it shouldn't have been. But it really was. In the past six months Vida had never commented directly on my romance with the sheriff. It hadn't occurred to me that she might not approve.

"I don't get it," I huffed. "You like me. You like Milo. What's wrong with liking us together?"

Vida's lips compressed as she steered the Buick up Front Street. "You're not suited for each other. You have very little in common. You enjoy classical music, movies, theatre, books. Milo fishes and reads gun magazines. What on earth do the two of you watch together on television?"

"Sports," I answered promptly. "We both like sports. We've got tickets to a Mariner game with the A's."

Vida sighed again. "I keep forgetting—you actually enjoy watching all those overgrown boys romping around in silly suits with various types of balls or pucks or other such missiles. But that's not enough on which to build a future."

"It's enough for now."

"Oh, dear!" Vida actually sounded despondent.

"Vida . . ." I paused, questioning the wisdom of having to defend my feelings. "Milo and I are very . . . comfortable with each other. We have more in common than you might think. Milo occasionally does enjoy a movie. I like some country-and-western music. We laugh at the same things. We can talk to each other. What's wrong with that?"

Vida was driving up Fourth Street, apparently taking me home. She didn't reply for a long time, not until she turned right on Fir. "It's not Milo himself. It's you. I truly don't believe you've ever gotten over Tommy."

"Vida!" I was appalled. For reasons I'd never fathomed, Vida clung to a belief that Tom and I belonged together. A few years ago, when we had been reunited, I'd found her attitude touching. After I'd decided to cut Tom out of my life, her persistence was amusing. Now I was downright disgusted. "What would be the point? Tom is never going to leave Sandra, and even if he did, can you see him moving from San Francisco to Alpine?"

"He could commute," Vida said doggedly.

I opened my mouth to argue that Tom owned a weekly-newspaper empire, all his family, business, and social ties were in the Bay Area, he was a city person through and through. But debate was pointless. Tom and I were finished; the only connection was our son. If Vida couldn't accept that, then I might as well shrug it off as one of her inexplicable blind spots.

"You're really convinced that Ursula was murdered, aren't you?" I finally said, changing the subject.

"Milo's divorced. He's a Protestant." Vida pulled up in my driveway.

"Milo and I have never discussed marriage," I replied testily. "Why are you so sure about Ursula?"

"Could Tommy get a—what do you call them?—an annulment?"

"I agree with you about the bottle. In fact, I think you're right about foul play." I was forcing myself to sound reasonable.

"I've heard that if you have money, you can buy an annulment from the Vatican."

Briefly closing my eyes, I let out a loud sigh. "That's not true. And I don't want to discuss it. Really, I don't."

Vida stared through the windshield, which was now covered with a fair share of dead bugs. "That's very foolish. But I'll keep my own counsel. For now. Goodbye, Emma."

I despised quarreling with Vida. However, her present mood was impossible to dent. I got out of the car and headed for my front door. It was only after I'd heard the Buick drive off that I realized my Jag was at her house. Running down the driveway, I waved my arms and yelled her name. But she had already turned onto Fourth.

It was too hot to walk all the way over to her house. There were more clouds moving in, which offered hope that the weather might cool off by late afternoon. Feeling tired and frustrated, I went inside. The phone was ringing.

The voice on the other end identified itself as belonging to Alicia Lowell. "Francine's daughter," she clarified. "Do you know where my mother is?"

Briefly I was speechless. "No. Isn't she at the shop?" Francine's Fine Apparel was open on Saturdays from eleven until five. It was now three-twenty.

"The shop's closed," Alicia said in a worried voice. "I'm at home—at Mother's, that is. I just got back from Snohomish."

Francine and I attend the same church, we belong to the same bridge club, we're both members of the Chamber of Commerce. I like her, and I think she likes me, but we aren't close friends. I'm a customer and she's an advertiser. There is more mutual dependency than intimacy in our relationship. Consequently I was puzzled by Alicia's call.

"I tried Mrs. Runkel first," Alicia said, as if she could read my mind. "But she didn't answer. Mother says Mrs. Runkel always knows everything about everybody. I thought she might be at your place."

"You mean Mrs. Runkel? She just dropped me off. But I don't think she knows where your mother is." I had carried the phone to the kitchen, where I took a Pepsi out of the fridge. "Have you called your father? Maybe she's helping him with the funeral arrangements." Only an emergency would make Francine close the shop. Her ex-husband's plight could qualify.

"I don't speak to my father." Alicia's voice had turned icy. "Who else would know where she might be?"

The first name that popped into my head was Roseanna Bayard. Over the years I'd gathered that the two women were good friends. "Try Roseanna at home. She doesn't usually work at the photography studio on weekends."

Alicia thanked me and rang off. Sipping my Pepsi, I, too, began to worry about Francine. My thoughts were interrupted by Vida, calling to me through the screen door.

"Goodness!" she exclaimed, bursting into the living room. "How addled can we be? It isn't as if I knew Ursula particularly well, certainly not in recent years. But her death must have unhinged my brain. Do you want to get your car now?"

I stared at Vida. Apparently she had dismissed our discord over Tom and Milo. There was no trace of anger in her manner as she paced between the green sofa and the stone fireplace, her eyes darting into every nook and cranny.

"That'd be fine," I finally said, grateful to be on good terms again. "How about something to drink first?" I held out my can of Pepsi.

Vida doesn't care for soft drinks, but she said that ice water would do nicely. A minute later we were seated in the living room and I was telling her about Alicia's phone call. To my surprise, she evinced no concern.

"Maybe the power went out. You know how often that happens around here." Vida calmly sipped her water.

Power failures, both massive and individual, were definitely not rare in Skykomish County. Sometimes the cause was lightning; often it was the wind; in winter, it was snow.

But the weather had been perfect, at least by some people's standards. "It just doesn't seem right," I murmured.

"Unexpected company, in for the Labor Day weekend," Vida declared. "The register broke. A rat got loose. Crazy Eights Neffel barricaded himself in the dressing room. Don't fuss so, Emma. Francine is very capable. Warren couldn't lose two wives in one weekend."

"Ursula wasn't his wife—yet," I reminded my House & Home editor. "Who was his second wife?"

Vida gave a small shrug. "Someone from Monroe. Warren was working in the sporting-goods store there at the time. I never knew her, except by name. They moved to Seattle. I don't believe it lasted very long. They divorced."

The annulment issue popped into my head. How had Ursula and Warren gotten permission to marry in the Church when he had been divorced twice? But I didn't bring up the question for fear of having Vida start in again on my romantic situation. Instead I asked if Warren had left Francine for the other woman, or if they had already broken up by the time he met Wife Number Two.

"I'm not entirely sure," Vida admitted. "Warren had been working for Harvey Adcock, but they didn't get on well. Warren took a job with a fishing-tackle store in Monroe. It was a bit of a commute, but he didn't mind. The next thing we heard"—as Vida spoke I had visions of Alpine's residents, ears attuned for any news that was whispered along Highway 2—"he was staying over now and then. Now, whether he quit Harvey's Hardware partly because he wanted to get away from Francine, I don't know. It might have been a kind of trial separation. When he married this other woman, *The Advocate* didn't run the story because the ceremony took place either in Monroe or Everett. I hadn't yet gone to work for the paper, and Mrs. DeBee wasn't much for reporting news that didn't fall in her lap."

Over time, I had heard occasional oblique references to Vida's predecessor. I knew little about the woman then called the "society editor" except that by the time Vida was widowed, Mrs. DeBee was in her eighties, and unwell. Still, Vida had hinted that she hadn't retired gracefully.

"And Alicia?" I inquired, trying to keep my worry over Francine at bay. "She told me she doesn't speak to Warren."

"That's true," Vida said equably. "Alicia was eight or nine when Warren and Francine divorced. She and her father had been very close. Then he was gone. Francine got custody, of course, and while Warren had visitation rights, he didn't exercise them. I suppose it was because of the new wife. Perhaps she hoped to give him more children."

I felt a breeze stir through the house. "Did she?"

"Not that I know of. Really, I don't think they were together more than four or five years. It's surprising that it took so long for Warren to find someone new." She set her empty glass down on the coffee table. "Shall we? I'm expecting Beth and her family for dinner. I believe I'll treat them at the ski lodge."

Beth was Vida's eldest daughter. She and her husband and their children lived in Seattle. Somehow the idea of a visiting daughter recalled Alicia Lowell. "That's odd," I said, grabbing my purse. "Alicia told me she'd just gotten back from Snohomish. But Francine said she was coming home last night."

Vida was already at the door. "Perhaps she made a second trip. Snohomish isn't that far away."

Vida was right. Some forty miles separated Alpine from the larger town on the Snohomish River. Maybe Alicia had more than one friend who lived there. Or she'd gone back to browse in the many antique shops. The Wells family's problems were none of my own.

Still, on the way back from Vida's, I took the long way home. Driving slowly down Front Street, I eyeballed Francine's Fine Apparel.

The sign on the door read CLOSED.

Marisa Foxx wasn't home, so I left a message for her to call me at her convenience. The temperature was dropping as the clouds periodically blotted out the sun, but I decided to barbecue anyway. I had no idea when Milo would arrive, but I knew he'd be hungry. At six-thirty I phoned Father Den.

"I thought I'd catch you after five o'clock Mass," I said. "Did you get a good voter turnout this evening?"

"So-so," he replied. "We had a lot of tourists. And we won't count the ballots until after Mass tomorrow. In fact, we probably won't count them until Monday. Jake and Veronica and I should do it together, to make sure nobody cheats." His usually ripe laugh was a trifle weak.

"Say," I said as if the idea had just popped into my mind, "do you know who put the pressure on Everett to speed up Ursula's autopsy? Milo indicated it was somebody from the chancery."

"It could have been anybody," Father Den responded.

"I try to avoid the chancery. With any luck, they'll forget that St. Mildred's exists."

In layman's terms, the chancery could be equated with corporate headquarters. Like an employee working in the field, parish priests often felt that farther was better. All of western Washington made up the Seattle Archdiocese's flock. If a parishioner in the city had a complaint, it was easy to pick up the phone and dial the chancery. Out in the boondocks, not only did Church officialdom seem remote, but voicing criticism by long distance cost money.

"Ursula must have had some influential friends," I remarked. "Will you be one of the celebrants at the funeral Mass?"

"I doubt it," Father Den replied. "I'm not sure who's in charge. I asked Warren, but he seems kind of vague. Besides, I still intend to go see my mother for a couple of days. Sister Mary Joan can handle a prayer service for the daily Mass goers. We only get about twenty during the week anyway."

Maybe I imagined the faint note of reproach in Father Den's voice. I was not among the twenty faithful who attended Mass on weekdays. "I've got to ask you a tough question," I said, anxious to change the subject. "This is strictly business. Do you have any reason to think Ursula's death was something other than an accident?"

"Oh, man." Father Den took a deep, audible breath. "Evil exists, no matter how much some contemporary Catholics try to downplay it. I won't bore you with theological or philosophical arguments, Emma. As an army brat, I saw—or heard—some pretty weird things. Some of them might technically have been accidents, especially when drinking or drugging was involved. But the result was the same. Evil—or sin, that old-fashioned word nobody seems to remember—played its part. An untimely death is often caused by sin, whether it's overindulgence, anger, jealousy, violence, whatever. It's not intended, but it happens. Does that answer your question?"

"No." I couldn't help being candid. "I mean, not with regard to Ursula. Unless," I went on, trying to sift through Father Den's words, "you mean that somebody unintentionally got Ursula killed. Is that what you're saying?"

"Yes. But that doesn't make it an accident."

I still wasn't sure what Den meant.

It felt like rain by the time Milo arrived at seven-thirty. Since I'd already started the barbecue, I put the burgers on the grill but decided we might as well eat inside. After I'd handed Milo his Scotch, he admitted that Vida had made an impression on him with her doubts about the manner of Ursula's death.

"I've gone over Dwight's notes with a fine-tooth comb," Milo said, referring to his deputy's interview with Warren Wells. "Doubles wasn't much help. He claimed he was in shock. I suppose he was."

Hearing Milo use Warren's nickname evoked a question: "Did you go through school with Warren?"

Milo shook his head. "He was three, four years ahead of me. But he was a pretty good ballplayer, shortstop, second base, sometimes behind the plate. The Buckers had a decent team in those years—Tank Parker got a look-see from a couple of major-league scouts and Dave Tolberg won a baseball scholarship to WSU."

The phone rang before Milo could get off the diamond and back on track. The caller identified himself as Murray Felton, a Seattle TV reporter. He was in town for the weekend, and his station had asked him to check out a couple of leads. Could he swing by for a few minutes?

I grimaced at Milo, who was watching me with mild curiosity. "Can't we do this over the phone?" I finally said, trying not to sound impatient.

Murray Felton chuckled, a rich, rather engaging sound.

"Ms. Lord, do you prefer doing phone interviews? Or maybe you do, but we're talking TV here, not print media."

My journalistic pride was on the line. "Okay," I relented. "Come on over. I can give you half an hour."

I could also give him directions, which I did. "I'll pull the burgers until he leaves," I grumbled to Milo. "Meanwhile you figure out if you're the sheriff or my secret lover from Sultan."

"Shit," Milo muttered, following me through the kitchen. "I don't want to talk to some Seattle TV guy. Maybe I should go home."

I turned around to look up at Milo. His long face was a mixture of annoyance, uncertainty, and yearning. Or so I thought until I noticed that his eyes rested not on me, but on the barbecue grill.

Slinging an arm around his neck, I used my other hand to poke him in the chest. "Are you hungry for dinner—or dessert?"

"Both." Milo grabbed me roughly, covering my cheek and neck with kisses. "I'll stay," he said into my left ear. "You got cheese?"

"I think so." I allowed myself to lean into him for a brief moment, then broke away to move the burgers. We had just returned to the house when I heard a car pull up in the driveway.

Murray Felton was much younger than he sounded, late twenties, with dark hair that was already receding, dazzling blue eyes, and a sharply etched profile that could have cut cake. At five-ten, muscular, and tanned, he exuded a playful masculinity that I found attractive and Milo seemed to resent. Or so I judged from the sheriff's suddenly truculent expression.

"Okay," Murray said after I'd given him a beer, "I understand you had an unexplained death here last night. Ms. Randall seems to have friends in high places. My boss thinks there's a story here somewhere. How are you handling it, Ms. Lord?"

"With kid gloves," I replied from my place on the sofa next to Milo. I'd introduced the sheriff by name, but not by title. "We don't know much yet."

The brilliant blue eyes seemed amused. "You must know more than I do, though. What was Ms. Randall doing here in Alpine?"

"Living. Until she died." A second bourbon was making me truculent, too.

Murray cocked his head to one side and gave me a skeptical look. "Come on, Ms. Lord. You can do better than that. Why do you really think she moved up here to this mountain aerie?"

"I told you—I don't know." By reflex, I edged closer to Milo. "She was getting married. She and her fiancé were both from Alpine. She'd bought a nice home here. She has family in town. What other reasons would she need?"

Carefully Murray poured more beer into his pilsner glass. "How about the fact that she was a lush? What about the old cash flow not being what it used to be? Or maybe the need to keep a low profile because she was running away from her late husband's legacy?"

As Murray calmly sipped his beer Milo and I exchanged puzzled glances. "What legacy?" the sheriff asked, speaking for the first time since being introduced to the TV reporter. Milo's tone was typically laconic but I could sense the underlying tension.

Murray regarded us both quizzically. "I guess you really don't know." He chuckled, but the sound wasn't as engaging as it had been over the phone. "According to my sources at the TV station, Dr. Wheaton Randall ran a real butcher shop. The malpractice suits are causing quite a logjam in King County Superior Court."

Again, Milo and I looked at each other, this time in

surprise. "Say again?" the sheriff said, pulling out a cigarette.

Murray shook his head in an exaggerated manner. "Those things'll kill you, Sheriff."

Milo paused in the act of flicking on his lighter. "Okay, Felton. How do you know who I am?"

Patting the pocket of his army-surplus jacket, Murray grinned. "We do our homework in the Big City. Milo Dodge, Skykomish County sheriff, seems laid-back, don't be fooled, a stand-up guy who goes by the book. Emma Lord, editor and publisher of *The Alpine Advocate*, objective, fair-minded, sexy in a cranky sort of way." Seeing my eyes spark, Murray put up a hand. "Hey, just kidding! I mean, that last part is a personal observation, and should be stricken as sexist and hearsay. Now don't tell me that neither of you knew about the late Dr. Randall's legal problems."

"How could we?" Milo exploded. "Do you think Ursula would advertise them in *The Advocate*?"

"Background," Murray said softly, now looking straight at me. "That's the name of the game in journalism, huh, Ms. Lord? But then again, maybe the good doctor's bungling doesn't have anything to do with his widow being found facedown in—what was it?—six inches of the Skykomish River?"

Milo waved his cigarette at Murray. "It probably doesn't. Look, Felton, get to the point. What do you want from us?"

Murray suddenly became self-deprecating. "Hey—not much, it seems. I'm beginning to think I'm trying to squeeze rocks through a sock. Humor me. How about that miracle?"

I was momentarily puzzled. "What miracle?"

Now Murray actually looked pained. "The old lady's vase." He reached into his pocket and pulled out a notebook. "A Mrs. Patricelli. Somebody leaked word to us

that she's got a picture of Jesus or somebody on it.
Well?"

Milo turned away in disgust. I shrugged. "I've heard
about it. But I haven't seen it. Polly Patricelli is old and
imaginative. I guess."

"I'd like to see it," Murray said, finishing his beer and
standing up. "How do I find her and Jesus?"

"Try the phone book," I snapped. "You won't find
Jesus, but you might find Polly."

"Fair enough." Murray gave me that engaging grin.
"Thanks for the beer. I'll be in touch."

"Hey!" I was off the sofa and following Murray to the
door. "How did you happen to be in Alpine in the first
place?"

For the first time there was a hint of vulnerability in
Murray's sharp features. "I'm a hiker. It's a three-day
weekend. And somebody I know told me to look up a
woman in Alpine. Only she's not around, so maybe I
wasted a trip—unless you can help me out with this Randall death or the miracle in the vase. As I said, we'll be in
touch."

"Who?" I shouted after Murray as he started for his
Mazda Miata. "Who is she?" Somehow I had a terrible
feeling that I already knew.

And Murray Felton knew that I knew. He laughed as
he reached the car. "Your star reporter—Carla Steinmetz.
Give her my love, okay? I hear she's hot."

Hot she's not, I wanted to say. But then Murray and I
probably had different standards.

Chapter Nine

"I'M GETTING OLD," Milo complained as he watched me turn the burgers on the grill. "I don't much like people under thirty anymore."

"It's the electronic media," I said. "They're different from those of us who work in print. Besides, all this guy really wants is to score with Carla. I wonder why."

"Why do you think?" Milo was frowning up at the dark clouds. "Carla may be dizzy, but she's cute."

My head jerked up. "You think she's cute?"

The sheriff gave a little shrug. "For a twentysomething girl. I like 'em fortysomething and cranky." He winked, a habit I always found annoying. Maybe that's because I'm cranky.

We took our burgers inside, where I'd already set the table in the dining alcove. I told Milo about the call from Alicia, asking after Francine. Like Vida, he seemed unperturbed.

"Maybe she gave herself a holiday," he suggested. "She deserves it."

"I might believe that if she was spending it with her daughter," I responded, "but she isn't."

The subject obviously didn't interest Milo. He took up where he'd left off before Murray Felton had called. Dwight Gould's report termed Warren's account "garbled." He hadn't seen much of his bride-to-be Friday, having played a round of golf with Clancy Barton, and then running errands, most of which he couldn't recall off

145

the top of his head. The last time Warren had talked to Ursula was on the phone, maybe around five P.M. He'd called her from the ski lodge after visiting with the manager, Henry Bardeen. Ursula had sounded fine. She always sounded fine. After that, Warren had stopped at Cal Vickers's Texaco station to get his brakes checked. Cal was calling it a day by then, so he'd gone with Warren to Mugs Ahoy for a couple of beers. When Cal decided he'd better go home before his wife, Charlene, began to worry about him, Warren stayed on and jawed with some of his other old chums. He'd eaten a burger and then taken off on his sightseeing trip around town. It was going on eight by then, maybe eight-thirty. He enjoyed driving without the hassle of city traffic. Alpine was a pretty little place, when you came right down to it.

The last part of Dwight's report had been relayed orally, and Milo didn't put much stock in it. "I dropped in on Abe Loomis this afternoon," Milo said, referring to the owner of Mugs Ahoy. "He said he didn't remember seeing Warren in the tavern after seven-thirty. But it was a Friday night, a three-day weekend with a lot of tourists. Abe isn't the most observant guy in the world."

"So where was Warren?" I inquired, handing Milo his second burger.

"Damned if I know. The classic scenario is that he went back to The Pines, got drunk with Ursula, and they ended up on the river, where she fell in and he passed out. But it doesn't make sense somehow." The sheriff shook his head. "Somebody was with Ursula, that's for sure. There were two highball glasses on the coffee table in the living room."

I lifted both eyebrows, never having mastered the art of raising only one. "Prints?"

Milo winced. "Smudged. Either by accident, or on purpose. The problem is, Dwight didn't cover all the surfaces. He was acting on the premise that Ursula's death was an accident. He only checked the glasses as an afterthought. Sloppy police work, but there it is." He avoided my gaze.

I wasn't about to criticize. "What about the neighbors? Did they see any visitors?"

"Dwight and Dustin were still interviewing at The Pines this afternoon. By the time I took off, I hadn't heard anything. But they hadn't talked to Debra Barton yet. She'd gone into Seattle for the day. The other nearest neighbors are the Carlsons and they went to the ocean for the weekend."

Chewing on a gherkin pickle, I tried to think why something was awry with Warren's story. Nothing came to mind, except the fact that Warren wasn't living with Ursula but up at the ski lodge.

"This is a dubiously enlightened age," I remarked. "If we were getting married, would you object to moving in with me?"

Milo dropped his burger, smeared mustard on his shirt, and turned pale under his tan. "Married? Hell, Emma, I don't know. . . . I mean, we haven't even . . . Isn't it too soon to . . . ?"

I was torn between annoyance and amusement. "Theoretical, Milo, it's theoretical. I'm talking about Ursula and Warren. Doesn't it seem strange that he was living elsewhere?"

Milo recovered the burger from his lap, along with his equilibrium. I handed him a dishrag to wipe off the mustard. "Well . . . Maybe. I figured it was some kind of Catholic deal. You know, keeping pure before marriage."

I gave the sheriff a rueful smile. "Ideally, that's what should happen. But it doesn't these days, at least not often. Ursula and Warren were mature people. I don't know—maybe it was a case of maintaining appearances, but it seems odd."

"Maybe it was that damned frilly bedroom," Milo said, now complacently chewing on his burger. "It'd scared the hell out of me. You see it?"

I shook my head. "I didn't get beyond the living room."

Milo was laughing. "I checked out the house on my way over here. You wouldn't believe it—lace and ruffles and a great big canopy, like out of the movies. Everything was moving in the breeze, like somebody's wash on the line. Is that supposed to be erotic?"

"Romantic," I said. "Sensuous, maybe."

"Crap," Milo retorted. "I like it better when you turn on a Mariner game and we hit the sack. There's nothing like a 6–4–3 double play to put me in the mood."

I didn't want to think what Vida would say about Milo's remark. And I sure wouldn't admit to her that I agreed with him.

The Mariners had played the Orioles back at Camden Yards that afternoon. As it turned out, we didn't need a baseball game to inspire us. But later, as we lay in bed sipping Drambuie, I thought about Ursula's elegant boudoir.

"Milo," I said, my chin resting against his upper arm, "why was there a breeze?"

"Hmm?" He turned a puzzled face to me.

"The breeze in Ursula's bedroom. Where did it come from?"

Milo shifted against the pillows. "Ah . . . the window, I guess. Why?"

"You mean it was open?"

"Yeah, I think so." He paused, apparently trying to visualize what he'd seen earlier in the day. "That's right. The window by her dressing table was open."

"Why?"

"Because it was hot." He nodded toward the window next to my bed, which was raised some four inches. "So what?"

I traced his profile with my index finger. When it reached his mouth, he bit it. Gently. "Because," I said,

"Ursula's house is air-conditioned. You tell me—why was that window open?"

I bit back. Not so gently.

Five minutes later Milo was dressed and gone, berating himself for being an idiot. If it hadn't been almost nine-thirty, I would have insisted on going with him while he personally interviewed Warren Wells. Of course he probably would have refused to let me tag along.

Still worried about Francine, I put on my light cotton robe and called her home number. To my relief, she answered on the second ring.

"What a tempest in a teapot!" Francine laughed. "I decided to take a break. It's a holiday weekend, remember? Labor Day tourists don't shop for clothes. They hike, picnic, camp, fish—whatever. I thought I told Alicia, but either I forgot or she didn't hear me." She laughed again, though I thought I detected a false note.

"Maybe I got it mixed up," I said, trying to sound confused. "Maybe I assumed Alicia was puzzled because you weren't home."

"I had a lot of catching up to do," Francine said blithely. "You know how that is—you're a working woman, too."

"I sure do." Now I sounded downright ingratiating. "And kids—well, they're not kids, but you know what I mean—they get so wound up in their own lives that they don't pay attention. Alicia was probably full of news when she came home last night from Snohomish."

Maybe I also imagined the faint hesitation at the other end of the line. "Actually Alicia stayed over," Francine said, not sounding as jolly as before. "I'll say one thing for the younger generation—if they've had a few glasses of wine, they don't drive. That's smart."

"Very smart," I agreed. "So is having a designated driver. As irresponsible as Adam has been sometimes, he and his buddies are always good about ..." Now I paused, hearing a noise that sounded as if it came from my bedroom. "Say, Francine, I'd better let you go. It's getting late."

"Thanks for worrying," she said, again on a breezy note. "See you in church. Vote early and vote often."

I kept the phone in my hand as I exited the living room, entered the small hallway, and tiptoed to the bedroom door. I'd left the bedside lamp on. Cautiously peering around the edge of the door, I saw nothing that alarmed me.

Except that when I entered the bedroom, I noticed that the window Milo had pointed out to me was now open almost a foot instead of four inches. Fleetingly I thought about looking in the closet and under the bed. But that seemed reckless. I left the room, closed the door behind me, went out onto the front porch, and called the sheriff.

Bill Blatt answered. Milo was at The Pines, talking to Warren Wells. It appeared that Warren had checked out of the ski lodge and moved into his late fiancée's house. Bill seemed in an unusually chatty mood, but I cut him short. My account of a possible break-in seemed to impress him. Vida's nephew knew I wasn't the hysterical type. Dustin Fong was on patrol; he'd be dispatched immediately. I stayed on the porch, reasoning that if someone was in the house, I could run to a neighbor's for help.

Dustin, however, arrived in less than five minutes, having just broken up a brawl at the Icicle Creek Tavern. He checked out the house thoroughly, found nothing of interest, and then came back into the living room, where I was anxiously waiting. I told him that this wasn't the first time I'd heard strange sounds, but figured it was an animal.

"Tonight was different," I said, wishing I'd had time to put on something more than my flimsy cotton robe. "Deer don't open windows."

Dustin allowed himself a small smile. He hadn't been in law enforcement long enough to be sure of what circumstances permitted humor. "You're positive that the window wasn't open that far earlier?"

"Definitely," I replied. "You can ask the . . . question over and over, and I'll give you the same answer." It didn't seem prudent to say that Dustin could ask the sheriff. Our romance might not be a secret, but neither of us cared to flaunt it.

"You were on the phone, out here." Dustin surveyed the living room. "This is a small house. But it's very nice. I like the logs," he added in his eager-to-please manner. "If someone had come in through the window, he or she could have heard you talking. Except that whoever it was might not have realized you were on the phone. The impression that you weren't alone may have scared the person off."

"Something did," I said dryly. "There's nothing worth stealing in the bedroom. My purse was out here." I pointed vaguely in the direction of the end table where I'd left my big shoulder bag when I came home.

"There's a lot of weird stuff going down lately," the deputy mused. "Some are tourists, some are kids, some are just plain troublemakers. Maybe it's the end of summer. You know—one last fling."

I knew from checking the crime log that Alpine seemed to be in the clutches of a veritable crime spree. The number of incidents during the past week had increased by more than half. "You probably expected a peaceful existence when you came up here," I said with a smile.

Dustin took me very seriously. "Well—no. You don't go into law enforcement because you want peace and quiet. It's just that there's been so much vandalism and domestic disturbances and rowdy teenage stuff. Not to mention Ms. Randall drowning. I've never had to deal with the Seattle media before. It seems like everything is

happening at once. Maybe it's because we're shorthanded. Maybe it's the weather."

After filling out his report, Dustin asked if I was afraid
to spend the night alone. While the idea wasn't appealing, I assured him I'd be fine. He promised that a patrol
car would come by at regular intervals. Knowing the
sheriff's limited resources, I figured that I'd be lucky if
they made it more than twice between now and three A.M.
On a Saturday night, the Icicle Creek Tavern brawl was
just the tip of the iceberg.

Even in the best of circumstances, I tend to short-
change myself on sleep. During the week I'm rarely in
bed before eleven-thirty; on weekends, I often stay up
well past midnight. After Dustin left, I read for a while,
but realized I wasn't absorbing much. At eleven I turned
on the news. By chance, the local network affiliate I'd
randomly selected was the station that employed Murray
Felton. The item before the commercial break leading
into the weather forecast was about Ursula Randall.

"The widow of prominent Seattle surgeon Wheaton
Randall was discovered drowned last night in the
Skykomish River near the town of Alpine," the dark-
haired anchorwoman intoned. "Ursula O'Toole Randall
had recently moved from Seattle to the small logging
community where she grew up." The screen showed
stock footage of Front Street, obviously taken some years
earlier before a Hollywood film crew painted *The Advocate* yellow. "Ms. Randall was well known in Seattle
civic and church circles for her generosity and hard
work. Skykomish County Sheriff authorities are investigating. Next, we'll see if rain is going to fall on the rest
of the three-day weekend. . . ."

At precisely eleven-thirty the sheriff scared me witless
by showing up at the front door. Dustin had told him
about my alleged prowler, and Milo had decided to spend
the night. It would be the first time that he had ever slept
over. I was pleased, as well as relieved.

After I had poured us each a nightcap, I told him about the TV news report, and inquired after his own investigation. "What did Warren tell you?" I queried.

"Zip." Milo took a deep drink. "The damned window was still open when I got there. Warren hadn't been in the bedroom. He's bunking in a guest room that doesn't look like it belongs to some Barbie doll."

"So who opened the window?" The question made me think of my own, and I couldn't help but shiver.

"Warren doesn't know. But you're right—you don't open windows when you've got air-conditioning. It defeats the purpose. What's more, the screen had been removed."

"So had mine," I said with a start. "It didn't dawn on me until now."

"It pisses me off," Milo complained. "Am I getting careless? I should have gone over to The Pines right away. Even after I got there, I should have noticed that open window from the get-go."

"Hey," I said, trying to soothe the sheriff, "I didn't notice that my screen was gone right away, either. I'm a trained observer, remember? All journalists are—or supposed to be. But oversights happen."

My words didn't have much effect on Milo. "Maybe," he mumbled, "it doesn't have anything to do with what happened to Ursula. It could have been kids. We've had about three times as many prowler reports this last week as we usually get. It's a good thing school opens Wednesday."

Kids. The thought was quasi-comforting. I tried not to dwell on my own intruder. "Was Ursula's window forced?"

"No. It's one of those vertical jobs that swings in. If it wasn't fastened right in the first place, it wouldn't be hard to jiggle open." Milo's mood had now changed from irascible to brooding. "I checked for footprints inside and outside, but didn't get much. Warren says the gardener—one of the Amundson kids—has been working there quite a bit. The place is kept well watered, except for the flower bed on that side of the house. Ursula wanted to put in a bunch of bulbs, and it's too soon for that, so the ground's fairly dry." Milo began to slide into gloom.

"Did you ever talk to Debra Barton?" I asked, trying to keep my voice bright.

Milo nodded without enthusiasm. "She was back from Seattle by the time I got to The Pines. The only thing she saw yesterday at Ursula's was Buzzy's van. That was around five, five-thirty. I'll check him out tomorrow, but there's no reason why he shouldn't visit his sister."

"He's living in that van," I said. "Is there any reason why he couldn't live with his sister?"

Milo squared his slumped shoulders. "Buzzy's living in the van? What happened? Did Laura throw him out?"

"Laura said he left." I shrugged. "Laura O'Toole isn't inclined to elaborate."

"Hell!" Milo whacked his thigh with the flat of his hand. "Just what we need—one more homeless Alpiner living in a car or a truck or a van or under the bridge or in Old Mill Park. Can't somebody build an all-purpose shelter in this stupid town?"

I thought of Ed and his Spanish "villa," of Ursula and her elegant house in The Pines, of a hundred other comfortable residents who seemed indifferent to the needs of the less fortunate. I thought of me.

"It's something we should consider at St. Mildred's," I said quietly. "The battered women's shelter isn't large enough to expand. Maybe that kind of new project was what Ursula had in mind when she talked about helping the rest of Alpine."

Judging from his vacant stare, Milo hadn't heard me. His face was in shadow, its planes and angles softened but not at ease. Even though I had closed all the windows, the house suddenly felt cool, almost chilly. In the midnight silence, I heard the first patter of rain.

"Sometimes I hate this place," Milo finally said, still not looking at me. "People call logging towns dead ends. They're right. Alpine is dead."

"No, it's not," I retorted, surprised at my own vehemence. I was a city girl, not inclined to boost small towns except in a professional, self-serving way. "The college is coming. Commuters are still moving in. Many of the loggers are trying to reeducate themselves. Alpine's not dead. It's in transition."

Draining his glass, Milo turned to look me in the eye. "I mean for me. Where am I going? Where have I been? Nowhere, except to college. I'm forty-nine years old. Every four years I have to bust my hump just to get reelected and keep my job. Some job! Hustling drunks, trying not to get killed by warring spouses, pulling bodies out of car wrecks, chasing a family of five out of an old barn where they've set up the only home they've got." Thrusting a finger in my face, Milo's features contorted. "You know what I did last Tuesday? I found the Almquists—Sid used to be the deckman at the old Cascade & Pacific Mill—living under the Icicle Creek Bridge. Mary Jean had a new baby, and there they were, less than a hundred yards from my house, with a bunch of dirty bedding, two old dinette chairs, a card table, and a tarp. I had to tell them and the three kids to move out, and the last thing I saw was Mary Jean, carrying that little baby and one of those damned dinette chairs with the plastic cover peeling off. I felt like the biggest shit in the world."

"Milo." I cradled his face in my hands. "Let's do something. Together."

"Like what? Screw?" For once, the idea didn't seem to appeal to Milo.

I shook my head. "I'll start an appeal in the paper. You can speak at the Chamber of Commerce, Kiwanis, all the service clubs and organizations. I'll ask Father Den to rally the other churches. Maybe Fuzzy Baugh can look into getting federal funds."

Milo wasn't energized by my enthusiasm. He looked tired and defeated. "It's a Band-Aid," he said dolefully.

"It's something," I replied. "Would you rather just sit and bitch?"

"No." But the sheriff's expression was rueful. I knew that the homeless and the unemployment and the economic inertia weren't the only demons he was facing. Ursula Randall's demise seemed as much of a dead end as Alpine itself. He was frustrated and weary and middle-aged.

But most upsetting was that in all of his unburdening, he hadn't mentioned me.

I wasn't used to waking up with someone beside me. Milo wasn't used to waking up with someone who had to get to church. Somehow he found the situation paradoxical. I didn't. Pointing him in the direction of the pancake batter I'd whipped up, I headed off to St. Mildred's in the softly falling rain.

Small knots of parishioners braved the weather to gather in the parking lot, presumably discussing Ursula's death, the school-board vote, and whatever else might have been going on under the camouflage of good Christian people attending worship. Inside, I gazed around the small frame building with its whitewashed walls, worn wooden pews carved from the forest's once limitless bounty, not-quite-life-size statues, and small stained-glass windows where the rain ran like tears. The church was full, with perhaps three dozen visitors. Two of them sat on my left, while the Bartons were on my right. Annie Jeanne Dupré thumped on the organ, signaling us to rise for Father Den's entrance in the green vestments that denoted what is known as "Ordinary Time" in the church calendar.

As so often happens, my attention strayed during Den's sermon. Next to me, Debra and Clancy Barton seemed transfixed—or maybe they were merely in a zone. The sleekly groomed duo of Francine Wells and Alicia Lowell were across the aisle, contemplating their sins—or the Paris collections. Polly Patricelli fingered her rosary and prayed under her breath. The Bayards, the Mullinses, the Daleys, the Luccis, and the Jake O'Tooles all faced forward with benign if vacant expressions. Ed Bronsky twitched and Shirley shifted. Ronnie Wenzler-Greene appeared deadly earnest, while Monica and Verb Vancich struck me as ill at ease. Or perhaps it was only Verb; on closer scrutiny, Monica may have been experiencing ecstasy or gas.

Reproaching myself for lack of attention as well as uncharitable thoughts, I tried to concentrate on Father Den. He looked drawn, and his usually smooth, if somewhat soporific delivery, suffered from occasional hesitation. Maybe he was worried about his mother.

Again, I drifted. So many different types of people, yet all here on this rainy Sunday morning, presumably honoring God. I knew their agendas were varied, and not always selfless. I was aware that there was ambition and pride and arrogance and pettiness under their pious exteriors. But they were here, and that must count for something. Nor did I kid myself that I was any better.

Discreetly I turned just enough to see who lurked in the rear of the church. There was no Laura or Buzzy O'Toole but that didn't surprise me. There were others who should have been there but weren't. Maybe they'd gone to five o'clock Mass on Saturday. Maybe they were out of town. Maybe they didn't give a damn.

But one face struck me as out of place: in the second to the last pew, I spotted Murray Felton. Everybody belongs in church, or so I've always felt.

But Murray didn't belong in St. Mildred's. I sensed that he was working, seeking background, studying the congregation. The brilliant blue eyes caught me staring, and I quickly turned away.

After Mass, I waited my turn to mark my school-board ballot. Ursula's name was there, indicating that the list of candidates had been run off on the school's venerable mimeograph machine before she died. The instructions said to vote for two. Feeling that memberships should be limited to Catholics, I skipped Derek Norman of fish-hatchery fame. I had faith in Debra Barton's basic good sense, so I checked her box with a certain amount of confidence. Then I came to Laura O'Toole and Rita Patricelli Haines.

Rita was of at least average intelligence, but I almost never saw her in church and I didn't know if her children were enrolled in St. Mildred's school. She could be stubborn as a mule; I had found that out in my dealings with her at the Chamber of Commerce. On the other hand, Laura O'Toole struck me as someone who might have trouble reading the ballot, let alone complex educational issues. But she was Nunzio Lucci's candidate, and while Luce might have a brain like a brick, he seemed rock-solid on basic Church doctrine.

Out of the corner of my eye, I saw him talking earnestly to Father Den. Della Lucci was standing awkwardly by the door that led from the vestibule to the crying room. She looked forlorn, and somehow her demeanor literally forced my hand. A vote for her husband's candidate was a vote for Della. I felt the need to appease Luce, if only because it might make life easier for his wife. I checked off Laura O'Toole's name, and handed the ballot to Ronnie Wenzler-Greene. The principal looked grim.

Still feeling sorry for Della Lucci, I went over to her and gave her a warm smile. "The forecast was right for once," I said, falling back on the weather as a topic of conversation. "It looks like we won't have to worry about water rationing."

Della Lucci's plump face brightened ever so slightly. "Isn't that the truth, Ms. Lord? Maybe summer is finally over." The light went out in her eyes as she saw her husband approach. Luce was limping, and he looked disturbed.

His nod to me was perfunctory and his tone was sharp as he spoke to his wife. "Come on, Della, let's go. I gotta start haulin' stuff over to Old Mill Park for the picnic tomorrow."

"What's wrong with your leg?" I asked, trying not to notice how Della cringed when Luce spoke to her.

Luce glowered at me. "It's the rain. That's the leg that got bunged up in the woods." He gestured impatiently at Della. "What're you waitin' for—Santa Claus? He ain't comin' till December, Del. Let's move it."

With a timorous smile, Della said goodbye. I watched the Luccis leave the vestibule, Luce limping, Della carefully keeping a couple of paces behind. I held back until they had descended the six wooden stairs. Then I, too, made my exit.

Ed and Shirley Bronsky waylaid me in the parking lot. Shirley held an umbrella over their heads. It featured the stained-glass windows of Notre Dame, and no doubt was a trophy from their European tour. Having grown up in Seattle, where the rain is usually as gentle as it is frequent, I eschewed umbrellas of any kind. I found them a nuisance, and easier to misplace than car keys.

"Hey-hey!" Ed exclaimed, beaming. "You and I have to take a meeting, Emma. How about Monday, say around ten?"

"Monday's a holiday," I reminded Ed with what I hoped was a friendly smile. "But Tuesday would be fine. In fact, I was thinking about calling you. Milo and I have a project in mind that might interest you. We've been talking about the problem with the homeless. We thought that if—"

Ed held up a beefy hand. "Put all that stuff on hold,

Emma. If you're asking me to get involved with any more volunteering, you'll have to wait." He gave Shirley a conspiratorial glance, then turned back to me and lowered his voice. *"I finished the book."*

I'd all but forgotten about Ed's autobiography. He'd started writing it the previous winter, and had nearly driven me crazy by asking for help. At one point he had begged me to ghostwrite it for him. But a combination of flattery and intimidation had finally persuaded Ed that he should be the sole author.

I tried to look thrilled. "Great, Ed. How did it turn out?"

Ed again looked at his wife, who giggled and jiggled and almost conked her husband with the umbrella. "It's absolutely fantastic," Shirley said with enthusiasm. "I couldn't put it down."

Ed's attempt to look modest failed miserably. "It's pretty good, I'll admit. That's why I want to talk to you, to set up an interview when I get the contract. I sent the book off Friday to Doubleday. Maybe I'll hear from them by the end of next week."

Having worked with a number of reporters who had tried to get books published, I knew a little about the industry. "I don't think they turn projects around quite that fast," I cautioned. "Maybe you should try to get an agent first."

Ed scoffed. "What for? Why lose fifteen percent off the top? This book will sell itself. Heck, the title alone is worth it."

"Which is?" I wasn't sure I wanted to know.

"I needed something that told the reader what the book was about, namely me," he replied, now very serious. "I wanted to keep it simple, but to have a familiar ring, so it would be easy for people to remember. I call it *Mr. Ed*."

"That's . . . good," I gulped, exerting every ounce of restraint to keep from laughing, smiling, or falling down in a coma. "Let me know what happens."

Shirley twirled the umbrella like a top. "Everyone will know. We'll give a huge party. The only thing is, we hope they don't rush it into publication before we get the house finished. It'd be so much better to host the gala in our new banquet hall."

I didn't know if the new Bronsky house actually had a banquet hall, or if Shirley was suffering from her usual delusions of grandeur. But the allusion to excess reminded me of my original intention.

"While you're waiting to hear from New York," I began, managing to keep a straight face, "you might think about how we can build a multipurpose shelter in Alpine. The number of homeless people is growing by the day. Maybe you could talk to Father Den about it."

Ed frowned and shook his head. "I don't know about that, Emma. Like I said, we should wait."

"Ed," I said, now growing impatient, "we can't wait too long. The good weather is coming to an end. We should get something up and running before the first snow. Believe me, it might take six months before you get a reply from Doubleday."

Ed obviously didn't believe me. "I can't take the chance. Besides, it's not a good idea to bring up any big projects right now. Things around here are kind of shaky. If you know what I mean." His small eyes darted toward the church, where Father Den now stood on the steps, bidding farewell to the stragglers.

"Are you talking about the school-board vote?" I asked in a puzzled tone.

Ed shook his head and took a couple of backward steps, forcing Shirley to move with the umbrella. "I mean Den. I've got a feeling that his days are numbered here in Alpine."

I was shocked. While it was seldom wise to take Ed seriously, his pronouncement made an impression. "You can't mean he's being transferred," I said in an incredulous voice. "The chancery doesn't move priests this time of year, they do it in the spring."

The rain was coming down harder now. Ed looked over his paunch, apparently trying to see what effect the water was having on his black alligator shoes. "They'll move him if enough pressure is put on the archbishop. Or if he flat out resigns." Turning to Shirley, he placed a guiding hand on her shoulder. "Let's go home, Shirl. My feet feel damp." Over his shoulder, Ed nodded benignly. "See you, Emma. Don't worry, you'll get one of the first autographed copies of *Mr. Ed.*"

Trying not to feel appalled by Ed's cocky attitude, I trudged to my car. Murray Felton was leaning against the passenger door, holding a black umbrella over his curly dark hair.

"I recognized your Jag from last night," he said, giving me that big grin. "Want to take me for a ride?"

I couldn't quite summon up a smile. "Where? Why?"

"Don't forget who, what, and when." Murray reached for the handle and found the door unlocked. He shot me a look of mock amazement. "Talk about trust! You small-town folks really do feel safe from crime. Do you suppose that Randall babe got overconfident?"

"She wasn't a babe," I said stiffly. "Move it, Murray. I'm going home."

"Not quite." To my astonishment, he closed the umbrella and got inside the Jag.

Angrily I marched around to the other side. "Listen, jackass," I barked, leaning across the steering wheel, "get out of here! Or do you want me to call the sheriff?"

Murray's expression was insolent. "What do you call him? Quick Shot or Slow Draw?"

Rarely have I had the urge to throttle anyone. To keep from doing Murray Felton bodily harm, I flew out of the car, slammed the door, and stomped off in the direction of the rectory. Separated from the church by a covered walkway, the modest frame building is set off from the parking lot by a small garden. I galloped up to the front porch and punched the bell, hoping that Father Den had had time to change in the sacristy.

Apparently he hadn't. There was no answer. The era of the full-time housekeeper had ended a few years earlier, forcing the pastor to rely on sporadic help. Frustrated, I started back to the parking lot.

To my relief, Murray Felton had gotten out of the Jag. He met me halfway back to the car. "Okay," he said in a cheerful voice, "so I trash-talk sometimes. It's the cynical reporter in me, so what? Meet me at Starbucks. I'll buy you a latte, and explain how Ursula Randall managed to get herself drowned."

"I thought you needed a ride," I said in an irritable voice.

Murray shrugged. "Just kidding. My car's over there." He nodded across the lot at the red Mazda Miata that was the only other remaining vehicle besides my Jag. "In fact," he continued, now turning more serious, "I thought maybe we could go see Mrs. Patricelli together. She wouldn't let me in last night."

I wasn't surprised. Polly was a nervous, suspicious widow who lived alone. A stranger who appeared on her doorstep after dark would not be welcomed. Finally calming down, I considered my options.

"I'll lead the way to Mrs. Patricelli's," I said, brushing wet hair from my forehead. Now that Murray was putting on the pressure, I decided it was time to take a look at the miracle vase. "If you've really got a viable theory about Ursula, you can come with me and tell the sheriff."

Murray seemed appeased. His Miata followed me closely along the two blocks to the Patricelli house on Tyee Street. From the outside, it seemed impossible that nine children had been raised in such an old crackerbox. Vida, however, had told me that the inside, especially the second story, was a veritable rabbit warren of rooms.

Eight cracked and chipped concrete stairs led through

an overgrown rockery. An ancient lilac, which looked as if it had been split down the middle by lightning, stood at one end of the porch; at the other, a towering yew blotted out the daylight from the front windows. Boards creaked underfoot as we approached the front door, a solid slab of oak that had been varnished until it looked congealed.

Predictably, Polly opened the door only a crack. "Yes?" she said, her filmy dark eyes wary.

I identified myself, and introduced Murray. Slowly Polly undid the chain and let us in. "I know you, yes," she said to me, her small, wrinkled face looking worried. "But him"—Polly gestured at Murray—"I never seen him before until last night. I don't talk to strangers. I tell my children, don't talk to strangers. But sometimes they do. They grow up and think they know everything." She shrugged helplessly, a small, insignificant figure in a shapeless black dress. "You want to see my vase?"

I was vaguely startled. "How did you know?"

"Everybody wants to see it. Maybe God wants me to show it to other people. I don't know. Come, it's in the living room." She always moved slowly, but now she was down to a crawl. Murray bumped into me as I tried not to do the same with Polly Patricelli.

The heavy, worn drapes were closed, and the only illumination on this rainy Sunday came from a dozen votive candles on the mantel. My gaze flickered over the shabby furniture, much of which was covered with specimens of Polly's needlework. A small but exquisite Venetian chandelier hung from the ceiling, along with a collection of cobwebs. The walls were covered with familiar, if sentimental, religious pictures: the Holy Family, the Sacred Heart of Jesus, St. Francis, St. Clare, St. Cecilia, the Good Shepherd.

As Polly approached the fireplace with its smoke-blackened tiles, she crossed herself. I waited for her to speak, but she said nothing, merely standing there with her head bent. Murray and I stood on each side of our mesmerized hostess, trying to examine the vase in the flickering light of the votive candles. There was definitely a crack—five or six of them in fact, all radiating from a faded cluster of flowers that might have been wild roses. There were three in number, on a background of thin, pointed leaves. The vase had cracked in such a way that the center of the flowers could have been taken for two eyes and a mouth, while the other squiggly lines might—with a great stretch of the imagination—suggest a nose, a beard, longish hair, and something across the brow that could be construed as a crown of thorns. The leaves seemed to form no part of the picture, and if anything, might have been taken for ornamental head feathers. I was reminded more of Montezuma than Jesus, and didn't know what to say.

Murray, however, wasn't so tongue-tied. "When does it cry?" he asked.

Polly didn't respond. I gathered she was praying. At last, she crossed herself again and turned slowly. "What did you say?" she asked in a hushed voice.

To Murray's credit, he was respectful. "I heard the vase cried. Does that happen often?"

Polly gave a small shake of her head. "He won't cry now." The cloudy old eyes gazed first at Murray, then at me. "That's because you don't believe. But later, when you are gone, He will weep. For both of you."

Chapter Ten

"IT'S NOT WORTH it," Murray declared as we sat down with our beverages at a window table in Starbucks. "I couldn't see squat. My producer won't waste footage on anything that lame."

"It was kind of obscure," I admitted.

"Screw it," Murray said, taking a sip of his double-tall. "It was just a side issue. I don't even know who told us about it. Probably some Catholic bleeding heart. How's your mocha?"

"Fine," I replied, though I hadn't yet tasted it. I was still smarting from Polly's denunciation. Or so I interpreted it. Had she meant that I didn't believe in her vase? Or that I didn't believe? Either way, was she right? There were times when I wondered. But I'd never say so out loud, not even to Ben. "Let's talk about Ursula. The sheriff's not around, so you can tell me." I'd tried to call Milo on my way from the rest room, but he hadn't answered at my house or his. I'd also phoned the sheriff's office, but Bill Blatt hadn't seen him all day. Maybe Milo was following up a lead.

Murray was giving me that engaging grin. "I lied. I do that a lot, to get people's attention. You know what I mean—ninety percent of them are brain-dead. Like, which makes you tune in—'So how are you doing?' or 'You got tits to die for'?"

"Murray . . ."

"Just kidding! So I'm not PC. Not in private, anyway.

Forget what I said, even if ... I'm not kidding." He sipped some more at his latte, then wiped foam from his upper lip. "As for Ursula, I'm going after this from the legal angle. Four malpractice suits have gone down so far, three settled out of court, one went to trial. The plaintiff lost that one, but the other three collected a total of five million bucks, give or take a few hundred grand. Two of those took place before Dr. Randall died three years ago. Yes, he had malpractice insurance, but only up to twenty-five mil. With eleven more cases out there totaling close to forty mil in damages, that wouldn't leave his widow with a lot of cash flow. It might not leave the plaintiffs with much, either. So who decided that revenge was better than money?"

Trying to put aside my spiritual quandary, I turned a perplexed face to Murray. "I don't get it. Why kill Ursula? She didn't perform botched surgeries."

"Hey—did I claim people are rational?" Murray leaned back in his chair. "Let's say you've got a kid with spinal problems. You send Junior to Dr. Randall, who screws up and the little guy ends up walking on his hands. You're number ten on that list of eleven plaintiffs, and if you've got more than four brain cells, you figure you're not going to get enough to buy Junior a pair of padded gloves. Then you find out that Wheaton's eatin' dirt in some cemetery, so who do you go after? Mrs. Randall, that's who. It's human nature." Murray gave me a smug look.

"So Mom or Dad waits until Ursula moves to Alpine, follows her up here, has a few drinks with her, and hauls her off to the Sky. Glub, glub." I shook my head. "No sale, Murray."

"Emma!" Murray gazed at me with mock astonishment. "I thought you had brains to match those tits! Just kidding!" He put both hands in front of his face as if he needed to fend me off, which wasn't a bad idea on his

part. I was feeling fairly dangerous. "How many sur-
geons have you got in Alpine?" Murray asked between
his fingers.

The question took me aback. "Both Doc Dewey and
Dr. Flake perform some surgeries. But they aren't sur-
geons per se," I admitted.

Murray allowed his hands to fall back onto the table.
"You got it. I'm heading back this afternoon since the
babelicious Carla isn't around and the vase is a dud. But
I'll keep in touch. Meanwhile take a hint from Felton's
Fabulous Files and find out who got fucked over by Dr.
Randall. There are four thousand people in this town, and
I'll bet you a hop in the hay that at least one of them got a
referral to Wheaton's Wacky Weed-Whacker."

There was some merit in Murray's argument. Maybe
I'd look into it. I had nothing better to do on this drizzly
Sunday afternoon.

But even as Murray rose from the table he was off on
another tangent. "Look at it from another angle—who
benefits from Ursula's death? You know anything about
her will? Rich people always have wills."

"There were no children," I said as we went outside
and stood under the shelter of the green Starbucks mar-
quee. "There are her two brothers here in town, of
course. But maybe Warren Wells gets everything."

"Assuming there'll be anything left to get," Murray
said with a grim expression. "If Ursula had been smart,
she'd have left the country, not the county. That's what
doctors—and their widows—usually do when they're
faced with big lawsuits."

My gaze traveled across Alpine Way to Old Mill Park,
where the Labor Day picnic banners sagged in the rain.
Several people were braving the weather to work on
preparations for Monday's event. Red, white, and blue
bunting decorated the original mill, which dated from
World War I and now housed the local museum.

I looked again at Murray, who seemed indifferent to

our little festivities. "Money is always a good motive," I remarked.

"Money, revenge, sex, fear," he said with a nod. "There's not much else. But I'm betting on revenge. Trust me."

I didn't, not completely, but I waved him off with a show of cooperation. As the red Mazda Miata headed down Alpine Way for the bridge over the Sky, it seemed to me that the money motive would be a hard one to track from this end. Undoubtedly, Ursula had an attorney in Seattle. On the other hand, she had consulted with Brendan Shaw about her insurance. Maybe I could do some nosing around after the holiday.

But I didn't need to wait that long to start working on the malpractice angle. Doc Dewey and his wife, Nancy, had taken off for part of the weekend, and I didn't want to disturb Peyton Flake, who was on call. Consequently, I phoned his nurse, Marilynn Lewis, who also happens to be Carla's roommate. Marilynn is originally from Seattle. She is Alpine's token African American—along with Father Den—and is rumored to be engaged to Dr. Flake, who is Caucasian by ancestry and a retro hippie by choice. My question about referrals to Wheaton Randall stumped Marilynn, and with good reason: "I've only been here a little over two years. Hasn't Dr. Randall been dead longer than that?"

Marilynn was correct. "But I thought you might have noticed the referral on somebody's chart," I said. "Of course it could have been a patient of Doc Dewey's."

"Some days I handle both," she replied in her usual thoughtful manner. "I know I've seen Randall's name, but I can't remember where off the top of my head. Do you want me to check Tuesday if I have time? I can't promise much, because we'll be really busy after a three-day weekend."

I started to say yes, but decided to press my luck. It was a long shot, but there was something in Murray's argument that was compelling. "If we could go into the office now, I'll treat you to dinner at Café Flore."

Marilynn laughed. "Now that's an offer I can't refuse. You must have some hot leads on this story. How did you know I was dying of boredom this weekend?"

"Just a guess," I said glibly.

Marilynn agreed to meet me at the clinic at four. I called Café Flore to make a reservation for six o'clock. Then I wondered if I should include Vida. I didn't believe her assertion that she was abandoning the story as a hopeless Catholic cause.

I was right. When I reached her at home five minutes later, she was annoyed. "If you wanted to check the medical records, why didn't you call me? You know perfectly well that my niece Marje Blatt is the clinic's receptionist. She could have searched the files and saved Marilynn the trouble."

"Well," I replied, "why not ask them both? It'll save time. Then you can treat Marje to dinner while I pick up the tab for Marilynn."

Vida emitted a beleaguered sigh. "Because Buck and I are going to dinner in Marysville at The Village," she responded. "And Marje has a date. Or so she told me at church. Really, I think your Catholic notions are contagious. We have some very queer ideas going 'round among some of our younger Presbyterians. Criticizing John Knox, indeed! Why, the man's a veritable saint! Or would be, if we had them."

I decided not to rise to the bait. John Knox was the least of my religious problems. I started to tell her about Murray Felton, but decided against it. Vida would see Murray's intrusion as big-city meddling. Worse yet, she might be jealous of any cooperative ventures I shared with the TV reporter. If—when—she heard that Murray had been nosing around Alpine, I'd dismiss his involvement as trivial. It wouldn't do to anger Vida again. When describing my visit to Polly's house, I omitted mentioning that I hadn't gone alone.

"I must see that vase," Vida murmured. "I have some spare time now. . . ." Her voice trailed off.

"Maybe you'll be more receptive to the vision or whatever than I was," I said with a trace of asperity. Polly's comment still rankled.

"I'll try to keep an open mind," Vida promised, and rang off.

An hour later I was watching Marilynn unlock the clinic door and marveling at, as well as envying, her cool, classic beauty. Most of all I admired her courage. She'd traveled some rough roads in recent years, but had emerged stronger and wiser.

The first thing she did was to check both doctors' referral lists. "I don't expect to find Wheaton Randall," she admitted, "because Marje tries to keep these current."

"Does that mean that if you don't find him you'll have to check all the charts?" I asked, staying on the other side of the reception desk in order to give Marilynn professional privacy.

"Not exactly," she replied, then shook her head. "No, he's not here. Let me look him up in one of the older King County medical listings. It'll help to see what kind of surgery he did."

It turned out that Wheaton Randall was an orthopedic surgeon who had practiced out of a prestigious address on what is known in Seattle as Pill Hill. He had performed his surgeries at a reputable hospital in the same neighborhood, specializing in knee replacements.

"Let me think," Marilynn said with a thoughtful expression. "Who's got new knees?" She started writing names down on a notepad. "Offhand, I can recall at least a dozen patients, but not all of them were referred to specialists." She paused, then jotted a few more names. "Now I'll look at the charts and hope for the best. Frankly I don't know all the possibles. Does it matter?"

It did, but I decided not to say so. As it was, I had asked a big favor of Marilynn. While she searched through charts I opened a copy of *Sports Illustrated* and caught up on the pro football exhibition season. I was becoming depressed by the Seahawks' prospects when Marilynn leaned back over the counter.

"There were four referrals to Dr. Randall, one in 1989, one in 1990, and two in 1991," she said. "I can't give you their names, but they're definitely locals." Marilynn's beautiful face conveyed apology. "There may be more earlier, but I might not know the patients. Let's face it, they're often elderly, and they could be deceased."

I was silent for a few moments. "Dr. Randall died in 1993," I finally said. "Or thereabouts. Is it odd that no referrals were made after 1991?"

"Not necessarily," Marilynn replied, "but it could indicate that our doctors lost confidence in Randall. Is that what you're thinking?"

I nodded. "There were a bunch of malpractice suits filed against him. They'd be a matter of public record. I suspect someone is already checking out that angle." I thought of Murray Felton.

"Lawyers don't do anything for free. You have to have money to file a malpractice suit." Marilynn's expression was enigmatic.

I knew she was trying to tell me something. Unfortunately I couldn't figure out what it was. If Marilynn was hinting at someone in Alpine who lacked financial resources, she could have meant half the population.

"Do you want me to keep looking?" she asked as I remained mute.

"No. Without names, it's hopeless." Seeing Marilynn's face fall, I hastened to amend my statement. "I mean, knowing that there were more referrals wouldn't help. It's sufficient to find out that Alpine patients were sent to Wheaton Randall."

Marilynn and I arrived early for our dinner reservation

at Café Flore. Located a few miles out of town on Highway 2, the restaurant was popular with diners from as far away as Seattle. On this Labor Day weekend, we had to wait a few minutes for a table.

"Once in a while Peyton and I come here," Marilynn said as her eyes roamed around the simple French country decor. "He doesn't like to dress up, but he enjoys good food. There aren't a lot of choices in Alpine."

I started to ask Marilynn what it was like to date the boss. But I knew: I'd met Tom Cavanaugh while I was an intern at *The Seattle Times*. "You've been going together quite awhile," I noted, a typically unsubtle female remark phrased to elicit the depth of a relationship.

As always, Marilynn was candid. "We're starting to think long-term. It's a huge decision."

Neither Marilynn Lewis nor Peyton Flake would take it lightly. "Do you mean marriage or something less official?" I inquired over the top of the handwritten menu.

Marilynn gave me her big smile. "I don't think you need to live together if you work together. Believe me, we know each other's flaws by now." The smile faded. "It's not a question of how we feel about each other. It's . . . the other."

"Other what?" There are times when I'm quite dense.

Fine lines appeared in Marilynn's forehead. "The racial thing. It always comes back to that."

"I wish we'd put all that behind us," I said. "This is almost the twenty-first century."

"Not in Alpine." Sadly she shook her head. "I've already been a pioneer, I was the first African American to live permanently in Alpine. I don't know that I want to spend my life breaking ground."

I was surprised. Marilynn's courage was one of the things I admired most about her. "You'd give Peyton Flake up because of a bunch of bigots?"

"I didn't say I'd give him up. But we don't have to stay in Alpine."

"Oh." A small wave of resentment washed over me, and I was ashamed of myself. I knew that Alpiners looked upon people who moved away as defectors. The departure was taken as a personal affront. Was I acquiring a small-town mentality? Or did I take offense because Marilynn and Dr. Flake were free to leave, and I was not? Even Milo was thinking about a move. Had Alpine become a life sentence for me?

"Peyton's not from the city originally," Marilynn was saying as I mulled over my reaction. "There's so much he likes about living at the edge of the forest. But we could do that closer to Seattle, out in the 'burbs. I have to admit I miss the city."

Marilynn had been raised in the Bay Area and had lived in Seattle for several years. I understood how she felt. Too well. That was my problem. "I'd hate to see you go," I said. "Flake, too. He's a good doctor."

Marilynn smiled again, but this time her expression conveyed a wistful quality. "I'd miss you and Carla and Doc Dewey and Marje Blatt and so many of our patients. I've grown fond of them all. Even," she added, suddenly looking mysterious, "strange old ladies like Darla Puckett and Grace Grundle and that sourpuss county commissioner Alfred Cobb and rednecks like Nunzio Lucci."

Occasionally I may be dense, but I'm not stupid. Again, Marilynn was trying to tell me something. In fact, she just had.

When I got home that evening, there was a message from Milo on my machine. His ex, Old Mulehide as he called the former Tricia Dodge, had telephoned to remind him after the fact that Saturday was their youngest daughter's birthday. To make amends, he had gone to Bellevue to take Michelle to dinner. He'd see me tomorrow. Probably.

Since Marilynn and I had gotten to Café Flore early,

we had returned to Alpine shortly after seven. On a whim, I decided to drive out to the spot where Ursula's body had been found. Figuring that death must have occurred somewhere between six and eight, I wanted to see what the place looked like under approximately the same conditions that she'd drowned in the river.

Except, of course, that the conditions weren't the same. It was raining, a steady downpour that discouraged me from prowling the Sky. At seven-thirty on this Sunday night, it was considerably darker than it would have been Friday with the late-day sun shining. What little I could see in passing didn't provide any insights. I headed for home.

Just past Icicle Creek, I noticed that the gas gauge was hovering around the quarter mark. I have a fixation about running out of gas, tending to panic when the indicator is anywhere under half-full. Cal's Texaco might or might not be open, so I pulled in to Gas 'N Go.

The chinless young man who worked the register looked smarter than the usual specimens I'd seen at the combination gas station and convenience store. "You're . . . ?" I said with an encouraging smile.

"Craig," the young man responded. He had a luxuriant brown mustache that would have served him better if he'd extended it to his short chin. "Craig Rasmussen. I know you. You're the newspaper lady."

"That's right." I kept smiling. "Emma Lord. I have a son about your age. Say, Craig," I said on a sudden inspiration, "were you working here Friday night?"

Craig nodded. "I pull a weekend shift. I'm going to Everett Community College. I wish they'd hurry up and build the one here, so I wouldn't have to drive so far."

Briefly I sympathized with the hundred-mile round-trip commute. "Who did you wait on in the early evening?"

The clever brown eyes registered understanding. "You mean the night they found that lady in the drink? Dang, there were a lot of people I didn't know—tourists, I guess. But there were some locals, too. Let me think—Norm Carlson, the dairy guy, Mr. Bamberg, from the video store, Tim Rafferty—he tends bar next door at the Icicle Creek Tavern, Mrs. O'Toole, from the grocery store, and . . ." He paused. "How far into the night do you want me to go?"

I congratulated Craig on his recall. "Eight o'clock?"

"That's it, then." He held up his hands. "I'm not sure I got them in order, though."

Vaguely I recalled Betsy O'Toole mentioning that she'd stopped at Gas 'N Go Friday evening. "What time was Mrs. O'Toole here?"

Craig thought. "Seven? Seven-thirty? No—it was earlier, maybe before seven. I remember because some guy came in at the same time and wanted to use the rest room. I had to give him the key. I thought he was a tourist because I didn't recognize him or the cool red Z3 he was driving, but Mrs. O'Toole did."

"Did she call him by name?" I asked eagerly.

"No, but she acted as if it was somebody she knew." Craig glanced outside as a rattletrap of a truck with boards instead of panels pulled up to the pumps. "He wasn't very tall, maybe five-nine, about the same age as Mrs. O'Toole, or a little older. I think he was losing his hair."

The description fit any number of men in Alpine. Warren Wells was just one of them. But he was the only one I knew who owned a red BMW Z3. I paid cash for my gas and thanked Craig for his help.

"No problem," he said, then clapped a hand to his head. "I forgot—the rich babe! She was here around six-thirty. Does that count?"

"It could," I said, again sounding eager. Was it possible that Ursula O'Toole had stopped in at Icicle Creek Gas 'N Go?

It wasn't. Craig's description was of a much younger

woman, and at first I assumed he was talking about a tourist. I suggested as much, but Craig shook his head.

"She knew her way around town," he insisted. "She mentioned something about how nice it was to have a Starbucks here, and that she wondered if when they built the new bridge by here, they'd have to tear down this place and the tavern."

"What made you think she was rich?" I inquired as the heavily bearded owner of the patchwork truck entered the store.

Obviously not one to jump to conclusions, Craig considered. "She was driving a new Chrysler LHS, and her clothes looked expensive. You know, like how women dress in the movies and on TV. She didn't look like she belonged in Alpine—if you know what I mean."

The bearded man laughed richly. "*I* know," he said. "Alpine broads look like two hundred pounds of dog meat."

Craig flushed and I bristled. The man with the truck realized his gaffe. "You must be a visitor, sweetie. You look pretty nice."

I didn't, but that was beside the point. "Thanks," I muttered, then smiled at Craig. "I'll pass your information along to the sheriff." Glaring at the bearded man, I departed.

Warren Wells and—who? Only one possibility came to mind: Alicia Lowell. Had Alicia and her father both been at Gas 'N Go within the same two-hour time span? Coincidences aren't rare in a small town like Alpine. But it also meant that Warren and Alicia had both been near the spot where Ursula had been found.

So had Betsy O'Toole. I drove back along Railroad Avenue in a pensive mood. Had Milo interviewed the residents along the Sky? Some of them were virtually his neighbors. Surely he or one of the deputies had talked to the inhabitants of the houses along that stretch between Icicle Creek and the dirt road. But had they learned anything of significance? If so, the sheriff hadn't told me. Irked, I headed home.

Ben had called, leaving an unfamiliar number. When I dialed it, Adam answered. Despite my annoyance with him, my voice was flooded with maternal warmth.

"Uncle Ben's not here right now," Adam said, somehow sounding older and vaguely distant. "We're staying in a trailer, just outside of Tuba City. Uncle Ben's visiting somebody who's real sick."

"How's he managing?" I inquired, trying to tone down the rush of affection. Maybe Adam had sensed it and felt overwhelmed.

"He's okay. He said Mass in the school hall. The people mobbed him afterward. It was pretty emotional. I served."

From the time that Adam was ten until he reached about fifteen, I had encouraged him to sign up as an acolyte. My son had resisted, citing various reasons, including an allergy to the cigar smoke that clung to one of our assistant pastors in Portland. Naturally I was surprised to hear that he'd assisted his uncle by serving at Mass.

"When did you learn to do that?" I asked in a bemused voice.

"Uh . . . I don't know. A year or two ago. Uncle Ben taught me. Say, do you think it'd be okay if I didn't come to Alpine until Thanksgiving? Uncle Ben needs all the help he can get."

If ever Adam had offered an excuse for not visiting his poor old mother, that was it. I stifled my disappointment and assured him that it would be fine. "But what about school? Aren't you due back in Tempe in a couple of weeks?"

The hesitation was fractional. "I'm not going back. Not this term, anyway. Uncle Ben's work is more important. As soon as we get funding, we'll start rebuilding the church. The goal is to have it completed by Christmas, maybe sooner."

Not coming to Alpine was one thing; dropping out of school was another. "Ben will have lots of help," I pointed out. "Come on, Adam, don't lose sight of your future. You've almost got your degree."

"I can get my degree later," he said doggedly. "This is more important. Don't fight me on this. It's too big."

I felt frustrated, defeated. Then, reminding myself that time was often a mother's greatest ally, I tried to soften my tone.

"See what happens in the next couple of weeks," I advised, sounding almost genial. "Ben may find himself inundated with volunteers." *And,* I thought to myself, *you, my son, will be bored and ready to return to Arizona State and the beer and the girls and the other joys of college life.*

"That's not what I mean," Adam said in that semi-somber voice that was so unlike his usual flippant style. "Uncle Ben doesn't need just moral and physical support. He needs somebody to prop him up spiritually, too. You know, Mom, even priests can hit a low ebb sometimes."

Did I hear sarcasm in Adam's tone? Or irony? Was my son trying to kid me or impress me? I was confused. "Are you telling me that Ben's having a spiritual crisis?" I asked with a lame little laugh.

"Not a crisis, no," Adam replied, his patience sounding strained. "He's tapped. But everybody still leans on him. So he needs someone he can lean on. I'm here for him. Is that a problem for you?"

It shouldn't be, I told myself. Then I told Adam the same thing. He seemed to believe me.

But did I believe it? I wasn't sure. Suddenly there appeared to be a number of things about which I had doubts.

* * *

That night I watched the news on one of Murray
Felton's rival TV stations. To my horror, the feature that
closed out the telecast showed Polly Patricelli and her
vase. Judging from the wan light and the heavy rain in
the exterior shots of Polly's house, the TV crew hadn't
arrived in Alpine until late afternoon, perhaps while
Marilynn and I were at Café Flore.

"Attending Sunday services isn't all that the little town
of Alpine has to offer in the way of religious experiences," the dapper TV newsman announced as Polly's
dark old house loomed behind him in the background.
"Appollonia Patricelli has her own shrine, which may or
may not be some kind of miracle."

The camera moved inside, showing Polly in her living
room. In spite of the TV crew's efforts to light the interior of the house, it still looked gloomy.

"A few weeks ago," the newsman recounted as Polly
piously approached the mantel, "Mrs. Patricelli discovered that her precious family heirloom vase had cracked.
But the pattern formed by the cracks was no ordinary
damage."

A microphone was put in front of Polly, who was obviously startled as an off-camera reporter asked what she
could see in the vase. "Jesus," she said simply. "I see
Jesus."

Now the cameraman zoomed in on the vase. Under the
TV lights, the vase took on mellow gold and sepia tones.
Try though I might, the cracks still looked like cracks
to me.

"Not everyone may see what Mrs. Patricelli sees," the
newsman said in a voice-over as the camera lingered on
the vase. "But if the longtime Alpine resident is a woman
of simple faith, she also has some reasons for believing
in her little miracle."

Again, the microphone was thrust at Polly. "I come
from Italy, the town of Assisi, where St. Francis lived,"
she said, obviously in answer to a question posed by the

reporter. "The first time I noticed Jesus' face was Friday, the eleventh of August. It is the feast of St. Clare, St. Francis's dear friend in God."

We were back to the vase and the flickering votive candles. "Skeptics may scoff," the voice-over continued, "yet in this small logging town with its hard-hit economy, any sign of hope is welcome. Polly Patricelli's vase may not be a miracle, but as she herself might put it, maybe Alpine isn't the town that God forgot."

The screen abruptly changed to a shot of the news desk with a smiling crew wishing us good night. Angrily I clicked off the set. My phone rang almost immediately.

"Screw the competition," Murray Felton said in a furious tone that matched my mood. "Where did those jerks from that other freaking unmentionable station come from?"

"It was your choice not to use the story," I snapped, sparing no sympathy for Murray. "How do you think *I* feel? I've been scooped in my own hometown!"

"I drove all the way to Alpine and back for nothing," Murray fumed, as lacking in compassion for me as I was for him. "I didn't get a freaking thing on the Randall death, I came up empty on your crackpot's cracked vase, and I didn't get laid! This three-day weekend sucks!"

I agreed. Trying to calm down, I made an attempt at doing something positive. "Check out these names from Alpine and see if any of them have sued Randall." I gave him the four patients that Marilynn had mentioned in her not-so-subtle fashion at dinner.

Murray seemed slightly mollified. "Okay, but I'll have to wait until Tuesday. Everything's closed tomorrow because of Labor Day."

I understood. We made mutual, grudging promises to help each other on the Randall story.

"What about the vase?" I asked. "Are you still interested?"

"Hell, no," Murray replied. "Put a fork in it, it's done.

In TV, when a rival station uses a feature like that, the rest of us back off like a guy on a bad blind date. Mrs. P can take that vase and stick it."

My attitude couldn't be so cavalier. "Okay. Give me your number so I can call you if I find out anything."

"Generous!" His tone was mocking, but I knew he was appreciative. He had to be; he was a journalist. Murray might be a pain in the butt, but he seemed to have his priorities right when it came to tracking down a story. "Don't call me, I'll call you, probably Tuesday, around noon. See ya."

Still feeling angry about having the Seattle media pull a local story right out from under me, I checked the doors and windows before going to bed. It was still raining, and the house had finally cooled off. I wasn't really afraid that the alleged prowler would return, but there was no point in taking chances.

Yet as I lay awake I realized that theft and assault weren't always physical in nature. However unwittingly, my brother had robbed me of my son. A Seattle TV station had stolen my story. And Polly Patricelli had attacked my capacity for faith. All in all, it had been a bad day.

I almost wished the prowler would come back. I was in a combative mood. Recklessly I got out of bed, turned on the light, and went to my closet. Under the low shelf where I kept my shoes was a combination jewelry case and music box I'd received as a present on my fifteenth birthday. It was white, with a small ballerina on top. When wound up, the little figure twirled to a Tchaikovsky strain. I'd liked the music, but I'd hated the case. In fact, I'd taken the interior apart many years ago. In its altered state, it was a perfect repository for my dad's old Colt .45.

I removed the gun along with a box of bullets. Then I loaded all seven of them into the magazine and pushed it into the well. I chambered a round by pulling the slide back, then put on the safety. My father had taught me how to shoot, but warned that I should never pick up a weapon without being prepared to use it.

On this wet, lonesome September night, I not only felt that I could, but that I wanted to.

Chapter Eleven

THE NEXT MORNING I reached Milo at his office. He spent the first minute or two yawning in my ear and complaining about driving on a rainy night in heavy holiday traffic between Alpine and Bellevue.

"We need the rain," I pointed out.

"Yeah, sure, I know that," the sheriff replied. "But we don't need all those damned cars, and half of them are from out of state and they don't know how to drive in the rain in the first place."

I waited for Milo to finish grumbling before I broached the subject of Warren and Alicia Wells and Betsy O'Toole being in the Icicle Creek vicinity Friday night. The sheriff wasn't much interested.

"Emma, give it up," he said with a weary sigh. "You're not a detective. Three-day weekend or not, Cal closed his Texaco station around six. Warren mentioned having a beer with him at Mugs Ahoy, remember? With Buzzy's BP shut down, where else would people go to get gas except Icicle Creek?"

"Exactly." I felt smug. "Warren and Cal went beer drinking together because Warren had stopped at Cal's to get his brakes checked. If he needed gas, why didn't he get it there? Besides, Craig Rasmussen didn't say Warren bought gas. He just said he came in to use the rest room."

The silence at the other end indicated that I'd hit home. Milo, however, wasn't giving in gracefully. "So he had to take a leak. Big deal. Or are you trying to say that he drowned his girlfriend, and it upset him so much that he felt like wetting his pants?"

"That's not funny, Milo," I retorted. "As a matter of fact, it could have happened that way. Never having killed anyone, I wouldn't know."

It was the wrong thing to say. Milo exploded in my ear: "*I* know! Didn't I save your ass last winter by blowing away a perp? I may not have wet my pants, but I had some damned strange dreams for months!"

I knew about the dreams. It wasn't long after the fatal shooting that Milo and I had become lovers. He hadn't talked about the incident for a while, and I'd hoped that he'd put it behind him. That hope was not just for Milo, but for me. I'd always felt guilty about the shooting. It wasn't *Catholic* guilt, as Leo would put it; guilt can be nondenominational.

"I'm sorry," I apologized. "I didn't mean to be a smart-mouth. But let's face it, Milo—how often do you guys stop at a service station to use the bathroom if you're near the woods?" I had long ago become accustomed to the sight of fishermen and hikers and just about any other male relieving themselves on the outskirts of Alpine. Expediency often won out over privacy.

"Doubles has become citified," Milo replied, no longer sounding angry. "Somehow I don't think Ursula would approve of him whizzing in the International Fountain at the Seattle Center."

"Probably not," I allowed. "But I still think it's a little bit of a coincidence. If you're not going to ask any of those three people what they were doing at Icicle Creek, I am. I've nothing better to do today."

"Go ahead," Milo said on a note of resignation. "You know I've got to work. Will you be at the picnic?"

I'd forgotten about the picnic. "I don't know. Will you?"

"Maybe. If they need crowd control." Milo sounded cagey.

"At a Labor Day picnic in Old Mill Park? What do you expect—a riot between the wienies and the dill pickles?"

"Hell, these days you never know. Everybody's so damned touchy. But," he admitted, "it's raining, which means there won't be such a big turnout. They've got canopies, though."

"Vida's taking pictures, so I don't need to attend." I paused, contemplating the long, empty day. "I'll see."

As anticipated, my House & Home editor proved more intrigued by Craig's sightings at Gas 'N Go. "I think," she said in her most ingenuous tone, "that we should drop in on Francine and Alicia. It isn't right not to have a visit while Alicia's here. I'll bring cookies. You offer a beverage."

I bridled. "I'm not *offering* a beverage." It was bad enough that Vida would haul along a package of cheap cookies from the Grocery Basket. "Why don't we ask them over here?"

"What a nice idea!" Vida exclaimed, and I knew I'd been conned. "Try to make it around one. I'd have them here, but Roger is staying with me while his parents are in Seattle. I don't like disrupting his schedule."

I kept mum, but thought how much I'd like to disrupt Roger—permanently. Vida's spoiled grandson was the apple of her eye, and a colossal pain in the butt. No doubt she meant that trying to drag him away from the TV set would unleash a tantrum. Or, since Roger was now going on twelve, a world-class sulk. Maybe he'd even threaten to run away. I liked the concept.

But the cozy get-together with Francine and Alicia wasn't to be. Vida called back ten minutes later, saying that mother and daughter were going to the picnic. Maybe, Francine had said, they'd see us there.

I was stuck. It's not that I despise communal picnics, but after five years I was tired of the Labor Day event. The high-school band would play, Mayor Fuzzy Baugh and at least one of the three county commissioners would give a boring speech, somebody from the unions would drone on about the virtues of hard work and brotherhood, a designated old-timer would talk about what it was like when the woods were full of trees, the mills were full of jobs, and Alpiners' pockets were full of money. Finally Bucker Swede, the stuffed dummy dressed in logging togs that serves as the high-school mascot, would be trotted out and hauled around in a mule-drawn wagon. If the mules would deign to budge.

I was doing my best imitation of housework when Laura O'Toole had a flat tire in front of my house. She knocked timorously on my door shortly before noon and asked to use the phone. Glancing outside through the rain, I saw a battered maroon Plymouth Fury listing in the direction of my mailbox.

"Come in," I urged. "Are you calling Cal Vickers?"

Laura, who wore a shabby blue jacket over shapeless green slacks, looked bewildered. "I don't know. Should I?"

"Well ... You were going to call *someone*. Who was it?" I tried to make sure that my voice conveyed kindliness.

In the wan midday light, Laura's thin face looked much older than her forty-odd years. "Mike," she finally said. "He knows how to change a tire. If we've got a spare." She chewed on her index finger.

"Does Mike drive?" Laura and Buzzy's children were a blur to me. There were four or five of them, maybe even six, and none seemed to have a distinct personality. I thought Mike was the eldest, perhaps sixteen, and therefore old enough to have a license.

"Yes," Laura answered. But I was only half-right: "He flunked his driving test, though. But he could borrow a car."

"Don't let him do that," I cautioned. "I'll go get him. Is he home?"

"I don't know." Laura looked utterly at sea, a leaky boat caught in a summer squall.

I considered the options. "Is the spare in the trunk?"

"Ummm . . ." Laura's gaze wandered around my living room, as if I had a prompter somewhere that could give her the answer. "It could be. I didn't look."

Grabbing my jacket, I led the way back outside. "Let's see. If it is, I'll call someone." Maybe, just maybe, Milo and his men weren't all tied up in Labor Day mayhem.

But there was no spare. The trunk was full of junk, beat-up shoes, dirty clothes, fast-food cartons and bags and boxes, old magazines and tabloids, rusted tools, and a bunch of road maps that bore the BP logo. When I studied the tire that had gone flat, I realized that it probably *was* the spare.

Recalling the various old cars and parts of cars that decorated the O'Tooles' yard, I posed a question: "Is there a good tire on any of those . . . ah . . . vehicles . . . um . . . parked by your house?"

Laura didn't know that either. She moved from one tennis-shoe covered foot to the other, with the rain trickling down her face. "Buzzy would know," she finally said.

"So where is Buzzy?" I was finding it an effort to keep the kindliness in my voice.

Laura slowly shook her head. "I don't know." Then she turned hopeful gray eyes on me. "In his van?"

I shrugged. "Could be. Where's the van?"

Laura considered. "Up in the woods?"

In Alpine, that's a vast amount of territory. Logging roads, many abandoned but still usable, snake along the mountainsides. I gave up. "Let's go inside," I suggested. "It's raining pretty hard."

Obediently Laura trotted along. Back in the living room, I offered coffee. She accepted, rather eagerly, I thought. Buckling under to what I presumed was misfortune in more ways than one, I also offered a sandwich. This time she declined, but I sensed that pride—or timidity—held her back.

"I'm going to make myself some lunch anyway," I insisted, though it wasn't true. "You might as well eat something with me while we figure out what to do next."

"Okay."

Laura followed me into the kitchen. Indicating that she should sit at the table while I whipped up a can of tuna, I worked for at least a full minute in silence. It was Laura who spoke first:

"If only she hadn't drowned first." A heavy sigh ensued.

I turned sharply. "Who? Ursula?"

Laura nodded. "She would have helped us. I know she would."

The incongruity of Ursula Randall being Laura O'Toole's sister-in-law struck me anew. The two women couldn't have been more different. Yet Ursula, Buzzy, and Jake had been born to the same parents. It wasn't so difficult to paint Jake and Betsy into a family portrait, but Laura and Buzzy simply didn't fit.

"I understand Ursula was very generous," I finally said, for lack of anything more cogent.

Laura nodded. "It was just a matter of minutes."

Once again I turned away from the tuna salad. "What was?" I asked, feeling puzzled.

"Her. Coming to help us. But Buzzy didn't know. Or maybe he did. I suppose that's why he came home."

Spreading the tuna mixture on bread, I added potato chips and the rest of the gherkins. Then I sat down at the table. "I'm confused, Laura," I admitted. "What are you talking about? With Ursula, I mean."

Laura crammed three potato chips in her mouth at once. "Money," she said, though as she chewed, it sounded like *mungey*. "Ursula was bringing money. She'd promised Buzzy. But she didn't come and didn't come and didn't come. I blamed Buzzy for not being nicer to his sister. That's when he left." She bit off a quarter of the sandwich, a defiant gesture indicating contempt for her husband, lingering hunger, or both.

I tried to cling to the narrative thread. "That was—when? That Buzzy left, I mean."

"Which time?" Laura asked after swallowing her food.

"How many times did he go?" At this point I wasn't sure that I knew what we were talking about. Nor could I imagine Laura serving on the school board. I might as well have cast a write-in vote for Crazy Eights Neffel.

"Twice," my unfit candidate answered. "Wednesday and Friday." A slight frown creased Laura's narrow forehead as she stared at what was left of her sandwich. "The first time we had a fight. About money. It's always about money. That's when Buzzy took off."

"Is he still working at the Grocery Basket?" I didn't want to stray from the original topic, but it seemed to me that Jake probably paid his brother a fair wage.

"I guess." The question didn't seem to hold much interest for Laura.

"So Friday, Ursula was supposed to come to your house with a . . . loan?" I felt as if I were playing a word game, Fill in the Gaps.

Laura nodded once. "Buzzy talked to her, and she promised to give us some money. She was coming over around seven. But she never did."

"So you and Buzzy were waiting for her?" It seemed like a logical supposition.

Laura nodded again, then brushed crumbs off her jacket. The sandwich was almost gone. "We waited and waited. Like I said, she never came."

That figured. Ursula couldn't come because she was dead. But I didn't make the obvious statement to Laura. "What time did Buzzy come by to wait for Ursula?" I inquired, hoping to sound casual.

Laura scowled. "It was after seven-thirty. I was getting mad, because he was late. He's always late. It wouldn't be right to keep his sister waiting, not when we were asking for money." Laura paused to gobble a few chips. "So then we waited together. But Ursula never showed up. I figured Buzzy had made her mad, too. I told him so. That's when he left. But he forgot his keys, so he had to come back. The sheriff came then and told us Ursula had drowned. Buzzy went off without saying another word."

In the brief silence that followed, the rain pummeled the kitchen window. Canopies notwithstanding, the weather wasn't conducive to a picnic.

"Did you talk to Ursula Friday?" I asked, offering the bag of chips to Laura.

Taking the bag, she shook her head emphatically. "No. Why would I do that?"

"Well . . . to arrange the time." I knew my smile was artificial. "To see when it was convenient for all of you to get together."

"Buzzy talked to her." The gray eyes struck me as slightly furtive. "Didn't I say that?"

"Yes." Once more I hesitated. "Did you see much of Ursula after she moved to Alpine?"

Licking a piece of potato chip off her lip, Laura considered. "Twice. She had us and Betsy and Jake to dinner. Another time I ran into her at—"

A pounding at my front door interrupted Laura and startled us both. I rose, calling out that I was coming. Buzzy O'Toole stood on the porch, looking distressed.

"Emma?" he said, as if he were surprised to find me living in my own house. "Is Laura here? Or is it Mike?"

"It's Laura," I informed Buzzy, stepping aside to let him in. "She had a flat."

"I know." He nodded in a jerky fashion. His faded denim jacket was damp from the rain and his blue jeans had a hole in the knee. In Buzzy's case, I didn't think it was a fashion statement. "I saw the Fury in front of your house. That's why I stopped."

We were standing in the middle of the living room.

Laura remained in the kitchen, though I knew she could hear every word we said.

"Won't you join us?" I asked Buzzy. The polite request sounded fatuous in my ears.

Buzzy looked terrified. "No. No, thanks. I just wanted to make sure that . . . there hadn't been another . . . accident."

I was puzzled. "*Another* accident?"

Again, that jerky nod: "Yeah, like Ursula. This family's jinxed."

There was no point in urging Buzzy to stay or in arguing about his family's run of bad luck. I started walking him to the door when Laura's voice called out from behind us.

"He's got a spare. Tell him I need it."

I didn't say anything. It was annoying to be put in the middle of a domestic squabble.

Buzzy stopped but he didn't turn around. "Tell her it won't fit the Fury. It's for the VW van."

I still didn't say anything.

"Tell him to get one from Cal's and bring it back here." Laura's tone was surprisingly strong.

Another brief silence ensued, as if some invisible translator was relaying the messages between estranged husband and wife.

"Tell her she wouldn't know what to do with it if I did. Tell her she shouldn't be driving the Fury anyway. Tell her she shouldn't be driving at all, because she's too damned dumb to—"

"Shut up, Buzzy!" Laura's voice had acquired a rasp, like radio static. "You don't drive so good, either! What about the other night, when you said you were late because you couldn't start your stupid van?"

Now Buzzy did turn around. I stepped out of the way, seeking safety behind the sofa. "It was the carburetor, you moron! I can drive just fine—but I'm not a mechanic!"

"You sure aren't!" Laura screeched. "If you were, the

gas station might not have gone broke! You aren't much of anything, if you ask me! You don't even have the guts to stick around and support your family!"

Buzzy advanced on Laura, but she held her ground. "I gave you most of my paycheck! What did you spend it on—tabloids? Why don't you stop reading about Princess Di and find a job? Why is it always *me*?"

"I got kids to raise, that's why!" Laura's pointed chin jutted. "Like you ever stayed home with them, even when you could? I'm stuck there in that dump of a house while you go off drinking beer with your friends and working on your crummy cars! You're a joke, Buzzy!"

Buzzy lunged at Laura, his hands around her throat. She retaliated with feet and fists and ear-rending shrieks. I stood frozen, wondering what to do. Never in my life had I witnessed such a sight.

The O'Tooles were grappling and pounding and yelling in the doorway between the kitchen and the living room. Buzzy finally got a good grip on Laura's windpipe, stifling her cries. Her knees began to buckle; her face was very red. I thought about the Colt .45, thought again, and picked up my copy of *The American Heritage Dictionary*, third edition. With all my might, I brought it down on Buzzy's head.

The blow stunned him just enough to relax his hold on Laura. Staggering and gasping, she slipped out from under his hands. He whirled on me while Laura collapsed into a kitchen chair.

"What the hell are you doing?" he shouted, his gaunt features contorted.

"What the hell are *you* doing?" I shouted right back. "This is *my* house! How dare you come in here and act like you escaped from the zoo?"

Panting, Buzzy seemed to be trying to get himself under control. "We don't have a zoo," he mumbled, then pulled a red-and-white handkerchief out of his pocket and wiped his high forehead. "Sorry. But Laura ticks me off."

"Jeez!" I threw up my hands.

Stuffing the handkerchief back in his pocket, Buzzy turned to look at his wife. She was leaning against the chair, still gasping, still red in the face. "I'll go get your damned spare," he bellowed. "But I won't put it on!"

Laura made a small, scornful gesture with one hand. Buzzy squared his narrow shoulders and stomped out of the house. I retrieved my dictionary and set it back down on the desk.

If the pen is mightier than the sword, maybe a book is more persuasive than a gun.

But I doubt it.

Cal Vickers showed up twenty minutes later with his tow truck. He told me that he wasn't sure he had a spare to fit the Fury. With the picnic in full swing at Old Mill Park, there was a lull in business, so Cal had left the station in the care of his assistants and driven up to my house. It was no big deal, he said. The O'Tooles had had their share of hard luck. He didn't mind doing them a good turn. What were friends for, after all? I praised Cal for his generosity, but knew darned well that he must feel a twinge of guilt for helping put Buzzy out of business.

Meanwhile I had coped with Laura. She wasn't really hurt, though she might have some bruises on her throat in a few hours. I couldn't help but ask if Buzzy often got violent. But Laura didn't want to talk about it. She spent the remainder of the time under my roof drinking coffee and staring at the refrigerator door. I felt pretty helpless, and a little hopeless, too.

After Cal and Laura left, I decided to go to the picnic. The rain had let up to an intermittent drizzle. Since the Labor Day affair was potluck, I stopped at the Grocery Basket to buy a package of hot dogs and buns. Jake O'Toole was up front, doing something with the safe.

I was tempted to say something about Buzzy and Laura, but didn't know how to begin. It was Jake who brought up family matters, though it wasn't his brother he referred to but his sister.

"Ursula's funeral is Wednesday at St. James Cathedral," he said as I pulled out an empty grocery cart from the queue by the main entrance. "I guess you won't be able to have it in the paper beforehand."

"What a surprise," I said, though the irony was lost on Jake. It seemed that *The Advocate* was missing out on several news fronts in the past few days.

"Betsy and I'll go," Jake said, his face looking drawn. "I don't know about Buzzy and Laura." There was a question in his voice. He'd brought up the subject of the other O'Tooles. It was no good pretending that their problems weren't any of my business. Laura and Buzzy had brought them right into my living room.

"Your brother and his wife don't seem to be getting along," I said frankly. "They just made a scene at my place." Seeing Jake's dismayed expression, I held up a hand. "Don't worry, I won't put it in the paper." Briefly I summarized what had led up to the row. "Maybe," I concluded as Jake anxiously rubbed his forehead, "they'll be able to call a truce for the funeral. Of course, I don't know if fighting like that is typical, or if it's something new."

"They've always fought," Jake said, trying to keep a smile in place for passing customers. "It's not like Betsy and me—with us, it's kind of a . . . game. But the physical stuff with Buzzy and Laura is new. I don't like it."

"Nobody does." My eyes ran along the expanse of the front end, where all six checkout stands were busy. Despite the rain, there were still tourists in town, their carts loaded with foodstuffs suitable for camping, picnicking, and snacking. "Did Buzzy work today?"

Jake shook his head. "I gave him today off. He'd put in

six straight, seven to five. I thought he could use the overtime."

"They seem hard up," I remarked, hoping to sound more sympathetic than curious.

"Yeah, well . . ." Jake paused to answer a charcoal-briquette query from a young couple. "Buzzy's making decent money now," he went on after the young couple headed for Aisle A-2. "The trouble is, they got so far into a hole after the gas station folded. They're still playing catch-up. And Laura's no money manager. Betsy's tried to help her, but Laura either can't or won't get the hang of it. Friday was payday, so Betsy went over there to see if she could lend a hand paying bills. But Buzzy hadn't shown up with the money. Betsy got tired of waiting and left."

"Yes," I said matter-of-factly. "I gather Buzzy didn't get to the house until seven-thirty."

Jake regarded me with mild interest. "Is that right? Betsy didn't get home until around eight-thirty. She must have stopped someplace."

The small awkward silence was broken by a request for Jake's approval of an out-of-town check. I trundled my cart down Aisle F-2, in search of hot dogs and buns. Ten minutes later I was making my way through the drizzle to one of the picnic tables in Old Mill Park.

A three-piece jazz ensemble was playing, a sack race was under way, and a mime acted out something that looked like scalping a small child, but hopefully wasn't. The air smelled of wood smoke, barbecue, and damp earth. Some teenagers were climbing the bronze statue of Carl Clemans, Alpine's founder, and posing for pictures. According to the schedule Vida had posted in the paper, the official program wouldn't start until three. It wasn't quite two, so maybe I could eat and run.

By chance, the table I had chosen was also hosting Monica and Verb Vancich, Ronnie Wenzler-Greene, Greer Fairfax, and a pale blond man who I assumed was her husband, Grant. The Vancich children were playing under the wooden benches, bumping into the legs of anyone foolish enough to sit down, such as me.

Ronnie was the first to notice my arrival. "Are you covering the event?" she asked. "I'm giving a brief talk about education."

I said I was merely another carefree picnicker. Vida would cover the story, but it would be mainly a photo essay.

Ronnie was disappointed. "You really should include more text. What I have to say is rather important."

"Really?" I tried to look intrigued. "Then you should have mentioned it when I interviewed you Monday."

The parochial-school principal's fair skin flushed slightly. "I did, in a way. But I intend to make my points more forcefully today. Better quotes, you see. For you."

Aware that Ronnie was trying to pacify me, I smiled. "Then Vida will use them, I'm sure." Pulling my legs away from one of the rampaging Vancich children, I turned to Greer, who was on my left. "I don't believe we've officially met. I'm Emma Lord."

Greer nodded solemnly. "I gathered as much. You support the loggers, it seems."

"I've tried to be fair," I said. "My main concern is for people."

"People can't live in a world that they rape," Greer declared as two boys about nine and eleven came up and started pulling on the sleeve of her poplin jacket. "We have to address environmental concerns first, or there'll be nothing left to support life as we know it." She turned to the importunate boys, who were demanding food, while I pondered her last statement. Maybe life as we know it wasn't quite as good as Greer thought. At least not in Alpine, judging from the number of battered pickups, aging beaters, and rusting vans.

"The veggie burgers will be ready in a few minutes," Greer crossly informed the boys, then poked the man

who I assumed was her mate. "Grant, take them for a run
around the park. They need to expend some energy
before they eat."

Greer made their sons sound like a pair of dogs. But
Grant dutifully rose and led the boys away. They went
with reluctance, whining until out of earshot. Their
mother was still talking, now about the need to spare old-
growth timber. I tuned her out, having heard every possible argument from both sides of the logging dilemma.
My mind wandered to the Vanciches, who seemed lost in
their own little world at the end of the table. When Greer
finally ran out of steam, I asked if anyone had seen
Father Den.

The question caught Monica's attention. "He left right
after Mass yesterday," she said.

I recalled not getting an answer Sunday morning when
I knocked at the rectory. "That's right—he was going to
visit his mother in Tacoma."

Ronnie sniffed. "He claims she's ill."

I stared at the principal. "Isn't she?"

Ronnie shrugged, then her gaze locked with Monica's.
"He says so." The two women laughed softly.

Cringing as one of the Vancich kids whacked me in
the shin, I tried to think of something that would rescue
the conversation, then decided it wasn't worth the effort.
I needn't have worried. Vida was approaching with
Roger dawdling behind her.

"Well! There you are!" she exclaimed, though I wasn't
sure whether my House & Home editor referred to me or
the entire group. "Anyone for coleslaw?" Vida pointed to
a wicker hamper which she carried over one arm.

"Is it low-fat?" Greer inquired.

Vida fixed Greer with her owlish look. "Of course
there's no fat. I don't make my coleslaw with meat."

As far as I knew, Vida didn't make coleslaw at all. I
suspected that she'd bought it. Which, I reflected, was a
blessing. Escaping from the bench and the bruising by

the Vancich children, I informed Vida that I was going to find a barbecue pit and cook my hot dogs. Would she care to join me?

Vida gave Roger a dubious look. "Are you hungry, dearest? You just had a big bowl of chili and a pizza."

Roger studied the wet ground. Since I'd last seen him, he'd grown, both vertically and horizontally. His light brown hair was much longer than I remembered, though his manner was as truculent as ever.

"Where are the other kids?" he asked, straining to look around the milling crowd.

Vida bent down to peek under the table. "Too young," she murmured, espying the Vancich duo. "Well, now . . ." It was her turn to scan the picnickers. "Ah!" she cried as Grant Fairfax returned with his two panting sons. "Here are some nice boys, just about your age."

Roger curled his lip. Vida, however, persevered. "Now run along with these fine fellows and play some games. The three-legged race is set for two-thirty."

I shuddered for whoever got stuck with Roger in a three-legged race. It would have been more appropriate if they'd held a two-headed contest. Roger would win hands down—or heads up, so to speak. Thus my uncharitable train of thought ran on, whimsically and nastily.

"How," Vida demanded after Roger and the Fairfax boys had formed a wary alliance and gone off, "did you end up with that dreadful crew?"

We were making our way to the nearest barbecue pit. "It was the first table I saw. By the time I got close enough to see who was there, I couldn't turn around and leave."

The jazz trio had been replaced on the bandstand by a barbershop quartet. I recognized Norm Carlson and Ellsworth Overholt, but not the other two. As I unwrapped my hot dogs, I brought Vida up to speed on my latest bits and pieces of information, including the ruckus between Laura and Buzzy O'Toole.

She was only mildly surprised. "Frustration, failure, a sense of hopelessness, all the besetting sins of a town under economic siege. By the way, the newly appointed dean of students for the college is going to speak today."

"What newly appointed dean?" I asked sharply. "Carla hasn't written a word about him. Or her."

"Now, now," Vida soothed. "It's not Carla's fault this time. I understand it won't be officially announced until this coming week. His name is Ryan Talliaferro, from Spokane Falls Community College."

"So how do you know?" I asked.

Vida shrugged. "A little bird told me. Do you remember Faith Lambrecht?"

I did, vaguely. Her husband had been the pastor at Vida's church years ago.

"I called to tell her about the outrages committed by our younger set," Vida continued, her eyes, as ever, skipping from group to group around the park. "She lives in Spokane, and her podiatrist's neighbor's son is married to Ryan Talliaferro's sister."

I didn't try to follow the connection. It was sufficient that Vida had nailed the story. "His appointment is no secret if he's speaking at the picnic," I noted.

"He's not speaking in his new capacity," Vida replied. "He's representing the state community-college system. But he's the goods, I assure you."

With any luck, we might announce the new dean in *The Advocate* before the story hit the rest of the media. Feeling slightly mollified, I turned the hot dogs on the grill. When I looked up, Vida was talking to Alicia Wells Lowell.

"Well," Vida cried, "you made quite an impression on Craig Rasmussen the other night! He's not used to seeing such sophisticated young women at Icicle Creek Gas 'N Go."

Alicia, who was wearing a quilted jacket over tailored

navy slacks, gave Vida a modified smile. "Craig Rasmussen? Who is he?"

Vida explained. Alicia was nodding in comprehension when Francine joined us. "I hear Ursula was drunk as a skunk when she fell in the river. What a surprise. Ha-ha."

Vida tapped her chin. "Now, Francine, how did you know that Ursula drank? I never heard any such thing." The idea of such a juicy snippet eluding my House & Home editor clearly unsettled her.

The question clearly unsettled Francine. "What? Well . . . I hear things, from Seattle. I have contacts there. I know someone in the chancery. Oh, trust me, those rich Catholic families try to keep things like that under wraps. They're very protective. But word leaks out all the same." Her tone was defensive.

I was bothered by Francine's assertions. Not that I doubted what she said about wealthy Catholics circling the wagons, but I had to wonder about her omission when she was trashing Ursula the previous Wednesday while I was in her shop. Such an obvious vice as drinking would have been tailor-made for Francine's critical tongue.

Vida was looking thoughtful. "You wouldn't think Warren would marry a woman who drank. Wasn't that the problem with his second wife?"

"Alexis?" Francine made a face. "I don't know. I think it was more of a stepson debacle. The kid was incorrigible."

Roger leaped to mind. I glanced among the picnickers but couldn't see him or the Fairfax boys. Maybe they'd gone into the Old Mill Museum and were playing with sharp instruments. I waited to see what scent Vida would pick up on next. She hadn't gotten very far with Alicia's stop at Gas 'N Go.

Naturally it didn't pay to underestimate Vida. She had put a friendly arm around Alicia and was leading her out of hearing range. "You must tell me all about your visit to Snohomish. Now, which Carlson girl is your old chum . . . ?"

Francine was eyeing me suspiciously. "What's Vida up to now? She's pumping Alicia. Why?"

I gave Francine a helpless look. "Do you think I know why Vida does what she does? Maybe she's trying to figure out what really happened to Ursula." Sometimes the truth serves better than a lie.

"By asking Alicia?" Francine was scornful. "Alicia wouldn't have known Ursula if she fell in her lap."

"Did you know her? Other than from church, I mean."

The barbershop quartet had stepped down, and was replaced by a rock group from Sultan. Either they were very loud, or I was getting rather deaf. I had to ask Francine to repeat her reply.

"Are you nuts?" she shouted, which should have been clear enough to me. "I wouldn't have spit on that bitch if she was on fire!"

A few yards away the three-legged race was being organized. I noticed that Roger and his companions hadn't yet shown up. "I thought Ursula might have come into the shop," I said, raising my own voice above the din.

"Never!" Francine snapped. "I'd have barred the door." As the bass pounded and the guitars thwanged and a young man made noises that sounded like someone was performing surgery without an anesthetic, Francine edged closer. "Look, the woman's dead. I ought to shut up. If she really was killed—though I don't see how—I don't want to be at the top of Dodge's suspect list. If you want to know what Ursula was really like, ask Warren. He knew her better than anyone, at least in Alpine."

"I ought to do that," I mused as the drums crashed and a great shout went up from the younger set, which had made its own mosh pit below the bandstand. "Do you think he'll stay on in Alpine?"

Francine opened her mouth to say something, then shrugged. "I don't know."

Another shout rent the air, but this time it didn't come from the mosh pit. Francine and I both turned to see Nunzio Lucci facing off with Bill Daley. Onlookers, including Vida, Alicia, Della Lucci, and Bill's wife, Kathryn, were moving out of the way, watching in frozen silence.

"So put your mouth where your money is, you SOB!" Luce yelled. "Admit it, you're all talk and no guts!"

Bill Daley was about the last person I'd expect to see in a fistfight. Nearly sixty, with a full paunch and almost no hair, he was a genial man who was respected as a pillar of the community.

"Now, Luce, be reasonable," Bill pleaded as his would-be opponent stomped around on gimpy legs. "I didn't mean any disrespect."

"You called me a bigot!" Luce shouted, revving up his fists. "I ain't no bigot! But where's your racial pride? You want some slope marryin' one of your granddaughters?"

"We don't have any slopes in Alpine," Bill shot back. "Except ski slopes," he added with an impish smile.

If Bill thought to disarm Luce, he was mistaken. "You called me a dago!" Luce cried, moving in on Bill. "Take it back or I'll clean your clock!"

"I did not! I only said that . . . oh, to hell with it!" Bill lunged forward and caught Luce with a haymaker to the midsection. Luce retaliated with two quick blows to Bill's head. The home-furnishings-store owner staggered, then collected himself and butted Luce in the chest. The former logger began raining his fists on Bill's head as the women shrieked and the men began to take sides. The loggers seemed to be rooting for Luce; most of the others rooted for Bill. Nobody seemed inclined to stop the fight.

"Oh, dear!" Vida exclaimed as she and Alicia moved back to where Francine and I were standing transfixed.

"This is no way to hold a Labor Day picnic!" Ever the professional, she began adjusting her camera to capture the brawl on film.

The two men were thrashing about at close range, missing more than hitting. Luce had just put a hammerlock on Bill when Milo entered the fray. "Cut it out!" he ordered, his long face grim. "Now!"

Neither combatant seemed to hear him, which wasn't entirely Bill's fault, because he was turning a peculiar shade of puce. Milo grabbed Luce by the back of the shirt and attempted to break his hold on Bill. He failed—and had to draw his baton, which made contact with Luce's skull, dropping him to the ground like a load of dirty laundry. Bill also collapsed. Della and Kathryn rushed to their respective mates' prone figures, both cursing Milo, though for what I wasn't sure.

And the band played on.

Chapter Twelve

IT WASN'T EXACTLY the most successful Labor Day picnic in Alpine's history, but it might have been one of the more memorable. Nunzio Lucci and Bill Daley were both taken to the hospital emergency room, as were two teenagers who had been stomped in the mosh pit. Vida used up four rolls of film before the day was out.

"Really"—she sighed as we sat at a table situated as far as possible from the bandstand where Fuzzy Baugh was pontificating—"I don't recall a Labor Day quite like this since Dust Bucket Cooper's shorts caught fire and he jumped in the river, forgetting he didn't know how to swim." Vida sighed again.

The rain was coming down hard, but it didn't bother the crowd, which seemed to have been energized by the fight between Luce and Bill Daley. While at least half the spectators paid desultory attention to the mayor's speech making, the rest appeared in a frolicsome mood. Around the fringes, there was much laughter, exuberant conversation, and diminishing half racks of domestic beer.

"I wonder what really set Luce off," I mused.

Vida, who was sipping a paper cup filled with plain water, shrugged. "It wouldn't take much," she said. "Luce is touchy."

"I hope it didn't have anything to do with St. Mildred's," I said, stepping aside as a Frisbee sailed past me. "Luce told me that he thinks Bill is something of a fair-weather

school-board member. He votes not for what's right, but
what's popular."

Vida seemed temporarily disinterested in the school-
board controversy. "Alicia Wells—Alicia Lowell, I should
say—is very much of a clam. It was difficult getting anything out of her—except for one slip on her part."

"Which was?" I tried to ignore Fuzzy's honey-and-
grits platitudes, even though the loudspeaker seemed
beamed in my direction.

"She's seen her father." Vida gave me one of her smug
little smiles. "I mentioned that Ursula's death seemed to
have aged Warren overnight—not that I actually thought
so, of course. Or, I suggested—just doing a bit of
fishing—was he ill? Alicia acted shocked, then said she
thought he looked all right, considering. But she added—
far too quickly—that she'd only seen him at a distance,
on the street. She was lying, though I don't believe she
realized I saw through her."

"So maybe they've patched up their long-standing
quarrel?" I suggested, noting the approach of Greer and
Grant Fairfax.

"Estrangement is more like it," Vida said, wincing as
Fuzzy went into one of his tried-and-true anecdotes about
arriving in Alpine forty years ago, fresh out of Baton
Rouge. "I really couldn't say. Alicia doesn't strike me as
the type who takes things lightly. Certainly her mother
doesn't. The question is not only *why* she saw him, but
where. Was it an accidental meeting? Or was it—"

The Fairfaxes looked upset as they descended on Vida.
"Where are our boys?" Greer demanded. "Have you seen
them in the last two hours?"

Vida's eyebrows raised above the tortoiseshell frames
of her glasses. "Why, no. They were with Roger. . . . Oh,
dear!" Now she, too, looked alarmed as her head
swiveled in every direction. "Where *did* they go?"

"We checked the riverbank," Grant said, tight-lipped. "Greer even walked over to the mall. Is Roger responsible?"

Vida drew back as if struck. "Of course! He's the soul of maturity!"

I felt like snickering, but didn't. In my opinion, Roger was as responsible as a rabbit in heat. And about as bright. But neither Vida nor the Fairfaxes were amused. As a mother, I didn't blame them. The fear of misplacing a child is always with parents. I still vividly recalled the occasion on which I'd lost Adam at Lloyd Center in Portland. He was six at the time, and I'd been caught up in Nordstrom's annual sale. After I'd notified security and contemplated a nervous collapse, we'd finally found him hiding under a table display for the Trail Blazers. My son had thought it was a big joke. I thought he was awful, but was too relieved to say so.

"Then," Greer said in the grimmest of tones, "where would your mature grandson have taken Byron and Lionel?"

Shoving her yellow rain hat higher on her forehead, Vida considered. "Youngsters love to fool adults. Perhaps they're sneaking about, hoping to dupe us." It was a viable theory, but my House & Home editor sounded uncertain.

Greer, however, shook her head. "We've looked everywhere. We separated, just to trick them if that's what they had in mind." Noting Vida's uncharacteristically helpless look, Greer turned to her husband. "We're going to notify the sheriff. Has anyone seen that big lummox?"

I bristled. "Milo has had his hands full this afternoon. He doesn't need to be bothered by parents who can't keep track of their own children."

The Fairfaxes and Vida all turned on me. "And grandparents, I assume?" Vida snapped.

"Now, hold on. . . ." I protested.

Greer waved a finger in my face. "*I'm* going to bother that moron! If he doesn't find our boys in the next thirty minutes, I'll have his badge! The next time Dodge runs for election, I'll see he's run out of office!"

Vida was already moving off in her splayfooted manner, apparently in search of Milo. Checking my watch, I noted that it was going on five. The speeches were winding down, with only our state representative, Bob Gunderson, and high-school football coach Rip Ridley left on the program.

Greer was still denouncing Milo, but I chose to ignore her. Grant, however, attempted to soothe his wife. She brushed him off as if he were a gnat. I let my eyes roam around the park and, in my imagination, cover a much larger area. There were dozens of places that might intrigue a trio of young boys. Alpine's woods were seductive, as was the river, the creeks, even the old buildings that lined the railroad tracks.

Five minutes later Vida reappeared with her nephew Bill Blatt. Bill was already looking harassed, and his aunt was chewing his ear off. Greer and Grant Fairfax eyed the young deputy as if he were some subhuman species.

"Where's Dodge?" Greer demanded, fists on hips. Despite her diminutive size, she almost seemed a match for Vida.

Bill looked apologetic. "There's been a bad accident just below the summit, possible fatalities. Sheriff Dodge went to check it out. My—Ms. Runkel has brought me up to speed about the boys."

Sure enough, the sound of sirens could be heard coming from the vicinity of the hospital. A moment later an ambulance raced down Alpine Way. Greer frowned as her eyes followed the emergency vehicle. I knew what she was thinking: will that be needed for the boys?

Bill—or Vida—seemed to have matters in hand, however. "My nephew is contacting the county Search and Rescue unit," she announced. "Several of the volunteers are already here."

Off the top of my head, I counted Coach Ridley,

Clancy Barton, Verb Vancich, and Garth Wesley, the resident pharmacist. Even as Bill Blatt got on his cell phone, Rip Ridley climbed to the bandstand and started talking about the high school's upcoming football season. Apparently his beeper went off before he finished assessing the linebacker situation: With a call to "Cut 'em up, you Buckers!" he signaled for the band to play the Alpine fight song.

Keeping one eye on Bill and the assembling members of the Search and Rescue team, Vida now steered me away from the Fairfaxes. "This is probably very silly," she murmured, "but it doesn't hurt to be cautious. I'm sure those Fairfax boys have led Roger into some harmless mischief."

I held my tongue. Before Vida could speak again, Monica Vancich approached with her two children trailing behind her. "Did I hear that Greer's boys are missing?" she inquired in an anxious voice.

"Not missing," Vida retorted. "Disappeared. With my grandson." Her steely glare reproached Monica for omitting Roger.

"I don't think I know your grandson," Monica said, looking vaguely apologetic. "Is he . . . um . . . a *sturdy* boy?"

Vida started to bristle, then regarded Monica with her full attention. "Roger is a husky lad, yes. Why do you ask?"

As ever, Monica seemed nervous. "Well . . . I saw the Fairfax boys and someone who might have been your grandson get into a car about an hour ago. It was after Verb and I had left the picnic table, so I didn't know anything about Byron and Lionel being missing until just now. I thought that they were getting a ride home with somebody they knew."

Vida looked as if she could pounce on Monica and swallow her whole. "A car? What kind of car? Who was driving? Which way were they headed?"

Monica gulped. "I told Verb, so he and the other Search and Rescue members will know what to look for. It was an older car, maroon—I don't know what kind. I didn't see who was driving, but I think it was a young person. A boy, maybe, with long hair." Monica was speaking faster now, obviously intimidated by Vida.

"Maroon," Vida said. "Old. Young driver. Hmm." She squinted through the rain and tapped one foot.

"You mustn't worry," Monica interjected. "The Good Lord will take care of them. We must learn to trust, not only Him, but each other."

"Oh, bilge!" Vida exclaimed, now stamping her foot. "Don't talk nonsense! Try to think instead what *kind* of car it was!"

Monica looked as if she didn't know whether to cower or be affronted. "But I told you I don't—"

"Laura O'Toole," I said suddenly. "Laura has a maroon Plymouth Fury."

Vida's head whipped around as if it were on a string. "Where's Laura? Is she here?"

I shook my head. "I haven't seen her since she was at my house."

"Ah!" Vida spun away, apparently searching for her nephew.

The conclusion of the Alpine fight song had signaled the official end of the picnic. Though the rain had let up a bit, the banners sagged and the bunting drooped. The high-school band was loading instruments onto the tired yellow team bus. About half the remaining crowd began to gather up their picnic items and head home. The rest lingered in small groups, some talking and laughing, some still eating, and those who apparently had heard about the missing boys were looking concerned.

My inclination was to join the departing picnickers. It had been a long, tiring afternoon. I was wet, if not cold. With only one day to get ready for Wednesday publication, tomorrow promised to be hectic.

But I didn't feel right abandoning Vida. I could see her hat bobbing above a knot of people near the tennis courts. Collecting my basket, I started for the little group. Before I could reach them, Vida marched off in the direction of the parking lot. My guess was that she was going in search of Roger on her own. Maybe it was just as well. I didn't think I could stand listening to her ascribe any more undeserved virtues to the little creep.

On the other hand, I was being mean. It *was* possible that something terrible had happened to Roger and the Fairfax boys. That was the trouble with contemporary life: the worst-case scenario was always feasible. I got into the Jag and tried to spot Vida's Buick. It was just pulling out of the lot, turning left on Park Street.

It seemed likely that Vida was headed for Laura O'Toole's. Now we were on Alpine Way, and I could see Bill Blatt's county car in front of the Buick. He turned on the siren just before making a right onto River Road. My hunch appeared to be correct. But to my surprise, he stopped short of the dilapidated old houses beyond Icicle Creek. We'd arrived at the holding pond by the only working mill in Alpine.

The smokestacks were dormant on this holiday, and the logs floated listlessly in the man-made arm of the river. As I saw Vida and Bill get out of their cars, my heart sank.

"What is it?" I shouted, hurrying across the sawdust-covered ground.

Vida peered out at me from under her hat. "Roger's fascinated with the holding pond. We came down here several times this summer. I thought he might . . ." One gloved hand fell away at her side.

For the moment it appeared that Bill Blatt felt more secure talking to me than to his aunt. "We're getting some dogs," he said. "But I honestly think the kids are just driving around. Aunt Vida tells me that the O'Toole kid does that, even if he hasn't got his license."

"I don't know why you haven't arrested him," Vida declared angrily. "Surely you must recognize him."

Bill gave a helpless shrug. "He hasn't done anything wrong behind the wheel. How do we know he hasn't passed his driving test?"

"You ought to know these things. I do." Vida scoured the pond again, as if she could will Roger to pop out of the murky water.

A search of the area showed no evidence of any trespassers. Certainly there was no sign of the Fury. With a faint sigh of relief, Vida trooped back to her car.

"I'm going to see Laura," she called to Bill. "You keep driving around town. Where are the Search and Rescue people?"

Bill didn't know, though he guessed they were waiting for the dogs. Vida snorted in apparent contempt, then got into the Buick and drove away. I sidled up to Bill Blatt.

"Where would you have gone at Roger's age?" I asked.

Bill, who was in his mid-twenties but looked much younger, scratched one ear. "Walk the railroad trestle. Swing on a rope over Burl Creek. Sneak a smoke under the old loading dock." He gave me a sheepish grin. "It sounds kind of tame now. Kids can get into a lot more trouble these days."

I nodded. "Yes, they can. Are you sure Mike O'Toole's never been collared?"

Bill thought, his earnest face still showing a few freckles under the summer tan. "I think Dwight or somebody gave him a warning for shoplifting at Harvey's. Dustin caught him and some of his buddies drinking beer up on Second Hill. That's about it. We busted his brother, Kenny, for breaking into cars a while back. Shoot, he's only thirteen."

"Betsy said the other O'Tooles had been in quite a bit of trouble," I noted. "But you think not?"

Bill shrugged. "Maybe with the park rangers. There've

been a ton of problems this summer. But you know that from the reports."

I did. Some of the misdeeds that plagued tourists included theft, vandalism, harassment, a couple of assaults, and an attempted rape. The Icicle Creek campground in particular had been a hotbed of wrongdoing. Many of the young offenders were local kids, but some were imported. Almost all had been drinking or doing drugs.

Bill got into his squad car and drove off. Not having been invited to join Vida in her visit to Laura O'Toole, I considered going home. But as I sat tapping the steering wheel and mulling over my options, I saw Buzzy's van ease onto a short spur off the holding-pond road. He pulled up at the west edge of the pond but didn't get out. Perhaps he hadn't noticed my car through the rain. I waited a full minute, then sloshed my way over to the van and called his name.

The rusting door slowly opened. I could glimpse blankets and an air mattress in the rear section. Buzzy's home-away-from-home looked meager and sad.

"Okay, Emma," he began in a tired voice, "if you're going to chew me out for—"

I put up a hand to silence him. "That's over. You already apologized. Just don't do it again. I wanted to ask you a question."

Buzzy's haggard face showed surprise. "You want to come inside? It's raining pretty hard."

I shook my head. "It'll only take a minute. It's for my story on Ursula's death," I said, exaggerating only a bit. "I understand you were at your sister's late Friday afternoon. Did she seem okay to you then?"

The query seemed to puzzle Buzzy. "Well . . . that depends. Yeah, she seemed . . . okay. Sort of in high gear, you could say."

"Like how?" I asked, brushing my wet bangs from my forehead. "As if she were expecting someone?"

"Not that." Buzzy paused, obviously thinking hard. "I mean, maybe she was. But when Ursula drinks . . . *drank*, that is . . . she'd get all revved up. Sort of . . . what do you call it? Hyper, I guess."

"You came to talk to her about a loan, isn't that so?"

Buzzy didn't exactly blush, but his face changed color. "We would have paid her back. When we could." There was a defensive note in his voice.

"I'm sure you would," I said soothingly. "Was she agreeable?"

"Yeah." Buzzy nodded with unexpected vigor. "I think she liked being able to be a big shot like that."

"So you celebrated with a drink or two?" I was on thin ice, but had to ask.

Buzzy, however, shook his head. "Heck, no. If I was going to show up . . . at home, I wouldn't want to have liquor on my breath. Laura was mad enough as it was."

So Buzzy had not been Ursula's drinking partner. "But she never came, right?"

"No." Buzzy let out a big sigh. "Laura got mad at me all over again, as if it were my fault."

My feet were sinking into the muddy dirt spur. "Thanks, Buzzy. Is this . . . where you usually park your van?"

"I don't have a special spot. Yet." His face grew rigid.

I thanked him and trudged back to the Jag. It was depressing to think of Buzzy O'Toole, living inside that old van and searching out a secluded place to rest his head. Going home to my cozy log cabin was very appealing, but I had started out in search of Roger. Recalling the little wretch's sometimes ghoulish personality, I continued down River Road.

Vida's car was parked outside of the O'Toole place. There was no sign of the Fury. I kept going until I reached the spot where Ursula's body had been found.

While the gray clouds still hung low over the mountains, the rain had almost stopped. I pulled up short of where Vida and I had parked on Saturday. I didn't want to spoil any new tire tracks.

To my satisfaction, there was a fresh set in the muddy dirt. Close scrutiny indicated that three of the tires had the same tread; the fourth did not. Cal's spare, I figured, and stood by the side of the road gazing thoughtfully upriver. Roger would have enjoyed seeing the site where Ursula Randall's body had been found. The kid had a morbid streak, though perhaps no more than most of his peers.

However, the Fury was gone now. Nor did I notice any sign of the car having turned around, at least not within a fifty-foot radius. Rather, the tracks reversed just slightly, then veered back onto the road. Given the rainy conditions, it wasn't hard to follow the car's path into the woods.

I lost sight of the river after less than a quarter of a mile. The relatively flat terrain also disappeared as the road began to climb and twist up the face of Mount Sawyer. It was typical, a treacherous corridor that always made me marvel at how those huge rigs navigated the rugged switchbacks, the makeshift bridges, the narrow passages gouged out of the mountains with a thousand-foot drop on the sheer side. Loggers were a different breed, men who embraced danger, for whom a mill whistle was their siren call; the damp woods, their aphrodisiac.

Through the trees, I could see across the valley, though my view of Mount Baldy was obscured by the low-lying clouds. The road became more rugged, with potholes and an occasional rock to dodge. The Jag didn't seem to like the ride. I sensed it would have preferred gliding along the M40 between London and Oxford. Coming out into the open on a hairpin curve, I felt the same way. Here, at the four-thousand-foot level, the second-stand timber had been cut within the last five years. Young alder grew among the logging slash, and a family of jays

chattered noisily in the branches of a Douglas fir that had
been left standing. But after another curve in the road,
wild blackberry vines took over, creeping among the
stumps and rotting logs. I spotted a brown bear nosing
around for food. He moved ponderously between the
logs, indifferent to my passage. If not tame, many of the
wild animals have grown bold as civilization encroaches
upon their habitat. I almost expected to see the bear's
mate and a couple of half-grown cubs.

I didn't expect to see the four motorcycles. Indeed, I
heard them first, a gathering roar like the sound of a
waterfall. They careened around a blind corner, two and
two, forcing me to swerve into the bank. I braked just a
little too late but not too hard. The Jag nestled into the wet
earth, sending a cascade of rocks and mud tumbling onto
the bonnet. The bikers roared on down the mountainside,
heedless of my dilemma.

It was only after the noise had faded and my engine
died that I realized I was shaking. Had I made the wrong
choice, I might have gone straight over the cliff on the
other side of the road. I sat motionless for at least two
minutes, trying to collect myself. A jagged flash of lightning further unnerved me, followed by a rolling clap of
thunder. I waited, trying to calm down, steeling myself
for another burst. Nothing happened, except that the
clouds seemed to encircle me like an eerie pall. I started
the car again and backed slowly out onto the road. A
more confident driver might have risked turning around
on this narrow stretch, but I was too upset to try. With
the rocks rolling off the bonnet, I crept along through
the gathering mists, still climbing, still winding, still
bumping over potholes. At last I found a spot that was
wide enough to turn the Jag in the opposite direction. My
personal and professional curiosity had been stifled.
Whatever lay ahead on this hazardous logging road
wasn't worth jeopardizing my life—or my Jag. For all I
knew, a swarm of bikers might be camped among the

crags of Mount Sawyer. My eyes darted between the road ahead and the rearview mirror. I didn't need any more surprises coming up behind me. Briefly I thought about the Colt .45. But I doubted that it would have done me any good had I brought it along. If the bikers were armed, they would have been much quicker on the draw.

It began to rain again as I made the descent, and I realized that somewhere after the first quarter mile, I had lost sight of the Fury's tire treads. In the parts of the road that were heavily sheltered by trees, the ground hadn't turned completely soft. If Roger and company had gone all the way up the road, they might still be there. With the bikers. I hardly knew who to root for.

I breathed a sigh of relief when I reached the pavement shortly before the turnoff to Ed and Shirley Bronsky's construction site. A minute later I was passing Laura and Buzzy O'Toole's house. Vida's Buick was gone. Wondering if she had driven to the sheriff's office, I headed for Front Street. There was no sign of her, but Milo was just getting out of his patrol car. He saw me and waited on the sidewalk.

"What a weekend!" he exclaimed, removing his regulation hat and tugging at his graying sandy hair. "The emergency room's so busy, Flake had to call for backup from Monroe."

"I don't think doctors call it backup," I said with a sympathetic smile. "Are you still on duty?"

Milo had put his hat back on, which was a good thing because another flash of lightning and clap of thunder heralded a real downpour. "Let's get inside," the sheriff said, grabbing my arm. "Maybe this rain'll cool everybody down."

Toni Andreas, the department's receptionist, and Deputy Jack Mullins were behind the big curving desk in the outer office. Toni nodded and smiled in her vague, pretty way, and Jack grinned impishly.

"What did you do for fun on Labor Day when you

lived in Portland?" Jack asked me. "Go out to the skating rink at Lloyd Center and watch people fall down? I'll bet it was pretty tame compared to Alpine."

I merely shook my head as Milo led me into his private office. He hadn't directly answered my question about still being on duty, but since we were in his place of work instead of the bar at the Venison Inn, I figured it out for myself.

"Really ugly accident up near the summit," he said, shaking rain off his hat. "Four cars, nine injured, two may not make it. Jeez, I wish people would smarten up when they drive on a three-day weekend. In fact, I wish the dumb bastards would all stay home."

Briefly I commiserated with the sheriff. Then I went over to the wall map of Skykomish County, where I found the logging track that took off from River Road. "Milo," I said as my finger traced the zigzagging red line, "what's at the end of this?"

"See for yourself," he replied. "It peters out near the start of Deception Creek."

"I don't mean the topography." I tapped the map with my index finger. "I'm talking about . . . well, I'm not sure. Have you found Roger and the Fairfax boys yet?"

Milo waved an impatient hand. "They've been spotted at least five times, cruising around with Mike O'Toole. The last sighting was by his mother. They shot past Laura O'Toole about an hour ago, doing sixty-five. I'm going to bust Mike's butt real good."

I was still at the map. "I think they might be up here. I followed their tracks to the place on the river where Ursula's body was found. They took off from there, up the dirt road. I ran into some bikers."

"Bikers?" Milo's hazel eyes showed a spark of interest. "How many?"

"Four. They were coming down Mount Sawyer. Lots of leather, a ton of studs, fringe all over the place. They ran me off the road." Suddenly I sounded sulky.

"Jeez! Are you okay?" Milo was leaning on the desk, eyeing me with concern.

"Do I seem okay?" Now I was surly.

"Bikers." Milo stroked his long chin. "I wonder . . ."

"What?"

The sheriff didn't answer immediately, then he shook himself. "Nothing, maybe. But we've wondered . . . you know, about all the vandalism and assaults. Several witnesses described perps who didn't sound like they belonged around here."

"Did they sound like bikers?" I asked, finally sitting down in one of Milo's visitors' chairs. More thunder rolled, and the lights flickered briefly.

"A couple did. But you know how witnesses overreact. If some guy's wearing a leather jacket, he's automatically a biker. Anybody who has a hog is a bad guy as far as the loggers are concerned. They hate bikers almost as much as they hate the environmentalists."

The logger-biker feud was long-standing in timber towns. Over the years the Icicle Creek Tavern in particular had been the site of some violent clashes. I had grown silent for a few moments, but finally offered the opinion that Milo or his deputies ought to go up the Mount Sawyer road and see if Roger and his newfound friends were there.

"Before it gets dark," I added somewhat hastily. I didn't want Milo to think I was telling him how to do his job. Occasionally he returned the favor, and it infuriated me.

Milo started to shake his head, then checked his scanner. An apparent calm had settled in over Alpine, along with the clouds descending through the trees and onto the rooftops. "I could send the Search and Rescue guys," he said. "They could bring Bill Blatt with them, in case they need a sidearm."

It appeared that Milo had taken me seriously.

"Where's Vida?" I asked, knowing that she wasn't sitting around twiddling her thumbs.

Milo's tan grew even deeper. "She's . . . ah . . . well . . . she insisted on joining the Search and Rescue team. Actually she's with her nephew Bill. She left her car out back, on Railroad Avenue."

I tried not to smile. "Isn't it illegal for a civilian to go with a deputy?"

Milo's skin grew ever darker. "Bill asked her to sign a waiver."

"I'm surprised he had the nerve," I said. "Did she do it?"

"I don't know." Milo leaned back in his chair, arms behind his head. "I don't want to know."

Again, I grew silent. The clock on Milo's wall told me it was going on seven. "If you go off duty in the next hour, do you want to eat some dinner at the Venison Inn?"

Milo stretched and yawned. "Sure. But I won't leave until those damned kids are rounded up. Vida'd kill me if I did."

"Understood. I'm going home now and change. I'll call you between seven-thirty and eight."

Milo nodded. I left, bidding farewell to Toni and Jack on my way out through the front office. It appeared that Toni was also leaving, slipping into her jacket and wrapping a scarf over her short black curly hair. I considered waiting to accompany her outside, but she took her time. Toni is a very deliberate sort of person. Some, such as Adam, who once dated her, might say *slow*—but the sheriff wouldn't have hired her if she couldn't do the job.

I'd barely gotten through the door when the maroon Fury pulled in next to my Jag. To my amazement, Vida exited from the driver's side. Peering through the rain, I could see a trio of heads in the backseat. Before I could say a word, Bill Blatt's squad car also came to a stop. He, too, had a passenger. I guessed it to be Mike O'Toole.

"I'm going to get my car and take Roger home," Vida declared in an angry voice. "Milo can do what he likes with those odious Fairfax children. If I were him, I'd put them in juvenile hall."

Bill Blatt was escorting Mike O'Toole. I recognized the teenager now, a medium-sized kid with long brown hair that fell over much of his nondescript face. His attempt at a swagger was shattered by a bolt of lightning that startled all of us. The crash of thunder followed at once, indicating that the storm was directly over Alpine.

"Excuse me," Bill said apologetically, steering Mike through the door.

I had stepped aside and started after Vida. Roger and the Fairfax boys remained in the Fury's backseat. "Where were they?" I shouted as more thunder and lightning hit.

"On Mount Sawyer." Vida kept tromping straight down Third Street, impervious to the pelting rain. "Roger's soaked. I'm bringing the car around so that he doesn't get any wetter. I'm afraid the little fellow is going to take a chill."

If I had thought Vida's anger had been partially reserved for her grandson, I was wrong. Apparently all her ire was directed at Roger's companions. I caught up with her while she opened the Buick's door. Our eyes met across the top of the car.

"Get in," she commanded. "I've something to tell you. I can do it while I drive around to Front Street."

I obeyed, as I always did, despite the fact that I was the employer, Vida, the employee. Our situations often seemed reversed. Vida sat behind the wheel, removed her hat, and ran her fingers through her unruly gray curls. Then she yanked off her glasses and rubbed furiously at her eyes.

"Ooooh! It's a good thing I called on Laura O'Toole. She'd seen those boys headed up that logging road and hadn't done a thing to stop them. That's the trouble with parents nowadays—they're afraid to discipline their children."

It was hardly the moment to point out that Roger needed as much discipline as any Fairfax or O'Toole. Nor would Vida have believed me if I'd said so. "But you didn't go after them directly," I noted. If she had, I would have passed her on the road.

"No." Vida shook her head, the curls hopping around her face. "I went back to get Billy and have him alert the Search and Rescue team. The Fairfaxes are with them. They should be back by now, too. Such a pair! Grant's a meek, spineless sort, and Greer's unbearably opinionated, especially about modern child rearing. No wonder their children are so hopeless."

Having put her glasses and hat back on, Vida started the car. "So what did you want to tell me?" I inquired.

"Oh!" For once, Vida seemed to have lost track of her thought processes. "Two things, which Billy is reporting to Milo even as we speak. I hope. First, that area up at the end of the logging road is nothing more than a party place for all sorts of disreputable creatures, many of them teenagers."

My guess appeared to be on track. "And some of them bikers?"

Vida hesitated, braking for the arterial onto Front Street. "Perhaps. The crew I saw was mostly made up of fifteen-to-twenty-year-olds. Liquor. Drugs. Heaven only knows what else. Milo must clean them out. It's a catastrophe. No wonder we've had so much crime this summer!"

"Did you recognize them as locals?"

"Generally, no." Vida frowned at the slashing windshield wipers. "Maybe four or five, out of twenty. One of them was a Lucci. Another was a Gustavson." Vida's mouth turned down. The Gustavsons were somehow related to her, as were so many of Alpine's residents.

"Mike O'Toole must have known about it," I mused.

"It's a wonder nobody's found out about the place until now."

There were no empty parking places near the Fury, so Vida stopped in the middle of Front Street. "They've probably had lookouts posted along the road. I'm quite sure that some of the hikers who've had difficulties encountered them in that area. But of course Milo had no specific reason to search there. Until now."

Vehicles were beginning to line up behind Vida. Someone honked. Vida scowled. "If you move your Jaguar, I can pull in next to that dreadful O'Toole car. I hope they throw the book at Mike. Such an instigator! Showing off, of course."

I opened the passenger door, then tried to ignore another blast on somebody's horn. "Two, Vida. You said two things. What was the other?"

Vida's mouth set in a tight line. "While I was chasing . . . ah . . . encouraging Roger to come along with Grams, I stumbled upon something rather interesting." Her gray eyes gleamed behind the big glasses. "A satin shoe, a sling-back wedgie. Doesn't that beat all?"

The horns kept honking. But I was oblivious to the cacophony as I got out of the Buick. Ursula's shoe. Halfway up Mount Sawyer. In a teenage party place. What did it mean?

Maybe nothing. Maybe everything.

I got into my Jag just as a large man got out of the car behind Vida and began shouting at her. Vida rolled down her window and told him to go get the sheriff. She waved a gloved hand in the direction of Milo's headquarters. As I drove away I noticed that the man's car had Montana plates. He didn't know Vida. He also didn't know what he was in for. But he must have guessed. The man from Montana was in retreat when I saw the last of him in my rearview mirror.

Chapter Thirteen

THAT NIGHT, AS the storm passed over Alpine and headed west into the Puget Sound basin, I ate dinner alone at home. Milo had phoned me not long after I got in the house. He said he and his deputies had requested some state troopers and were heading up Mount Sawyer. I called Carla, who had returned from Seattle only a few minutes earlier. She expressed mild excitement over taking pictures of possible criminals.

"Just remember, if they're under eighteen, we can't show them," I cautioned my reporter. "Vida says some are older, and I saw four bikers coming down the mountain today. They had to be legal and then some."

"Bikers make good pictures," Carla remarked. The visual side of journalism always intrigues her far more than the written word. And with good reason—she is a much better photographer than she is a writer. "Hey—where's Marilynn? Was she at the picnic?"

I kept my Labor Day account brief. "The emergency room got hectic. I'm sure your roommate was pulled in for extra duty. Say," I added almost as an afterthought, "do you know a guy from Seattle named Murray Felton?"

Carla hesitated. "I don't think so. Should I?"

"Not necessarily. But he knows you. He's a TV reporter who was nosing around town about Ursula Randall's drowning."

224

"Who's Ursula Randall?" Carla sounded characteristically bewildered.

I'd forgotten that Carla had left town before the tragedy. Again, I tried to keep my recap short. "It's going to be a tricky story," I pointed out. "It may have been an accident, it may not."

"Gee," Carla said in a downcast tone, "you had some excitement around here for once. All I did was go to Bumbershoot. There were some good bands, though."

I felt a brief pang for city life. The only time I'd attended the Labor Day festival at the Seattle Center was six years ago, when Adam and I had gone together. He, too, had enjoyed the bands. I'd settled for a couple of literary readings and great quantities of Vietnamese food.

At seven thirty-five I was about to check back with Milo when the phone rang in my hand. It was Ed Bronsky, sounding as gloomy as in days of advertising yore.

"I'm delivering used clothes at the battered women's shelter," Ed announced, his voice low as well as sepulchral. "Holiday or not, Monday's my usual volunteer day to fetch and carry." A note of martyrdom also crept into his tone. Or maybe it was virtue. "Della Lucci's here. What do we do about *that*?"

Puzzled, I blinked at the receiver. "What do you mean? Is Della helping out on the wrong day?"

"No!" Ed barked the word, then again lowered his voice. "She checked in. Luce came home from the hospital and threatened to kill her."

"Jeez!" I cried. "What's going on in this town? Everybody seems to have gone nuts at once."

"I know," Ed replied, very subdued. "It's like somebody pulled a cork out of a bottle." He paused, and I heard him take in a quick little breath. "Say! That's not bad! I should have used a phrase like that in the book. Maybe I can add it when I do the revisions—if there are any, of course."

The last thing I wanted was to get Ed sidetracked, especially about his autobiography. "Did Luce beat Della? Or just threaten her? How come they released him from the hospital so soon?"

"They release everybody too soon these days," Ed said, reverting to gloom. "Last spring, when my back went out, they wouldn't let me stay—"

"What did you mean about us doing . . . whatever?" I interrupted. I recalled Ed's back problem, which had been caused by his attempt to dance with a thirty-pound ham. "About Della, was it?"

Another short intake of breath, then a whisper. "I'll be right over. Debra Barton can cover for me." Before I could say a word, Ed clicked off.

Wanting to inform Milo of Ed's imminent arrival and thus avoid a potentially awkward situation, I dialed the sheriff's number. He was out, apparently still up on Mount Sawyer. The thought of Milo facing a bunch of irate bikers and juiced teenagers made me uneasy. Of course the sheriff laid his life on the line every day. It was part of the job description, even in a rural area like Skykomish County. We had been friends for a long time; since becoming lovers, my apprehension level for him had increased.

Five minutes later Ed came puffing into my living room. "I don't suppose you have a spare sandwich? I haven't eaten since three o'clock."

That probably meant five or six, but I used the rest of the tuna to meet Ed's request. He also accepted a bottle of beer. "It's like this," he began, sitting at my kitchen table. "Luce didn't hit Della, as far as I know. But he made really scary threats, so she left and brought two of the kids with her. Now, here's the problem—Luce is on the parish council, and when word gets out that his wife is in the shelter, how's that going to look for us at St. Mildred's? Haven't we had enough bad press already?"

My initial reaction was that we weren't image makers.

But I felt a need to help Father Den. "It's not a news story," I hedged. "We never run names of people who go to the shelter. You know that."

Ed waved a beefy hand. "Sure, sure. But you know how people talk. The vote will be announced tomorrow on the school-board election. Everybody in town is watching St. Mildred's. I say we impeach Luce."

I gave a little start. "Is that legal?"

Ed grew indignant. "It's got to be. If you can impeach the president of the United States, you should be able to impeach some creep on the parish council."

"You'd have to check the bylaws and talk to Father Den and—"

"Den's not here. We've got to move fast. I say we call a meeting tonight. We can hold it at our house, unless Monica Vancich will let us into the rectory. She's got a key."

"Hold it, Ed," I cautioned. "You can't act without the pastor. The parish council is a consultative body, remember? And you're not on it."

"I should be," Ed said, very serious despite the hunk of tuna plastered to his chin. "I could let them appoint me to Luce's place."

"Ed . . ."

"You'll cover the story, right?" He took a big gulp of beer; the tuna fell in his lap; Ed didn't notice. "Think you could get some decent pictures?"

Ed knew I wasn't any great shakes as a photographer. "I could—no, Ed," I interrupted myself, "this is a terrible idea. If you call this maverick meeting—and you've no authority to do so—you'll have the chancery all over you. Father Den will be angry. So will half the parish."

Ed finished his sandwich, took a last swig of beer, and stood up. "No, my mind's made up. I'm calling Jake right now. Mind if I use your phone?"

I threw up my hands. "Go ahead. Jake's going to tell

you the same thing I'm trying to get through your . . . head."

But Jake succumbed to Ed's badgering. I had forgotten how my former ad manager could—upon rare occasion—steamroll over prospective advertisers. The parish-council president would try to get the other four members rounded up by nine o'clock. If Luce had any idea what was going on, he might refuse to show, Jake cautioned. On the other hand, they didn't dare leave him out.

Ed was looking very smug as he hitched up his pants. "I have clout, see," he declared. "I've been a Eucharistic minister for five years, I give a ton of money, I volunteer all the time. Father Den couldn't get along without me. I might as well be the associate pastor—if we had one. There's only one thing," he added, a touch of gloom returning.

"What?" I inquired, feeling helpless in the face of Ed's dogged determination to undermine our church. Or so I viewed his backhanded, illegal, and just plain stupid attempt at a parish coup.

Ed gave a shake of his head. "This should go in the last chapter of the book. Do you suppose I ought to write an epilogue?"

To my amazement, all five members of the parish council were assembled in the rectory parlor by nine o'clock. Ed and I were the only outsiders. I still hadn't heard from Milo, which increased my apprehension level.

At least Jake didn't try to impress us with big words. Apparently we were too small a group. The setting was informal, with everyone seated on an eclectic collection of chairs and the aging, sagging sofa. Jake tried to give himself an aura of officialdom by pulling a side chair into the middle of the room and using a chipped and scratched mahogany coffee table as his forum.

True to my observer's calling, I kept to the back of the

room, standing next to an old-fashioned Victrola that had been Father Kiernan Fitzgerald's pride and joy. Directly opposite me, Monica Vancich was perched on an old cut-velvet armchair. I gathered it had taken some cajolery on Jake's part to get Monica to let us into the rectory. Even as we stood on the steps and the small porch, the parish secretary and director of religious education had expressed grave doubts as she fiddled with the key. Now her gray eyes darted around the parlor, from tense Jake to wary Luce, to the alert if suspicious Francine Wells, and finally to the guarded countenance of Brendan Shaw.

"We're meeting tonight in emergency session," Jake finally said, then looked over to where I stood with camera in hand. "Emma, I'm not sure this is a public meeting."

"It either is or it isn't," I responded. "You decide."

Apparently fearing ejection, Ed spoke up from the mohair armchair favored by Father Fitz during his long pastoral tenure. "A secret meeting looks bad, Jake. We'd better go public with this baby."

Jake's expression grew pained. "It's not a *secret* meeting, it's *private*. There's a difference."

"No, there's not," Ed countered. "A meeting's either open or closed. What'll it be, Jake? I'm with Emma."

Church politics make strange bedfellows, I mused, and waited for Jake's decision. "Well . . . the results have to be made public, I suppose." Again, he looked at me. "You'll handle this fair and square, right?"

I nodded. Jake smoothed his wavy hair and cleared his throat. "Okay—we're assembled here to consider the matter of one of our members' . . . um . . . conduct. Does anybody know if the bylaws provide for . . . what's the word?" Jake looked vaguely miserable as words, even the wrong ones, failed him.

"Censure," Francine snapped. "Spit it out, Jake." She turned on the sofa to Luce, who was at her left. "You've been tearing up the town today. First you got into a fight

with Bill Daley. Then you sent poor Della to the shelter.
What's wrong with you, Luce? If you ask me, you're
nothing but a damned bully."

Nobody could accuse Francine of not laying it on the
line. Luce, however, didn't roar back as expected. He had
a bandage on his head and another on his forearm. I had
noticed that he'd been limping badly when he arrived at
the rectory.

"Listen up, Francine," he said, more in self-defense
than belligerence. "Daley pissed me off today. He starts
in on how everybody should be one big happy family,
black and white and yellow and red, all intermarryin',
and havin' these butterscotch and hopscotch and whatever kind of kids, and when I told him he was full of it,
he got all huffy. Well, I know that deep down Bill
Daley's prejudiced, too. He made a big deal about askin'
Father Den to play golf with him here in Alpine, but
when Father said somethin' about goin' over to Everett
to play, Bill had about ten excuses. Now, whaddaya think
of that?"

"I think," Francine said archly, "that you still haven't
explained why you tried to punch out Bill Daley."

"Awww!" Luce threw his hands up in the air. "You
don't listen, Francine! You're just like Della, always
hearin' what you wanna hear and nothin' else!"

"Let's stick to the issue, folks." Brendan Shaw smiled
ingratiatingly and made a steeple of his fingers. "I think
what we're trying to determine is if a parish-council
member's conduct is reason for dismissal. Do we have
any rational discussion?"

Monica raised a tentative hand. "I think we should
try to understand Mr. Lucci's reasons for being upset.
It's not right for us to be judgmental without knowing the
circumstances."

Luce didn't seem grateful for Monica's qualified support. "I told you, Bill Daley pissed me off—"

"Stick it, Luce!" Francine broke in. "I'm voting

against you, so you can save the bullshit for your court date when Bill sues your butt off."

"Sues *me*!" Luce roared. "I'd like to see that chickenshit try it! I've sued bigger fish than him!" He rounded on Brendan Shaw. "I shoulda sued you, too, you cheap weasel! Tryin' to screw me out of my workmen's comp!" Next he glared at Jake. "And you, O'Toole—when was the last time you gave me credit at your freakin' store? Cash on the barrelhead, that's all you know! Some Christian!" Staggering slightly, Luce got to his feet. "You bastards won't can me! I don't want to have anything to do with any of you two-faced pansies! I quit!" Luce limped out of the parlor.

"Oh, dear!" Monica gasped.

"Good riddance." Francine sneered.

"I volunteer to fill the vacancy," said Ed.

Jake stared at Ed. "Ah . . . is that legal?"

"I'm not sure," Monica said.

"I'm confused," Jake admitted. "Maybe we should wait until Father Den gets back."

"We can't do that," Ed declared. "We're already in a mess with this school-board deal. How can we operate while we're short a parish-council member? I say, strike while the iron is hot."

"Strike *what*?" Francine demanded. "Come off it, Bronsky. You're on a power trip."

"Ed has a point, though," Jake began.

"On his head," Francine snapped, and glared at Ed, who glared back. "Father Den will be here in a couple of days. What can happen between now and then?"

Brendan was fingering his fleshy chin. "Something sure happened to Ursula Randall between the time she announced her candidacy and the actual election. Maybe we shouldn't take any more chances."

Jake darted a look at Ed, then at Brendan. "Ed's just trying to do us a favor." Now he dared to meet Francine's dagger-eyed gaze. "I mean, it's not like this is Congress, or something."

"Go ahead," Francine said with ill grace. "It's late. I'm tired. If we could impeach Luce, we can always impeach Ed."

Ed started to bluster, but Jake had risen to shake his hand. Brendan joined them, all three men standing in the middle of the room. I hurriedly shot a few obligatory pictures.

Monica had hung back, her pale face increasingly troubled. "Did Mr. Lucci really try to kill his wife?"

"I doubt it," Francine said, gathering up her Sharif handbag and London Fog raincoat. "Della's got no spunk. Luce is the kind that if you call his bluff, he'll roll over. He's different from Buzzy."

An awkward silence engulfed the little parlor. "What do you mean?" Jake asked.

A flush rose in Francine's fine skin. "I heard about the little episode at Emma's today. Betsy called me. I guess Laura told her."

"Damn!" Jake held his head.

"Don't get worked up, Jake," Francine counseled. "That's what I mean about Buzzy—he got out of control because he's like a cornered animal. His back's against the wall, and he lashes out. But he's really harmless. That's not true of Luce. He can be mean—in the way that bullies are." Slipping into her coat, she poked Ed in the paunch. "You win, Bronsky. Welcome aboard. Enjoy the ride—while it lasts."

Monica burst into tears. I happened to be standing next to her, and automatically put out a comforting hand. "What's wrong?" I asked as Ed stared and the rest of the group looked only mildly surprised. I suspected that it wasn't unusual for Monica to lose the grip on her emotions.

"It's . . . nothing." Monica sniffed as she wiped at her eyes with the sleeve of what appeared to be a handmade cardigan. "It's just that . . . I can empathize . . . with

Buzzy. I mean . . ." She sniffed again, trying to get herself under control. "What we need is more understanding. That comes from the Holy Spirit. Why can't people realize that?"

The garbled response seemed to bewilder all of us except Francine. "Get a grip on it, Monica," she urged quietly, though her sympathy had a hard edge. "It's fine to let the Holy Spirit sail around over your head, but keep both feet on the ground, okay?"

Monica's swimming gray eyes hovered on Francine's face. "Will you come with me?"

Francine took an abrupt backward step. "Come where?"

Monica swallowed. "To Mrs. Patricelli's. I want to pray at her vision."

"Oh, hell!" Francine twirled around, colliding with Brendan Shaw. "No, Monica, I won't. That vase isn't the only thing that's cracked around here. I'm going home. Good night." Francine's Chantal high-heeled boots carried her quickly across the faded carpet.

Though she didn't say a word to me, I saw the appeal in Monica's teary eyes. "I'll go," I said, surprising myself and probably Monica as well.

It turned out that she had gotten a ride to the rectory from Brendan Shaw. Since I had discovered that the Vanciches lived so close to me, I insisted that it would be no trouble to drive Monica to Polly's house and then take her home.

We had gone only one of the two blocks between St. Mildred's and the Patricelli residence when I realized that there was nowhere to park on the street. As I slowed in front of Polly's I saw why. There were at least two dozen people threading their way up the broken front steps that led through the rockery. Some of them carried candles, which flickered and sputtered in the rainy night.

"Oh, my!" I breathed. "Polly's drawn a crowd. I suppose it was the TV exposure."

"Pardon?" Monica seemed puzzled.

"One of the Seattle stations featured the vase on the news last night," I explained, preoccupied with trying to find a parking place. "Damn! I wonder if this has been going on all day?" The thought of missing another story annoyed me.

"Wonderful," Monica murmured, her hands clasped together. "The Spirit *is* moving. How dare I doubt?"

I dared to ease the Jag into a tight spot around the corner on Fourth. At least I had the camera with me. Hopefully the flash would work. It had functioned in the rectory parlor, but sometimes it was unreliable.

"It's like a pilgrimage," Monica said in an awed voice, not moving from the passenger seat. "Like Lourdes. Or Medjugorje."

"I've seen the vase," I said, wrestling with the camera and my handbag. "You go ahead and do your thing. I'll stay outside, take some pictures, and interview people."

Monica didn't seem to hear me. Wearing a beatific smile, she slowly got out of the car and walked off as if in a daze. Clutching my things, I hurried after her. I had my own vision, of Monica stepping in front of an oncoming car.

But she made it safely across the street. A moment later she was at the end of the line, which now stretched onto the sidewalk. I searched through the rain for a face I recognized, but found only one: Buzzy O'Toole.

Apologizing for pushing my way up the uneven stairs, I greeted Buzzy with what a few dark looks told me was inappropriate enthusiasm. Buzzy, however, made a brave effort to smile.

"This is for *The Advocate*," I warned him, fumbling with a notebook. "What made you decide to visit the vase?"

The smile disappeared quickly. "My sister. I want to pray for her soul."

"Ursula?" I said stupidly. "Of course." Given Buzzy's

other troubles, it struck me as very generous that he was thinking of someone other than himself.

Buzzy nodded faintly. "Yeah. I think Ursula needs some prayers. She wasn't always ..." He stopped, staring at the notebook. "Sorry. I forgot you were taking this down."

"It's okay," I assured him. "I won't mention anything personal."

The line moved up as three people edged past me on their way out. The too-thin woman behind Buzzy was a stranger. Introducing myself, I asked why she had come to the Patricelli shrine. Cancer, she replied through taut lips. The ascetic-looking young man in front of Buzzy had AIDS. A couple from Everett were praying for their daughter who was in prison. Another set of parents wanted to ask Jesus to help them find their son who had disappeared three years ago. The litany of human burdens went on, all the way to Polly's front door.

Buzzy was now at the bottom of the porch. After clicking a few pictures, I tried to spot Monica. She was about where I had first encountered Buzzy. I decided to slip inside the house and ask Polly some questions about the phenomenon. Announcing "Press" in a discreet voice, I entered the dark hallway. The living room was jammed. Muffled sobs reached my ears, as did the muttering of a few prayers. I refocused the camera, but thought better of it. This wasn't the place for flashbulbs.

Polly was standing by the arched entrance to the living room. Her eyes were downcast and she was fingering her rosary. I waited, but she didn't look up. At last I put a gentle hand on her arm.

"When did all these people start coming?" I inquired in a hushed voice.

Polly's cloudy old eyes scanned my face. "Oh. Mrs. Lord." She sighed. "This morning, after Mass. They were waiting when I came home." She signed herself with the silver crucifix, then kissed Christ's broken body.

Again, I glanced into the living room, where long, wavering shadows trembled against the walls. In the crush of worshipers, I could barely see the votive candles. An old couple, weeping and clinging to each other, came out into the hall. A Vietnamese woman in her thirties carrying a baby moved into the room. So did a Hispanic man who held a holy card of Our Lady of Guadalupe.

"They've been coming all day?" I asked Polly.

"Yes. Pete will be here soon so that I may go to bed."

I stared at Polly. "You mean—you'll let them in until they stop showing up?"

Polly's gaze was uncomprehending. "What?"

"I mean . . ." I fumbled for words.

Polly's bowed shoulders shrugged. "It's not a store."

I pressed my knuckles against my lips. An ancient African American woman supported by a tall, graying middle-aged man who might have been her son, came out into the hall. "No. Of course it's not."

A silence fell between us, deep as the gap that divides generations, wide as the chasm that separates cultures. The ebb and flow continued. Buzzy, with a brief nod to Polly and me, now entered the living room. I wondered about Ursula, with her smug, self-centered sense of religion. Where was she now? Would Buzzy's loving intentions move her? Would she laugh? But I had no idea of how the dead responded to the living, or if they responded at all. I wasn't even sure of what was going on in Polly Patricelli's living room.

"Ma." It was Pete, a man I knew primarily as an advertiser for Itsa Bitsa Pizza. He leaned down to peck at his mother's cheek. "You're drawing quite a crowd, huh?" His gap-toothed grin took me in. "Hi, Emma. What do you think? A little stand down on the sidewalk, hawking rosaries and statues and prayer cards?"

I didn't know if Pete was serious. But his mother made a sharp, slashing motion with one gnarled hand. "No, no!

Don't blaspheme, Pietro! Why is it always money with you?"

Pete hugged his mother and chuckled. "It's not, Ma. You know that. I'm only joking. Go to bed. I'm here for the next shift. Rita will be along about sunup if you've still got customers. *Pilgrims*, I mean," he corrected himself hastily.

I'd forgotten about Rita, the dark horse in the schoolboard election. I was about to mention her candidacy when Monica Vancich glided along in her pious daze to the living room. Someone near the shrine was wailing, a heartrending, keening sound that made me wince.

It bothered Polly not at all. Maybe she'd already heard similar cries earlier in the day. Or even before. I had to admit that I was woefully ignorant of what had passed previously in this house. Pete was kissing his mother good night. Polly gave me a tentative smile and headed for the staircase in the deep, dark recesses of the hall. Pete took up her post, rubbing at one eye and belching discreetly.

"I ought to be selling pizzas to this crowd," he said in a tone that I suspected was only half-joking. "They must get hungry waiting out there. I heard some of them had come all the way from British Columbia."

"I should interview more of the visitors," I said, and failed to suppress a yawn. I couldn't see my watch in the dark, but knew it must be going on eleven. "What do you think, Pete?"

Pete laughed. "Heck, I don't know. That vase looks like a bunch of cracks to me. I guess when it comes right down to it I'm not real religious."

Buzzy O'Toole was emerging, along with a teenager who had obvious Slavic features and a startlingly beautiful woman in a sari. Impulsively I touched Buzzy's arm. "Do you . . . feel better?" I inquired for lack of anything more profound.

Buzzy, however, took the question very seriously. "I

feel . . . more at peace. But I don't think Ursula does."
His pallid blue eyes fixed on my face. "I think she hasn't
come to rest. Her soul is all messed up. I guess that's
because she was murdered." With a slight shake of his
head, Buzzy walked away.

Pete's chuckle was jagged. "That's putting it on the
line. What do you think, Emma? I heard it was some
dumb accident."

I shook my head. "I don't think the sheriff knows for
sure. It's a problem I have to cope with tomorrow when
we get ready to go to press."

"Wow." Pete leaned against the wall with its peeling
floral paper. "Why didn't Doubles figure it out before he
brought that woman up to Alpine?"

I regarded Pete with a curious stare. "Ursula? What do
you mean?"

"Oh . . ." Pete now looked embarrassed. "My delivery
kid, one of the Gundersons, dropped off a pizza Friday
night at Francine's. He said Warren came to the door and
paid for it. So what was Doubles doing with his first wife
when the bride-to-be was sitting around in her fancy
house in The Pines? It sounds kind of funny to me."

It sounded more than funny. I was about to press Pete
for details, if any, when a weeping Monica Vancich
shuddered her way into the hall. She didn't seem to
notice me, so I swiftly excused myself and followed her
out onto the porch.

"Are you okay?" I inquired, aware that she obviously
wasn't.

Monica kept walking. It was only when we reached the
sidewalk that she answered. "I was praying for Verb,"
she said, finding a tissue in her purse. Then she turned
her tearstained face to me and fell into my arms. "Oh,
Ms. Lord! I'm so frightened!"

"About what?" Vaguely I noticed that the line of pilgrims now reached the end of the block.

Monica didn't respond, and I felt her sag against me.

She is slight, but at five-four and a hundred and twenty pounds, I'm not exactly big. I staggered, trying to hold her up. It was only when my back struck the overgrown rockery that I realized Monica had fainted.

A recovering alcoholic from Bremerton and a heart patient from Tacoma helped me lower Monica onto the sidewalk. Both seemed to know more about first aid than I did. While they tended to the unconscious woman I satisfied the curiosity of concerned onlookers and wondered if I should make a run to the hospital emergency room.

But Monica had come 'round, and was sitting up, begging the recovering alcoholic and the heart patient not to fuss over her. "Thank you, thank you," she said repeatedly. "Bless you, bless you."

I escorted her to the car while she murmured apologies and expressions of dismay. My offer to take her to the emergency room was rejected, however. "I do that sometimes," she said in an abject tone. "When I'm upset."

"You're upset about Verb?" I asked as we drove off through the rain.

"Yes." Monica sat up straight, her hands folded primly in her lap. "I prayed for him at the vase. I felt so . . . moved."

But apparently not reassured. Monica had said she was frightened. "What's wrong with Verb? I mean, besides having those bikes stolen."

Monica didn't answer directly. "It's very difficult to earn a living in Alpine these days. Sometimes it seems as if everything is against us. But you have to have hope. It's a Christian virtue, you know."

I knew. I hoped. I was often disappointed. "Does Verb feel hopeless?"

"Maybe." Monica sounded vague, even more so than usual. But at least she wasn't crying and it appeared that she wouldn't pass out again. We were turning onto Fir.

My house lay to the left; the Vancich residence was on the right.

"The ski season is coming," I said after a moment of silence. "Verb's store does well in the winter, I would think."

"Fairly well." Monica's slim body gave off a small tremor. "He hasn't had much competition. Until now."

Up ahead, I saw the Vancich house with the low clouds looming above the roof. The threat of Warren Wells also loomed over Verb and Monica. His proposed sporting-goods store definitely would cut into Alpine Ski's business. I didn't blame Verb for being worried.

"He can diversify," I said, pulling into the driveway. "It'll take Warren several months to get up and running. Verb can beat him to the punch."

Monica didn't say anything. As before, she was slow to get out of the car. Finally, with her thin fingers clutching the door handle, she turned to give me a pitiful look. "Why did it have to be Warren Wells? Why has it always been Warren Wells? I feel haunted. Why didn't God take Warren instead of that awful woman? God rest her soul."

Monica moved with unexpected alacrity, ignoring my plea for an explanation. To my astonished eyes, she seemed to evaporate into the rain. But of course she merely went inside the house. I chided myself for having too much imagination.

Or maybe not enough.

Chapter Fourteen

IT WAS AFTER eleven-thirty when I got home. Anxiously, I checked my machine for a message from Milo. The red light showed the number "2." Vida's voice came through on the first call.

"Roger just got picked up by his parents. Naturally they're relieved that everything turned out so well. I warned him that he mustn't take up with children who don't know how to behave. I especially cautioned him to keep away from teenagers. But the little fellow seems to have overcome his misadventure and is quite his lively self again. I just wanted to reassure you, because I knew you'd worry about him."

Like I'd worry about Mussolini, I thought, waiting for the next message. I couldn't imagine that Roger had turned a hair over his escapade. I wished—no doubt futilely—that his parents might show more mettle in disciplining their son. So my thoughts were running when I heard Carla's voice on the machine.

"You should have come with me," she declared in a breathless voice. "The sheriff and the state troopers brought in twelve suspects. They've been charged with reckless endangerment, possession, vandalism, and . . . I forget. There was a big confrontation up on Mount Sawyer, I guess. Some of the partygoers or whatever resisted arrest. Oh—they got charged with that, too. Anyway, a couple had guns and threatened to shoot it out with the sheriff and the troopers. But they finally brought

241

them in, around ten. I wish I'd gone all the way up the
mountain, but I got some good shots of the perps being
hauled out of the squad cars. I got a totally cool close-up
of Milo, bleeding. By the way, he's in the hospital. See
you tomorrow. 'Night."

I was too upset to actually run out and strangle Carla.
Instead I struggled into my jacket and headed back into
the night. The hospital is located about halfway between
my house and the newspaper office. It took me three minutes to get there.

A weary-looking Marilynn Lewis was behind the desk,
talking on the phone. She saw me at once and nodded.
I glanced at the waiting room, where a young couple
sat with a fidgety two-year-old, an older man held his
head while his grim-faced wife stared at the opposite
wall, and Ginny Burmeister Erlandson leaned against her
husband, Rick.

Despite my concern for Milo, I rushed over to Ginny.
"What's wrong?" I asked, fearing that the worst can
happen in the early stages of pregnancy.

Ginny pointed to her left ankle. "I fell. There was a big
hole in the street by Videos To Go, but you couldn't see
it because of all the rain. Rick wants to make sure it's not
broken."

With a sigh of relief, I patted Ginny's arm, then turned
back to the desk, where Marilynn was hanging up the
phone. "The sheriff?" I asked in a whisper.

Marilynn rolled her dark eyes. "He'll be fine. Somebody hit him with a beer bottle. He's had about ten
stitches and there'll probably be a scar, but he can go
home in a little while. Dr. Flake wants to keep him under
observation just to make sure there's no concussion."

"Oh." My shoulders slumped in relief. "Should I stay
so I can drive him home?"

Marilynn, like everybody else in town, knew that Milo
and I were a duo. "If you want," she said, sounding faintly
frazzled as she gathered up a chart. "But it might be

another hour. Kelly Amundson?" Marilynn had raised her
voice as she smiled at the couple with the two-year-old.

I sat down next to Ginny and Rick. "The city should
fill those holes," I said, wishing that the Erlandsons
would make their big announcement so that we could
speak of more important things, like babies.

"I really don't think it's broken," Ginny asserted. "But
Rick fusses over me like a mother hen." She gave her
husband a fond smile.

"It's always better to be sure," I said somewhat
vaguely, for Milo was coming out of the examining-
room area. He saw me and made a face.

"What's wrong with *you*?" the sheriff demanded.
There was a large diagonal bandage above his right eye.

"Nothing," I said hastily. "I heard you got hurt and
came over to see if I could take you home. With me," I
added in a whisper.

"Oh, hell! Why not? This is a bunch of bullshit." The
sheriff led the way out of the hospital, oblivious to the
stares of the older couple and the Erlandsons.

If Milo had given in without a struggle, he was also
giving up—at least for the night. "No damned reporter's
questions about those bums up on Sawyer, no dingbat
ideas about what happened to Ursula, no running commentary on the frigging picnic. Give me a stiff shot of
Scotch and let me zone out. We can jabber like a pair of
jays in the morning."

I met all of Milo's not unreasonable requests, as well
as one he hadn't mentioned. The Scotch restored him, if
briefly. Lying in his arms while he slept deeply, I felt
secure and almost happy. Milo might be damaged goods
in many ways, but he was safe. I, too, slept.

We both woke up grumpy. Less than six hours of sleep
hadn't revitalized either of us. Milo had hoped to take
some time off after the three-day weekend, but couldn't
because of the arrests on Mount Sawyer—and Ursula's

mysterious demise. I had a paper to put out, and a ticklish lead story. We didn't really discuss any of those things over breakfast. Once we put on our professional faces, we would deal with the harsh realities of our jobs.

The rain had dwindled to a drizzle by morning. Since Milo's Cherokee Chief was still parked on Front Street, I drove him to work. He could see me around ten, after filling out all the paperwork necessitated by the bust on the mountain. There'd be a transfer of prisoners involved, since Skykomish County didn't have adequate facilities, especially in the case of juveniles. While Vida might glibly talk of juvenile hall, the only holding area we had in Alpine for young people was a bleak room in the courthouse basement. Over the years it had been used more as a drop-off point for parents who wanted to party all weekend. They dumped their kids, and let the county pay for them from Friday night until Monday morning when Mom and Dad arrived with world-class hangovers. The sheriff had mixed emotions about the practice, but figured in the long run that the children were better off under county supervision than they would be if left alone.

None of our photos from the weekend would be back from Buddy Bayard's studio until noon, so I concentrated on writing the story about the fight between Luce and Bill Daley. I kept it short, not wanting to offend or humiliate either man. As usual, Vida would handle basic picnic coverage.

I had also assigned myself the task of doing the article about Polly's vase. It would be the second lead. I was mulling over the angle to take when Vida came into my office.

"I still haven't seen that thing," she said, shaking her head at my offer to sit down. "Now I hear that half the state is showing up. I drove by there this morning on my way to work and there were people standing out on the stairs. Really, Emma, don't you think it's a humbug?"

I uttered a deep sigh. "I don't know. I mean, I can't see anything unusual. But then Polly thinks I'm sort of a heathen."

"Polly!" Vida waved her hands in dismissal. "The woman's addled. She always has been wanting. She simply gets worse with age. I'm certainly not going to stand in line to see that vase. All of her crockery is cracked. I know, years ago I covered your Legion of Mary meetings at her house. Honestly! The dishes she used to serve that funny striped ice cream! All chipped and none too clean, if you ask me. She'd better ask God to send her a dishwasher."

Vida stomped out, but before I could write a lead, Leo wandered in. He looked as tired as I felt, and I wondered how he'd spent his weekend. It occurred to me that I hadn't seen him around town. "Where do you want to run this?" he asked, setting a full-page layout in front of me.

It was a formal portrait of Ursula Randall, with her name, dates of birth and death, and the inscription, BELOVED WIFE OF THE LATE WHEATON ALBERT RANDALL, M.D., CHERISHED FIANCÉE OF WARREN WILLIS WELLS, ADMIRED AND RESPECTED BY ALL WHO KNEW HER. REST IN PEACE.

It was not uncommon for families to pay for the privilege of running a memorial for their dear departed ones. However, a full page was a first during my tenure on *The Advocate*. I stared at the portrait, which showed Ursula from the waist up, seated in a Victorian brocade chair, and wearing an artfully draped off-the-shoulder evening gown.

"Who brought this in?" I asked.

"Wells. First thing this morning." Leo didn't sit down, but paused to light a cigarette. "He was waiting for me at the door."

"This is overkill. Excuse the expression." I gave Leo a wry look.

He merely shrugged. "It helps pay the bills."

"Well, yes," I said, trying to sound as impersonal as Leo. "But it really is too much. If Fuzzy Baugh dropped dead tomorrow, I wouldn't run a full page of him, mayor or not."

Leo was beginning to look peeved. "Do you want me to pull a Bronsky and discourage advertising? Come on, Emma, this is revenue. It doesn't reflect your editorial stand on dead people, for chrissake."

"Okay, okay," I said hastily. "We'll run it. But you can take all the heat. And there *will* be heat. A lot of people will resent the fact that Ursula gets this kind of space. She may have been a native, but she defected years ago and only returned within the last couple of months. Then she rubbed quite a few folks the wrong way after she got back. Furthermore," I added, tapping at the layout, "there's no mention of her first husband, and even if his family's not around anymore, people in Index and Alpine will remember. And what about her brothers? Warren should have included Jake and Buzzy."

Leo puffed on his cigarette. "I asked him about that. He didn't take well to the suggestion. I gather there's some bad feeling involved."

"Maybe so." I gazed again at Ursula's portrait. Her smile seemed enigmatic, her manner, complacent. "I wonder why they're at odds with Warren."

"Money," Leo said, taking the layout from me. "Isn't it always money?"

"Often, yes." I was inclined to interrogate Leo again about his standoffish attitude, but thought better of it. "We'll run the thing on page nine, across from Vida's House & Home section."

Leo gave a single nod, and left in a cloud of smoke. I resumed tackling the article on Polly's vase. *Miraculous vision or maudlin misconception?* I typed, then deleted the words. They were too harsh. *Is seeing believing?* Too flippant. *Could the face in the vase be Jesus?* Too irreverent.

Maybe I was trying too hard to be clever. A simple, straightforward lead would serve me—and our readers— better. *Polly Patricelli thinks she has a miracle in an old cracked vase, and people from all over western Washington and British Columbia agree with her.* That was better, if less colorful. I typed away, sticking to the facts, remaining the observer. By the time I finished the story, it was going on ten, and Ginny was delivering the mail. She limped, but said that her ankle was neither broken nor sprained.

"It was just a bad turn," she reported. "Dr. Flake didn't even put an Ace bandage on it."

I expressed my relief, waiting for Ginny to make a more exciting, if not unexpected, announcement. But she didn't. Sighing, I began opening the mail.

Carla turned in her interview with a University of Washington forestry professor, which she'd done Friday after arriving in Seattle, and which allowed her to charge the paper for mileage. At twenty-six cents a mile for a total of a hundred and seventy miles round-trip, I was out over forty-four dollars. It wasn't worth it. The forestry prof had hemmed and hawed, and Carla's conclusion was that old-growth timber was . . . really *old.* I insisted that she call him and try to get some kind of opinion or insight. My reporter started to argue, but must have seen the fire in my eyes. While I no longer was inclined to strangle her, I was still miffed over her breezy message about Milo.

I was getting ready to head for the sheriff's office when Murray Felton called. "Early bird and all that," he declared. "Do I have news for you!"

"Such as?" I tried not to sound too skeptical.

"Such as your logger buddy sued Wheaton Randall for a million bucks. How's that for openers?"

"I'm not surprised," I said as Carla ambled into the office. "Luce mentioned having sued somebody last night while we were at a meeting. Did he win?"

"The suit's still pending," Murray replied. "Now how do you suppose an out-of-work logger paid a high-priced lawyer to file said suit?"

"I did wonder about that," I admitted, indicating that Carla should sit. "Do you know?"

"I've got a good guess. At least four of the unhappy patients don't have the proverbial pot to etcetera. What I figure is that somebody who really had a hard-on for Wheaton backed this crippled quartet. In other words, Lovely Lady Lord, somebody was out to get him."

I couldn't help but roll my eyes at Carla. "The old conspiracy theory, huh? Murray, I expect better of you."

I saw Carla give a little jump. She immediately began to scribble something on a spare piece of paper.

"Hey—rebuke me not," Murray retorted. "This stuff happens, at least in the Big City. Doctors make big bucks, they spend said bucks on many things, sometimes property. Wheaton and Ursula Randall bought and sold houses the way you and I change our underwear. You *do* change your undies, don't you, sweetheart?"

"Knock it off, Murray," I snapped, glancing down at Carla's note, which read, *Is this the guy?* I wrote back, *Yes, but forget him.*

"So now we're looking at a slightly different motive— maybe," Murray said. "Somebody who wanted to get both Randalls, one way or another. I'm still digging. What's going on at your end?"

Carla had now written *Why?* and underlined it three times. I waved a hand, trying to tell her to wait. "Not much here, Murray. I'm going to see the sheriff as soon as I get off the phone. The only new development is that Ursula's missing shoe was found at a party site on Mount Sawyer. But that may not mean much."

"I'll be in touch. Talk to you tonight or first thing tomorrow." Murray rang off.

I took a deep breath. "Carla, he's a real jerk. You

wouldn't be able to stand him for five minutes. But he's trying to be helpful with this possible homicide. I think."

Carla, however, wasn't convinced that I had her best interests at heart. "You probably have different standards. I mean, Milo Dodge isn't exactly a Nineties kind of guy."

"That depends on what century you're talking about," I said with a straight face. "Now I must dash. Trust me, Carla—you can do a lot better than Murray Felton. He's already losing his hair." Halfway to the door, I remembered to tell Carla about the imminent appointment of the new community-college dean. "Call Olympia and get the details. I think his name is Talliaferro."

"How do you spell it?" Carla called after me.

"Ask Olympia," I shouted, and was gone.

Milo's mood had improved only marginally since breakfast. "I can't give you much," he announced, looking as if he were trying to hide behind his NRA coffee mug.

"You've got Ursula's other shoe now," I pointed out. "Doesn't that mean something?"

Milo put the mug down on his littered desk and sighed heavily. "That's the problem. I don't know what it means. We're still trying to build a case."

"What kind of case?" I asked, feeling puzzled.

"Against one of these morons up on Sawyer." Milo pushed some papers around, flicking one of them into the wastebasket. "You can't print this, but half the crew we hauled in were high on dope or alcohol or both. They've been growing marijuana up there, and one guy had an assault weapon and some grenades. I can't believe we didn't know what was going on."

I frowned at Milo. "You mean I can't print that you're dumb? When did I ever do that?"

"Very funny," Milo said, but he didn't crack a smile. "I'm not talking about the guns and the grass and the grenades. That's a matter of record. I mean the part about the possibility of them being involved with Ursula. Let's say that somehow she ended up sitting by the river in her fancy clothes. One or two or twelve of these crackheads decides to mug her, only to discover too late that she hasn't brought a purse. They get pissed off, and leave Ursula to drown. End of story."

I looked askance at Milo. "They also leave Ursula's egg-sized diamond on her finger but take one of her shoes?"

Milo shrugged. "They're dopers, drunks. You expect them to be rational?"

"It doesn't make sense."

"Of course it doesn't." Milo seemed less tense. Maybe talking through his so-called case had improved his spirits. One of the benefits of our newfound intimacy was that he was more inclined to candor about his job. "The problem is nailing the right perps," Milo went on. "Somebody has to give somebody up. It'll happen, but it'll take time."

I gave the sheriff my most sardonic look. "As it is, you have a shoe theft. At least as far as Ursula's death is concerned."

Milo was unperturbed by my sarcasm. "We've already charged some of them with reckless endangerment. That's not because of Ursula, but some of the campers who were—"

I held up a hand. "Hold it. The way I see it, reckless endangerment is the most you could charge them with *if* they were at fault in Ursula's death."

"That's true, but—"

"Sheriff, you haven't got *jack*. Neither do I." Standing up, I grimaced at Milo. "Now let me get out of here to write my nonstory."

Milo half rose from the swivel chair. "What are you going to say?"

"I don't know yet. What is there to say? 'Ursula Randall accidentally drowned in the Skykomish River Friday night. Sheriff Milo Dodge is investigating.' What else can I say?"

Milo gave me a crooked little smile and stood up. "Not much. Keep it that way. You want to see a picture of the corpse?"

I cringed. "I do not. Why would I? Ugh!"

But for perverse reasons known only to Milo and God, the sheriff shoved an eight-by-ten glossy across the desk. "This was taken at the scene. There's something about it that bothers me. Can you figure it out?"

Since Milo was asking for help, I steeled myself and gazed at the photograph. It was grainy, dark, and not as gruesome as I'd feared. Ursula was lying facedown in the river, just as Richie Magruder had reportedly found her. She could have been a hiker, pausing for a drink of cool water. I kept staring at the picture, wondering what Milo had meant.

"The main thing that's wrong," I finally said, "is that she's dead."

The sheriff wasn't amused. "Keep looking. Of course I could be nuts."

Then I saw it. "Ursula's got the left shoe on the right foot." Excitedly I pointed to the glossy photo. "See, the ankle clasp is fastened on the inside."

"Ah!" Milo took the photo from me and nodded several times. "That means that somebody took off her shoes—or she did, and put one of them back on the wrong foot. Weird."

I agreed. "Why? Because they were in a hurry? Because somebody came along and they—whoever it was—had to run?"

"Could be." Now satisfied that he hadn't been nuts, the sheriff tossed the photo onto a filing cabinet. "We'll figure it out. Maybe. By the way, I talked to Buzzy."

"So did I." We exchanged notes; the accounts meshed. "Ursula was supposed to come by Friday night and give Laura and Buzzy some money. But of course she never showed." I moved back to Milo's desk. "Do you think Ursula may have asked someone to drive her there but they got sidetracked? She'd been drinking, though not with Buzzy, and maybe she realized she shouldn't be behind the wheel."

Milo considered. "I hope she'd figure that way. Ursula had her license pulled three months ago for one too many DWIs."

"No kidding!" I shouldn't have been surprised, but I was. "Yet she drove that Lexus around Alpine."

"Very carefully, I imagine." Milo gave me a dour look. "So who gave her the lift out to Buzzy's end of town?"

"Whoever left her to drown by the river," I replied, and made my exit.

The story I wrote about Ursula Randall wasn't much longer than the abbreviated version I'd recited for Milo. Vida was handling the actual obituary, so I added only a brief paragraph of identification and the barest of details about the discovery by Richie Magruder. It was only after I'd hit the *send* key on my computer that I realized I hadn't filled Milo in on Murray Felton's latest digging. I started to phone the sheriff, but thought better of it: Murray was speculating, a pastime that Milo despised when it came to investigating crime. Again, I thought of telling Vida about our Seattle source, but my House & Home editor wasn't in a receptive mood.

"Honestly!" she fumed, plopping herself down in one of my visitors' chairs. "This Ursula thing is such a mess! I had to stop by Parker's Pharmacy just now, and I saw Billy, heading off in his squad car. He told me along what lines Milo's mind is running. If you ask me, he's been derailed."

"You mean the theory about the losers up on Mount Sawyer?"

"Exactly. Now I asked Billy if any of our youngsters were involved." Vida was looking very prim. "As it turns out, none of those who were charged came from Alpine. But of course you know that from checking the sheriff's log."

"Carla did the checking," I replied as the phone rang. "But you're right—she said there were no locals." I picked up the receiver and heard Francine Wells at the other end.

"Have you seen Betsy O'Toole?" she asked in a furtive voice.

"Betsy? No, not today, Francine. Why?" I arched my eyebrows at Vida, who looked as if she'd like to snatch the phone out of my hand.

"She was in here five minutes ago and she's on her way to the—Emma, could you meet me for lunch? Or better yet, in private. Your office, maybe. Alicia can watch the shop." Francine sounded desperate.

"Sure. It's almost noon. Come on by." My second line now glowed, and I picked it up before answering the obvious question on Vida's face.

"We've counted the votes," Veronica Wenzler-Greene said. "The new school-board members are Debra Barton and Derek Norman."

"Oh." I scribbled the information down and passed it to Vida. "Was it close?"

"Fairly. Debra was a clear-cut winner, but Derek beat out Rita by only eleven votes. Laura O'Toole trailed. Badly." The principal seemed pleased by Laura's defeat.

I took down the actual tally, thanked Ronnie, and started to say goodbye. "Hold it—this is odd. Even with everyone voting for two candidates, there are at least— what?—fifty more votes than the number of people who usually show up for the Saturday and Sunday Masses. Did the ballot box get stuffed?"

"Not precisely," Ronnie replied in a strained voice. "But you must realize that many of the parents either aren't Catholic, or if they are, they don't attend Mass regularly. They voted, however, by stopping in at the vestibule and picking up a ballot."

"I see. Thanks, Ronnie. Bye." I gazed at Vida. "The pro–private school parents—as opposed to pro–parochial school—put Derek Norman on the board. Debra Barton was the top vote-getter, no doubt because of name familiarity with the family shoe store. Rita and Laura are out."

"Yes." Vida was studying my scribbles. "You expect Debra to act more conservatively?"

"Maybe. I don't know her very well. You do, though." I made a rueful little face. "How do you think she'll perform?"

"With a certain amount of integrity," Vida answered promptly. "But she can be swayed by a stronger personality. Debra's not stupid. Not quite."

I grew silent for a moment. "So we've got Bill Daley, Buddy Bayard, Greer Fairfax, and these two newcomers. Bill and Buddy *should* be reliable. Greer and Derek are the opposition. Neither are Catholic. Debra's the swing vote."

"It could have been Ursula." Vida sat back in the chair with her arms folded.

"That's true. I'd almost forgotten. She wouldn't have been swayed by anything." The thought bothered me. "Nobody gets drowned over a school-board election, right?"

"Arthur Trewes was kidnapped in 1961 when he ran for president of Rotary Club," Vida said blandly. "His foes hid him in the Overholt barn for two days. Arthur ended up getting very friendly with one of the pigs and made him an honorary Rotary member."

I'd grown accustomed to the vagaries of Alpine life. "Did Arthur win?" I asked without turning a hair.

"Yes, by acclamation. The pig was voted in as secretary." Having made her point and digested the school-board vote, Vida now backtracked to Francine. "What bee does she have in her bonnet now?"

I shook my head. "I don't know, but she'll be here any minute. If you have time, go on a scouting expedition for Betsy O'Toole. That's who put the bee in Francine's bonnet."

"Well!" Vida was galvanized into action. "So I shall. But I haven't quite finished my wedding-and-anniversary copy. Carla should be back with the pictures from Buddy's by now."

Carla wasn't, but Francine came rushing into the office just as Vida left. "Can I close the door?" she asked breathlessly.

No one was in the outer office at the moment, but I expected both Carla and Leo to return momentarily. "Go ahead," I said. "Have a seat."

"Betsy's a snake," Francine asserted, slumping into the chair Vida had vacated. "I've never liked her much. I can't remember when she ever looked at anything in my shop that wasn't on sale."

As Francine stopped to catch her breath I reflected that she hadn't come to see me about Betsy's spending habits. "So what's wrong?" I inquired, noting that Francine's carefully applied makeup didn't hide the circles under her eyes.

Francine let out a ragged sigh. "Betsy came by to tell me that she was on her way to the sheriff's—to do her duty, you see." The rose-hued mouth grimaced. "It seems—if you can believe Betsy—she saw Warren and Ursula drive past her house Friday night around six-thirty. They were headed east, which could mean they were going to the river."

I stared at Francine. "Do you believe her?"

Francine put both hands to her smart blonde coiffure. "I don't know what to believe. Betsy never liked Warren. She and his second wife were friends, you know. They took some classes at Everett Junior College together. Betsy thought Warren treated Alexis badly, but when Warren left me, I didn't see Betsy wringing her hands." Bitterness had invaded Francine's voice.

"Six-thirty," I murmured. Later, maybe as much as an hour, Betsy had run into Warren at Icicle Creek Gas 'N Go. I wondered if Francine knew that. There was no point in keeping secrets, I decided, and told her about the encounter that Craig Rasmussen had reported.

Francine's eyes widened. "Really? Oh, damn!" She put her head down on her arms.

Bewildered, I offered a comforting hand. "What is it, Francine? I'm confused."

There was a long pause before Francine raised her head and spoke again. "Okay." She sighed. "Emma, this is one of those sad old stories you won't believe. Warren and I were together Friday night after eight o'clock. Does that shock you?"

"No." I almost laughed. "I'd heard as much."

Francine's jaw dropped. "You did? From . . . oh, that damned pizza kid! I told Warren not to go to the door!"

I nodded. "You know what gossips people are in this town. Sometimes I wonder why I bother putting out a newspaper."

Francine was leaning back in the chair, looking spent. "It didn't take long for Warren to figure out he'd made a mistake getting engaged to Ursula. He tried to break it off before she could move to Alpine, but you can imagine how Ursula reacted. It was as if he hadn't said a word. A whim, the usual cold feet, feeling strange about going home again—that's what Ursula told him. He'd get over it, once they were settled. Oh, she could have run right over a small army. Warren came back to town on a temporary basis, which is why he was staying at the ski lodge. Meanwhile he called me. I tried to be indifferent, to put him off, but the truth is . . ." Francine lowered her eyes and shook her head. "This is the really idiotic part, Emma. It sounds like a bad soap opera. Despite everything, despite Alexis, despite Ursula, despite virtually abandoning our daughter, despite the way I heard he treated his stepson by his second wife, I still loved the bastard. Can you believe that any woman would be stupid enough to love a man who behaved so badly after over twenty years?"

I simply stared at Francine. "Yes," I said. "I can believe it."

I could. I did. I had been stupid, too.

I didn't unload on Francine. She was in no mood to hear my sad story, and in any event, I'd written *finis* to it. But Francine had not. She went on to tell me how Warren had been with her when I'd called Friday night about Ursula's death.

"That's why I sounded so strange," she explained. "That's why Alicia didn't come home that night. She knew her father was coming to see me. We—all three of us—hoped to iron things out. But Warren had to figure out how to deal with Ursula. He'd tried to talk to her earlier in the day, but she was drinking. She was always drinking. Frankly I think if Warren had stayed with her, he would have become an alcoholic, too. He's not a strong man, but he's not dumb, either, and he understood that much. Now I'm scared to death that Betsy's blabbing to the sheriff will make it look very bad for Warren. What on earth can I do?"

Scarcely knowing Francine's ex-husband, I was loath to give advice. "Where were Ursula and Warren going when they went by Jake and Betsy's house?"

Francine regarded me with a helpless expression. "I don't know. I haven't talked to Warren since Betsy came in the shop. He didn't tell me they'd gone anywhere. He said he was having a beer with Cal Vickers."

"Is Betsy lying?" It was possible, though it seemed out of character. Betsy was as forthright as Francine. But, I reminded myself, Francine had been practicing her own brand of deceit.

"Jake and Buzzy may have quarreled with their sister," Francine finally said in a weary voice. "I honestly don't know. Family rows are so common in this town, they're like an epidemic. But that doesn't explain why Betsy would lie about Warren."

Francine was right. There was no explanation. I racked my brain, trying to sort out the O'Toole internecine dilemma. At a loss, I asked what seemed like an irrelevant question.

"Whatever happened to Alexis?"

"She died." Francine made a face. "Not long after the divorce, actually. She had leukemia."

I paused just long enough to pay my respects to the memory of Alexis Wells, a woman I had not known, but who had clearly played a big role in Francine's life. "So Warren would have had to get only one annulment," I said at last. "From you. How did Ursula plan to do that?"

"Who knows?" Francine let out a dry little laugh. "It wasn't Warren's problem—not after he decided he couldn't marry her. Besides, Warren's not Catholic."

I hadn't realized that. "Hadn't Ursula converted him?"

"Not yet. I'm sure she was working on it." Francine again slumped in the chair. "What should I do, Emma? Go tell Milo all?"

"I don't see why. I mean, if you're giving Warren an alibi, it doesn't play." My half smile was apologetic. "He wasn't with you during the period that Ursula ended up in the river."

"But I could tell Milo that Warren didn't harm Ursula," Francine said with fervor as her usual energy returned. "He wouldn't. He couldn't. Warren's not like Luce or even Buzzy. He doesn't hit women. He just . . . walks out."

"He should have walked on Ursula," I noted, but didn't wait for Francine's argument. "Oh, go ahead and tell Milo. It might help."

"Help!" Francine snorted. "He shouldn't need help.

But of course he does." None too steadily, she got to her feet. "This is all so crazy. Here Warren and Alicia and I were trying to sort out a way to be one big happy family again. We thought maybe we finally had something. Now it turns out that we have nothing. Except for Warren."

I didn't quite get the gist of Francine's words. "You mean . . . ?"

"I mean," she said, turning towards the door, "that Warren has a motive. For getting rid of Ursula. I'm going to see the sheriff."

Chapter Fifteen

VIDA HAD FOUND Betsy O'Toole, not at the sheriff's office, but in the Upper Crust Bakery. Betsy had already talked to Milo, and was certain she'd seen Ursula and Warren in his sports car around six-thirty. Betsy could pinpoint the time because she was getting ready to go over to Laura and Buzzy's to help pay bills. She'd just gone into the living room to get her purse when she saw the red car race by her house.

Vida and I were eating a hurried, late lunch at the Burger Barn. Carla still hadn't returned with the photos, which meant that we were going to be right up against deadline before the afternoon was out.

"Warren and Ursula could have been going to Laura and Buzzy's," I noted between bites of my hamburger dip. "That was supposed to be Ursula's evening destination."

Vida laid aside the fork with which she'd been attacking her meat loaf sandwich. "Let's sort this out, and correct me if I'm wrong. Betsy saw Warren and Ursula at six-thirty. Betsy was seen at Icicle Creek Gas 'N Go around seven, as was Warren. They spoke, in a courteous manner, according to Craig Rasmussen. What did they say?"

I thought back to my conversation with Craig. "Not much. I gathered they just greeted one another."

"Betsy didn't ask after Ursula? It would have been the natural thing to do, having just seen her with Warren."

If she did, Craig hadn't overheard her. I mulled over

this while Vida consumed meat loaf. "That half hour or so doesn't allow much time. I wonder if Milo has talked to Cal Vickers about Warren's alibi between five and eight."

Vida chewed thoughtfully. "Cal usually leaves work around six. Would consuming two beers take more than half an hour?"

"Probably not. But Milo did talk to Abe Loomis," I said, smiling vaguely at a middle-aged couple I recognized from church. "Abe thought Warren was still at Mugs Ahoy around seven-thirty."

"Abe!" Vida was scornful. "The man's a mental midget. What would you expect of a tavern owner?"

I repressed a smile. Vida was broad-minded in many ways, but she retained a strict Presbyterian outlook on people who were involved in the dispensing of alcoholic beverages.

"Warren could have left and come back," Vida pointed out, daintily wiping catsup from her lips. "On the other hand," she continued in a more somber tone, "Betsy may have her own ax to grind. As she made clear when we lunched at their house, Betsy doesn't like Warren."

"Betsy's not fond of any of her in-laws," I said, picking up my bill. "I'm surprised she was willing to help Laura."

"Betsy's good-hearted." Vida was gaping at her own bill. "Six dollars! And they call it the special?"

"That's why," I replied dryly. "How was it?"

"Passable." Vida dug in her purse, then carefully counted out a dollar in change for her tip. "If Betsy's telling the truth, the explanation could be simple. Warren and Ursula drove to the river, quarreled, and Warren left in a huff. Ursula was inebriated, and passed out in the water. That does make it an accident. Naturally Warren isn't willing to talk about it. The encounter might be construed as something more sinister, especially since he was courting his ex-wife."

I had told Vida about my closed-door session with Francine. We seemed to have run out of ideas about Ursula's demise. Scurrying back to the office, we found Carla with the contact sheets from our various rolls of film. She had some excellent shots of the Mount Sawyer perps being carted into the sheriff's headquarters. My photos of the pilgrims at Polly's were merely adequate. Vida, however, stole the show.

"Ah!" she exclaimed, pointing to one of the picnic punch-out shots. "That's Dutch Bamberg's left arm. There's Clancy Barton's elbow. Can you make out Norm Carlson's nose?"

As usual, I was in awe of Vida's ability to identify her fellow Alpiners, even when it came down to body parts. The actual pictures of the combat between Luce and Bill Daley were very good, but I hesitated to use them.

"Nobody's filed charges," I pointed out. "I don't want to cause more problems."

"Emma!" Vida was flabbergasted. "This is *Alpine*! What's a community event without a little excitement?"

"It's news," Carla asserted. The astute comment was out of character, and it swayed me.

"Well . . . everybody knows what happened," I temporized. "Maybe we could use a shot of Milo, breaking up the brawl. A kind of happy-ending photo."

Vida eyed me with disdain. "Luce wasn't happy. I can't imagine that Bill Daley was happy. Milo certainly can't be happy about having to hit his constituents over the head."

We debated for the next five minutes. Finally Leo arrived. He swiftly scanned the contact sheet, then pointed to a shot that showed Luce and Bill grappling manfully, if awkwardly.

"Run this one. They could be hugging. You can hedge in the cutline. 'Picnickers engage in old-fashioned horse-play' or some such ambiguous bullshit. It's a good crowd scene, too. You can pick out at least six locals. A couple of them might even be sober."

Vida's disdain turned to contempt. "Really, Leo, that's no way to talk. Kathryn Daley and Della Lucci are not only sober, but practically hysterical. They'll be mortified."

Leo shrugged and sat down at his desk. "Do what you want. The one thing you can't do is ignore the fight." His brown eyes swerved from Vida to me. "It'd make *The Advocate* a laughingstock. If anybody should be worried, it's me. I have to deal with Daley as an advertiser."

In the end we chose the frame that depicted Milo holding up Bill while standing over Luce's prone form. It wasn't exactly an action photo, but it conveyed a relatively peaceful conclusion. In my short article, I referred to the confrontation as "a fracas," and tried to keep the wording lighthearted.

It was close to five by the time we finished laying out the paper. I sent Carla to check on the visitors to Polly's shrine while I walked over to the sheriff's office. This was one week when I didn't want to miss any loose ends.

When I arrived, Milo was closing up shop for the day. "Don't try to seduce me, woman," he said with a wry little grin. "I'm going home and sleep for ten straight. Besides, I need to take out the garbage. I missed the pickup this week."

"The only thing I'm putting to bed tonight is the paper," I assured the sheriff, not taking time to sit down. "Anything new on Ursula or the Mount Sawyer gang before we lock it up?"

"Court appearances are scheduled for tomorrow, both here and in SnoCo," Milo replied, taking his regulation hat from the top of a filing cabinet and settling it on his head. "We're trying to track down witnesses, but some of the campers who were assaulted are from out of state. We may not end up with much."

Accustomed to the tightrope of law enforcement, I sympathized briefly. "What about Ursula?"

"Zip. I suppose you heard about Betsy O'Toole. I saw Vida chewing off Bill Blatt's ear this afternoon." Milo tossed his jacket over one shoulder. "Betsy's so-called tip doesn't mean a damned thing. I don't know why she bothered."

I frowned at Milo. "But it puts Warren with Ursula not long before she died, right?"

"So? I talked to Warren less than an hour ago. He says Betsy's full of it. At six-thirty, he was waving Cal Vickers out the door of Mugs Ahoy, and he can prove it. Which he did. Cal swears it's true. He didn't get home until almost a quarter to seven, and Charlene was furious. Her pork chops had dried out."

Mystified, I leaned against Milo's desk. "Could someone have taken Warren's car for a spin? I gather it's a pretty hot little sports number."

"The Z3? Sure, it'd be a temptation for just about every kid in Alpine. But would they take Ursula with them?" Milo dangled his keys at me. "I'm leaving. You want to stay and man the office?"

I gave an impatient little shake of my head. "Betsy's not a liar. I don't think."

"Money," Milo said, putting a firm hand on my back and pushing me toward the door. "She probably thought Warren was going to get everything. Betsy should have waited a couple of hours before perjuring herself."

I came to a dead stop right on the threshold. "What are you talking about?" I whirled around, coming chin to chest with the sheriff. "Are you holding out on me, Dodge?"

Milo darted a quick look out from under the brim of his hat, saw that Toni Andreas and Dustin Fong were both absorbed in phone calls, and kissed me. "I don't think so. Didn't Bill tell Vida what Brendan Shaw told him? Or was that after Vida collared her nephew?" Milo's long face grew puzzled.

"No," I replied, my annoyance only slightly tempered by Milo's quick kiss. "What did Brendan have to say?"

With an arm draped over my shoulder, the sheriff steered me into the outer office. "Ursula changed agents after she got to Alpine, but she hadn't yet changed beneficiaries. She was supposed to do that today, after Brendan finished doing the paperwork. It's a million-dollar policy, and I guess something that big takes time to work out. Hell, I wouldn't know, I'm lucky to have a measly—"

"Milo!" I attempted to shake the sheriff, but only managed to wrinkle his shirt. "Who gets the million bucks?"

Milo grinned at me. "You can't use this. What's the rush?"

I gritted my teeth. "Don't be a jerk."

"Warren was supposed to get it," the sheriff answered as Dustin tried to get his attention, "but like I said, the forms never got signed. The million bucks is split right down the middle, between Jake and Buzzy O'Toole. See you, Emma. I've got a date with a garbage can."

I chased after Milo, but Dustin's tone was even more urgent. The sheriff stopped at the door, his good humor suddenly erased. "Now what?" he called to his deputy.

"It's Verb Vancich, Sheriff," Dustin replied, a shielding hand over the telephone receiver. "He says Nunzio Lucci tried to shoot him. Can you go up there right away?"

"Up where?" Milo barked, and then swore under his breath.

"Mr. Vancich is calling from the Bjornsons', next door to the Lucci place. He says the Lucci kids have his stolen bikes." Dustin's expression was apologetic, as if it were bad manners to report a crime to the sheriff.

"Hell!" Milo whirled around and pushed one of the two swinging doors so hard that it shuddered on its hinges. The last I saw was an angry figure charging through the rain with the regulation jacket waving like a warning flag.

"You know," Dustin said in his mild voice, "sometimes he gets too worked up over things. Do you think he's tired of his job?"

I thought back to the other night when Milo had expressed discontent with just about everything, except— but not necessarily excluding—me. "He doesn't always feel appreciated," I said somewhat vaguely. "And of course he hates having to put his job on the line every four years. It's unsettling."

"Not all counties elect their sheriffs," Dustin remarked. "Why does it have to be that way here?"

I studied Dustin's pleasant, serious face for several moments before I replied: "It doesn't. Maybe that should be my next editorial campaign." In other counties the sheriff was appointed. Why not here in SkyCo? The voice of the people was often capricious, ill informed, and just plain dopey. Obviously I was gathering steam for my leadoff editorial.

Dustin was like-minded. "That's a good idea," he said as the phone rang again.

I hurried out, half running down the street to *The Advocate*. Kip MacDuff was just finishing an in-store poster job for Stuart's Stereo. Since Carla had nothing new to report except that there were still pilgrims lining Polly's front steps, I told Kip we were ready to roll. Then I beckoned Vida into my office and informed her about Ursula's insurance policy.

She listened to the news with keen interest. "So Milo thinks that Betsy acted out of spite because she thought Warren was going to become a rich man. Tsk, tsk."

"I don't know anything about a will," I put in. "If Milo has found out, he hasn't told me. He's too busy trying to keep Luce from killing Verb Vancich. Verb says the Lucci kids stole those bikes."

"Oh?" Vida was only mildly intrigued by this bit of

information. "Perhaps. They're very unpleasant children. I wonder . . . Did Milo say if Jake and Buzzy know about their windfall?"

"No. I told you, Milo was in a rush. It seems strange, doesn't it?"

"That Ursula should die before she changed her beneficiary?" Vida tipped her head to one side. "Of course it does. It also seems strange that she hadn't made the change sooner."

"Not really," I countered. "I wouldn't own this newspaper—or my Jag—if my ex-fiancé had remembered to delete me from his Boeing insurance policy. Almost twenty years went by, and he never bothered to do anything about it. Of course, he was an engineer. They're not quite like real people."

"Mmm. Yes." Vida had heard the tale of my unexpected boon many times. "And Ursula was an alcoholic. Muddled. Goodness, what luck for the O'Toole boys—especially Buzzy. Perhaps he can piece his life back together." She grew pensive, apparently considering how Buzzy and Laura could mend their marriage and stabilize their family. Or, knowing my House & Home editor, maybe she was thinking of the ways that the O'Tooles might squander their windfall, and further self-destruct. "Timing, they say, is everything," she concluded, and I realized I had been wrong about her thought processes. "Who knew about Ursula's insurance?"

"Brendan Shaw, for one," I answered promptly. "His wife, Patsy. And Warren, I suppose."

"The Shaws are merely tools," Vida noted. "And for all of Brendan's heartiness and Patsy's outgoing manner, they're quite discreet."

"So they wouldn't have gossiped, even about a million-dollar policy, which must be rare in Alpine?"

"I think not," Vida responded. "Over the years, I've . . . tested them. Brendan and Patsy are really remarkable."

In other words, they had resisted Vida's relentless

probing. Not only were they remarkable, but rare. "So Warren might be the only one who knew what Ursula intended to do," I said. "But it wouldn't have been in his interest to kill Ursula before she could make the change."

"Heavens, no!" Vida exclaimed. "The four O'Tooles have the motive. Yet I doubt very much that they knew anything about the policy. Unless . . ."

"What?"

Vida removed her blue felt cloche, then put it back on and repinned it to her head. "Unless Ursula told them. Drinkers blurt things, you know. Especially foolish things."

Ursula had mentioned hosting her brothers and their wives on at least one occasion. The image of the family get-together in The Pines struck me as incongruous, yet it had taken place.

"Betsy," Vida murmured. "I really should stop by this evening. Aren't she and Jake going to the funeral service tomorrow in Seattle?"

"I think so," I replied. "Do you want me to come along with you?"

Vida, however, shook her head. The cloche tilted precariously, indicating that the pins hadn't quite done the job. "It would be better if I went alone. Girl talk, you know." She stood up and fiddled again with the hat. "Which reminds me, did you ever get in touch with Marisa Foxx?"

I'd forgotten about Marisa. "I left a message, but she never called back."

"Try again," Vida urged, heading for the door.

It struck me as odd that Vida would encourage my friendship with another woman. Usually such relationships tended to make her jealous. "Why?" I asked bluntly. "Do you think I'm lonely?"

Vida glanced over her broad shoulder. "I think she's an attorney. A Catholic attorney. If Ursula switched insurance agents, she'd also engage a local law firm. Call Marisa. It's the friendly thing to do."

The rain had almost stopped by the time I got home around six-fifteen. There were no messages on my machine and nothing of interest in the mail. I'd hoped to hear from Ben or Adam by now, but of course they were busy. After taking some frozen shrimp out of the freezer, I dialed Marisa's number. She answered on the second ring, and immediately became apologetic.

"I'm so sorry I didn't get back to you, but I went away for the weekend," she explained in her brisk voice. "Naturally, work had piled up and I was swamped all day. How can I help you?"

Suddenly I felt awkward. Possessing none of Vida's guile, I found it difficult to approach a virtual stranger and ferret out information under the guise of friendship. "Are you representing Ursula Randall's estate?" I blurted.

There was a sharp intake of breath at the other end of the phone. "Is this for publication?" Marisa asked.

"Not really. I'm trying to piece some things together. Deep background, you could call it." The quasilie made me wince into the receiver.

"Ms. Randall had scheduled an appointment for Wednesday. Tomorrow," Marisa clarified. "I've no idea what she wanted to see me about, and even if I did, I couldn't say. You understand, of course." The lawyer attempted to soften her words, but I could sense the underlying steel.

"Oh. Well, that's okay," I said, sounding mealy-mouthed. "Ah . . . I don't suppose you'd like to get together some time for a drink or dinner?"

"To what purpose?" Marisa was nothing if not direct.

I squirmed a bit, then tried to sound as straightforward as Marisa. "You've been in town for going on two years, and it seems stupid that we've never gotten acquainted. Yet we've got so much in common. We're both career women, single, Catholic, nonnatives, about the same age. It's my fault. I've been remiss in extending an invitation."

Marisa laughed. "After two years we're both remiss. Let me check my daily planner."

I don't know what there is about the term *daily planner* that raises my hackles—but it does. Maybe it's the implied self-importance, maybe it's the penchant for organization, maybe it's just one of my peculiar quirks. Chiding myself, I waited for Marisa to come up with a date.

"This week's already booked," she said with what might have been regret. "Tomorrow's a client dinner in Everett, Thursday is Father Den, Friday we have a partners' meeting, and Saturday I'm going to see my parents in Yakima. How's Monday, the eleventh?"

I had no daily planner, just a Monet Giverny gardens calendar on which I scrawled notes that I often couldn't decipher two days later. "It sounds fine," I said. "By the way, when do you expect Father Den to get back?"

"I'm not sure—tonight?" Marisa replied somewhat uncertainly. "We've had this meeting set for over a week, so I'm sure he plans to be here for it."

"You're not a canon lawyer, are you?" It was possible. I'd known other laypeople who had studied church law and were highly regarded canonists.

"No," Marisa answered warily. "I'm strictly family law. But I can sometimes offer advice on other matters as long as the issues are sufficiently broad."

I sorted through Marisa's careful legalese. "Like Father Den's rights as a pastor?"

Marisa laughed again, though the sound was strained. "Now, Emma, you're probing. Priests are people. They're not concerned solely with issues pertaining to their vocations."

"Maybe you can help him sort through the mess the parish council got into last night," I said, with a touch of acerbity.

"What mess?" Marisa's tone indicated that she was taken aback.

I, too, could play the professional. "It's in tomorrow's edition of *The Advocate*." I didn't point out that the information was buried at the end of the school-board story. "Nunzio Lucci quit the parish council, and Jake appointed Ed Bronsky in his place. Or something like that," I hedged, still not quite clear on how the agreement had been reached.

"I don't believe—from my interpretation of the parish bylaws—that Jake can do that," Marisa said in a thoughtful voice. "The other members can recommend dismissal of one of their peers, but the pastor has the final authority. It's also up to him to appoint a replacement or call for an election. Unfortunately some parish councils naively—or egotistically—believe they hold the power. It doesn't work that way. I hope St. Mildred's council behaves sensibly so that this doesn't grow into something that will cause further schism in the community."

"I thought they acted kind of high-handed," I said, inwardly chortling over Marisa's revelation that she had reason to be conversant with St. Mildred's bylaws. "Of course they felt pressured. I hope Father Den isn't too upset when he finds out."

"So do I." Marisa's tone had turned grim. "I should go now, Emma. I brought work home. Practicing law is a demanding taskmaster."

After hanging up, I waited thirty seconds before dialing the rectory. Sure enough, the line was busy. I then redialed Marisa's number. It, too, was engaged.

I may or may not have taken a step toward a new friendship. But I'd set off an alarm bell in Marisa's mind. I wished I knew why.

The shrimp sat in a colander on my sink counter, pink and plump. But I'd eaten a late lunch and wasn't hungry. Putting the shrimp back in the refrigerator, I left the house and drove downtown. Sure enough, Milo was pulling up with Nunzio Lucci and Verb Vancich. Jack Mullins was with them, and he had Luce handcuffed to his wrist.

Verb kept his distance from Luce while Milo met me at the curb. "I hate to charge Luce, but this is two days in a row," the sheriff said, removing his hat and wiping perspiration from his forehead. Now that the rain had stopped, the air had turned muggy.

I glanced at Verb, who seemed absorbed in a nearby light standard. "Did he really try to shoot Verb?"

"He threatened to, then he resisted arrest." Milo shook his head. "Luce is out of control. Della wasn't there, and he wouldn't tell me where she was."

"She's at the shelter," I said. "She went there last night."

"Shit." Milo turned to Verb. "Come on, you have to fill out a statement."

Verb, however, drew back, clinging to the lamppost. "I don't want to go near that creep. He's nuts."

"Jack's putting him in the holding cell," Milo replied none too patiently. "Let's go, I don't have all night."

"I want my bikes," Verb said, not moving. "Why didn't you bring them with you?"

"Damn it, Verb, we'll get the bikes later," Milo shouted. "Move your ass inside or I'll have to let Luce go."

With great reluctance, Verb trooped through the double doors. Milo stayed on the sidewalk, taking a roll of mints out of his inside pocket. "So what's the deal with Della?" he asked.

Feeling like a snitch, I told the sheriff about the Luccis' most recent conflict. "She took two of the kids with her. Not the ones who swiped the bikes, I'd guess."

Milo started to put the mints back in his pocket, then belatedly offered one to me. "I hate this kind of crap," he groused. "Not the bike deal—that's kid stuff. It's these husbands and wives and so-called friends and neighbors.

The last couple of years that Mulehide and I were married, there were times when I wanted to strangle her, but I never so much as raised my hand, not even when she beaned me with a Ping-Pong paddle."

I'd never heard that story, but this wasn't the time for juicy details. "Go book your perp," I said, giving Milo a poke in the arm. "I'm going to check out Polly's pilgrims. There's more of a story there than the cursory one I did in such a rush for tomorrow's paper."

Milo gave me a quick hug, then went inside. I was starting up the Jag when Verb came out onto the sidewalk, waving a hand. He needed a ride out to the Luccis' house, where he'd left his car. Could I give him a lift?

Nunzio and Della Lucci lived just off the Burl Creek Road. Their nearest neighbors were the Bjornsons, who owned a small, neat farm populated mostly by chickens, a couple of cows, and a horse that was doted on by their teenage daughter. By contrast, the Lucci property was overgrown with tall grasses, vine maples, and wild blackberry vines. A dirt path led from the road to what had once been a comfortable two-story house, but was now run-down and ramshackle. Old railroad ties, discarded toys, shoes, tools, and a hot-water tank littered what could only charitably be called the front yard. While the door stood open, there was no sense of welcome. If Della and the two younger children were still at the shelter, I suspected that the older offspring were hiding from the sheriff.

Verb's car was parked by the mailboxes that served the Luccis, the Bjornsons, and two other families. During the five-minute ride, Verb had griped in a subdued, almost puzzled voice against Luce, the Lucci children, and the world in general. He ran down only when I pulled up in back of his blue Hyundai.

"Thanks, Emma. That was nice of you," he said, looking more meek than usual. "I should have driven back to the sheriff myself. But when Dodge told me to come along, I just followed orders."

It occurred to me that that was the trouble with Verb: he always followed orders, and seldom thought for himself. "Tell me something," I said, ignoring his sudden look of apprehension. "How did you happen to know Warren Wells before he moved back to Alpine? Monica mentioned it the other day."

Verb's narrow shoulders relaxed. "Oh—that. It was a long time ago, before Monica and I got married. Warren and I worked for a sporting-goods store in Seattle, in the Ballard area."

I thought I knew the store, which was part of a large chain. "I gathered from Monica that Warren gave you a bad time."

Verb uttered a small, choked laugh. "In a way, I guess. I was just out of high school, and let's face it, I wasn't too sharp when it came to handling the credit-card customers. I screwed up a few times, and Warren told the manager. I got fired." Verb stared at his shoes.

"That seems a bit severe," I remarked. "Why didn't Warren simply get you squared away?"

Verb's lifeless brown eyes moved slowly to my face. "Looking back, that's what he should have done. But I was barely nineteen, and thought it was the way people acted on the job. The funny thing was, he seemed like a nice guy. I guess he had problems of his own. Later I ran into one of the girls who'd worked there, and she said his stepson was getting into a lot of trouble and his marriage was on the rocks. That wasn't Ms. Wells, of course. I mean it was, but not Francine."

I knew what Verb meant. "Alexis," I said. "She was from Monroe. I understand she died a short time after the divorce."

"Really? That's too bad." Verb seemed genuinely touched. "I only met her once, when she came in the store to pick up Mr. Wells. Warren, I mean. She had the kid with her, and he did seem kind of nasty. You know, a real smart-mouth. He must have been about twelve at the time. I hadn't thought of him in years, but the other day somebody reminded me of him."

Naturally I thought of Roger. "Maybe," I said darkly, "he's in a federal penitentiary by now." Visions, quite delightful, danced through my mind wherein Roger was baking under a hot sun on a chain gang in a remote penal colony. I needed to refocus my brain. "Did you know Monica then?" I inquired as the penal colony faded into a dismal, alligator-infested swamp.

"We met in high school. I went to O'Dea. Monica was at Holy Names." Verb referred to two private Catholic high schools in Seattle, one for boys, the other for girls. Though separated by gender and about four miles, the students mingled on social occasions. "Monica and I went together for quite a while before we got married," Verb continued, smiling softly at the windscreen. "We wanted to be sure. There are too many divorces these days, even among Catholics."

"That was very wise of you," I said, though my mind was again elsewhere. "So the stint in the Ballard store was the only time you worked with Warren?"

Verb nodded. "That's right. The only other time I ever saw him—until he came to Alpine this summer—was a couple of years later when I was working at a sportswear shop in one of the malls. One of the other clerks had caught some kid sneaking out with a Pittsburgh Steelers jersey under his coat. It turned out to be Warren's stepson. Warren came in to talk to the manager and . . ." Verb grimaced. "I don't like raking up all this old stuff, not when Warren's just lost his fiancée. Do you suppose I could collect my bikes now?"

"Where are they?" I asked.

"Out back. At least that's where the kids dumped them after I chased them up the Burl Creek Road." Creases appeared in Verb's high forehead. "Maybe they've hidden them by now."

"Wait," I cautioned. "The sheriff will get the bikes back for you. Those kids might be out there in the trees somewhere. If they're as feisty as their father, you don't want to tangle with them alone."

Verb's expression was uncertain, but ultimately he decided that discretion was the better part of valor. Just as he started to get out of the Jag, I detained him with one last question: "What did Warren do when he came in about the jersey?"

"Oh . . . he insisted that his stepson didn't try to steal it." Verb nervously fingered the door handle. "Then he saw me, and told the manager I'd tried to get the kid in trouble to settle an old score. Luckily the manager knew I hadn't been at work when it happened. I went into the back and stayed there until Warren and the manager sorted things out. We had quite a few shoplifters there, especially teenagers. Those team-logo items are pretty expensive, and the kids just couldn't resist trying to swipe them." He opened the car door and gazed at the vine maple, alder, and fir trees that surrounded the Lucci house. "Like bikes. Kids can't keep their hands off them, either. Sometimes it seems as if everybody's trying to keep me from earning a living. It's not fair." Verb got out of the car and didn't look back.

I drove across town to Polly's house, trying to think of insightful questions to ask the pilgrims. In order to put together a serious article, I'd have to interview Father Den at length. His earlier, off-the-cuff comments didn't do him or the subject justice. I'd also talk to some of the locals who had visited the vase, preferably at least one who believed in its mystical properties and one who was merely a curiosity seeker.

My plans, if not my prayers, seemed answered when I saw Veronica Wenzler-Greene and Warren Wells in the line that went up Polly's steps. I would wait until they emerged from the house and interview them individually. Parking my car a half block away, I decided to remain in place for a few minutes. Less than thirty seconds passed when I noticed that Vida's Buick was pulling up across the street. My House & Home editor got out, along with the odious Roger. Naturally Vida spotted my car at once.

"Roger's parents have come down with flu," she announced in a worried tone. "I told them he shouldn't be exposed to germs, especially after getting so wet yesterday up on Mount Sawyer. He and Grams are going to have an overnight, so that he's fresh and rested for his first day of school." She beamed at her grandson, who looked sullen and was plugged into a Walkman. "Chocolate marshmallow treats and big bowls of—what was it, darling?—bubble-gum ice cream? A special video about the Dance. What was the name of the little show you picked out, dearest?"

"*Showgirls,*" Roger replied, not looking at either of us.

"Yes," Vida said blithely, "a musical. Roger said he preferred it to *Carousel*, but then he keeps up with the latest films and Grams doesn't, I'm afraid."

I could have sworn that Roger snickered, but when I looked at him he was still staring at the sidewalk. Vida was still talking. "I called ahead, to ask Polly if we might sneak in just for a peek at the vase. She wasn't sure— she's never sure of anything, such a muddleheaded woman—but finally suggested we come 'round the back, through the alley. Do you want to join us?"

I hesitated. "I've seen it, of course." On the other hand, it would heighten the atmosphere of my story if I had another look. "Okay, let's go."

Roger lagged behind, so that by the time we'd gone around the end of the block and entered the alley, he was nowhere to be seen. "Really," Vida murmured, as close to exasperation as she ever got with her grandson, "why must youngsters dawdle so? I suppose he's enjoying his little songs on his radio."

When Roger finally appeared, he was gyrating to what
I guessed was a rap number that would have taken all the
curl out of his grandmother's permanent. I considered
telling her that *Showgirls* wasn't exactly Rodgers and
Hammerstein, but a raw version of how to get to the top
by lying on the bottom, at least most of the time. My
opportunity fled, however, when Vida called to Roger to
hurry along, as she was holding the rickety gate of the
picket fence open for him.

It took forever for Polly to reach the back door. We
stood waiting amid piles of newspapers, two plastic
garbage cans, and stacks of empty cardboard boxes. At
last Polly opened the door a crack, then hesitated for
almost a minute until she recognized us.

"Mrs. Runkel. Mrs. Lord," she said in a low voice.
"And the boy."

The boy sauntered into the kitchen as if he owned it, or
perhaps he was so self-absorbed that new experiences
bounced right off his stocky frame. Polly, who had had at
least one child go wrong, ignored Roger. "This way," she
murmured, leading us into the long hall.

As before, the worshipers who filled the living room
were representative of every age, ethnic, and economic
group. I saw a man in a turban and a woman in a kimono.
I also noticed several local residents, none of whom was
Catholic.

"There's a Pidduck," Vida hissed, "from *our* church.
Goodness!"

The darkened room, which had smelled stale when I'd
first visited with Murray Felton, now reeked of sweat and
candle wax and more exotic, if not entirely pleasant,
odors. I held back while Vida took Roger by the arm and
led him toward the mantel. The supplicants parted with
only mild grumbles of protest, though at least half of
them could not have recognized Vida. She stopped in
front of the fireplace, fingering her chin. Roger, still
plugged into his Walkman, fidgeted at her side. After a

few moments Vida leaned down and spoke to her grandson. He dutifully gazed up at the vase, then shrugged. Vida said something else to him and started to turn away, smiling demurely at the waiting pilgrims. Roger, however, remained in front of the mantel. Then he picked up the vase, juggled it experimentally, swayed to the music only he could hear, and dropped the hallowed object onto the hearth.

It smashed into a hundred pieces.

In the pandemonium that followed, I was never quite sure what happened next. Hysterical shrieks, heartrending moans, and angry curses filled the Patricelli living room. Those waiting in the hall and on the porch and even down the steps charged forward, creating a dangerous crush. Someone—perhaps the man in the turban—tried to grab Roger, but Vida was doing her best to drag him out of harm's way. She got as far as the arched entrance to the hall before she encountered Polly.

"Lucifer," Polly whispered in a shaky voice, and collapsed into the arms of Veronica Wenzler-Greene.

"Oh, good grief!" Vida cried, hauling Roger down the hall and toward the back door. Given Roger's bulk, it was no easy task, not even for his stalwart grandmother.

Briefly I thought about following them, but realized that my place was inside the house. That was my story. It wasn't what I'd planned, but it was certainly big news. Noting that Polly seemed in capable hands, I circumvented the stampede and went upstairs in search of a phone. First I had to find a light switch, for it was dark when I reached the second floor. Luckily there was a phone on a small wooden stand. It was the old-fashioned rotary-dial type, and my fingers didn't want to track properly. On the third try, I reached Kip MacDuff in the back shop.

"Is it too late to stop the press?" I shouted over the din that roiled up from the lower floor.

"What? Ms. Lord? What's that?" Kip sounded as if his mouth was full.

"Stop everything. I'll be right there." I hung up and raced back downstairs. Pushing and shoving my way out of the house, I slowed on the uneven cement steps, lest I take a nasty fall. Halfway down, Warren Wells grabbed my arm.

"What's going on in there? I got out of line to have a cigarette and now it sounds like all hell's broke loose."

"It has," I panted. "The devil broke the vase. Or so Polly would have us believe. Excuse me, Warren, I've got to dash."

"But . . ." Warren let go of my arm, though his blue eyes were stunned as he watched me leave. Then, cutting through the muggy night, I heard him cry out: "Alicia! Help me!"

As far as I could tell, Alicia was nowhere in sight. Under any other circumstances, I would have queried Warren hard and fast. But not now. I had to salvage *The Advocate*. Five minutes later I was in the back shop, consulting with Kip MacDuff. He had only just begun the press run, having gone over to the Burger Barn to get his dinner.

"I ran into a couple of guys I knew from high school," he began in apology, "and that's why I was kind of late getting started."

"Never mind," I said hurriedly. "It turns out to be a blessing in disguise. Wait here, I'm going to write a new lead for the miracle-vase story."

It didn't take long, though I realized I was missing various details, including Polly's fate. In deference to Vida, I didn't include Roger's name. We could sort out the fine points in next week's edition. The hardest part was cutting enough of the original story so that the copy would still fit without having to redo the page one layout.

Kip was finishing a large Coke when I rejoined him in the back shop. "I never did see that vase," he said in a musing voice after he read my new lead. "Was it really special?"

"I don't know," I replied in a tired voice. "There were a lot of people who thought so."

Kip ran a hand through his wavy red hair. "I guess we'll never find out now."

In my mind's eye, I saw the long lines of old and young and black and white and rich and poor who had come to Polly's house. "Maybe not," I said after a long pause.

Kip eyed me curiously, then set to work. A few moments later the press was humming. I watched for a while, and then left. On the way home, I drove by St. Mildred's. The church was dark, as I'd expected. All the same I stopped the car and sat for a few minutes, staring up at the single wooden spire that was outlined faintly against the September night. My eyes traveled up to the cross, which legend said was made of iron fashioned from a piece of machinery in the original Alpine mill. During the past few days I had been so caught up in my work that I hadn't taken time to think about the makeshift shrine in the Patricelli living room. My concerns had all been worldly, the outward signs of a life caught up in material goals. Did we purposely make ourselves so busy that there was neither time nor room for spiritual contemplation? It was much easier to think about deadlines than death.

I had not seen Christ in Polly's vase, but I could see the cross. Maybe, I thought, there are many things we cannot see.

But they are still there.

Chapter Sixteen

VIDA WAS CASTIGATING herself. "I should have driven to the funeral in Seattle," she fretted that Wednesday morning. "Someone should represent the paper. Hardly anyone from Alpine is going as far as I know."

"It's a workday," I pointed out. "Ursula hadn't kept up with her old friends here. You said so yourself."

Vida pursed her lips. "That's not important. Now. Oh, Jake and Betsy went, perhaps Laura and Buzzy. Warren, of course, with Alicia."

"Alicia?" I gave Vida a curious look. "Why not Francine?"

"Francine has to stay at the shop." Vida glanced at the clock, which showed that it wasn't yet nine. "I could still make it if I left now." She stood up, grabbing her purse and camera. "I'm going. I'll see you later this afternoon."

Leo watched Vida make her exit. "The Duchess wouldn't miss a good funeral for anything," he remarked. "Do you suppose she'll take pictures of Ursula in her coffin?"

"I hope not," I replied rather vaguely. My thoughts were elsewhere, at St. James Cathedral. I wondered if Murray Felton would be on hand, studying the mourners. I also wondered if I should call him to pass on the news about Ursula's insurance policy. But then I remembered that I didn't have his number. Perhaps I could reach him through the TV station. "No," I said suddenly, returning to reality. "Vida doesn't photograph dead people. It's in poor taste."

Carla looked up from a news release she'd been perusing. "What's being dead got to do with poor taste? Death is part of life."

Leo grinned at Carla. "That's deep, sweetheart. Don't tell me you've been thinking?"

Carla made a face at my ad manager. "Leo, sometimes you're a real jerk. I think all the time. Like now, I was thinking you're a jerk."

The comment made no dent on Leo, who, I noticed, was acting more like himself this morning. A few minutes later, after Carla had left to interview the county commissioners about progress on the new bridge over the Sky, I came out of my office and sat down next to Leo's desk.

"So what's new?" I asked in a lighthearted tone.

Leo set aside a mock-up for the local General Motors dealership. "Not much. How about you?"

"The same. Except that it's been hectic around here lately." I gave a little shrug. "I had to stop the press last night for the first time since I bought the paper."

Leo took a bite out of a sugar doughnut Ginny had picked up at the bakery. "The vase deal? Yeah, that was a hell of a thing. What really happened?"

I was still loath to name names. Vida had called me late last night, asking how I intended to handle the story. I'd informed her that it was a *fait accompli*, but I hadn't mentioned Roger. Naturally she had defended him, insisting that his youthful curiosity—such a fine attribute in a young mind—had triggered the incident. I had said nothing. Word would get out soon enough. Indeed, it probably had within an hour of the disaster. I wondered if that was the real reason that Vida had been anxious to get out of town.

But apparently Leo hadn't heard the details. I was reluctant to tell him, since I knew that his opinion of

Roger was as unfavorable as mine. On the other hand, I didn't want to upset Leo's newly regained good humor. Certainly he would find out the truth before the day was done.

Leo, however, changed the subject before I could reply. "That Kelly's pretty sharp," my ad manager said, brushing sugar from his plaid sport shirt. "How come you never told me about him?"

"What are you talking about?" I asked in surprise. "I've mentioned Father Den often, and usually with praise."

Leo fingered his upper lip. "Hunh. Maybe I wasn't paying attention."

"Maybe you didn't want to hear it." As a fallen-away Catholic, Leo wasn't inclined to take in anything positive about the Church. "So now you two are chums?"

"Not exactly," Leo replied. "We had a little talk last night. I happened to run into him at Cal Vickers's station after work. Kelly had just come back from Tacoma."

I regarded Leo with amusement. "So you yukked it up around the gas pumps?"

Leo stretched in an exaggeratedly casual manner. "Actually I went over to the rectory and had a drink with him. He's really down-to-earth. I guess it's his army-brat background. He doesn't go around with his head in the clouds like some of the priests I've known."

"You've met my brother," I retorted. "Ben's as real as they come."

Leo tipped his head to one side. "Ben's okay. But he's like you—kind of indecisive. Neither of you likes taking a stand."

That much was true. In my case, I called it journalistic objectivity, and being fair in print. As for Ben, he acted out of Christian charity, unwilling to judge. To observers, we sometimes seemed wishy-washy.

I wasn't about to argue with Leo. "Talking to Father Den seems to have improved your mood," I said lightly.

Leo's gaze was ironic. "Are you asking if I unburdened myself?" Before I could answer, he chuckled. "Maybe I did, in a way. But we didn't have much time. He got a phone call that seemed to throw him. I decided I'd better split."

I recalled the busy lines at Marisa's and at the rectory. "Do you know who phoned him?"

Leo looked perplexed. "No. It was none of my business. It's not like Kelly's my new best bud. We just had a drink and yakked for a bit. Who do you think called him? The Village Harlot?"

"Hardly." My tone was priggish. "In case you haven't been reading *The Advocate*, and since you don't attend church, you may have missed the controversy that's going on at St. Mildred's."

Leo feigned terror. "Wow. Which is the greater sin, missing Mass or skimming your stories?"

My ad manager's disposition may have improved, but mine was deteriorating. "Look, a member of the parish was found dead last Friday night. Maybe it was an accident, maybe not. But if somebody deliberately drowned Ursula Randall, then it could have something to do with what's going on at St. Mildred's. Don't tell me you haven't noticed, Leo, or I'll have to cut your salary."

"Relax, babe. I've noticed. Parish politics are a pain in the ass. Even in those dark, dim days when I used to go to church, I kept out of that crap. It's pure poison. If people want to backstab and spread scandal and incite hostilities and screw up basic ideologies, then they should join the Democratic party. The trouble is," Leo went on, now looking quite serious, "you've always got a bunch of the Little People in any group who have to prove they exist by causing trouble. The bigger the institution, the nastier the attack. They're not only weasels, they're hypocrites. Fuck 'em, I say. That's another reason I don't go to church."

I was sure that Leo's list of reasons for staying in bed

on Sunday morning was lengthy. But he was right about
parish troublemakers. "I should go see Father Den," I
said, more to myself than to Leo. "I've felt all along
that there's more to this parish conflict than meets
the eye."

"It wasn't all Liza's fault." Leo made the statement
while staring at the GM mock-up.

"What?" It took me a moment to recall that Liza was
Leo's ex-wife.

"The breakup." Now he did look at me. "I was an asshole. It's a wonder she put up with me as long as she
did."

I knew that Liza had left Leo for another man, or so he
had told me. I also knew that the reality was that Liza had
left, period. The other man may have been waiting in the
wings, but he wasn't the reason that the marriage had
failed. Leo had had difficulty keeping a job, he had been
an unsatisfactory parent, he had neglected his wife, he
had drunk too much. All of these things he had acknowledged, but never had admitted what a disastrous impact
his flaws had had on his marriage.

I didn't know exactly what to say. "You're not an asshole now," I finally allowed. "Not often, anyway." I
smiled.

"People don't change," Leo said, his voice a little
ragged. "But maybe they sort of mutate."

The phone was ringing in my office. "Maybe." Gin-
gerly I patted Leo's shoulder. "I'm glad you finally sat
down with Father Den."

"Yeah. Me, too." Leo returned to his mock-up.

I returned to my office and caught the call just before it
trunked over to Ginny. Della Lucci's anxious voice
touched my ear.

"Could I see you, Ms. Lord? I need . . . some advice."

Giving advice is a trap. If volunteered, it's usually
scorned. If sought, it's rarely taken. People don't want

advice, they want sympathy and reinforcement of their own beliefs and actions.

But Della was pathetic. She was still at the shelter, so I said I'd meet her there in twenty minutes. Unlike larger cities, where anonymity is more easily achieved, there is nothing secret about Alpine's shelter. It's located in an old three-story house on First Hill off Highway 167. Officially run by the town's churches, the staff is made up of volunteers. When I arrived just after ten-thirty, Shirley Bronsky met me at the door.

"Emma!" she squealed, jiggling around in her lime-and-black-striped tank dress. "Have you come to lend a hand? We could use it—Mrs. Bartleby from Trinity Episcopal and I have been here since six this morning. The place is jammed—as usual. Do you know that we've got women who've come all the way from Wenatchee?"

Female figures skittered in and out of doors along the narrow hall while children yipped and skipped around the living room, which had been turned into a play area. With a twinge of guilt, I informed Shirley that I hadn't come to relieve her or the wife of the Episcopalian rector, but to see Della Lucci. Since I wasn't a volunteer, Shirley immediately became officious. Had Della sent for me? Did she expect me? How had the meeting been arranged?

I explained about the telephone call, adding that I understood Shirley's insistence on security. Seemingly satisfied, she led me to the old-fashioned, high-ceilinged kitchen, where Della was preparing a vat of macaroni and cheese.

"I kept the kids out of school today," Della said shyly as she wiped her hands on a dish towel and sat down at the long trestle table. "It's the first day, and they won't miss much."

"Probably not," I agreed.

"Is it true that Luce is in jail?" As soon as she asked the question, Della lowered her eyes.

"He was last night," I said. "He got into a row with Verb Vancich over those bikes."

Della looked up and blinked. "What bikes?"

"The bikes that were stolen from Verb's store. Verb believes that your kids may have taken them." I saw no point in softening the blow.

But Della was indignant. "That's dumb! Luce bought those bikes for the twins' birthday."

The last thing I wanted to do was get into a dispute between the Luccis and the Vanciches. "Verb thought otherwise," I said, dumping the burden where it belonged. "In any event, Luce threatened Verb, and Verb called the sheriff. I suspect that your husband will be released today."

"Mmm." Della cupped her round chin in her hand. "So where does that leave me? Not here—I hate it. The kids hate it. But I won't go back to Luce. I hate him."

The words were spoken without rancor, a simple statement of fact, which made them all the more jarring. "So you plan to leave Luce?" I asked.

Della sighed, her plump bosom heaving under the same stained shift I'd last seen her wearing at Sunday Mass. "I guess. I just don't know where to go, Ms. Lord. That's what I wanted to ask you."

I began by quizzing Della about her family. She was from Skykomish, but her parents were dead and her only sibling, a brother, had moved to Montana years ago. There was a cousin—she thought—in one of the Seattle suburbs, Renton or maybe Maple Valley. She'd lost track of him some Christmases past. Luce's mother was also dead, and his father was in the local nursing home. The three Lucci sisters were scattered around the West, and their brother hadn't really kept in touch. It sounded to me as if Della was on her own.

"If," I began, feeling on very shaky ground, "you could work something out with Luce, at least for a while, you might consider reeducating yourself when the new community college opens. Then you'd have some marketable skills if you wanted to make a move and look for work."

Della was aghast. "Me? Go to college? Oh, Ms. Lord! I'm not that smart."

It was pointless to enumerate the borderline morons I'd known who had been given degrees by supposedly reputable institutions of higher learning. "The college will offer vocational training," I pointed out. "I've heard that food services will be among them. You've had experience, cooking at the high school." Indeed, I wondered why Della wasn't there now. Perhaps it was because the first day was usually over at noon. "Think about it, Della. And please stop calling me Ms. Lord. We must be about the same age."

"But you're ..." Della's spindly voice trailed off. I knew she was going to say that I was a college graduate, a newspaper editor, a *writer*, for God's sake. In her eyes, I was virtually canonized as a secular saint.

"Never mind," I interrupted. "The point is, can you reconcile with Luce?"

Before Della could answer, her two youngest children raced into the kitchen, the boy chasing the girl. He was around nine and had a garter snake in his hand. I let out a little yelp while the girl screamed and flung herself against Della.

"He's got a poison snake!" the girl cried. "He's going to kill me! Help!"

Della retained her implacable air. "It's just a garter snake, Megan. Put that down, Joe-Joe, or I'll cook it in the pot."

Joe-Joe waved the snake over his head. "You can't cook it. It's full of poison. If you eat it, you'll die, just like Pa said he wished you'd do."

Della's plump shoulders sagged. "Pa was making a joke. He doesn't mean what he says. Put that snake back outside, or I'll have to use this." She pointed to the

wooden spoon with which she'd been stirring the macaroni. "Go on now. Don't make me mad."

Whether Joe-Joe believed that his mother could exert
herself sufficiently to become angry, or whether the
squirming snake was beginning to lose its charm, I didn't
know. But the boy thrust the snake one last time at his
sister, was rewarded with another shriek, and left the
kitchen. Megan continued to cling to her mother until
Della pried her loose.

"Go play with those nice girls from Skykomish,
Megan. They're building a castle for their dollies."

Reluctantly Megan moved away, her big brown eyes
riveted on me. She looked about seven, with an intelligent face that must have been a throwback to a previous
generation. Certainly neither Della nor Luce seemed
overly bright.

"Let's go away and leave Joe-Joe here," Megan said,
slowly backing toward the door. "He's mean."

"Joe-Joe's a tease," his mother declared. "Pay no
attention. He'll stop."

Megan looked dubious, but finally left the kitchen. I
wondered if her mother's advice grew out of the way
she'd handled Luce over the years: maybe Della had pretended that her husband was only kidding. Maybe she'd
never acknowledged the mean streak, the latent violence,
the bully in him.

A sudden thought popped into my mind. "Is it money?
I mean, would you get along better if Luce wins his
suit?"

Again, Della looked blank. "What suit?"

"The malpractice suit against Dr. Randall's estate."

"Who's Dr. Randall?" Della seemed utterly mystified.

So was I. "Ursula Randall's late husband. I understand
that he operated on Luce a few years ago. Apparently the
-surgery wasn't successful and . . ."

Della was shaking her head. "Luce never had an operation. That's why he limps. After the doctors told him

there were some risks, he wouldn't take the chance. Luce got real disappointed in doctors. The only person he ever sued was the logging company, but he lost because the accident was part of the job. What do they call it? An 'occupational hazard,' I think."

I thought back to my conversation with Murray Felton. He had assured me that Luce was one of the plaintiffs in the outstanding malpractice suits filed against Wheaton Randall. Had Murray been mistaken? Or had Luce not told his wife about taking the late surgeon to court? But certainly Della would know if her husband had had an operation. My confusion grew.

"I'm not going back to Luce," Della was saying, her plump hands now made into fists and resting on the table's worn fir planks. "If the twins want to stay with him, fine. But Megan and Joe-Joe are going with me. If I went to Monroe, where would I stay?"

"Monroe?" I echoed. "Why Monroe?"

"Seattle's too big. I'm scared of cities. Even Everett has grown too much." Della's lower lip protruded and I thought she was going to cry. "Monroe is just about right."

"Talk to Father Den," I said, feeling inadequate. "He can put you in touch with Catholic Community Services. Will you do that?"

Della looked uncertain. "Won't Father think I'm terrible for leaving Luce?"

"Father doesn't judge people," I said firmly. "He tries to help them. He knows about the resources that you have at your disposal. Go see him. Today, if he's free."

"Ohhh . . ." Della's helplessness enveloped her like a straitjacket. My mind flashed back to a similar encounter at a kitchen table, with Laura O'Toole. But Laura had more backbone. She had stood her ground, and thrown Buzzy out. Della had less courage, and only enough initiative to bring her as far as the shelter.

"Look," I said as Della continued to dither, "I'll go see

Father Den. Then I'll have him get in touch with you,
okay?"

Judging from Della's frightened expression, the idea
was about as okay as third-degree burns. Change—any
kind of change—clearly terrified her. She could turn her
back on Luce, but she couldn't face something new.

I left her, staring at the vat on the stove. Shirley was
nowhere to be seen, though a trio of toddlers scampered
after me down the hall. They seemed happy. I marveled
at their resilience, or perhaps it was ignorance. What
ghastly domestic situation had brought them to the
shelter? I could drive away without fear, but the sordid
home lives of these little exiles would go with me.

St. Mildred's was halfway between First Hill and *The
Advocate*, so I stopped at the rectory. I didn't like calling
on Father Den unannounced, but I also didn't like having
Della Lucci on my plate, quivering like leftover Jell-O.

Monica Vancich was on duty in the small office just
off the parlor. She seemed remarkably cheerful on this
overcast September morning. I couldn't resist asking
her why.

"We had the most wonderful liturgy this morning, for
the opening of the school year," she said, her usually pale
face aglow. "Sister Mary Joan and Ronnie Wenzler-
Greene arranged it. Women are so much better at creating a meaningful religious experience—we're truly in
touch with our feelings. Each child was given a piece of
bark."

"Bark?" I echoed. "Why?"

"To symbolize the external." Monica picked up a
small chunk of bark that looked as if it had come off of a
cottonwood tree. "We all have outward signs of protec-
tion, whether it be pride or intolerance or a sharp tongue.
When these things are peeled away, our innermost being
is revealed. Just like a tree." She gazed up at me with a
sublime expression.

I tried to imagine how children under ten had related to

this analogy. "Did the students find it . . . meaningful?"
When in buzz, speak as the buzzworders do.

Monica's face tightened. "Well . . . you know how
children can be sometimes. Especially boys. We had a
little problem with them throwing the bark around the
church."

"Really." Hoping to deflect any more of Monica's
liturgical anecdotes, I asked if Verb had gotten his bikes
back yet. She said he hadn't, and was becoming rather
cross with Milo Dodge. Not wanting to hear the sheriff
criticized, I hastened to ask if Father Den was available.

"He's in his office," she replied stiffly. "I'll let him
know you're here."

Dennis Kelly was going over the school enrollment
figures when I arrived. He looked frazzled, even a little
haggard. I wasted no time telling him about Della and her
apparent needs. He expressed concern, promising that
he'd try to help. If she was serious about moving, he
knew of a Seattle parish that was searching for a cook.

"Della's afraid of big cities," I said with reluctance.
"She was thinking of some smaller place, like Monroe."

"Della doesn't have unlimited choices," Den pointed
out bluntly. "If she takes the cook's job, she'll still have
to find a place to live. She can stay with the kids at the
Sacred Heart shelter down by the Seattle Center for a
month until they get themselves squared away."

"I don't think she'll go," I said apologetically, as if
Della's fears were my fault. "She doesn't have the
nerve."

"That's up to her." Den jabbed at the papers on his
desk. "Her two younger kids are absent today. She can't
keep them out of school forever."

I stood up, my gaze taking in the cramped office, which
still showed evidence of Father Fitz's long tenure as
pastor. During that time the square little room had been
called the study. Many of the volumes in the open book-
cases had belonged to him, along with the old-fashioned

brass pedestal ashtray, the painting of the Agony in the Garden, and a letter of commendation from a bishop in County Cork. Though Father Fitz's worldly possessions had been few, I suspected that there was little room for more than the necessities in the nursing home where he was living out his last days.

"I'm sorry I bothered you with this," I said. "I tried to get her to come to see you, but she was afraid of that, too."

"Why?" Father Den's glance was ironic. "Am I such a monster?"

"What are you talking about?"

The priest let out a big sigh. "I was never a pastor until I came here. You know that. I was a teacher, and a damned good one, if I may be honest instead of modest. But you can't teach invisible students. When there are no vocations, there are no classrooms." He clapped his hands together. "Bang! The seminaries close their doors, and become wineries or resort complexes or mental institutions. You know what bugs the hell out of me, Emma? I'll bet it bugs your brother, too. Guys like us give our lives to God, and we think it's a great thing to do. But we aren't conveying that to young men. These kids look at us, and all they think about is that we can't go to bed with a woman. Or that we do, on the sly—when we're not playing games with little boys and other men." Den's expression became rueful. "Sorry, I don't usually rant like this. I wouldn't do it now if you didn't have a brother who's a priest."

I had sat back down in the old oak chair with its straight, uncomfortable back, which would have enhanced any nun's job of encouraging correct posture. "It's not your fault, or Ben's. It's that the world is too much with us."

"I know, I know. TV, movies, books—the material and sexual messages are clear. Maybe," Den went on, the familiar spark of humor finally surfacing in his dark eyes, "they ought to show commercials with priests surfing or skiing or drinking beer."

I laughed. "We could get Leo to put together an ad showing you with ski equipment from Verb Vancich's store."

The humor fled. "Verb." Father Den groaned softly. "Oh, he's all right. I guess."

"Monica?" The name slipped out.

Den pressed his fist against his lips. "They want me out," he finally said.

I jumped in the chair. "Who?"

But Den wouldn't say, at least not specifically. "Some parishioners feel they can inject themselves into every facet of their church. Liturgy, budget, building—you name it. And the school, of course. That goes without saying. After Vatican Two, when the laity was encouraged to take a more active part, the floodgates were opened. Oh, changes were needed, they still are, no doubt about it. But unfortunately many Catholics got some weird ideas about participation. They don't—or won't—understand that the Church hierarchy is still in place, which means that on the parochial level, the pastor retains command. If that weren't true, there'd be chaos. The Church isn't a democracy. Americans, especially, sometimes find that galling."

Searching for his views on the latest parish-council debacle, I tried to sort through Father Den's soliloquy. "Are you saying that Jake and the others usurped your powers at the emergency meeting?"

Father Den waved an impatient hand. "Oh, sure, of course they did. But they weren't being mean-spirited." He gave me a sickly grin. "Another typically American response—if something's broken, we have to fix it. Now. That's what they did. And I'll have to try to unfix it, by doing the right thing, which will be to remove Ed and have him run for Luce's spot." His hand fell away to his side and his face sagged. "It's just one more pain in the neck. There are days when I wonder why I bother."

"You're not thinking of leaving, are you?" I asked in alarm.

"I don't know." Den stared through the small window that looked across the parking lot to the church. "I won't stay if I'm a bone of contention, like some icon for evil. The truth is, I may be a lousy pastor. I've never been very organized, and finances aren't my strong suit. In fact, I'm not entirely sure what I do have to offer the faithful."

"Faith," I said. "Maybe that's enough."

Den responded with something like a cross between a snort and a sneer. "You know," he said, putting the school enrollment papers aside, "last week I dreaded the idea of Ursula Randall getting on the school board. I saw nothing but trouble. Now I wonder. She would have been a force, possibly for good. I'm glad I'm not preaching her funeral homily. I would have made a lot of people mad."

"Why?" I asked, though I could guess.

But Father Den kept his own counsel. Not having publicly uttered his condemnation of certain mind-sets among the laity, he wasn't about to do so privately. Thus we changed the subject, and I brought him up to date on Ben's misfortune in Tuba City. As he walked me to the door of his office, Den promised to try to raise some funds for a new church.

"I hadn't thought about it before," he said in wonder, "but your brother's in a situation similar to mine."

"How so?" Ben had been pastor in the home missions for almost twenty years.

"He's the wrong race," Den replied. "He can never be one of them."

"I don't agree," I said. "Faith binds us together. That's what being children of God means. We're all the same."

Father Den held out his dark brown arm next to my pale white skin and smiled sadly. "No, we're not."

*   *   *

If the funeral Mass for Ursula was held at noon, then the service and the reception should be over by three. On the chance that he'd attended one or both, I'd wait until four to call Murray Felton at the TV station. Maybe he could clear up the misunderstanding about Luce's lawsuit.

On my way back from St. Mildred's, I'd stopped at the mall and bought teriyaki takeout for lunch. It was never very good, perhaps because the concession was run by a Norwegian and a Dane, but it was a change from the grease at the Burger Barn and the Venison Inn.

I was stuffing myself with chopped cabbage and boiled rice and minuscule strips of beef when Ed thumped into my office. "Don't tell me you forgot about our meeting? I've come prepared." He waved a file folder under my nose. "Promotional stuff, marketing concepts, big PR plans. Do you want to start with the TV spots?"

I honestly couldn't recall having set a specific time for getting together with Ed to discuss his book publicity. Maybe by being vague, I'd hoped he'd forget, too.

"Ed," I began, "I don't have time for—"

"Sure you do, it's Wednesday." Ed's familiarity with my work schedule was an obvious drawback—for me. "I don't have much time, actually. I'm supposed to meet Father Den at two. I suppose it's about my appointment to the parish council." Ed's buoyant humor faded a bit. "Have you talked to him about it?"

I hedged. "Not in detail. I saw him just now, but we got off on other things."

Ed nodded sagely. "The school board, I'll bet. Derek Norman and Debra Barton are a standoff. They might as well not have bothered adding the new members."

I considered the complexities of church politics. Ursula Randall had been what I'd call an archconservative, a pre–Vatican II Catholic of the old school who'd just as soon hear the Mass in Latin with the priest's back turned to the congregation. Veronica Wenzler-Greene was poles apart, a liberal who interpreted anything the pope said as "optional." The Monica Vanciches of this world were somewhere in the middle, or nowhere at all except in a spiritual la-la land where they viewed life, death, and the religion that guided them through rose-colored glasses. "You figure Bill Daley for the swing vote?" I asked. The conclusion was fairly obvious.

"He always has been," Ed replied, shuffling papers. "Greer Fairfax and Buddy Bayard never agree on much of anything. It's like Monica and Luce on the parish council. Complete opposites. They way I see it," Ed went on, settling his elbows on the desk and leaning forward, "Luce was unpredictable, what I call a loose cannon. Hey!" Ed sat up and beamed all over himself. "That's good! A Luce cannon. Get it?"

I nodded. Ed kept talking. "I could put that in the book somewhere, like the epilogue, where I'll write about how I saved the parish or whatever I do once I get going on the council. Where was I? Oh, now that Luce is out, the politics are harder to figure. Francine and Jake both like to put their fingers in the financial pie. They haven't always sided with Father Den, especially when it comes to money. Brendan Shaw's like Bill Daley—he sits on the fence. And of course the only thing that Monica likes about Den is that he's colored."

"What?" I thought that I hadn't heard Ed correctly.

"Monica always upholds minorities," Ed asserted in his condescending newly rich man's way. "Blacks, Indians, Indian Indians—you know, the ones from India—Orientals, the whole shot. So Monica has to *say* she likes Den, even though she doesn't because they don't agree on much of anything."

I thought I understood what Ed was trying to say. I also thought that Monica was practicing reverse prejudice. But that wasn't the issue. "So you're bringing the voice of reason to the council?" I said in solemn tones.

"Sure," Ed replied, sitting bunched up like a Kewpie

doll in my visitor's chair. "I back Den most of the time, so he can't lose with me on his side. But I don't know about the others. I guess I'll have to talk turkey to Francine and Jake and Brendan, just like I did when they were my advertisers."

If Ed meant that he was going to support Dennis Kelly through thick and thin, then I wished him well and hoped that his appointment would stick. I suggested, however, that he might have to run for the post.

The prospect didn't please him. "That would be two special elections in two weeks. Not good, it's like a merchant holding two sales back-to-back. People think something's fishy."

I'd managed to finish my lunch and was anxious to get back to work. "Say, Ed, why don't you leave your folder here and I'll go over it this evening. I want to get a head start on my editorial for next week. Research is required for this one. I'm beginning a campaign to make the sheriff an appointee, rather than an elected official."

"Oh, Emma!" Ed's disappointment was, I felt, for my lack of eagerness in discussing his promotional plans. But I was wrong. "You don't want to do that, not when you're . . . uh . . . well, you know . . . with Milo." A hint of pink touched his chubby cheeks.

I'd listened to Ed's criticisms of my conduct with the sheriff before. He was always quick to point out some imagined conflict of interest. For once, I fought fire with fire.

"That's ridiculous, Ed. My relationship with Milo—not that it's anybody's damned business—has nothing to do with the philosophy behind how Skykomish County chooses its sheriff. If people want to talk, I can't stop them. I imagine half the town is saying that you bought your way onto the parish council."

"Whoa!" Judging from the quiver of his triple chins, Ed was definitely taken aback. "I haven't heard anybody say that. Yet." The familiar doleful expression returned.

"Anyway, I'm not the only rich parishioner these days. Jake and Buzzy are getting a pretty big bundle. In fact, they could end up richer than I am." Ed became downright morose.

"Hardly," I remarked, knowing that all of Ed's self-esteem was tied up in his net worth. "It's only half a million each, which is quite a bit less than you inherited from your aunt."

Ed's cocker-spaniel eyes stared at me. "That's just the insurance money. They get everything, including the house in The Pines. Or haven't you heard?"

I hadn't. "How do you know that?"

"Doubles told me," Ed answered. "I stopped by this morning before he left for the funeral. Since Shirl and I weren't going, I thought I should at least pay my respects."

I dumped the Styrofoam carton that had housed my teriyaki into the wastebasket. "So Warren comes out with nothing?"

Ed nodded, the chins now merely bouncing. "It's a shame, really. He's never had much luck when it comes to women. At least he got some money from that second wife."

"He did?" My voice was faint, as I remained stunned by Ed's bombshell.

"That was an insurance deal, too. Alexis, I think that was her name, wasn't rich or anything like that, but she had a fairly good-sized insurance policy. When they divorced, it was set up so that if anything happened to either of them, the surviving spouse would get the life insurance to help raise the kid. That's common, according to Brendan Shaw."

"You mean the stepson?" Ed had me muddled again.

"Right. Except that Warren couldn't stand the kid, and he went to live with an aunt or somebody." Ed was now speaking fast, as if bored with the subject. His pudgy fingers were sorting through his file.

"What about the boy's father?" I asked as an odd, almost sinister feeling seemed to seep into the atmosphere of my crowded little office.

"I don't think he was ever in the picture," Ed said, handing me several sheets of paper that were stapled together. "It was one of those deals where the guy walked as soon as the girl got pregnant. For all I know, they weren't ever married. Some people have no sense of responsibility." Apparently Ed saw my face tighten. "Hey, sorry, I don't mean . . . that is, I've never asked . . . everybody's different." The last words came out in a mumble.

I moved quickly to take the rest of the file from Ed. "Don't call me, I'll call you," I said, trying to keep my voice light. "See you, Ed."

For once, Ed left without another word.

Ursula Randall's funeral Mass had been impressive, Vida grudgingly admitted when she returned to work around three-thirty. She'd been tempted to stay for the reception, but had felt obligated to head home. Of course she had some quibbles about the ceremony.

"Such gaudy costumes—really, I don't see why priests and bishops and such have to dress up like something from the Middle Ages. A simple black robe—that's what Pastor Purebeck wears, no matter what the occasion. And never, *never* anything on his head. Honestly, I half expect to see one of your high muck-a-mucks show up with fruit on his hat, just like Carmen Miranda!"

Assuming that Vida was referring to a miter, I asked if the archbishop had celebrated the Mass. Vida thought so—she rather fancied that she recognized him from his photographs. Naturally she had observed much more than the liturgy and its participants. The eulogy had lauded Ursula for her support, both moral and financial. The pallbearers had been unknown to her, though she assumed they were old friends from the Seattle area.

Warren had behaved in a dignified manner, with Alicia at his side. All four of the O'Tooles had been in attendance, sitting *en famille*. Vida assessed their demeanor as appropriately sorrowful. The cathedral was almost full, evidence of Ursula's impact on the community. There had been no untoward incidents, which clearly disappointed Vida. Her manner seemed to suggest that things would have gone differently in Alpine.

I called the TV station at four and asked for Murray. "Not here!" the breezy young voice responded, and disconnected me with a decisive click. I'd try Murray again in the morning. There was no rush.

A few minutes later Vida returned to my office. She had started getting caught up on phone messages that had accumulated in her absence. One of them was from her niece Marje Blatt, the medical clinic's receptionist.

Polly Patricelli was in the hospital. According to Vida, the old lady had suffered a mild stroke. I waited for my House & Home editor to exhibit some kind of remorse for her grandson's carelessness, but none was forthcoming. Vida reiterated her belief that Roger had merely been curious, and who could blame the inquiring mind of a child? As ever, I marveled at Vida's blind spot.

I decided to stop by and see Polly on my way home from work. The local hospital is small, with only fifty beds. Even so, many of them were empty. The recent changes in medical coverage didn't permit anyone to take up space for very long.

Polly seemed to take up almost no space as she lay in the narrow hospital bed. Though always small, she appeared to have shrunken in the last twenty-four hours. Her cloudy old eyes were open, but she neither heard nor recognized me. I stayed for only a few minutes, then left her in the maze of monitors and IV tubing.

Dennis Kelly was out in the hall, talking to Doc Dewey. I kept my distance, not wanting to interrupt. After a couple of minutes Doc returned to the nurses' station and Den turned in my direction. He looked pleased to see me, though still haggard.

"Is she awake?" Den asked as I noted that he wore his stole under the black clerical jacket. I assumed he had brought Holy Communion to Polly. "Is she alert?"

I shook my head. "Her eyes are open, though. Do you know when they admitted her?"

"Pete Patricelli called for an ambulance this afternoon," Father Den replied. "Rita had spent the night with their mother, and couldn't rouse her. I suppose it was that damned vase." His expression was rueful.

"You never saw it, did you?" I inquired.

"No. I meant to, but I was gone for part of the weekend." Father Den sighed. "In a way, I'm not sorry it got broken."

I was surprised. "What do you mean?"

Father Den's pleasant, if unremarkable, features hardened. "Those so-called miracles often cause more harm than good. People get caught up in superstition, they mistake magic for grace. Why is it," he went on, growing more quizzical, "that we can talk about cracks in a piece of ceramic, but not about God? Sidle up to a bar, get yourself a martini, and start in on 'How about that vase?' and everybody chatters like chimps. But mention that you've been reflecting on your commitment to Jesus Christ, and people look at you like you're some kind of circus freak. I don't get it. But it's true. Even among Christians, God's not a conversational topic."

"Religion is private," I remarked. "It's like talking about sex or money."

"Oh, Emma!" Den's dark eyes were full of irony. "And I thought priests were supposed to be living in the Dark Ages. Everybody talks about sex and money these days. But they still don't talk about God."

I felt myself blush. "*I* don't talk about sex and money."

Den uttered a choked little laugh. "You probably don't talk about God, either." He held up a hand. "Sorry, this isn't the place for a homily. I'm out of line. Maybe you're not like the rest of them."

Maybe.

Milo had let Luce out of jail that afternoon. The charge had been reduced, and the judge had ordered the prisoner released on his own recognizance. Luce also had received a stern warning, which would probably do no good. I had conveyed Father Den's message to Della via Jack Mullins's wife, Nina, who was working the afternoon volunteer shift at the shelter. Nina, an eternal optimist, assured me that Della would jump at the chance to move to Seattle. I held my tongue. Della wouldn't jump out of a ring of fire if it meant leaving her own comfort zone.

It was still cloudy and had grown cooler, though I knew that autumn had not yet set in. September and early October often brought Indian summer. On the off chance that Milo might drop by later, I put on my better bathrobe, which was the one without the cigarette burns and the permanent grease stains.

Glancing down at the aqua chenille that had long ago lost its fluff, I thought about Ursula and her satin lounging pajamas. I also thought about dry-cleaning bills. Only the rich could afford to sit around the house in glamorous outfits. Only the foolish would wear satin wedgies to the Skykomish River.

But Ursula hadn't intended to go to the river. I realized that now, doubting that even an intoxicated woman would wear such footgear to walk along the Sky. When she unexpectedly found herself there on the rocky banks, she had removed those shoes. That was the only explanation for having one shoe on the wrong foot. Ursula had taken them off, but someone had put one of them back on after she was dead. He—or she—hadn't finished the task. There had been an interruption, or some kind of scare. The other shoe had somehow found its way up Mount

Sawyer. How? I marveled that I hadn't thought through this scenario before.

Milo wasn't home. It was not yet eight, so I assumed he'd stopped to eat dinner. I tried again five minutes later, but there was still no answer. I called Vida instead.

"Well." My House & Home editor was suitably impressed after hearing my theory. "You've come to the obvious conclusion, I see. Ursula was definitely murdered."

Chapter Seventeen

I GRIMACED INTO the receiver. "It *could* mean that she was murdered. Or that whoever brought her to the river left without her and somebody else came along. Before Richie Magruder, that is."

"Too complicated," Vida declared. "Simple explanations are usually best. I've felt all along that Ursula's death wasn't accidental. The problem is that homicide by drowning is so difficult to ascertain. According to Buck, who encountered a similar situation when he was in the military, it's only detectable if there's evidence of a struggle. In that case, there was, and the killer was apprehended. I'm beginning to think Ursula's murderer will go free."

So was I. Except for that curious, eerie feeling I'd had while talking to Ed. I wasn't sure at the time what had caused the sensation, and I tried to explain it to Vida.

"You felt strange while speaking with Ed?" Vida exclaimed. "I should think so! Conversations with that ninny make me queasy. Everything is always about *Ed*."

"This was different." I couldn't put my finger on what had set me off. "It was something he said, about Warren and his second wife, the one who died. Vida, are you sure she had leukemia?"

Vida grew testy. "I told you, I know nothing about her." The admission came hard. "Mrs. DeBee had no sense of news gathering. If Warren married someone from out of town—and in this case, out of county—she

306

simply paid no attention. Our readers were ill informed until I came to work for *The Advocate*."

There was no bravado in Vida's tone, just a statement of fact. "It was Francine who told me," I said. "I *think* it was Francine."

"If you have reason to doubt, we could check through the *Times*," Vida said, simmering down. "I assume she died in Seattle, though she may have returned to Monroe. Better yet, we could call the paper in Monroe. They would have posted a notice, since she was a local woman. The obituary might list cause of death, or name a charity associated with whatever disease she suffered from. If indeed it was a disease," Vida added darkly. "Are you thinking what I'm thinking?"

"I guess." I didn't like thinking it, though.

"I know the present editor," Vida said. "I'll call him tomorrow."

After I hung up, I tried Milo's number again. He still wasn't home, so I left a message. Now that I was off the phone with Vida, my fancy about Alexis Wells seemed foolish. Searching back through the exchange with Ed, I tried to recall what might have triggered my rush of anxiety. We had talked about Warren's bad luck with women, about his second wife's insurance, about the stepson, about the disposition of Ursula's estate. It was all tragic, but not exactly sinister.

By nine o'clock, I'd given up on Milo. There was a movie on TV that seemed worth watching, so I settled in front of the set with a glass of Pepsi and my second cigarette of the day. I hadn't managed to quit smoking, but I'd definitely cut down. Before the first intermission, I was disenchanted with the plodding story line. Turning off the TV, I went into the kitchen to get more Pepsi.

That was when I heard the noise.

At first I thought it was coming from the bedroom, and that my intruder was back. I froze in front of the refrigerator, then realized that someone was knocking at the door, instead of using the bell. Maybe it was Milo.

It was Murray Felton. In my surprise, I spilled Pepsi on the floor. After I let him in, Murray laughed, insisted on getting a towel from the bathroom, and finally sauntered over to my dark green armchair while I wiped up the puddle. I offered him his choice of beer or Pepsi, but he declined.

"I came up here to give you some professional advice," Murray said, making himself comfortable. "You've had a real human-interest story fall in your lap. Don't assign it to a staffer, write it yourself. It's all about opportunism, and how it doesn't always pay off."

I had thought at first that Murray was talking about Polly's vase. But now I realized he wasn't. The problem was that I didn't know what he meant. "Luce? Ursula? The town itself?"

"No, no." Murray shook his head, somewhat deflated by my obtuseness. "Warren Wells." A small smile played at the corners of his mouth. "Here's a guy who hits middle age and is going nowhere. He's never been able to make it on his own. Finally he meets a rich babe who falls for him, and suddenly everything looks cool." Murray paused, his eyes roaming to the open beams of the ceiling. "That meeting was no accident. You can take that to the bank. Warren and Ursula had known each other here in Alpine, when they were young. Maybe they had something going then, maybe not, but he went after her, like a hunter stalking a deer. Fast-forward to this summer: Ursula wants to move back to Alpine, maybe because she sees a new world to conquer, maybe because there's a buzz around Seattle about her late husband's malpractice fiasco. I don't know if Warren was hot to trot to Alpine, but he didn't have much choice—Ursula was used to getting her way, and she did. And that's when the wheels started falling off." Murray fixed me with a wry smile. "Agreed?"

I thought of Warren and Francine. "I gather things didn't go as planned."

"It was a bad plan," Murray declared. "They should have stayed in Seattle. Maybe it would have turned out differently. But I doubt it." There was bite in his tone.

"Warren might have felt his sporting-goods store would have less competition in Alpine," I said somewhat dubiously. "Besides, real estate is cheaper here than in the city."

"Oh, sure." Murray chuckled softly. "But you still need start-up money. Which Warren now doesn't have. In fact, what Warren has is zip, *nada*, the old goose egg, instead of the big nest egg. And that's why you have such a fascinating study of human nature that'll keep your readers glued to the page. This town has a loser's mentality; they would have liked to kill Warren if everything had gone thumbs-up for him. A triumphal return, the defector comes out on top, the jerk who walked out on his first wife and kid ends up with a rich wife and a house to die for. It wouldn't have played in this burg, Emma Lord. In some ways, Warren's lucky it folded. Disgruntled guys like Lucci and Vancich might have lynched him."

Bemused, I sat back against the cushions of my sofa. "So what you're saying is that I should write an article that'll make the rest of Alpine feel good. Warren's a loser just like the rest of you. Is that it?"

Murray leaned forward in the armchair. "A *bigger* loser. The higher you climb, the harder you fall. That's the important part. He finally got what's coming to him."

I didn't respond immediately. Rather, I sipped my Pepsi and tried to understand Murray's angle. Oh, he had one, but it was small-minded and vindictive. Certainly it wasn't the tone I tried to set for *The Advocate*. While I considered a less damning way to write the story, Murray got up and strolled over to the mantel. Out of the corner of my eye, behind the sofa, he picked up a Wedgwood candy dish that had belonged to my mother.

"Don't drop that," I warned him, and was suddenly reminded of Roger's disaster with Polly's vase.

And was suddenly reminded of Verb, talking about being reminded of another troublesome young boy. "Oh, my God!" I gasped.

Murray turned, and I swiveled around on the sofa. "My mother's best friend bought that for her in London," I said in a jagged voice. "I cherish it. My parents died young, in an automobile accident."

Carefully Murray replaced the candy dish. "It's safe. What's wrong?"

"You haven't heard about Polly Patricelli's vase? I should have told you, it would have made a good story, a follow-up to . . ." My brain seemed to have stalled; I was having difficulty finding words. "I mean, it wasn't your station that carried the original feature on the vase. But you might have beat them with the news that the vase was broken Monday night." I thought of my call to Murray's workplace. What *had* the brusque voice at the Seattle TV station barked when I'd asked for Murray? "Not here!" Did that mean not there at the moment—or not there at all?

Murray had returned to the armchair but hadn't yet reseated himself. "It's old news now." He shrugged, but his eyes remained fixed on me. "So what's up? You're acting kind of weird. Have you got something more than pop in that glass?"

"No, no." I laughed, a forced, unnatural sound. "No," I repeated, making a valiant effort to get a grip on myself. "It's just that I'm sort of paranoid about that Wedgwood dish. My mother always wanted one so much, and she'd only had it a few months before she was killed. I wouldn't mind a drink, though. How about you?"

My return to an apparently normal state seemed to satisfy Murray. "No, thanks. I've got another call to make. You will write that story, won't you?"

"It's news," I replied, trying to sound like a true muck-raking professional. "You're right. Warren's failure will make people around here feel better about themselves. That's terribly important."

Murray looked relieved. "Okay. I'm off." He started for the door. "Chenille bathrobes aren't sexy," he said over his shoulder. "You're sexy, but the bathrobe kills it. I hope Dodge isn't stopping by tonight."

"Oh, but he is." I smiled bravely. "The sheriff is an old-fashioned kind of guy. Victoria's Secret catalogs terrify him."

"I figured," said Murray. He left.

As soon as I saw the red Mazda Miata pull away from the spot by my mailbox, I called the sheriff's office. Where the hell was Milo? I demanded. According to Jack Mullins, he should be home. He'd worked late, held hostage by yet another domestic flare-up, out by Cass Pond.

Sure enough, Milo answered on the first ring. "Sorry, Emma," he apologized. "I just got home. You don't have a spare steak, do you? I'm starved."

Instead of a steak, I offered Milo specific instructions. He balked at first, as I knew he would, then listened with mounting interest. By the time I'd finished, he'd agreed to follow my instincts. Prevention, after all, was the first rule of law enforcement.

For the next minute I sat with my head in my hands, wondering what hath Emma wrought? Then I called Vida. She shushed me after less than ten seconds, and said she'd be right over.

She was, arriving at two minutes to ten, just as I finished dressing. "Now—what is this?" she demanded, adjusting her very ugly purple turban.

"I'm not sure," I admitted. "It's about Warren and
Verb and Murray Felton."

From under the folds of the turban, Vida stared. "Who
on earth is Murray Felton?"

I'd forgotten that I hadn't told Vida about Murray. "I'll
explain on the way," I said. "I think we should drive over
to The Pines."

Vida didn't ask why, though she insisted we take her
Buick. Five minutes later, we were approaching Ursula
Randall's house. There was no sign of the sheriff. I
cursed under my breath, and was reproved by Vida. She
had now been sketchily filled in on Murray and hadn't
yet had time to condemn me for my alleged oversight in
not informing her sooner.

"Should we wait for Milo?" she asked, peering
through the windshield.

"I don't know that we can," I said in an anxious voice.

Vida displayed what was reasonable caution under the
circumstances. "But this could be an explosive situation,
could it not?"

Grimly I patted my purse. "We aren't without
resources," I said darkly.

"Oh, good grief!" Vida was aghast. "Don't tell me
you've done something stupid! Do you have a *weapon* in
there?"

"Yes." I opened the car door. "Let's go. If nothing
else, we can create a diversion."

Vida, however, protested. "I absolutely refuse to let
you fire a gun." She grabbed the purse and put it in her
lap. "You'll shoot me or yourself. When was the last time
you fired a pistol or a revolver or whatever you have in
there?"

"Vida . . ." I tried to wrestle the purse away from her,
but she held firm. "Look, my father taught me how to
shoot—"

"Twenty years ago? Thirty is more like it." Vida's face
was set. "You've always claimed to have no knowledge

of firearms. My experience is more recent. I had to use
Ernest's thirty-eight to scare off a cougar two years ago.
The wretched animal was trying to get at my bird feeder.
Perhaps you remember the incident. Now, let's sit here
quietly and wait for Milo."

"We can't," I insisted. "Really, Vida, a life may hang
in the balance."

Vida rolled her eyes. "Oh, good grief!" she repeated.
"This sounds so dramatic! How could anyone I don't
know get into such a mess in Alpine?"

Having thus categorized Murray as negligible, Vida
got out of the Buick, which she had parked on the main
road, presumably to give Milo free access to the driveway. While she might fear for our safety, I knew that
nothing could deter Vida from finding out what was
going on inside the handsome house that now apparently
belonged to Jake and Buzzy O'Toole. The neighborhood
seemed very quiet, yet I sensed that the air of serenity
was deceptive. The red Miata was pulled up by the
double garage, which I assumed housed Ursula's Lexus
and Warren's BMW Z3.

We approached silently, heading straight for the front
door until Vida veered off and tiptoed toward the big
arched window in the living room. The recently planted
shrubs offered a minimum of hiding places, but Vida
managed to duck behind a rhododendron. I sidled up to
her, not daring to look through the glass. But Murray
Felton was shouting, and I knew his target was Warren
Wells.

"You're back to selling tennis balls and salmon eggs,
asshole! I hope you have to stand behind some crummy
counter in a two-bit store peddling ammo until you're
ninety!"

I heard Vida make a clucking noise with her tongue,
but Warren's reply was muffled. Through the glossy oval
leaves of the rhododendron, I couldn't see Murray, but I

could make out Warren's profile. He seemed abject, but
I might have been wrong.

"Put a fork in it, Wells!" Murray shouted. "You're
done."

Anxiously I glanced toward the road. There was still
no sign of Milo. Had Jack Mullins thought I was kidding? That was the trouble with romancing the sheriff:
his colleagues stopped taking you seriously.

Vida leaned toward me. "The bedroom window," she
whispered. "It must open from the outside. Do you
think . . . ?"

The mental image of Vida and me crawling through
the window into Ursula's boudoir was ludicrous. "Why
don't we ring the bell?" I whispered back.

But for once, Vida seemed to have abandoned her
usual blunderbuss tactics. "Hmm . . . I don't know . . ."
She peered through the shrubbery. "Drat, I can't hear
Warren. Ah! He's moving. Maybe this Murray person is
leaving."

The Murray person wasn't going anywhere, judging
by the gun that Warren had pulled out from somewhere
that I couldn't see. Vida and I both froze behind the bush.
But we could now hear Warren, who had raised his
voice.

"You've ruined everything! You always did! You
were nothing but a little shit from the get-go!"

"You killed her, you bastard!" Murray yelled back.
"You're weak, you're cruel, you're nothing but a worthless prick!"

Even in the shadows, I could see that Vida's face
showed alarm. "We can't let Warren shoot that foul-
mouthed man! What shall we do?" She saw me glance
down at my purse. "Not that! Don't you dare, Emma!"

"I wasn't really—" My words were cut off as Murray
dove for Warren. The two men went down and out of
sight. Vida and I stared at each other, then both galloped
off to the double doors. The melodious chime sounded

just as we heard the shot. Vida pulled on the brass handle, but the doors were locked. A stunning silence ensued, broken only by the approach of Milo's Cherokee Chief.

I started to wave as he drove up to the house, but turned sharply when the front door swung open. A trembling Warren Wells stood before us. There was blood on his pale blue sport shirt, and he just stared, speechless. Then he saw Milo striding up to the porch, and passed out at Vida's feet.

"What the hell . . . ?" Milo glanced from Warren's recumbent figure to me. I had knelt down to make sure that the blood wasn't coming from Warren. Vida apparently had noted as much, and had already stepped over the unconscious man to go inside the house.

"Warren may have shot his stepson," I gasped. "I think it was self-defense. Get an ambulance. Murray may still be alive."

"Murray?" Milo stopped in mid-step, obviously dumbfounded. "You mean that smart-ass TV reporter?"

"Yes. No. I mean, I'm not sure he is a TV reporter." I, too, was shaking. "Go. Get help. Vida's inside with Murray. I'll stay with Warren." I had no desire to see what carnage had been wrought in the living room.

The sheriff jumped over Warren and disappeared. I could hear him talking to Vida. Murray wasn't dead, but she believed that the wound to his chest was serious. A moment later I heard Milo barking orders over his cell phone. Next to my knees, Warren stirred.

"It's okay," I said softly. "Milo's here, he'll take care of everything."

Warren made an attempt to roll over and look at me. "I didn't mean to . . . but he jumped me." Letting out a long, agonized sigh, he let me help him sit up. "Murray was about the worst kid I ever met. Why did he have to belong to Alexis?"

"She probably spoiled him," I said, thinking not only

of Roger, but of my own sometimes wayward son,
Adam.

Warren sat on the porch with his head on his knees. "I
left Alicia for him. My bright, beautiful daughter—
Murray's right, I'm a prick." He peered out at me over
his hunched shoulder. "Can you call Francine?"

"Sure," I replied, hearing the wail of the ambulance
siren in the distance. "Is Alicia still with her?"

"Yes." Warren rubbed at his temples. "We still have a
lot to talk through. . . . It didn't turn out to be much of a
Labor Day vacation for Alicia."

It hadn't turned out to be much of a holiday for several
people in Alpine. The ambulance came up alongside
Milo's Cherokee Chief. I recognized the drivers, though I
could never remember their names. They went straight
for Warren, but I waved them off.

"The wounded man's inside," I said as Warren and I
both got to our feet.

"I need a drink," Warren muttered, still rubbing his
head.

It sounded like a good idea to me. But mixing cocktails
at the baroque bar would be in poor taste until Murray
Felton was removed from the living room. "Let's walk a
bit in the garden," I suggested. "You can tell me about
your stepson."

As I suspected, Warren was easily led, especially by a
woman. Now that I wasn't concentrating on hiding in the
shrubbery, I could feel the dew in the grass. A breeze was
blowing down from Tonga Ridge, soft and benign. Out
of the corner of my eye, I noticed that some of the neighbors had gathered at the foot of the driveway. I pretended
not to see them; that was Milo's department.

"There's not much to tell," Warren began, finally
squaring his shoulders. "Alexis had raised him on her
own until she and I got married. He wanted a father, but
he resented a stepfather." Warren gave me a sheepish
look. "It sounds dumb, but that's the way it was."

"No," I said. "I understand. Murray wanted his real father. He felt rejected. A substitute couldn't cure that."

"Right." Warren nodded with a semblance of enthusiasm. "You got it. You understand people real well, Emma."

"Sometimes." What I understood was how I knew Adam would have felt if I had married someone other than Tom. "So you and Murray never got along. I suppose that caused problems with Alexis."

"Boy, did it! It got worse and worse. Finally it came down to him or me. Alexis had to choose. Murray was a teenager by then, and he was getting into all kinds of trouble. She expected me to handle him the way she always had—by standing up for him, making excuses, even giving him alibis. I'd gone along with her to keep the peace, but as Murray got older and into more serious stuff, I couldn't do it anymore. That's when we split up. Right after that, before the divorce was final, Alexis found out she had leukemia. That damned Murray was old enough to read stuff in the papers and magazines. He found out that sometimes diseases are caused or at least aggravated by stress. Naturally he blamed me. Still, I tried to reconcile with Alexis after she got sick. But she was one of those people who acts like a wounded animal—they just want to go off in a cave and die. Which is what happened a year or so later. By that time Murray was living with her brother and his wife in Kirkland."

Ed had told me about the insurance policy Warren had inherited, and the supposed provision for Murray. "Did you try to make contact with the relatives?"

"Once. They hung up on me. I had to get on with my life." Warren had lowered his head, eyes focused on the soft, wet new grass.

The ambulance attendants were wheeling the stretcher into their vehicle. I could see Milo standing by the open rear doors, gesturing and talking. Appropriately enough,

Vida had gone down the drive and was relaying information to the curious neighbors.

Warren also noticed what was happening in front of the house. "We can go back in now, can't we?" He seemed eager.

"Well . . ." I hesitated. "It *is* a crime scene. Let's wait to see what Milo does."

"Shit," Warren murmured. "Now I can't even get a drink because of that creep."

"You'll survive without it," I said, recalling Francine's fear that her ex-husband might have slipped into alcoholism under Ursula's influence. "When did you run into Murray again?" I asked, taking his arm and leading him toward the rear of the house.

"In June, just before we moved to Alpine. We attended a silver wedding anniversary reception for some of Ursula's friends. Murray was working for the local weekly and taking pictures."

"So he *was* a journalist," I said, more to myself than to Warren. "Did he know Ursula?"

Warren shook his head. "No, but he recognized me right away. He was real nice, which should have made me suspicious. He asked a bunch of questions, especially when he found out I was getting married again. But I didn't hear from him until he showed up tonight."

The garden at the back of the house sloped sharply upward into a rockery with a small waterfall. There was a fish pond and a gazebo, as well as a large patio furnished with an umbrella-covered table, a barbecue, and a hot tub. I tried to envision the Buzzy O'Toole ménage dining in alfresco elegance, and failed.

I let out a sorry little sigh. "It wasn't enough to get his revenge. He had to make sure you understood. That everybody understood," I added, thinking how Murray had wanted me to write about Warren's humiliation.

But I was a step ahead of my companion. "What?"

Warren stumbled over one of the flagstones in the patio. "You don't mean . . . ? Oh, no!"

Though I couldn't tell in the darkness, I was sure that the color had drained from Warren's face. "It was no accident," I said grimly. "I don't see how it could have been. To get his revenge, Murray had to make sure that Ursula died. He couldn't take chances, not when she planned to change her will and her insurance policy in the coming week."

"But . . ." Warren was still having trouble finding words. "How could he know?"

The ambulance siren sounded again, denoting its departure. "I doubt that he did at first. He came to Alpine looking for an opportunity. He was a reporter, remember. Believe me, Warren, it's not hard to ferret out information when you're a member of the press."

"Brendan Shaw wouldn't tell tales out of school," Warren protested. "Neither would Marisa Foxx. Her, especially. I don't believe it."

"All Murray needed to know was that Ursula had appointments with Brendan and Marisa. He could guess why. I went to see Brendan myself the same day that Ursula did. It was right after that when I first realized I had an intruder. Murray may have thought I'd found out something about Ursula that day. Or maybe he was doing some research on my reporter, Carla Steinmetz, to buoy up his alibi for being in town. He needed as much background as he could get beyond the feature on Ursula in *The Advocate*. Murray was pretending to be a hotshot TV reporter, remember. But he also broke into this house the evening that Ursula died." I gestured in the direction of the bedroom window. "He may have found her personal papers. I suspect he came back later, introduced himself as someone she'd met at her friends' anniversary reception, had a drink or two, and offered to take her for a spin in his Miata. They were seen driving by Jake and Betsy's. Betsy insisted it was you, but if you think about it, there's a passing resemblance between you and Murray. You're both dark and about the same size. Furthermore, Betsy admits she can't tell one car from another. Your Z3 and Murray's Miata are both red sports cars. That's close enough for Betsy O'Toole. She was familiar with your Z3, but she'd never seen the Miata before. Naturally she assumed it was you."

"Jesus!" Warren wiped his brow. "Murray killed Ursula! I can't believe it!"

I realized that Warren hadn't heard much of what I'd said. It didn't matter. We had now circled the garden and were back at the head of the driveway. The neighbors had dispersed, but Vida and Milo were standing on the front porch.

"There you are, Doubles," the sheriff said, somewhat gruffly. "You'd better come inside. You can tell us what happened down at headquarters."

"He went for the gun," Warren said, lifting his hands in a helpless gesture. "He actually grabbed it, and then we wrestled around on the rug and—"

Milo put up a hand as we moved indoors. "Hold it, Doubles. You're a suspect. I can't play the old-buddy game. We have to go by the book."

In the entry hall, Warren turned a puzzled face to Milo. "But . . . it was an accident."

The sheriff's temper was fraying. "Shut up. It isn't just my part of the job. If this Felton lives, he could file a civil suit against you. Does that sound like something he might do?"

Warren hung his head. "It sure does. He's a real SOB."

Standing on the threshold of the vast and showy living room, our eyes immediately fell on the bloodstained Portuguese carpet. A tortured groan erupted from Warren's throat.

"That rug cost a fortune. If Ursula could see that, she'd croak!"

Nobody reminded Warren that Ursula already had.

Chapter Eighteen

VIDA DRANK HOT tea, Milo sipped Scotch, and I nursed a bourbon and water. It was almost midnight, and we were in my humble living room, going over the finer points of the Randall case. Naturally the sheriff brought up the question of Ursula's shoes.

"That's not so difficult," Vida said a bit testily. She was still annoyed with me for not telling her about Murray. "Ursula probably thought she and that dreadful young man were going for a joyride in his sports car. It didn't occur to her that they would stop by the river. But when they did, she removed her wedgies. Perhaps she left them in Murray's car. When Ursula drowned, Murray had to get rid of the shoes, so he did the logical thing, and tried to put them back on. But he was rattled—he put one on the wrong foot. Then he either panicked, or something startled him. He drove away, with or without the other shoe."

Milo was still looking puzzled. "So what you're saying is that Murray could have driven up Mount Sawyer and dumped that shoe, or that my original scenario about the party gang may have been right. One of them found the shoe and took it with them."

"Perhaps," Vida allowed. "If they were on drugs or drunk, anything's possible."

"It's a moot point," Milo said unhappily. "There's no way to prove Murray killed Ursula. Doc Dewey thinks

he'll survive, which means he's going to get off scot-
free."

I heartily sympathized with the sheriff. "Wasn't there
some evidence of a struggle? He had motive, opportunity,
and probably some kind of record, at least as a juvenile."

"So?" Milo threw back the last of his Scotch. "The
ME's report showed minimal bruising, which could have
been caused from the rocks or the underbrush. What happened, I'm guessing, is that Ursula passed out by the
river. Murray either planned it that way, or took advantage of the situation. He held her under until she was
dead. Try to prove it. As for his previous record, that
doesn't count, especially not if he was a kid at the time."

"But Betsy saw them drive by," I pointed out, getting
up to refill Milo's glass.

Milo grimaced. "Betsy thought it was Doubles. She'd
make a lousy witness on the stand. Did Murray admit to
you that he even met Ursula, let alone killed her? Did he
admit it to Doubles?"

"No," I replied glumly. "I'm not sure Warren really
believes Murray drowned Ursula. Oh, he knows what a
horror the guy is, but I don't think he wants to believe
that his former stepson committed murder just to get
back at him for allegedly causing Alexis's death."

With a rueful look, Milo accepted the fresh drink from
me. "That's another thing—it's a reverse motive. When
there's money involved, people usually kill for gain. In
this case, Murray killed to prevent somebody else from
getting the loot. It would sound damned odd in court."

"Revenge isn't odd," Vida noted. "That's the real
motive. I find it most credible. I'm sure that his mother's
death preyed on Murray's mind all these years. Ursula
not only was going to offer Warren a life of ease, but she
was taking Alexis's place. Murray must have resented
that usurping of his mother's place. If you interviewed
people who knew him, they might provide some enlight-
ening information."

"Maybe," Milo said. "Maybe not. Felton's a head case for sure. Which means he may have kept it bottled up. It could be that he never thought of actively taking revenge on Doubles until he ran into him at that party or whatever it was."

That struck me as likely. While Murray may have spent the last decade brooding over Alexis's tragic death, his quest for vengeance might not have manifested itself until he saw Warren again.

"He wants to be caught." The words tumbled out of my mouth and out of the blue.

Vida and Milo stared at me. "What do you mean?" my House & Home editor demanded.

"Murray never had to show himself to anybody in Alpine—except Ursula," I said in a rush. "Yet he wants everyone to know how clever he is. That's why he came here tonight to ask me to write that article. It wasn't just that he wanted Warren brought down, Murray also wanted the world to know how clever he was in managing it. If that meant being charged with homicide, so be it. He's never been punished for anything. A father would have disciplined him. Murray's crying out for a stern paternal hand." I turned to Milo. "I'll bet you five bucks you could get a confession out of him. He not only wants to brag, he wants attention, he wants to finally have some limits set. When we reprimand our kids, it's because we love them. Murray has never felt loved, except by Alexis, who abandoned him as surely as his real father did. He's still a little kid, misbehaving to see if anybody cares."

"Bull," said Milo.

"Rubbish," said Vida.

Neither could daunt me. "Trust me on this. Murray may not be aware of how his mind is working, it's probably all subconscious. That's why he's been a show-off all his life. It wasn't enough to be a weekly newspaper reporter, he had to pretend he was in television."

"I thought he wanted to meet Carla," Milo said, apparently not yet buying into my pop psychology.

"Carla was a ruse," I said. "It was a cover to get to me. I'll bet he never heard of her until he broke into my house and found her name in *The Advocate* or in my Rolodex."

"Really," Vida remarked acidly, "it's a wonder Carla didn't want to meet him! He sounds just her type."

I ignored Vida. "Come on, Milo. What have you got to lose?"

"Well . . ." He rubbed at one eye with the palm of his hand. "Nothing, I suppose. I'll have to wait until he's in better shape."

"If nothing else, you can charge him with breaking and entering," I said. "False representation, too." But I wasn't backing down.

Vida condescended to lend me a smattering of support. "Criminals must never go unpunished. Do you want the voters to lose confidence, Milo?"

The sheriff glowered at Vida, then raised his glass. "What the hell. I can give it a shot."

"I should hope so." Vida set her teacup down in its saucer. "It wouldn't do for the community—or Murray Felton—to feel that there are loopholes in the law." Vida sighed. "Such a nasty man. I can't think how his mother let him get away with being so naughty."

I kept my mouth shut. I didn't dare tell Vida that what had made me suspicious of Murray was Verb Vancich's comment that somebody had recently reminded him of his nemesis at the sportswear shop. It had been Murray himself, all grown up, but Verb's memory had preserved him as the wretched boy trying to swipe a team jersey. I had thought that Verb meant Roger. To say as much to Vida was pointless. I might as well fantasize about Milo grilling Vida's grandson as the unrepentant perpetrator of some heinous crime. In my dreams, the rubber hose and the thumbscrews were back. I leaned against the sofa and smiled.

Sometimes life has a strange way of resolving conundrums. Murray Felton did not confess to Milo. Instead he laughed in the sheriff's face. I lost my five-dollar bet. But meanwhile Milo had intensified his questioning of the Mount Sawyer crew. Two of them had biked down the mountain in search of weed that Friday night. They had seen Murray with Ursula. Thinking they had come upon a playful pair of lovers, the young man and the young woman from Sultan had hidden themselves in the woods, hoping to get a rush from watching riverside passion. Instead they had seen Murray return to his car, where he brought out a pair of shoes. In puzzlement, they observed him putting one of the shoes on the woman they had assumed was his willing sex partner. But the woman remained prone at the river's edge. Now disturbed, the couple called out to Murray, asking if something was wrong. Murray had bolted, jumped into his car, and driven off. He had dropped the other shoe in his wake. The young woman had picked up the shoe while the young man went down to the river. Discovering that Ursula was dead, the duo from Sultan had fled back up the logging road on their motorcycles. They had wished no involvement in what might be a capital crime. It was only during a plea-bargaining session that the truth had come out.

Milo was ecstatic. On Friday, the day after the revelation, he and I had lunch at the Venison Inn.

"Eyewitnesses, that's what it takes." He gloated over a double cheeseburger and fries. "Circumstantial evidence will only get you so far in front of a jury."

I was elated for the sheriff. "Does that mean you won't quit your job?" I asked with a wry little smile.

Milo's glee faded. "I have to serve out my term. Next

year, when the election rolls around, we'll see how I feel."

That was when I unveiled my editorial campaign. Milo seemed pleased, if dubious that such changes could be made. "Look at KingCo," he pointed out. "They haven't had an elected sheriff for years. But now they're talking about going back to the old way. The trend isn't for appointees."

"Screw the trend," I said. "This isn't KingCo, it's SkyCo. Let's face it, Milo—you're damned good at what you do."

Milo made a disparaging gesture with the hand that wasn't holding the cheeseburger. "What'd I do? Let some bastard break into your house so that you could figure out he'd shoved Ursula's kisser into six inches of the Sky?"

Emphatically I shook my head. "You did what any good law-enforcement official does—you kept after possible witnesses until you found somebody who'd seen something. Who else did you interview besides the Mount Sawyer gang?"

"Sheesh." Milo's eyes rolled up to the Venison Inn's grease-and-smoke-stained knotty-pine ceiling. "Between my deputies and me, we talked to about sixty people, forty of whom live along the route between Betsy and Jake O'Toole's house and the place on the river where Ursula was killed. Not one of those morons saw a damned thing, except Betsy, who IDed the wrong guy. Boy, does she feel like a dumb-shit."

"A *rich* dumb-shit," I pointed out. "She and Jake and Buzzy and Laura won't have any more money troubles. I don't know how much that matters to Jake and Betsy, but it may mean the world to Laura and Buzzy."

"You mean Laura'll take Buzzy back?" Milo inquired between french fries.

"She already has," I replied. "With them, it was always money, or the lack thereof. So often, that's at the root of marital problems. Not sex, not in-laws, not indifference, but paying the bills. Unfortunately there's no quick cure for the Luccis."

"Yeah," Milo said in a bemused tone. "I hear Della packed up and moved to Monroe yesterday. What the hell will she do there?"

"Who knows? It's too bad that the story about Luce suing Dr. Randall was a fabrication on Murray's part to mislead us. Money wouldn't have hurt there, either." I sighed, thinking of Della cast adrift on the social and economic waters of an unknown town.

"Hey." Milo leaned forward in the booth and grabbed one of my hands. "I can't come over tonight. I've got to drive down to Bellevue to meet Tanya's boyfriend. I kind of think they may announce that they're engaged. If it weren't serious, Mulehide wouldn't have asked me to come."

The imminent betrothal of Milo's elder daughter was sufficient reason to dump me on a Friday night. "That's fine," I said, then realized there was a lump in my throat. "You wouldn't leave Alpine, would you?"

Milo's fingers tightened around my hand. "Let's put it like this, Emma. I wouldn't leave *you*."

Ed called that night around seven-thirty. It was the old Bronsky, mired in self-pity. "I haven't heard from Doubleday," he moaned. "What should I do? Try another publisher? What's wrong with those people? Don't they know a hot best-seller when they see one?"

"Ed, I tried to warn you that publishers don't read manuscripts as soon as they arrive in the mail. Especially what they call over-the-transom, which means without representation by an agent. You're going to have to wait at least—"

"Random House," Ed broke in. "Wasn't that the one that Bennett Cerf headed up? I remember him from

What's My Line? He was sharp. I'll bet Random House would jump at the chance to publish *Mr. Ed*."

"Well, certainly," I said, knowing that any words of wisdom would be ignored. "Ship them a copy. They'll be agog." Visions of dismayed junior editors danced through my head, accompanied by an epilogue in which, after several pestering phone calls from Ed, they rushed to Manhattan window ledges and threatened to hurl themselves into traffic.

"Say," Ed remarked, apparently buoyed by my encouragement, "I have to run for the parish council after all. Did I tell you? Father Den said we broke some rules the other night."

"I thought so," I replied mildly. "Go for it, Ed. Father Den needs all the help he can get." And all that he deserves, I thought. There was no pat solution for the parish problems.

"It'll be another special election," Ed noted. "A week from Sunday, probably. Now here's my election plan— first, I'm going to hire a musical group to play outside in the parking lot before the Masses this weekend. I'll hand out banners and bumper stickers and buttons. Maybe I'll set up a little stand, with free hot dogs and popcorn and soda. Here's the slogan: 'I'm Onsky for Bronsky.' What do you think? Either that or, 'Better Ed Than Dead.' Then I could get a professional clown to . . ."

I tuned Ed out. There were enough amateur clowns in the parish community as it was. Finally, thankfully, a call came in on my second line. With what I hoped sounded like regret, I told Ed I'd better hang up and see who was calling me. It might be important, perhaps something to do with Murray Felton and Ursula's murder.

I was half-right. It had nothing to do with Ursula or Murray, but it was important. It was Adam, calling from Tuba City.

"Hi, Mom. Uncle Ben's saying Mass this weekend in a trailer. Cool, huh?"

It didn't sound cool to me. In fact, it sounded hot, especially in Arizona. "Well, I suppose it beats having a liturgy at the local truck stop."

"He did that last week," Adam informed me. "But Tuesday we found this really huge trailer that can hold about fifty people if you clear everything out. After Sunday Mass, we're going to officially lay the cornerstone for the new church."

"That's wonderful," I said, and meant it. "When are you going back to ASU?" I appreciated Adam's support for his uncle, but I was tired of having him put me off about his college courses.

"I'm not, not right now," he replied. "Uncle Ben needs a lot of hands. It's going to take a couple of weeks or more to put up the new building. It won't be anything fancy, just a kind of hall, like the old one."

I didn't want to discuss architecture. "Which means you'll miss the first week of classes?" Nor did I wait for an answer. "Which means you might as well skip this quarter and just loaf around the reservation? Damn it, Adam, you're too close to a degree to slough off now. Has it ever occurred to you that someday you're going to have to get a *job*?"

Adam made a noise that sounded like disgust. "I've got a job. Didn't I tell you . . . ?"

He hadn't. Not in so many words. He told me then.

I didn't want to hear it. But he told me anyway.

Milo returned from Bellevue Saturday afternoon. He wasn't keen on Tanya's fiancé. "A computer type," the sheriff declared as we lay in bed on a warm September evening. "A nerd. They met on the Internet. I don't get what she sees in him."

"Who knows, when it comes to love?" I traced his profile with my fingers, but felt distracted. "Who knows, when it comes to kids?"

"Tanya should finish college," Milo said with a frown.

"It's Mulehide who's pushing here. I think Tanya and this guy would like to live together for a while, but my ex won't have it. I know it's supposed to be wrong, but it makes sense these days. Find out what a person's really like. See if it's just sex. Get some of those dumb little problems out of the way before you make a commitment. Hell, if Mulehide and I'd done that, maybe we'd never have gotten married."

Ordinarily, I would have probed further into Milo's musings. Was he sorry he'd taken Tricia to wife? Did he regret the divorce? Was he hinting that the two of us should live together? But for once, I had no interest in male–female relationships. I rolled over on my side and stared at the sliding doors of my closet.

"Hey—what's wrong?" Milo poked me in the small of the back. "You don't agree? What if Adam showed up with some girl he hardly knew except on-line and announced he was getting married? Wouldn't you pitch a fit?"

I shook my head, but didn't—couldn't—speak. Milo tickled me in the ribs. "Adam has too many girls? Is that it? Are you afraid he'll never settle down and produce some grandkids?"

I burst into tears. In recent years Adam had become acquainted with his father, Tom. But it was Ben who owned him. Ben had been there at his birth, Ben had inspired him, Ben had wrapped him in a mantel of goodness that I could never understand, let alone imitate. Ben had held him captive down on the reservation, a willing hostage.

"No girls, no grandchildren," I blubbered. "No immortality for Emma Lord." I caught myself, then turned just enough to look at Milo. "Not the kind you're thinking of. Not the kind I planned." I swallowed hard, tasted the tears, and felt the smallest of smiles tug at my mouth. "Adam is going to be a priest."

Another blow for Emma. Another Lord for the Lord. Amen.